Michael Asher has served in the Parachute Regiment and the SAS. A fluent Arabic speaker, he lived for several years with desert nomads, and later made the first recorded crossing of the Sahara from west to east by camel and on foot. He is a Fellow of the Royal Society of Literature, and has won a number of awards for exploration, including the Lawrence of Arabia Memorial Medal of the Royal Society for Asian Affairs. Among his previous books are the bestselling *The Real Bravo Two Zero* and the autobiographical *Shoot to Kill: From 2 Para to the SAS*.

PRAISE FOR THE COLOUR OF FIRE:

'It's everything you'd expect: well plotted, taut, with fast flowing action, a believable and intriguing plot and very credible characters.' – John Sadler, author of *Blitzing Rommel*

'The vivid period details are so beautifully blended into the story that I felt that I was back in the war years. *The Colour of Fire* is what all good historical novels should be – an entertaining way to learn about the past.' – Edward Klekowski, author of *The Kaiser's American*

PRAISE FOR MICHAEL ASHER:

'Breathtaking bravery, astonishing feats of endurance, raids and battles described with terrific immediacy and pace. Compelling and definitive… will surely not be bettered' – *Sunday Telegraph*

'A staggering achievement. Asher has delivered a scintillating tale of a period of history that deserves to be remembered' – *Guardian*

'Extraordinary' – Damien Lewis

The Colour of Fire

Michael Asher

LUME BOOKS

LUME BOOKS

First published in 2018 by Lume Books
85-87 Borough High Street,
London, SE1 1NH

ISBN 978-1-83901-174-0

www.lumebooks.co.uk

INTRODUCTION

KL Natzweiler-Struthof was the only Nazi concentration camp on French soil. Opened by the *Waffen SS* in 1941, it stood on a bald panhandle in the Vosges mountains, thirty-one kilometres south of Strasbourg, capital of Alsace. The Alsace region, lying west of the Rhine, close to the German frontier, had been disputed between France and Germany for many centuries. Though its folk spoke various dialects of German, most remained staunchly loyal to France, and supported the Maquis – the active French Resistance – during the war.

It was for captured members of the Resistance – not only from France, but also from the Netherlands, Russia, Norway, Poland, Slovenia, and Germany itself – that Natzweiler had been built. Between 1941 and 1944, fifty-two thousand prisoners passed through its gates, many of them classed as *Nacht und Nebel* – Night and Fog – detainees, who were not intended to survive.

Since these prisoners were doomed, the SS decided to make their last days profitable – for the Nazis – by renting them out as slave-workers to industrial plants. Many of these factories were located in mines and tunnels against the threat of Allied bombing raids. One of the companies involved was Daimler-Benz, forerunner of Mercedes-Benz, which, in

1944, relocated its Berlin aircraft factory to a gypsum mine within the orbit of Natzweiler, where it was supplied by slave-workers from the camp. Daimler-Benz had maintained close ties with Hitler since the early 1930s. During the war its products ranged from aero-engines, to tanks, armoured cars, and parts for V2 missiles. Of Benz's sixty-three thousand wartime workers, about half were forced labourers, prisoners of war, or detainees from concentration-camps.

On its hilltop stump, Natzweiler was exposed to blasting arctic winds in winter, and, in summer, roasting heat. The prisoners, crowded together in makeshift huts, were starved, beaten, tortured, worked to death: those who refused to work were shot or hanged in public. They were riddled with sickness, ravaged by epidemics. Men, women and children were singled out for sadistic medical experiments: eighty-six Jewish prisoners were murdered in the camp so that their skeletons could be displayed as curiosities at the Strasbourg Anatomical Institute. The *Konzentrationslager* boasted a gas-chamber, and a crematorium for disposing of unwanted bodies. There were plenty to dispose of: almost half the prisoners who passed through Natzweiler were killed, or died of mistreatment, malnutrition or disease.

By late August 1944, though, the days of the Death-Camp were numbered. From the west, the American Sixth Army Group, with Free French forces under its command, was closing in on Alsace. To the south, ninety-one commandos of the British 2nd SAS Regiment had been dropped by parachute into the forests of the Vosges: they were helping the Maquis to mount aggressive hit-and-run raids on Nazi troops. France was crawling with secret agents of the Special Operations Executive (SOE) – many of them women – who had also arrived by parachute. Tasked to aid the Resistance in sabotaging vital industrial and military targets, they operated individually, passing as locals, speaking fluent French.

The *SS* staff of Natzweiler, terrified of the retribution that would surely follow, launched into a last frantic orgy of murder: between 31 August and 1 September, they shot or gassed a hundred and forty-one detainees from local Resistance groups. Thirty-one prisoners from the 2nd SAS Regiment, captured with their Maquis counterparts in the Vosges, were held at Natzweiler. In September, when the Nazis evacuated the camp, leaving only a few prisoners and a skeleton SS staff. Ten of the SAS men were moved by truck across the Rhine, where they were held at Rotenfels, a hastily constructed camp near Gaggenau, in the Baden-Wurttenburg region of Germany, directly east of Alsace. Most of the remaining inmates of Natzweiler were moved out on a death march into Germany. Some also ended up at Rotenfels, to be used as workers at Gaggenau, where there was another Daimler-Benz plant. In the meantime, Nazi-sponsored factories in France had moved their machinery discreetly across the Rhine, back to the *Fatherland*.

The rest of the captured SAS men remained at Natzweiler until November 1944, when the camp looked certain to be liberated by Allied forces. They disappeared. None of them was ever seen again. The SAS men held at Rotenfels, across the river in Germany, vanished at the same time. At least four female SOE agents were murdered at Natzweiler during that period: their bodies were incinerated in the crematorium, their ashes stored in nameless pots.

In July 1945, after Germany had surrendered to the Allies, the 2nd SAS Regiment formed a war crimes investigation team, to find out what had happened to their comrades who had disappeared in France and Germany the previous year.

CHAPTER ONE

Alsace, France. September 1944

Celia Blaney plummeted through the moonlight in free fall. It was the loneliest, most terrifying moment of her life. Then her canopy snapped open, and it felt as if a big, friendly hand had snatched her from certain death. Relief and euphoria flooded through her in equal measure. For a second, she felt she was actually floating through the night.

She'd jumped at eight hundred feet – if you could call flopping face first through a hole in the fuselage of a Halifax bomber *jumping*. The altitude was higher than normal, but the drop still lasted a mere forty seconds. Just enough time to release the catch on the leg bag holding her equipment. She let it go, felt the tug as it swung beneath her on its rope. She reached for the lift webs, bent her knees, forced her ankles together. *No wind drift,* she thought. The ground arched up to meet her, a rush of moonlit blue.

She heard the leg bag crump. Her feet hit the ground a second later. There were the remains of old furrows there that she hadn't expected. She rolled over, aware of a creasing pain in her left ankle that brought tears to her eyes. *Bugger.*

She came to a stop on her back. The ground was rough, grassy, uneven.

Ignoring her ankle, she whipped the clasp knife from her jumpsuit pocket, prized it open and sliced through the leg bag rope. Thank Christ it hadn't snapped. It had done once in training at Altrincham when she'd jumped from a Whitley in the grounds of Tatton Park. She'd been dreading a repetition on a real op.

She released her harness, rolled onto her belly and hauled in the canopy by the lift webs. When the parachute was a bundle under her, she packed it into its feather-light bag, removed the folded entrenching tool strapped to her right leg and the roll of sackcloth attached to her left. She unbuckled her helmet and goggles, started digging a hole right where she was. Too many ops, they'd told her, had been compromised by unconcealed parachutes; they were a dead giveaway to Jerry spotter planes. Her ankle was still smarting – the initial agony had subsided to an insistent throb. *It's not broken, just a sprain.* Ironically, the ground was soft. She unrolled the sackcloth to retain the spoil and started digging, piling the earth carefully onto the cloth. In ten minutes, she was down to a couple of feet. She enlarged the hole, laid the pumpkin-shaped bag inside, doffed her *striptease suit*, as they called it at Altrincham. Underneath, she was wearing a floral high-necked dress. She removed her .32 automatic pistol from the suit pocket, then placed the suit, helmet and goggles on top of the silk bundle. The leg bag lay only five yards distant. She hobbled over to it, coiled up the rope as she went. Pain jabbed her left calf: she cursed under her breath. She knelt down by the bag, opened her clasp knife, cut through the laced-up strings. She removed a small, battered suitcase. She carried the case and the bag awkwardly back to the hole she'd dug. She set the case down threw the limp bag into the hole.

Celia paused for a second, making sure she hadn't forgotten anything. *The spade. Can't take it with me. Wouldn't suit Giselle Tomalin from Paris.*

I'm a traveller in ladies' cosmetics, not a bloody gravedigger. She suppressed a giggle, folded the spade, laid it on top of the other items. She scooped in the spoil with her hands, tipped the last of it from the sackcloth then rolled the cloth up again – it could be thrown away. Her hands were dirty, of course, but she could wash them, and in any case, dirty hands were a lot easier to explain than a military entrenching tool. She almost guffawed, had to squeeze her nose to stop it coming out as a snort. They'd told her she might feel high after the jump – as if she'd swallowed a handful of Bennies. She recognized the symptoms, stood quite still, taking deep breaths, taking in everything around her. She glanced in each direction in turn. All her senses were on full beam, as they'd taught her. She stood drinking in the night like a long cocktail. The sky was speckled with stars. The moon three days past full, there was hardly a breath of wind. The Halifax that had brought her from Blighty was long gone. She couldn't hear even the murmur of her engines. She hoped the crew would get back to Tempsford in one piece.

She shivered, realizing for the first time how chilly it was. She knelt, opened the suitcase, drew out a ladies' Mackintosh and put it on. She stuck the .32 automatic in the right pocket, the clasp knife in the left. She surveyed the contents of the suitcase. She had only the basics – survival pack, first aid kit, a box of French matches, French cigarettes in the silver case Lurgan had given her before she'd left. He'd told her that in an emergency, she could sell it or pawn it for cash. In the money belt under her dress she had two thousand francs in small notes. The case contained neatly folded spare clothes, all with French or German labels – like her overcoat. She had a sheaf of forged documents – ID card, ration card, travel passes, together with a few carefully chosen cosmetics samples – mascara, lipsticks, eye pencils, powder puffs.

She closed the case, locked it. *Thank God I'm not a pianist,* she thought.

That was what the staff at Beaulieu – where she'd done most of her ten-week training – called wireless operators. Wireless was the weak link in SOE networks. W/T signals could be triangulated easily by Jerry: a pianist was reckoned to have a life expectancy of no more than six weeks.

The edge of hysteria had passed. Blaney didn't feel scared. Now she had her feet on French soil she realized that the flight had been much worse than the landing – butterflies as big as pterodactyls flapping in her stomach, the sickening stench of aviation fuel. The way the crate had lurched and wobbled as it jumped the French coast, dropped to tree level to slip under the enemy radar screen.

The RAF dispatcher, a cheery young chappie with plump, rosy cheeks had cracked jokes, made her rum toddies, opened the hole in the floor to show her the land flitting below the aircraft. Blaney had glimpsed the silver sheen of lakes and rivers, winding serpents of roads, railways, dark huddles of villages, brakes of dense forest, church steeples – a serene and magical fairyland bathed in soft blue, near enough, almost, to touch.

Blaney hadn't responded to the lad's banter though, and after a while he'd given up. *He'd seen it all a million times*, she thought. Even though the aircrew was from a Moon Squadron – one of SOE's own RAF Special Duties units – to them she was just a *Joe*. They knew where to deposit her, but they didn't know her mission. Only she and Lurgan knew that.

She'd sworn to herself that she wouldn't think about Tom Caine on the way. In the end, of course, he was almost all she *had* thought about. She tasted the soft touch of his lips on hers, felt his hands caressing her breasts, stroking her inner thighs. She flushed, suppressed a quiver.

Caine had been away on an op with his SAS squadron when she'd been recruited by SOE, and wouldn't know anything about it. *Was it brutal of me to go without telling him?* She imagined him arriving back in London, finding her gone. No one would tell him she was with SOE.

It was top secret, and not even her closest friends knew. Yet the chances were he wouldn't be home for months. He'd never told her when to expect him, almost certainly didn't know himself. She couldn't afford to wait. *The war might be over by then.*

The bomber droned on above the blue-silvered fields. She imagined him down there, blowing up bridges or railways, or whatever it was the SAS did. Not very different from what SOE did she guessed, except that for them it was a team job, not a one-man mission. SAS wore uniform. SOE spoke the lingo, blended in with the locals, wore civvies. She stopped herself from wondering if she and Tom would ever be together again. In these days, it was a silly question. She'd first met Caine when she was a field security officer with the Int. Corps in Cairo and had helped to coax him back to health and sanity. They'd met again in Algeria, where Caine had been in jail for treason. *Tom Caine, treason?* It never had made sense. As his defence at the court martial, she'd not only managed to get him off but also proved who the real traitor was.

It wasn't until they were both back in Blighty that they'd become lovers. Blaney had always known Caine was in love with her. She'd known it from the beginning, even if Caine hadn't known it himself. He'd only held off because of Betty Nolan, the G(R) courier he'd snatched from Jerry in the desert. Later, Nolan had taken a bullet, ended up in a coma. Not long after Caine got back from Algeria she'd passed away quietly in her sleep. Caine had been devastated but also released. Blaney had been there to support him, as she had been twice before. This time, their relationship had gone far beyond mere comforting, though – gone to the point of no return.

Caine probably wouldn't even recognize her now. She was no longer the girl with the flame-red curls he used to know. Her hair had been dyed mousy brown, the curls ironed out. Her startling blue eyes were concealed behind thick lenses of faux spectacles. They'd darkened her pink complexion with a stain that would take days of scrubbing to remove. In ordinary circumstances, most men would have called Blaney a *cracker*. A lot of SOE girls were, but it was a disadvantage. They didn't want women so pneumatic they stood out. In any case, she wasn't Celia Blaney anymore. She was Giselle Tomalin, born and bred in Paris, educated at French convent schools. She'd gone over her cover story so many times in training that she almost believed it herself. Actually, it wasn't that far from the truth.

She'd often asked herself why she'd gone for SOE when she was already serving with Int. The corps had even let her wear their cap badge and uniform, though officially she was a FANY – First Aid Nursing Yeomanry – something she shared with most female SOE agents.

Was it to prove she was as good as Betty Nolan? She doubted it. She might not have been on stunts like Nolan, but she'd proved herself in Egypt. She'd once been badly wounded in a shoot-out with deserters – she'd almost died. Nolan had saved her life that time, even though she'd been with the deserters. No, it wasn't rivalry with Nolan. It was the idleness, hanging around in England while millions of Allied troops were sticking their necks out for Europe – for the place she'd grown up in, France.

Blaney had a history few knew about. Her parents were a well-to-do British banking family, but she'd grown up in Paris, and she really *had* gone to a convent school in France before boarding school in England. Actually, she sometimes thought of herself as more French than British. Knowing how touchy the Brits were, she'd kept quiet about it though. She longed to do something for the ravaged country she considered, at least partly, her own. SOE was happy to filch her from the Int. Corps. Why waste a girl like that behind a desk in some dingy office, Lurgan thought, when, with her fluent French and counterspy experience, she'd be a peach in the field? Most female SOE agents were trained as pianists or couriers, but recognizing Blaney's special talents, Lurgan had had her trained intensively as a saboteur.

Blaney saw she was standing in a fair-sized field, once cultivated, now fallow. It was the relict plough furrows that had done for her ankle, damn them. *Never choose agricultural land as a dropping point*, they'd told her at Beaulieu. *Operational cock-up Number One.* She had no map and only a button compass, which she couldn't see without her torch. Flashing a light wouldn't be a good idea, so instead, she located the Pole Star. She'd been instructed to move south. She picked up her suitcase. Keeping the star behind her right shoulder, she waddled off the drop-zone until she came to a hedge.

It was blackthorn and looked impenetrable. She certainly wasn't going to push through or try to climb it, end up scratched to hell, coat ripped to shreds. Instead, she followed the line of the hedge, looked for a gate or a stile. There was a copse of trees at the corner of the field, swathed in deeper shadow. Blaney approached, sensed movement. It was nothing she could identify, more an intuition. Something or someone was concealed in the trees.

She stopped twelve paces away, set down her case. In a deft movement, she slipped the .32 from her pocket, cocked it, held it double-handed close to her hip, SOE-style, as she'd been taught. '*Qui est là?*' she demanded in a low voice. '*Montrez-vous.*'

First contact was the diciest moment of the op. It was the one time an agent was allowed to shoot. If it was the Resistance, it would be expected. If it was the Bosch, her only chance was to buy enough time to swallow her *L-ration* – her suicide pill. It was one thing being picked up on the streets when you had papers and could argue your way out of it. It was quite another to explain what you were doing in a field at two thirty in the morning, carrying an automatic weapon and special equipment, with a parachute they were sure to find, buried a few hundred yards away.

Two figures shuffled almost apologetically out of the shadows into the moonlight. One was taller than the other. Both had thick moustaches. They wore cloth caps and ragged peasant clothes. The taller one looked much younger than the other and might have been his son. Their hands were raised half-heartedly. Neither seemed to be armed, but she had no idea if there might be others hidden in the trees.

'*Êtes-vous l'Imperatrice Eugenie?*' the elder man asked in French. 'Are you the Empress Eugenie?' His voice was soft, low and had a dry quality as if he felt embarrassed asking such a silly question.

Empress Eugenie was Blaney's operational code name. Her impending arrival under that name had been broadcast on the BBC Resistance network sometime in the past twenty-four hours.

Blaney let out a slow, inaudible sigh of relief. She lowered the pistol, gave the prearranged response.

'*I wish I were,*' she said.

CHAPTER TWO

London, England. May 1945

Victory over Germany. It was written in big blue letters on a hoarding in Trafalgar Square. The war in Europe was over. The streets of London were a torrent of people singing, bawling, climbing lamp posts, making two-finger victory signs. A conga line of US sailors and local girls shuffled down the centre of Piccadilly. Bobbies watched and grinned.

Winston Churchill stood on the balcony of Buckingham Palace with an indulgent smirk on his face. On either side of him the king and queen waved to the crowd, the two young princesses gazed on. The cheer that rolled off the masses was roaring thunder. People held up babies with hair tied in red, white and blue ribbons. Bulldogs were draped in Union Jacks.

From his dingy room at the Victory Club, Captain Tom Caine heard the roar of the crowds, the firecrackers, the thump of marching bands. Millions were out there exulting, but somehow, he couldn't join in. He paced the room, knocking back whisky from a tumbler, getting slowly drunk. '*Like the arse dropped out of the world*,' his RSM had growled when they'd told him it was all over. That was how Caine felt. He'd served in the Commandos and the 1st SAS Regiment. He'd led missions

21

behind enemy lines no one thought he'd come back from – not even *he'd* thought he'd come back from. They'd given him the DSM and the DSO twice. He'd been busted from lieutenant to private for threatening a superior, worked his way up again to captain – he'd been acting major during the post-D-Day ops. Now he'd reverted to substantive captain again. He'd seen more combat than most. It wasn't that he enjoyed killing people, it was the sense of anti-climax you felt when the action and the danger stopped.

It wasn't just that, though. It wasn't just the fact that he had no family, no place to call home either. It was the weight of the dead. The enemy he'd shot, machine-gunned, bayoneted, mined, booby-trapped, blown to bits. And what about his own men? Men who'd trusted him. Men whose bleached bones were still lying in the desert, thanks to his bad calls. There wasn't any going back on that. The images were carved inside his head You could wave all the Union Jacks you wanted, cheer King George, do victory signs till the cows came home, but it wouldn't make them go away.

It wasn't just *those* dead, either. It was Betty Nolan, the G(R) special ops agent he'd whipped from under Jerry's nose in North Africa. She'd died in a military nursing home a year ago. Died without ever coming out of the coma she'd been in since a Nazi spy had put a bullet in her head in '43. Caine had been there, but he'd been too slow to stop that bullet. He'd never let himself forget that.

It was also Celia Blaney, the field security officer with the flaming red hair. The girl who loved him, who'd saved his arse more than once. He'd found out that she'd volunteered to parachute into France for SOE in '44, while he was away in Europe after D-Day. He'd come home to find her posted MIA – missing in action. Nothing had been heard of her since.

Caine halted in front of the full-length mirror on the wardrobe. He clocked a man there, medium height, smart BDs, medal ribbons, SAS wings on the breast. They'd officially banned the practice now. Parachute wings belonged on shoulders, they said, only RAF pilots could wear them on chests. Caine's commanding officer, the legendary Lt Colonel Paddy Mayne, had told them to fuck off. Caine studied the three pips in sky blue on his epaulettes. He saw a man with a slim waist and torpedo shoulders. A blunt face with freckles, grey eyes like polished steel. He saw the bags under them. The crows' feet. The wrinkles that hadn't been there when the war started. He couldn't believe he was still only twenty-five years old. He saw something lurking in those eyes, something that hadn't been there at the beginning either. Something that had possessed him. Something that wasn't himself.

A waft of *Rule Britannia* drifted in from the street. A wave of nausea drifted in with it. A blaze of fury exploded in his guts. He crushed the tumbler with a single squeeze. Glass shattered, shards stuck in his palm. He belted the mirror savagely, with bloody, whisky-soaked knuckles. There was a thud. A pattern of cracks spread across the mirror like a spiderweb. Ragged slivers of mirror smashed on the floor.

Caine stood back panting, shuftied the blood dripping from his fingers, the bits of glass embedded in his skin, grunted '*Shit. Shit. Shit.*'

At that moment, there was a rap on the door. Before Caine could breathe another word, a young major walked in.

CHAPTER THREE

Caine glanced up. The major stared at the dripping blood, studied the broken mirror. He didn't look surprised.

'Gets to you, doesn't it Tom?' he said. 'They're all out there, doing the hokey-cokey. The royals waving like puppets. Winnie smug as a beetroot, you'd think he'd won the war on his own. Looking down on the hoi-polloi. It was the hoi-polloi who won the war. The bodies lying in shallow graves, eh, Tom? The lads – and lasses – tortured, murdered, maimed, massacred… well, you know what I mean.'

The voice was officer class, but there was no hint of superiority. The words were harsh, irreverent – almost disloyal – but no trace of rancour. Caine flushed. It was as if the chap had just read his thoughts. He grasped his bleeding hand, tried to look unconvinced.

'Don't you usually wait till someone asks you in… *sir*?' he demanded.

The laugh was elvish. 'Not usually, no. Bad manners maybe, Tom – like calling you Tom, when you don't really know me – but then, that's just my way. Annoys some people. I'm sure it doesn't bother you.'

'Are you now, sir?'

What did the chap mean by *really*? Had they met? *There is something familiar about him.*

24

'Bill,' the major said. He advanced a step, ignored the hostile tone. 'Bill Backhouse. Major. DLI, ex-IO, 2nd. SAS Regiment… I *would* offer to shake hands, but… hey, let me take a look at that.'

He took a field dressing from his breast pocket. In seconds, he was picking bits of glass out of Caine's fingers. His hands moved with the touch of a skilled medic. Finally, he wrapped the bandage neatly round the fingers and tied it. Caine studied him.

He must have been the oddest, scruffiest-looking officer he'd ever met – and he'd met some dinkies. BD was the order of the day, but this bloke was actually wearing service dress. If you could call the wrinkled, worn, torn, faded, khaki rag of a suit a uniform at all. Looked like he'd slept in it… no, *been* sleeping in it… for weeks. He had SAS wings on his shoulder, squinted, hanging off, and sky-blue crowns on his shoulder straps. Instead of an SAS beret, he wore a peaked service cap, no badge. Long strands of dirty black hair fell from under it. There were winged dagger badges on his lapels – Caine knew the emblem was originally intended to be Excalibur, the Flaming Sword, but it had become the fashion to call it a dagger now. Maybe because SHAEF had pinched the Flaming Sword flash. Some of the major's tunic buttons were missing. His tie was skew-whiff, his shirt unbuttoned, the collar frayed.

The fellow had a long face, no moustache, two-day stubble on the chin. He was young – not much older than Caine, but there was a stern set to his jaw. His eyes seemed to change colour as you looked at them. The flesh around them was prematurely wrinkled, like Caine's, but there was a hound dog hint of sadness there. His expression was almost indignant as if he'd seen some terrible things he wasn't going to forget in a hurry and had every intention of putting them right. His manner was bright, warm, puckish, but Caine sensed iron under the surface. If this was a hound dog, he thought, it was one that could bite.

CHAPTER FOUR

They decided not to go down to the bar. It would be too rowdy – they could hear the drunken singing, the lurching off-key rattle of a piano, even from up here. There was whisky left in the bottle. Backhouse found chipped teacups and poured them each a measure. He held up his cup. 'To fallen comrades,' he said.

'*Amen*,' Caine nodded. They swallowed in silence.

'Ok,' Caine said. 'So, tell me, Bill, do you know me? How did you find me? And what're you doing here?'

Backhouse sat down on the bed. Caine settled in the single armchair. He slid a scratched cigarette case out of his BD blouse pocket, flicked it open, offered Backhouse a fag. The major took one. Caine took one too, tapped it on the case, put the case away. He lit both cigarettes with the Zippo lighter that he still carried in a condom. The lighter was his good luck charm. His mate Harry Copeland had once retrieved it from the body of a dead German paratrooper, weeks after the Jerries had swiped it from Caine. That was the second time he'd got it back from a dead Jerry. It had saved his life at least once.

He took a deep drag, blew out smoke. For a second, they both smoked in silence.

'Actually, we've met,' Backhouse said. He examined the glowing tip of his fag. 'I was part of the Int. team who briefed you for Op *Chafe* last year.'

Caine remembered. *Chafe* was a stunt of the old style. Its objective had been to assassinate Field Marshal Rommel in France. Six-man team. Apart from himself, all ex-Foreign Legion men from 2nd, 3rd and 4th SAS. One was Russian, one even a bloody *Jerry*, he recalled.

He snorted. 'I remember you, now. You looked a bit smarter. Never saw you at the debrief, though. Pity you didn't tell us Rommel had already bought one in an air attack before we jumped. Walked right into a trap.'

Backhouse didn't turn a hair. 'The int came from your lot. 1st SAS. As far as we knew, it was pukker. You did all right, though. Didn't lose any blokes.'

Caine sipped whisky, let a pencil line of smoke curl up to a ceiling already yellowed by years of cigarette smoke. 'Yep,' he said. 'Suppose you could say that.'

He watched the major questioningly, took another drag from his cigarette.

'Ok,' Backhouse said. 'How did I know where you were? Finding out things is my business. Why am I here? When I mentioned shallow graves just now, I wasn't kidding. A few days ago, the French authorities in Germany reported that they'd found twenty-seven bodies in a mass grave at a place called Gaggenau south of Baden-Baden. Some of them were tentatively ID'd as American aircrew, some French Resistance. Rest thought to be British. That's all they said, but I *know* they're SAS.'

Caine swallowed whisky, took another drag. On an Italian op two years back he'd found bodies buried in the woods. SAS men, captured and murdered by Gestapo troops. Hitler had ordered all special service troops slaughtered, whether they surrendered or not. Few people in Blighty had believed it then. It was against Hague Rules, they said. Caine's mates, big Fred Wallace and Taff Trubman had seen it first hand, though. Escaped by the skin of their teeth. Caine believed it all right.

'You *know* they're SAS?' he repeated. '*How* do you know?'

'I had a dream about it.'

Caine was about to scoff. *Bloody fruitcake*, he thought. *That's why he's dressed like a hobo. Escaped from the looney bin. Or they let him out to celebrate VE Day.*

Then he recalled the odd, out-of-body feelings he'd sometimes had in action. He'd once talked to his dead medic, Maurice Pickney, in a dream. *That was just the pressure of combat, though, wasn't it? Plays funny tricks on you.*

Backhouse was eyeing him. Caine felt the bloke was reading his mind. 'You can think what you like, Tom,' the major said. His voice was almost girlish. 'But Brian Franks – my CO – believes me. He authorized me to form a unit called the SAS War Crimes Investigation Team – WCIT. He's given me the green light to go to France and Germany and investigate the fate of every SAS man or SOE agent dropped into Europe after D-Day. Everyone that hasn't been accounted for, that is. If they were murdered by the Nazis, we're going to find the bastards who did it…'

His eyes blazed suddenly, burned tracer-round orange. His face contorted with a rage so furious it took Caine off guard. '*And then*,' he said slowly, his voice the voice of someone else altogether, '*they will pay.*'

Caine glanced at him. For a moment, Backhouse had looked just like he himself had, the instant before he'd smashed the mirror.

The major's face had resumed its calm contours, but he was still breathing heavily.

'Like you said, it gets to you,' Caine said, soothingly. 'Even if you're right, though, this… what was it… *Gaggenau*… discovery's only the thin end of the wedge. It could take years to find them all, and all the people responsible.'

'We'll just keep on till we find 'em…' The major knocked off his service cap, sent it scuttering across the floor. '…Don't think I always wear that crap hat. I've still got my beret, even if it's a maroon one now.'

Caine snorted. That was another thing that had rankled with SAS vets of North Africa and Italy. When they'd formed the SAS Brigade before D-Day – two British regiments, two French, one Belgian – they'd made SAS men wear the same maroon-red berets as the Paras. As usual, Paddy Mayne had given them two fingers, gone on wearing his sand-coloured beret. He was the only one who'd got away with it, though.

'What's this got to do with me?' Caine demanded, laying his teacup back on the table. He stubbed his fag out hard in the ashtray, stared up at Backhouse. 'I sympathize, but almost all the lads who went missing were 2nd Regiment, not my mates. Ok, I know about Franks and Op *Taunton* – he lost half his crew. I know the feeling, believe me. Survivor's guilt. Wanting to put it right. I'd feel the same. I'd call it a personal thing, though.'

Backhouse looked annoyed. 'We're *all* mates in the SAS, Tom,' he said. 'I thought you, of all people, would have understood that. It's personal for the lot of us. I've got three good men in the WCIT, but I could do with a few more. I want you in, Tom. I know you. Know all about you. Why'd you think I picked you for *Chafe*?'

'*You* picked me?'

'Yes, *I* picked you. That op was run by 2nd Regiment. You've got a temper…' he nodded at the broken mirror, 'but you've also got a conscience. You're a damn good man in action – a killer, in fact. You once killed three armed Brandenburgers with—'

'—A rusty knife, *all right*,' Caine rolled his eyes. 'Why the hell is that the only story anyone seems to know about me? It's not something I'm proud of.'

'That's my point, exactly. You're good at it, but you don't take pleasure in it. You've got no time for HQ wallahs, or red tape. You don't suffer morons, not even if they've got gold braid as thick as spaghetti on their hats. You're a straight arrow, Tom, and you're committed. Once you get your teeth into a thing, you don't let go. Like you never let go of Betty Nolan, even though they all told you she was dead.'

Caine flushed. 'You knew about that?' He felt a tear squeeze out of the corner of his eye, brushed it away. 'She *is* dead now. Died a year back. Never went to the funeral. Couldn't stand it. That's why I know how Franks must feel.'

'I heard. I'm sorry,' Backhouse said, 'but you're only proving my point again. Conscience, you see.'

Caine sniffed, stood up suddenly. 'Look, I appreciate the offer, Bill, but like I said, I reckon this is a personal thing – a 2nd Regiment thing. It's not for me.'

Backhouse also stood, faced him. 'So, what are you going to do? Back to the Sappers? Demob and start up your own garage in civvie street? You were an apprentice mechanic before the war, weren't you?'

'So what?'

'So nothing. Just that I know you better than you think. You hate the brass, but the army's home. It's all you've got.' He paused, examined Caine keenly. 'You say it's personal. Maybe it is. It could be personal for you, too.'

'Me? How?'

'There was another girl after Betty, wasn't there? Cracking redhead. Plucky young lady. Int. Corps. Field Security. Copped a bad one in a shoot-out with deserters in Cairo. Pulled through.'

Caine was staggered. 'You mean Blaney? Celia Blaney?'

'That's her,' Backhouse said without smiling. 'Turned out she grew up in France and spoke the lingo. They drafted her into SOE and dropped her into France last year. She's been missing ever since.'

'So what?' Caine growled again. 'I knew that.'

'Maybe you're not as bright as I thought you were,' Backhouse said. 'I told you the SAS War Crimes Investigation Team is charged with finding missing SOE personnel *as well* as SAS. SOE got it as bad as our boys, maybe worse.'

Caine pulled himself straight. 'So, you're offering me the chance to find out what happened to Blaney?'

Backhouse still wasn't smiling. 'Do you want to know?'

'Yes, I do.'

'Well, this is your chance. Because one of the bodies found at Gaggenau was a woman. They haven't identified her yet.'

Caine considered it for a moment. Backhouse had read him perfectly – action was just what he needed right now. 'All right,' he said. 'I'm in. There's just one condition...'

'...that you can take your old crew – Harry Copeland, Fred Wallace and Taff Trubman?' Backhouse nodded, his voice almost bored. 'You don't find that kind of loyalty every day...'

'What do you mean?'

'I've already been in touch with them at Hylands House. They all volunteered to join the War Crimes Investigation Team, on one condition – that you're on board.'

CHAPTER FIVE

Alsace, France. September 1944

They called themselves André and Rolande. Blaney guessed they were father and son, but she wasn't taking anything for granted. Those probably weren't their real names. Why should they be? They had no idea what *her* real name was.

'We'd best get moving,' André told her. 'Put the pea-shooter away, *Mademoiselle*. We've seen no sign of the Bosch, but you never can tell. We need to get to the safe house quick.'

Blaney stuck the pistol back in her pocket. 'Call me Giselle,' she said.

'Is your stuff well buried?' Rolande asked. He was strong looking, broad shouldered, chiselled, handsome features. Almost the opposite of the small, wiry, wizened-faced André. Yet while André exuded reassurance, there was a trace of anxiety in Rolande's voice.

Blaney nodded. '*Mais oui, naturellement.*'

'But you are hurt?' André said. 'You were limping.' There was a hint of reproach in his voice as if she'd done it on purpose.

'It's a sprained ankle, that's all,' Blaney said. 'I've got a first aid kit, but we don't have time for that.'

Rolande took her suitcase. They showed her to a wooden gate that opened onto a road. Blaney saw two bicycles propped against the hedge. André rode one and took the lead. Rolande rode the second, with Blaney perching on the luggage rack behind, one arm round his waist, the other balancing the suitcase awkwardly on her knees. She thanked God again she wasn't a pianist. Their suitcase-radios alone weighed eighteen kilos.

She knew the safe house was only a mile away – no, about a kilometre and a half – she corrected herself. From now on she had to eat, sleep, breathe and think French. She'd heard the stories at Beaulieu. Agents who'd betrayed themselves by pouring milk into teacups before the tea, or going into coffee shops and ordering *café noir,* when there wasn't any other kind. She'd been brought up here though, so it wasn't that hard. She'd got a bit rusty over the last years, maybe, but she was still French at heart.

The road passed through deep woods, where the branches made a tunnel over their heads. The men peddled through zebra-skin moon dapples. The bicycle wheels creaked. An owl hooted somewhere close. For no apparent reason, Blaney felt a sudden wave of terror. She imagined wild animals, not Jerries, jumping at her out of the night. She took deep breaths, the fear dissolved. Momentary panic fits like this were another thing she'd been warned about.

The safe house was in a clearing in the woods – two-storied, thatched, timber beams in plaster, smoke issuing from the chimney. It was a fairy-tale cottage. A dog barked as they rode up to the door. André silenced it with a curse. She stumbled off the bike, still balancing the suitcase. She smelt pigs, heard the squawk of chickens. The door opened and two women stepped out, both wearing shawls and simple peasant dresses. Like André and Rolande, one was older than the other. Both looked careworn and solemn. They reminded Blaney of Red Indian squaws in a cowboy film.

The women were called Ginevre and Violette. They didn't say much, but they seemed friendly and they ushered Blaney inside. The interior was tiny and sparse: hard chairs, a small table pushed into the corner. It was lit only by a smoky fire. André had Blaney sit down on a chair by the hearth. He told her to get out her first aid kit so that he could dress her ankle. The older woman – Ginevre – stirred something savoury, cooking in a metal pot that hung on a hooked chain over the fire. Rolande had stayed outside. On watch, perhaps. Or maybe gone to squeal to the Gestapo, Blaney thought suddenly. It was an ungenerous idea, considering these men were probably risking their lives for her. On the other hand, she had to stay alert, keep an open mind.

When she removed her shoe, she found that her ankle was swollen, but not as badly as she'd feared. André's hands were rough but surprisingly deft as he wrapped the bandage round her. He seemed to know what he was doing. Blaney stared at him in the smoky light. Was he what he appeared to be? She put the idea aside – only time would tell.

'It was a mistake landing in that field,' he told her. 'You should have dropped into parkland. Didn't they tell you that?'

There was a patronizing note in his voice that niggled her. She fought against it. André was talking as if she were a naïve child, but she guessed it was because she was a woman. Women didn't rate very highly in France – even less than in Britain. They didn't even have the vote. The idea of a woman dropping by parachute, carrying a weapon, organizing a dangerous sabotage stunt, was probably hard for him to take. Who cared? She was here to do a job – an important job. She intended to do it. It didn't matter what he thought.

The older woman ladled soup into a wooden bowl and handed it to her, together with a wooden spoon. It was mostly onions and potatoes, flavoured with herbs, but it was hot and delicious. Blaney was glad of it. The woman left two more bowls and spoons on the tiny table in the corner, then she and the younger woman crept silently up the stairs. They didn't say goodnight.

Blaney watched them go. She scraped the bottom of her soup bowl, laid it down on the hearth. André finished dressing her ankle with a sigh. Without making any other comment, he fetched a bowl and spoon from the table, ladled soup into it. He squatted on a stool opposite her. His eyes never left her as he ate.

'I chose that place because it was near the safe house,' Blaney told him. 'It didn't appear to be a cultivated field on the map, probably because it's fallow. All right, it was a mistake, but I'll live. There are always mistakes.'

André's eyes were bright in the firelight. 'Mistakes can get us killed,' he said. Then, as if realizing he was being pessimistic, added, 'We're going to need some special stuff for this job. They didn't drop it in with you. So, when's it coming?'

Blaney hesitated. 'You know what the mission is?' she demanded, a little too bluntly.

André finished his soup, put his bowl down on the hearth next to hers. 'Of course I do,' he scoffed. 'Who do you think supplied the intelligence? I'm the circuit chief – *Circuit Boxer*. My wireless code name's *Larroque*. Didn't they tell you that, either?'

'Yes, they did.'

'The operation is called *Ramboule*,' he went on. 'It's…'

'No need to say it,' she hissed. 'Does *he* know?' she nodded at the closed door.

André shook his head. 'Not yet. When the time comes, he will.' He raised an eyebrow as if repeating his previous question.

Blaney took a breath. 'The ICL containers will be dropped four days from now, same time, same place.'

'Four *days*? You realize we've only got a couple of weeks to do this job? The American Sixth Army is getting close.' He paused, shook his head. 'And dropping the containers in that field? We'll need more than two men to retrieve them. The Vosges are crawling with Bosch. Some of your parachute boys were holed up there. Them and the Maquis were demolishing railway lines, roads, bridges, staff cars, convoys, like nobody's business. The Bosch are hopping mad. Got a whole division after them. Captured some of them already.'

Blaney looked up at the mention of *parachute boys*. That could only mean SAS – the Airborne proper weren't trained to fight in small groups behind enemy lines. Could Tom Caine be there? No, that would be too much of a coincidence. There was a whole brigade of SAS troops operating in Europe now. Caine could be anywhere.

'What happened to the ones they bagged?' she asked.

'Sent them to KL-Natzweiler – only concentration camp on French soil. The Bosch don't see it like that, of course. To them, Alsace is part of Germany now. Administered directly from Baden.'

He paused, ruminated for a moment. 'It's awkward for us, though.'

'Why?'

'The SS have got captured parachutists working at our… target. Whether it was because they needed workers with some practical ability, or because they thought that if word got out, the Allies would think twice about bombing it, I don't know.'

'You mean hostages?' Blaney said.

'Exactly.'

'I don't think so. I'd have been told.'

'Maybe, maybe not. They only tell us what they think we need to know.'

Blaney considered it. Would SOE be ready to write off SAS soldiers? She doubted it, but there were other forces at work here. Like the SIS – the Secret Intelligence Service. They had labelled SOE *amateur, dangerous* and *bogus*, Lurgan had told her. The truth was, SIS was jealous as hell of SOE and hated them for queering what they regarded as their pitch. Making bangs was what SOE did; the SIS way was silence and eyeball. It was only the support of Churchill that kept SOE going. *Well, SIS isn't in charge of this operation. I am. And I'm not sacrificing any SAS men. God, what if one of them really* was *Tom Caine?*

'They can't work round the clock,' she said. 'They must have rest time and days off.'

André nodded. 'The place is shut down at night and on Sundays,' he said. 'That would be the time to strike.' He hesitated. 'I just wish they hadn't decided to drop the containers in that field. There'll be high explosive. Detonators. Incendiaries. If anything goes bang when they hit the dirt, our goose will be cooked.'

Blaney was about to say *you worry too much* but stopped herself. André would probably take it as an affront to have his courage questioned by a girl half his age.

Later, he gave her a tot of apricot brandy and showed her to a tiny room on the ground floor. There was nothing but a cot bed in it. She closed the door, lay down, covered herself with blankets. A while later, she heard Rolande come in, heard the creak as he sat down in front of the fire. She got very little sleep. The men's voices droned on in Alsatian dialect till sunrise. There were bedbugs in the sheets.

CHAPTER SIX

Paris, France. June 1945

'It's in the *French* Zone,' Colonel Kemp repeated, as if explaining to mentally deficient infants. 'Do you think the French are going to be pleased to have amateurs poking their noses in there?'

Caine and Backhouse both bristled. They exchanged glances. Caine saw a venomous look come over Backhouse's face – the same look he'd seen at the Victory Club when the major had told him '*They will pay.*' He'd got to know Bill pretty well in the intervening weeks. Floated like a butterfly until he was riled. Then you had to watch it. Talk about *pack a punch out of proportion to its size.* Whatever happened from now on, Caine thought, Colonel Kemp was likely to end up an unhappy man.

They were at SHAEF local HQ in Paris, where they'd been ordered to report en route to Germany. It was meant to be a five-minute courtesy visit. Instead, they seemed to have run into a brick wall.

Kemp was a beef-faced, bulky officer of the Royal Artillery, who wore the fiery sword-and-rainbow sleeve flash of SHAEF on his arm. Bulging BDs, bloodshot eyes. He looked as if he might have ridden out the war behind a desk, but the row of medal ribbons on his breast said otherwise. He'd probably just forgotten what it was like to be a field soldier. Either that or he had a good reason for standing in their way.

Caine and Backhouse were sitting on hard chairs in front of Kemp's desk. Both were wearing camouflaged Dennison smocks over their BDs with '44-pattern web belts in jungle green. Both carried automatic pistols in webbing holsters but no other equipment. They wore badges of rank clipped on their epaulettes and SAS wings clipped on their shoulders. Both had on regulation maroon-red berets with the SAS winged-dagger badge – not much different from SHAEF's fiery sword insignia, except that, rather than upwards, their blade pointed down. Backhouse had transformed himself since his first meeting with Caine. He had even shaved and trimmed his hair. Yet when they'd entered Kemp's office and saluted smartly, the colonel had eyed them as if they were some species of vermin.

If anything looked amateurish, it was this place, Caine reflected. Kemp's desk was piled high with papers. The office was shabby, cobwebbed, dusty – a chaos of documents and files. If this mess represented the smartness and efficiency of Supreme HQ, Allied Expeditionary Forces Europe, no wonder the colonel was put out.

'*Amateurs?*' Backhouse repeated.

Here it comes, Caine thought, almost wincing. He could hear the acid in Backhouse's voice. The major leaned forward. 'God forbid that I should be construed as boasting, Colonel, but I took part in six ops behind enemy lines after D-Day. All of our men are veterans, some of them from North Africa days, most of them decorated, some with multiple decorations. Captain Caine here, by the way, is one of the most highly decorated soldiers of the war.'

He paused for breath, his eyes burning. Caine realized he wasn't finished. 'Have you ever heard of Hitler's *Commando Order*, Colonel? At least thirty-one SAS men are presumed murdered by the Jerries, *after* they'd been taken prisoner, in contravention of The Hague Convention. Those are war crimes. The number of SOE operatives murdered – men and women – is still uncertain, but they reckon about one third of the agents they sent into the field never came back. We have authorization and orders to investigate the deaths of those people. Some of the dead men at Gaggenau were almost certainly comrades of ours.'

For a moment the colonel looked uncomfortable. Then, composing himself, he picked up the typed and stamped sheet Backhouse had given him, held it between finger and thumb, as if it was infectious. 'You call this *authorization*? Who is this… Brigadier Calvert? Never heard of him.'

'Brigadier Mike Calvert is Commander, Special Air Service troops,' Backhouse said. 'Former Second-in-Command, Chindit Brigade, Burma. DSO and bar.'

Kemp slammed the paper down on the desk with his palm. His thin lips creased into a grimace. '*Special Air Service? Chindits? Commandos? Popski's private bloody nutcrackers?* Bands of thugs raised in the confusion of war by people with friends in high places. Excuses for insubordination, ill-discipline and sloppiness. Thank God we're back to some *real* soldiering. The days of sloppiness are past.'

Caine couldn't help chuckling. He glanced round at the filthy, chaotic office.

'Yes, sir,' he grinned. 'I can see that.'

Backhouse laughed, his furious expression now vanished.

The colonel's face tightened. 'I ought to have you both on a charge for insubordination. Coming here, expecting to be given a free hand to swan around anywhere you like, in any zone, on the strength of this rag signed by a nobody.' He turned to glance at the map of Europe on the wall behind him. It seemed to afford him some effort. 'You've no idea how confused it all is,' he said. Caine noticed his voice had taken on a plaintive note. 'We've got SIS, American Intelligence, Yank War Crimes Teams…'

'Ah,' Backhouse cut in. 'So, the Americans can investigate war crimes, but we can't?'

The colonel stared at him, scarcely able to contain his irritation. 'They're *authorized*,' he boomed. 'I mean *real* authorization, man. From the War Office or its equivalent. Signed by somebody important.'

'I think you'll find that Brigadier Calvert is important enough,' Backhouse said.

Kemp stuck his chin out. 'Oh you do, do you, Major? Well, I don't. And as I'm the ranking officer here, and I command this branch of SHAEF, I think you'll find it's *my* opinion that counts.'

He picked up the receiver of the telephone on his desk and dialled a number, stabbing a thick finger into the dialling holes.

'Give me the OC Military Police,' he snapped, his eyes riveted on Backhouse.

'Where are your vehicles, Major?' he demanded. 'In the motor pool?' Backhouse nodded. 'Yes, sir.'

There was a scarcely audible squawk from the receiver. 'Sarn't? I'd like to speak to Major Sears-Beach.'

The hairs on the back of Caine's neck prickled. A cold shiver ran down his spine. *Sears-Beach? No, it couldn't be.* The MP officer who'd had him beaten up in a Cairo cell? The MP officer who'd tried to sell his patrol to the Germans in Tunisia? Sears-Beach had been transferred in disgrace to the Provost Corps – the army's prison guards. He'd last seen him the night Paddy Mayne had knocked him down the stairs of Shepheard's Hotel. That had also been the last night he'd ever really spoken to Betty Nolan. The night they'd crashed into the Nile.

His mouth went dry. Sears-Beach wasn't a common name. It was him all right, Caine was sure of it. Sears-Beach was the last person they needed on their case right now.

He kept his face straight. Backhouse stared at him suddenly. He had a disconcerting knack of sensing things.

'Major,' the colonel was saying. 'Colonel Kemp here. There are some vehicles in the motor pool, manned by... er... Special Air Service troops. Chaps with maroon-red berets...Yes, SAS, that's it.' He paused, listened for a moment. 'Look, I don't want to debate the colour of their headgear. Maroon-red, take it from me. I want those vehicles impounded... The men? No. Just make sure those vehicles don't leave the park.'

He slammed the receiver down. There was a look of triumph on his puffy face.

'I don't think you'll be going anywhere without transport, do you? May I suggest you find billets in Paris for the night and at the earliest opportunity head back to... where was it you came from?'

'Wivenhoe.'

'Exactly.'

Before he could dismiss them, both Caine and Backhouse were on their feet. They stamped to attention, saluted in unison, turned and marched out of the office. As soon as the door closed behind them, Backhouse said, 'I think it's *Who Dares Wins*, don't you Tom?'

'Spot on,' Caine replied.

Without another word, they sprinted down the corridor, heading for the stairs.

CHAPTER SEVEN

Sitting at the wheel of one of the two WCIT jeeps in the motor park, Lt Harry Copeland was getting impatient. He turned to Fred Wallace, lodged sideways on the seat beside him so that his hippo-sized legs had room to stretch. 'So much for five minutes,' Copeland said. 'What the hell is the skipper doing in there?'

Wallace, a huge bulk of a man with a blue chin and Neanderthal features, was about to comment when the driver of the jeep parked alongside spoke. 'Probably Backhouse. When Bill gets goin', 'e's like a dog with a bone.'

Copeland glanced at him. Sergeant Major 'Dusty' Rhodes was Backhouse's assistant. A tall, clean-shaven, wiry man, he'd served in 2nd SAS during the war, and, like Wallace, he'd won the MM twice. He was a tad younger than Copeland, lean to the point of bantam-weight. Apart from that, they might have been brothers. Same prominent Adam's apple, same stubbly straw-blonde hair. Cope understood why Backhouse had chosen Dusty as his right-hand man. Rhodes had personally known a lot of the 2nd SAS boys who'd vanished in the war. Like Backhouse, he was determined to find out what had happened to them. He was tough, focused, keen.

Behind Rhodes in the jeep sat a hefty corporal called Dick Swan – a reserved Second SAS vet – ex-11th (Scottish) Commando – who'd seen action in North Africa, Italy and France. Another 2nd SAS Trooper – 'Flint' Ronson, was lounging in the cab of the Bedford three-tonner behind them. The lorry and two jeeps were the sum total of the team's transport.

Suddenly, another voice piped up from behind Copeland. It was Corporal Taffy Trubman, the bespectacled Welsh signaller who'd been with Caine on most of his ops in North Africa. ''*Allo*,' he said. 'I think we got company, boys.'

Wallace, Copeland and Rhodes all looked up. A wedge of Redcaps, with scarlet cap covers and armbands, white webbing and gaiters, were moving towards them at the double, swinging pick helves. They looked as if they meant business.

'Not the bleedin' rozzers,' Wallace sighed. 'Never can seem to get away from those berks.'

Wallace was legendary for the run-ins he'd had with Redcaps. It wasn't that he had anything particular against *them*, he would say. It was just that he'd been in clink in civvie street before the war and had developed claustrophobia. He'd rather fight than go back there.

He slipped out of his seat with surprising agility for such a giant. He had a Colt automatic holstered in his belt. A Bren gun – his favourite weapon – was clipped in the dashboard brackets, made safe. His first reaction was to draw his pistol. He had to remind himself that the war was over. These blighters weren't the Hun.

'I don't like the look of this,' Copeland said.

The MPs were advancing in a rough arrowhead. There were ten of them. *Ten MPs against six SAS men. Hardly fair – on the Redcaps*, Cope thought. On point was a barrel-chested bull of a warrant officer, with a ferocious look on his face. He wasn't as big as Fred Wallace, but he had biceps like boulders, built like a barn door.

Wallace was standing, feet apart, slab-like chin raised, black piggy eyes narrowed, pan-sized fists clenched: *repel boarders*. Copeland knew that stance. He jumped out of the jeep and stood next to Wallace, giving him a nudge on the arm. Rhodes made to follow, but Cope turned and winked at him. 'Better get ready to pull out,' he said. Rhodes hesitated, as if he didn't like being told what to do by a 1st SAS Officer. The War Crimes Investigation Team was a 2nd SAS creation, and at the outset, there'd been some rivalry. As a lieutenant, though, Copeland was the senior rank present. He wasn't officious or snooty, and Rhodes liked him. He gave a private hand signal to Ronson in the three-tonner: *Prepare to start motors*. In the other jeep, Taffy Trubman adjusted his glasses, then, without being told, crawled over the seat and plonked himself solidly behind the steering wheel.

By now, the bullish WO2 had come to a halt in front of Cope. He eyed the maroon-red beret, the SAS wings and the two sky-blue pips clipped on Copeland's Dennison smock with suspicion. Then, as if remembering where he was, he snapped to attention and saluted. Cope returned the salute.

'Sorry, sir,' the MP growled, 'but I've got orders to impound your vehicles.'

The peak of his cap was pulled down tightly over his eyes. He looked more smug than sorry, Copeland thought.

'From whom, may I ask, Sarn't Major?' Cope asked.

'From my OC, Major Sears-Beach.'

Copeland and Wallace exchanged astonished glances.

'*Not that piece of cr…*' Wallace gasped. Cope's stern look silenced him.

'Of course,' Copeland said. 'But where did the orders come from originally?'

'Colonel Kemp, I believe, sir. GSO1.'

Cope recognized the name. Kemp was the officer Caine and Backhouse had had an appointment with. It meant they were in trouble.

'Now if you wouldn't mind moving aside, sir,' the MP said, 'and telling your men to stand down, I'll carry out my orders.'

Copeland didn't shift. 'I'd be glad to, Sarn't Major,' he said, 'but you see, we're under orders too, and to execute them, we require these vehicles...'

'But...' the MP started.

'And the fact is,' Cope cut in on him, nodding towards Wallace, 'my friend, this trooper here – double MM, by the way – doesn't care for military policemen. Says they leave a sour taste in the mouth.'

'Yeah, like the on'y good Redcap's a dead 'un,' Wallace snarled.

For a split second the MP looked from one to the other, as if unable to believe what he was hearing.

In that moment there was the patter of rubber-soled boots. Copeland saw Caine and Backhouse haring towards them from the direction of the main building. Caine was making the hand signal for *start motors. Pull out.*

The MP sergeant major suddenly understood what was happening. He began to raise his pick helve, his eyes fixed on Copeland. Before it was even halfway up, Wallace had lamped him twice in the face with fists as big as anti-tank mines. They weren't hard punches by Wallace's standards – he'd been the heavyweight boxing champion of the Middle East Commando – but they were hard enough to knock the MP off his feet.

The motors of all three SAS vehicles gunned with a single roar. They rolled forwards, accelerating fast in first gear, directly towards the group of MPs. The Redcaps scattered frantically. Cope sprang aside as his jeep passed, grabbed the roll bar and swung into the seat next to Trubman. Wallace just had time to kick another helve-waving rozzer in the balls before diving into the back. At almost the same time, Caine and Backhouse vaulted into the passenger seat of the jeep Rhodes was driving, squashing themselves together. '*Hit the throttle*,' Backhouse yelled.

Rhodes and Trubman jockeyed for lead all the way across the motor park, their tyres crunching on gravel, heading for the main barrier. The three-tonner trundled close behind. The windows of the SHAEF building gazed down at them like blank eyes. A few MPs chased them, brandishing pick helves. Others just stood and gaped.

Security at SHAEF wasn't as tight as it should have been. The red-and-white striped barrier was up. Realizing the threat at the last moment, the MP guards tried to close it, but too late. They had to hurl themselves aside as the three SAS vehicles hurtled through in a tight convoy, almost nose to tail. Wallace, crouching in the back of the jeep, felt something was missing. Then he realized what it was: the double Vickers K machine guns that SAS jeeps had carried in wartime. Those guns, originally designed for aircraft, had got him and his mates out of tight scrapes a score of times. Wallace had always preferred the gunner's place in the back to the confinement of the driving seat. He'd half-expected the MPs to shoot at them. He kept having to remind himself that the war was over. It was back to fisticuffs with your own lot now.

CHAPTER EIGHT

Paris hadn't been as badly bombed as many other European cities during the war, but still its streets were full of gaping wounds. Magnificent apartment buildings had been reduced to jagged wedges of stonework, crumbling walls, piles of rubble. One church they passed was nothing but an empty shell. The top section of the Eiffel tower had been sliced off. Even Notre Dame had been damaged.

The streets were crowded though. Boys pedalled bicycles with wooden crates mounted on the back, painted with the legend *Cycle-Taxi*. There were queues everywhere – men and women in down-at-heel clothes formed lines outside glass-fronted shops marked *Patisserie*, *Boucherie* or *Latte-Beurre-Oeufs*. Men in dirty aprons shifted milk churns to and fro.

Backhouse seemed to know the city. He led the little convoy through side streets, to avoid checkpoints. When they'd put some distance between themselves and SHAEF, the major had Rhodes turn into a boulevard that had been badly hit. The buildings were wedges of masonry; outer walls without interiors, or multi-storey blocks where the walls had fallen down, leaving the rooms exposed. The road between what had been blocks of flats was an impenetrable mass of debris – piles of brick, stone, shattered roof tiles, sticks of smashed furniture, twisted roof beams, broken window frames.

Backhouse ordered the men to debus. They squatted among the rubble in their Dennison smocks, chugged water, lit cigarettes. Caine offered Backhouse a fag and took one himself. He lit them both.

'Not exactly a smooth kick-off,' he said.

'Oh, I don't know,' Backhouse replied. It was as though nothing of note had happened back at SHAEF. 'Your trooper Wallace punched an MP who was swinging a pick helve at a commissioned officer…' he broke off, stared at Wallace.

The giant beamed back bearishly. 'Only tickled 'im. If I'd really 'it 'im, 'e wouldn't of got up.' He glanced at Copeland. 'Did you 'ere what that rozzer said? 'E reckoned 'is OC was Sears-Beach. Now they've even got bloody *traitors* workin' for 'em.'

Backhouse nodded. 'Now is the time for all good traitors to crawl out of the woodwork,' he said. 'German, British… what about the *Milice* – Frenchmen who collaborated with Jerry? Anti-partisan units who tortured and murdered their own countrymen.'

''Anging's too good for the bastards,' Wallace said.

Backhouse turned to Caine. 'So, this Sears-Beach is a traitor?'

'He might have played a part in selling David Stirling to the enemy,' Caine said, 'and he certainly planted deserters on us in Tunisia, who—'

'—Me and Fred there ended up behind the wire because of that so-and-so,' Trubman said indignantly, adjusting his glasses. 'Almost snuffed it, both of us, see. Jerry pulled us through, then tried to—'

'—That's a story for another day, Taff,' Caine cut in. 'Sears-Beach was never court-martialled. No real proof. Let's focus on what we came for.'

Backhouse held his cigarette elegantly between two fingers, watched the way the smoke curled with interest. 'The way I see it,' he said, almost absent-mindedly, 'Colonel Kemp had no right to countermand our orders. They were signed and stamped by a superior officer in the UK.'

'Yeah,' Wallace croaked. 'I mean, what would Stirlin' 'ave done? Or Paddy Mayne, eh?'

Caine gave him an exasperated glance. 'That was *war*, Fred.'

'The war ain't over till we find out who bumped off our mates,' Rhodes commented.

'The big fellah's reaction might have been a wee bit unorthodox,' Sergeant Swan said, speaking for the first time. 'But isn't that what we're trained for in the SAS?'

The men cackled, especially the 2nd SAS lads. They obviously respected the soft-spoken Scotsman, Caine thought.

'Question is, why would he *want* to stop us?' Copeland demanded, looking at Caine. 'I mean, was it just too much trouble, pushing papers about, or what?'

Caine shook his head. 'I don't know, Harry. Kemp's seen service all right. He was wearing a whole bunch of campaign medal ribbons. Did you notice that, Bill?'

'Yes, I did.' Backhouse was still examining his cigarette. 'But if it's not about top-heavy red tape, then Colonel Kemp – or somebody he's taking orders from – doesn't want us poking our noses in…'

'And if they don't want us poking our noses in,' Copeland said, 'it means they're hiding something.'

Backhouse stopped observing the cigarette, looked at Cope with new respect. He was aware the officer had been a schoolmaster in civvie street and had worked his way up from Driver First Class in the Royal Army Service Corps to decorated SAS lieutenant. Caine had told him that Copeland was sharp and would be an asset to the War Crimes Team. Backhouse was starting to see what he'd meant.

'We're here to find out what happened to our mates after they was captured and who did it,' Rhodes cut in. He flashed Caine a sidelong look. 'And whoever else the Jerries did in after they'd been bagged, of course. All the bleedin' Redcaps in the army ain't goin' to stop us doin' that.'

The men cheered and whistled.

'Good man, Dusty,' Backhouse said. He ground the half-smoked fag underfoot, caught the attention of the men. 'Now, I want you all to do something you won't like. Get out the black Tank Regiment berets you were issued with. The crap hats, you know. Remove the SAS insignia from your smocks.'

There was a murmur of discontent. The major had been right – SAS men regarded their winged dagger badge as their sacred talisman. They'd earned it. To don the insignia and headgear of another unit was like blasphemy.

'Come on,' Caine said. 'It's not like we've never done it before.'

They'd worn Royal Tank Corps berets during the last days of the war. If they'd got captured, they wouldn't have been subject to instant execution as saboteurs or special service troops.

'It's only temporary,' Backhouse said. 'Let's keep a low profile till we see what the real picture is.'

'You know the drill,' Caine said. 'Once we get going again, drivers, take it easy. No one does anything to get us noticed. When we're out of Paris, we'll go like the clappers till we make the German frontier.'

'There'll be a heck of a lot of Allied checkpoints between here and there,' Copeland said.

'So what?' Wallace cut in. 'There was a million checkpoints in Italy and France when we was workin' behind the lines. Still got past 'em, though.'

*

It was almost dark when they set off, the sun a last fizzle of dying orange between the fractured and rubble-strewn avenues. Caine and Backhouse sat together in the leading jeep, smoking.

'What about this Sears-Beach, fellow, Tom?' Backhouse asked quietly. 'Do you think he'll come after us?'

'I have a bone to pick with Sears-Beach,' Caine said. 'If he finds out it's me, he might come after us, just for spite.' He paused.

'You heard what Kemp said. Europe's in chaos. A score of different int and counter-int services getting wires crossed. Squabbles over jurisdiction between us, the Yanks, the Ivans, the Frogs. War criminals lying low among the civilian population, trying to escape to other countries, cover up their past. Ex-POWs making their way home, Nazi collaborators trying to dodge retribution. Millions of folk trying to get themselves together, get back to normal. There's probably never been such confusion in Europe.' He paused again, took a drag from his cigarette. 'Kemp will probably contact Calvert at UK Base to report us, find out we're legit and get a bollocking. Calvert's thick with Churchill… and don't forget Winnie's son, Randolph, was a good mate of Stirling's in the early days. Churchill loves the SAS.'

Backhouse considered him with narrowed eyes. He pulled on his cigarette, blew out a long trail of smoke.

'That may be true, Tom, big wheels are turning. Stirling missed most of the war in Colditz. He's got no official position in the SAS. Calvert's acting brigadier, but he's only a half-colonel really. Even Churchill might not be PM forever. The wind is changing. There's a general election coming up.'

Caine flicked his cigarette butt into the street. 'I'm here to find out what they did to Blaney,' he said. 'If she's dead, and if there's evidence

they murdered her while she was a prisoner, whoever's responsible will…
well, there won't be any trials or lawyers involved, let's put it that way.'

Backhouse smiled.

CHAPTER NINE

Alsace, France. September 1944

The Daimler-Benz factory at Wallenbach was similar to scores of such plants the company had built all over Europe to increase war-production, but the only one in France. It was a five-storey block of steel, glass and concrete, standing on the stump of a hill. Its high gates could be approached only by an iron suspension bridge. The bridge spanned a ravine with steep sides, scooped out over millennia by a fast-flowing river. It was heavily guarded. There were sentries in towers, machine gun posts – even 88mm anti-aircraft gun emplacements on both sides.

'One thing's for certain,' André muttered, 'we're not going in *that* way.'

Blaney suppressed a chuckle. She, André, and Rolande lay side by side at the edge of a wood overlooking the factory. They had cycled up from the nearest safe house, setting off two hours before sunrise. They had leopard-crawled through the wood and were in place by first light. It was almost a week since Blaney had jumped, and the swelling on her ankle had gone down. She could ride a bike now. She was wearing a dun-coloured boiler suit over her usual floral dress and had her hair tied back in a bun, under a stocking cap. They had left their bicycles on a dirt track a couple of kilometres behind them,

54

hidden by leaves and branches, guarded by the fourth member of their crew, *Le Gars* Paul.

A convoy of twelve lorries in camouflage paint with SS markings was passing through the gates of the factory, under the eyes of guards, perched in high watchtowers. The lorries had canvas covers over the backs and were sealed at the rear, but Blaney knew they carried labourers – male and female prisoners from the Natzweiler-Struthof concentration camp about sixteen kilometres away. At a rough estimate, a dozen lorries meant several hundred workers – a thousand at most. Blaney knew KL-Natzweiler was reserved mostly for the Resistance – Maquis fighters, or men and women from all over north-western Europe, Poland, Norway, even Russia – who had worked actively or passively against the Nazi regime. There was also a peppering of Allied prisoners, but not run-of-the-mill detainees – special-service troops, commandos, pilots, SOE agents like herself.

Blaney glanced at her ladies' watch. It was an elegant Swiss timepiece that had been a present from a rich aunt – if anyone asked. It had *actually* been issued by the SOE quartermaster, along with all the rest of her gear. 0630 precisely. *Right on time.*

She was taking turns with André and Rolande to observe the Benz plant with the pocket telescope André had brought with him. The 'scope wasn't much use. It lacked magnifying power; it was hard to focus – a toy really. Blaney would have preferred a good pair of binos, but André had been against it. With two lenses instead of one, lens-flash was more likely to be spotted. In any case, if they were stopped and searched by the police, how would they explain away a pair of high-powered binoculars? Privately, Blaney had thought a telescope would be almost as difficult to explain and just as likely to be seen, but she'd given way. In the end, the day turned out overcast, so the chances of lens-flash were small.

She adjusted the focus as best she could, watched the convoy crawl inside until the gates closed behind it. She traversed the scope, taking in each watchtower, each guardhouse, each barbed-wire entanglement, each AA gun emplacement. André's remark had been sarcastic, but true – there was no getting into the works that way. The Bosch had certainly pulled out all the stops when it came to protecting this one. Frontal assault on the Benz factory was quite definitely not an option.

'Looks pretty well sewn up,' she agreed. 'You sure you know how to get in?'

André grimaced. Blaney realized she'd blundered, bit her lip. She'd tried to be careful, but it wasn't the first time she'd put her foot in it. These Frenchmen were such chauvinists, she thought. She reminded herself once more that, though she'd been brought up in France and at times regarded herself as more French than British, to them she was still a foreigner. She had to adapt to their ways. After all, she was only risking *her* life. André and his *Boxer Circuit* were risking their lives *and* those of their families. 'Sorry,' she said. 'You know I didn't mean it that way.'

André seemed placated, but there was a lingering look in his eyes that she'd seen before. It worried her. It wasn't unknown for Maquis to turn informant. And though the people of Alsace seemed staunchly French, and spoke French when they wanted to, their own dialect was a variety of German. Blaney sometimes found that unnerving, even though she knew the real Jerries couldn't understand the dialect any better than she could.

'I told you, I'm a miner by profession,' André said. 'They roped me in to help build that place. All done by slave labour, a few press-ganged locals like me – *experts* – but mostly prisoners from Natzweiler. They preferred them because they didn't have to feed them, you see. Worked them to death on purpose. It was a way of getting rid of them without wasting bullets. Hundreds dropped dead on the spot from starvation.

Some got so weak they couldn't work. The bastards beat them to death. Some refused to work and were hanged. I used to see the corpses being carried out. I still have nightmares about it.'

He gulped, turned away.

'I swear, if I ever see anyone driving a Mercedes-Benz in London after this, I'll spit on it,' Blaney said. 'If I see one parked in Mayfair, I'll slash the bloody tyres.'

As if on cue, André spat sideways. 'Oh, you can bet Mr Daimler and Mr Benz, or whoever owns the place won't suffer,' he said. 'They'll just say, *please, sirs, Mr Hitler forced us to do it.*' He snuffled, almost choked. 'And your Allied bosses will say, *oh we understand perfectly. Just as long as our rich people can go on having your nice motor cars, the tens of thousands of Frogs who died working for you in the war can rot in hell.*'

'They won't let them get away with mass murder,' Blaney said. She blinked back tears from her own eyes, knowing that what André had said was almost certainly true. They *would* get away with it. Tom Caine always said that the war was about money. Despite the palaver they made, the flag waving, the calls for patriotism, the high-ups didn't really care how many people died in battle, of starvation, of torture, of disease caused by the war, as long as they stayed where they were. Well, that didn't matter, because Caine cared, and so did she.

André took a breath, went on in a steadier voice. 'Anyway, whatever they're making there, it isn't motor cars. The top levels of the building – the ones there – are a façade. Offices for pen-pushers. The administration. The production line is underground, in a grid of cross-tunnels, all numbered. Protected from bombing raids, you see. If it was all above ground, Allied bombers could have wrapped it up weeks ago.'

Blaney grunted assent, but the thought troubled her. At Beaulieu, she'd heard that the RAF had developed an incendiary bomb. When it exploded, it released some kind of liquid fire that could pour into tunnels like hot lava. It had been created with the specific purpose of clearing underground bunkers. She'd been told that they'd used it successfully in other places. Why not here? Why send a sole female agent in to do the job, with a handful of Maquis fighters? She was honest enough to herself to admit that they only had a fifty-fifty chance of success.

Did it mean that the SOE and Bomber Command were working at cross purposes? Blaney was aware that there was friction between them. She'd heard Lurgan raging about it. The RAF begrudged the squadrons they'd had to detach for special duties when they could have been pounding the shit out of European cities. SOE was the Prime Minister's own baby, though – *Churchill's Private Army*. There was nothing they could do.

'That's what they *invited* me to help with,' André said wryly. 'The production line is worked by slave labour too, of course. You've just seen the transport bring them in. They had to be more choosy with the special workers, though, because they need a certain level of technical skill. Those skills are valuable, so they can't work them to death. I wouldn't fancy their chances when the job's finished though, would you? It's a Daimler-Benz factory, yes, but they work for the Nazis. The commandant of Natzweiler supervises the whole operation.'

Blaney was surprised. 'What do you mean, *supervises*?'

André paused. 'I mean he runs the show from beginning to end. Bloke wears an SS uniform but acts like a civilian. I used to see him sometimes when I was working on the cross-tunnels. Forty-odd, dark hair, clean-shaven. A scientist or an engineer most likely. He knows what he's doing, all right, because I heard he designed the tunnel grid and the production line himself. I know he chooses the line workers and that some of them are Allied prisoners of war. Anyway, he must be well in with Hitler because he wears the Knight's Cross ribbon on his jacket.'

Blaney filed this data away for future reference. *An SS concentration camp commandant, who's also an engineer or scientist. That must be something unusual*, she thought.

'Ever hear his name?' she asked.

André screwed up his face. '*Boelcke*, I think it was. That's it. I heard it only once, but I memorized it. *SS-Standartenführer* Franz Boelcke.'

'A full colonel,' Blaney mused. She stopped and thought for a moment. 'And did this… Boel…'

'Boelcke.'

'Boelcke. Did he go along with the beating and the hanging and… all that?'

'*Go along with it?*' André scoffed. 'It was him who ordered the starvation *and* the killings. He didn't do it with his own hands, maybe, but he was responsible.'

Blaney took a long breath. 'So, what *are* they manufacturing there?'

It was an old question. One they'd pondered endlessly, smoking cigarettes, crouched around safe-house fires. At first, André said, he'd been sure it was aero engines. One of his informants in the factory, though, had told him that, if so, they weren't like any aero engines he'd ever seen. Since none of the production line workers got to experience more than a small part of the process and none saw the finished product, no one could be sure. There were rumours about Nazi secret weapons, about a new type of aircraft – a rocket-powered plane that flew without propellers. Maybe that was what they were producing. 'All we can be sure of is that it's something vital,' Rolande said. 'Something the Bosch reckon will give them the upper hand. The Americans are closing in – or will be when they get their logistics sorted out – and the Germans are short of everything. They wouldn't spare these guards and weapons if they didn't consider it of crucial importance.'

Blaney nodded. Her first impression of Rolande had been of a brawny farm boy, more biceps than brains and windy to boot. In the past week, she'd got to know him better. Every night they'd moved to a new safe house. They'd organized the retrieval of the ICL containers. To her relief, the RAF had dropped them on schedule, and nothing had blown up as André had feared. They'd unpacked the sabotage kit, stashed it in various places, disposed of the containers. Rolande had worked with dedication and quiet efficiency. Before the war, he'd been a law student at the University of Strasbourg. He was astute but modest. What she'd mistaken for nervousness, that first night, was professional caution. He had to be very careful, for instance, to avoid being drafted into a slave-labour force. He was registered as a farm labourer and played the part well. After all, he told any official who enquired, *someone* had to grow the food, didn't they?

André was equally circumspect. That didn't arise from windiness, either. He was solid as a rock, as tough as his gnarled and pitted miner's hands. Years of work in the mines had made him lean and stooped but had not dulled his spark, nor suppressed his brilliance as an organizer. He sometimes moaned; he could be awkward, critical or sarcastic, but then, unlike Rolande, he'd been made that way by years of working for the Nazis, by the horrific things he'd seen in those tunnels. In any case, his tendency to pessimism was offset by his dry humour.

'They can't have perfected it, either,' Rolande went on, 'because we've kept a strict watch on the place. We have informants on the inside. No product has been shipped out.'

'Could they be smuggling it out through an underground tunnel?' Blaney asked.

Rolande shook his head. 'A tunnel that long would take some

constructing. True, they might have got military engineers to do it, but André took part in most of the tunnel building, and he never saw or heard of anything like that.'

She noted that Rolande never referred to André as father. There wasn't much resemblance between them, and she was never sure if they were really father and son. The women she'd met on the first night weren't their wives, either. She knew very little about them – not even their real names. It was better that way. If she got captured, God forbid, she wouldn't be able to tell the Bosch what she didn't know.

'What if they're storing up the product for a last-ditch effort?' she suggested. 'Wait till the Americans arrive, then take out the lot with a final bang?' She remembered Tom Caine telling her about a mission he'd been sent on in Libya in 1942. The Nazis had produced a disorienting gas that they'd planned to drop on the Allies, just as they began their advance. Caine's SAS patrol had blown it up before they could use it, but Caine himself had been affected by the stuff. He reckoned he'd never quite been the same since.

'It doesn't matter what they're making,' André said. 'The question is how we're going to get in there.'

CHAPTER TEN

André passed the telescope back to Blaney. 'All right, now I'll show you what we're going to do,' he told her. 'Focus the 'scope on the right side of the bridge… That's it… Follow the edge of the ravine till you come to a bunch of Aleppo pines.'

'Ok,' Blaney said. 'I've got the pines.'

'Have a look at the ravine there,' said André. 'It's as steep as the rest, but we can get down without using ropes.'

Blaney couldn't make it out as clearly as she'd have liked, but she estimated the drop to be about seventy-five feet.

'All right,' she said. 'The river looks formidable.'

'It's fast flowing, but not deep at this time of year… Now, you'll see, the other side of the ravine is just as steep.'

Blaney traversed the lens up the ravine on the other side, flinched suddenly. She'd reached a ledge festooned in barbed wire, with a German sentry standing behind it. She had the impression that he was looking straight at her. She lowered the scope hastily.

'There's a guard,' she said.

André chortled. 'Of course there is. And you know why? Because at that point, there's a ventilation shaft that penetrates right into the heart of the factory. I know, because I was one of the blokes who built it.'

Blaney took another shufti at the guard. The idea that he was looking at her was silly, of course – just an illusion. She focused the lens behind him. In the rock face, she could make out what looked like an iron grille.

'There's some kind of barrier there,' she said.

'Naturally. The Bosch don't want just anyone wandering into the shaft, do they?'

Blaney let the telescope down again. 'How do you know the shaft isn't blocked?'

André tapped his nose. 'Why place a guard there if it was? Why install a grille? I mean, why not a door? No, like I said, I worked in that place. They've got turbines in there, running day and night. It's as hot as an inferno. Believe me, they need all the ventilation they can get.'

Blaney took another deep breath. It was a long shot, full of pitfalls: she'd always known it would be. What if the tunnel was mined? What if there were alarms? Still, it was an audacious plan, she had to admit that.

'If we go in on a Sunday night, there won't be any line workers,' he said. 'Only the guards and they're not first-class material. If they were, they'd be at the front. They'll be half asleep after the first half hour, like all guards, anyway. We'll have to deal with that sentry, of course. That's your job.'

Blaney thought he was joking. '*Mine*? Why the hell should *I* do it?'

'You've been trained for it, haven't you?'

'Yes, but…'

'Well since they sent *you* to knock out the factory, *you* ought to have the honour.'

A cold finger passed down Blaney's spine. André was getting her back for the inadvertent remark she'd made. He hadn't forgiven her. This was his way of rubbing it in.

She wasn't going to make a fuss, though. She'd signed up for this, and yes, it had been part of her training. *Kill a man in cold blood with a Sykes-Fairburn fighting knife, though? What if I muck it up?*

'We'll have to blow the grille,' André said.

'That's going to have the guards buzzing like bees.'

'We'll only need a small charge. The turbines are so deafening they won't hear a thing.'

Blaney gave him a doubtful look, didn't speak. André nodded at her.

'There's just one little problem you haven't considered,' Rolande said. 'The floodlights.'

Blaney lifted the telescope again, focused on the sentry. Moving the lens left and right, she noticed, for the first time, that there was a necklace of tripod-mounted floodlights; she estimated them to be at two hundred-pace intervals along the barbed-wire fence.

'Do they keep them on all night?' Blaney asked.

Rolande nodded.

'It's going to be bloody daylight.'

For a second, André looked put out. He swallowed, stared at Rolande wide-eyed. Blaney realized he really had forgotten about the lights.

His face relaxed suddenly. 'We'll send a group to knock out the transformers,' he said. 'They aren't guarded. That should be easy enough.'

Rolande frowned. 'Yes, but if we knock out the transformers, the turbines will stop, and the guards will hear our charge go off.'

André watched him blankly. For the first time, he had no answer.

'We'll have to work that one out,' Blaney said. She glanced at her watch again. It was already 0706 hours. She nudged André. 'We've been here long enough. Any longer and we'll take root.' She jerked her head back the way they'd come. Slowly, very slowly, hardly disturbing a leaf, they withdrew from their positions.

Paul was waiting for them by the bikes. He was a youth of no more than sixteen or seventeen: large cow eyes, prominent teeth, acne, a chin the shape of a spatula.

'Well?' he demanded, his voice almost girlish. 'Did you see it?'

'Yep,' Blaney said. 'It's a good plan. If it weren't for those damn floodlights.'

The thought had been plaguing her all the way out of the forest. *Explosive charge or floodlights. Floodlights or explosive charge. You could have one or the other, but not both.*

They stripped off their overalls and stocking caps, stuffed them in a canvas bag and buried it nearby. They covered the hole carefully with foliage, then brushed each other down, ran fingers through their hair, retrieved their bicycles.

They squatted in the lee of a hedgerow and lit cigarettes. Paul was going to be one of the assault team; they explained the problem.

When they'd finished the youth nodded, stubbed his cigarette out underfoot.

'That's easy,' he said. 'We send a man up in advance and cut the floodlight cables on that stretch, just at the right time.'

They stared at him, searching for flaws in his suggestion. There were some blindingly obvious ones, Blaney thought, with a chuckle. Since the man who cut the cables would have to scale the ravine in the glare of the floodlights, how was he going to make it up there? Even if he succeeded, when the lights cut out, someone would come to investigate.

She was just about to speak when they heard footsteps. Blaney looked up to see two men in sloppy battledress loping towards them. The men wore boots, gaiters and black berets with a badge that looked like the Greek letter *gamma*. The men were unshaven and untidy and had cigarettes dangling from their mouths. They were carrying bolt action rifles at the ready. The men stopped a few yards away, dropped their cigarettes. Their berets – the size of pancakes –gave them a slightly ludicrous air.

Blaney and the others rose slowly.

There was nothing ludicrous about the men, Blaney knew that. She'd been trained in recognition of enemy forces. These were members of the *Milice* – French collaborators charged with anti-partisan duties. The Maquis feared them more than the Gestapo because they were locals who knew the dialect, the people, the country.

Blaney hoped to God they hadn't been listening. She cursed her lax security. *Never talk about operations in public, even if you think there's nobody around.* It was an elementary precaution. She'd neglected it.

One of the *Milice* was young and smooth-faced – about Paul's age, Blaney thought. The other, older, with weasel-like features, narrow eyes. He was slim, slightly stooped. Like André, he had the coarse-grained hands of a labouring man.

The older man studied each of Blaney's companions in turn. His eyes came to rest on Blaney. He ogled her figure unashamedly. Blaney blushed. She thought about the telescope in André's pocket.

'Well, this is an interesting little gathering,' the man said, in French, not dialect, Blaney noted. He stared at her, grinning, showing bad teeth. 'Who are you, *Mademoiselle*? I don't think you are from round here.'

CHAPTER ELEVEN

France and Germany. June 1945

Outside Paris, the landscape rolled on, a patchwork of fields surrounded by hedges and trees. Some fields were overgrown, some cultivated. Cottages were dotted across the countryside. There were dense copses, and in places, deep woods covered low hills. Peasants were at work, rebuilding fences, clearing out dykes, tending cattle, driving hay carts yoked to pairs of big-boned horses. For a while, you could convince yourself that life was going on as it had done, uninterrupted, for centuries, Caine thought. Just when you'd been lulled into this idea, though, you'd be jerked back by a reminder of the horror of war. Woods where the trees were burned and blackened skeletons. Crashed aircraft, like great dead insects, lying in circles of scorched earth. Once, they passed a huge bomb crater in a field, with rotting carcasses of cows and horses scattered round it. Fred Wallace insisted on stopping the jeep to examine the dead animals. 'Poor buggers,' he muttered.

For a moment, Caine thought the big man was going to demand that they bury them with full military honours. 'Millions of human beings died in this war, Fred,' he said gently. 'These are just animals.'

Wallace glared at him. 'That's what I meant,' he said. 'What did they do to deserve this?'

Many of the small towns they passed through were reduced to heaps of debris, with only a handful of buildings left standing. They saw cars and tractors upended, lying in rusting bits amid the ruins as if a vast hand had picked them up and hurled them there. There were telegraph poles tilted and shattered, fractured steel-girder bridges, railway stations that had been razed to the foundations, lengths of railway track that were nothing but ligaments of grotesquely buckled steel. They saw men and women sitting among the ruins of what had been their homes, staring blankly. They saw children wandering around in dazed circles or poking in the debris. Whenever they stopped, hordes of people gathered around them, jabbering, begging for money, food, cigarettes. Backhouse would chatter to them in fluent French, but always he ordered the team to move on quickly. There was no resupply in this job. They needed everything they'd got.

In one village, a crowd was gathered around a group of young women, jeering and snickering. One by one, the women were being jostled onto a stool in the midst of the crowd to have their heads shaved. This time it was Caine who insisted on stopping.

He and Backhouse marched up to the crowd. 'What's going on here?' the major demanded.

Caine glanced at the women whose heads had been shaved. Most were young girls. They looked miserable and afraid. An old man in a cloth cap, with a drooping moustache, answered Backhouse.

'He says all these women had… *liaisons*… with the Jerries,' the major told him. 'This is their punishment.'

Backhouse spoke to the young woman now squatting on the stool. She answered him in a rush, her voice trembling, tears pouring down her cheeks.

'She says her husband was taken away for slave labour,' Backhouse said. 'She had four children to bring up and no money. A German soldier took a fancy to her. She didn't want to do it. She was thinking of her children. She said, "*What else could I do?*"'

Caine felt a surge of pity. 'Tell them the war's over,' he said. 'Tell them to leave the women alone.'

Backhouse told the villagers something, but Caine had no idea if he'd translated his words right. The crowd stared after them as they returned to the jeep.

'Tom Caine strikes again,' Copeland chortled, as they pulled out of the place.

'You ain't seen nothin', Major,' Wallace shouted across to the major in the other jeep. ''Ere's the man as lost 'is commission in the Sappers over some Itie women that was bein' molested by our own troops. Put 'is pistol to the CO's skull and told 'im if he didn't order 'em to stop, 'is 'ead'd be partin' company with 'is shoulders.' He broke into deep-chested laughter.

'It's always women and children first, with Captain Caine,' Copeland grinned.

Backhouse made no comment, but it was no surprise to him. He'd been through Caine's file carefully and joined the dots. Caine's mother and sister had been abused by his stepfather. Aged sixteen, Caine had injured the stepfather badly in retaliation, whether by using his fists or with a smithy's hammer, it wasn't entirely clear. The police had offered him a choice: join the army or go to borstal. He'd ended up in the Royal Engineers. That hadn't been the end of the story, though. A few years later, when Caine was away, his mother had taken her own life and his sister had run off – disappeared. Caine had never forgiven himself for it and as a result, couldn't stand to see women mistreated. That was why Backhouse had been almost certain that the mention of Blaney's name would get him on board.

The major kept the little convoy off the main highways, hugged the farm roads and the white tracks. He rode in the leading jeep, with Rhodes driving, a folded map on his knee. Although checkpoints and roadblocks weren't marked, he seemed to have an intuitive idea where they might be. Caine was impressed. He'd acquired a reputation as an ace navigator in the desert, but that was a different kettle of fish, he thought.

In the weeks they'd spent preparing for the expedition at Wivenhoe, he'd got to know Backhouse quite well. The major was physically tough – tough enough for special service, anyway – but more of a dreamer than a fighter. He was a sort of David Stirling minus the aristocratic background – not lacking in courage, but without the ruthless killer instinct of men like Paddy Mayne – maybe, some said, like Tom Caine himself. Some people said Backhouse was eccentric, some called him a mystic, others dismissed him as completely off his rocker.

Caine didn't believe that, nor did he doubt Backhouse's ability to fight. When Bill got mad, he was like a doodlebug – everyone in range had to watch out. It was more that he sometimes drifted off into a world of his own – a voyage to a distant planet, where no one could reach him. On occasions, he seemed completely unaware that the army was an organization with rules and a command structure. He talked to brigadiers as if they were imbeciles and to troopers as if they were his mates. He'd think nothing of taking enlisted men for a drink in the officers' mess. When fellow officers pulled him up for it, he didn't seem to know what they were talking about. It didn't bother Caine. He had little reverence for the command structure, either. Backhouse's antics made him laugh.

Only once or twice on the way, did Backhouse seem flummoxed.

Then he'd have them unload a Matchless motorbike – that Caine and his crew hadn't even known was there – from the back of the three-tonner. The bike had a 500cc engine, knobbly tyres and high mudguards, designed for rough country. He'd send the three-tonner driver, Flint Ronson – a wiry man with a ragged moustache and a face like old tree bark – ahead to have a shufti. Flint would be back in half an hour to report if the road was clear.

'Hope you weren't spotted,' Copeland had commented on Flint's first recce.

Flint gave Cope such a look of contempt, he almost pulled him up for it.

'Don't take it personally,' Backhouse told him quietly. 'Ronson's a motorbike ace – used to be a cross-country champion before the war. Knows just when to cut the engine so the guards won't hear it. He's a trained sniper, too. Knows how to conceal himself.'

They spent nights in the copses or deep woods, away from air spotters, or anyone intent on trailing them, cooking compo rations on primus stoves. It wasn't a war zone anymore, but they knew that it was best to keep a low profile. In any case, old habits died hard.

They skirted Strasbourg and found no problem crossing the German border. There were Free French convoys about, but as usual they steered clear of them. No one stopped them or asked to see their permits. Both Caine and Backhouse knew the real problem was going to be crossing the Rhine. Gaggenau lay on the opposite bank. Only months before, in March, Allied troops had invaded Germany by crossing the river on Op *Plunder* and Op *Varsity* – the last big push of the war. Monty's 21st Army Group had led the attack, with the US Ninth Army, under General Omar Bradley. Tens of thousands of Airborne troops had been dropped on the German side of the Rhine. That had been much further north, though. While the Baden-Wurttemberg area, directly across the river from Alsace, hadn't emerged unscathed, it hadn't taken the same pounding as the regions up north, either.

Luckily, they came across a pontoon bridge that had been built by British Sappers and was guarded by a detachment of the Cheshire Regiment. The sergeant in charge had a good dekko at the papers Caine handed him and studied their maroon-red berets and Dennison smocks.

'You Airborne, sir?' he asked.

'Yeah, that's it,' Caine said.

'What do you want at Gaggenau?'

'Some of our boys were POWs in a camp there,' Caine told him. 'They never came back. We think the SS murdered 'em in cold blood. We're here to find their bodies and make sure they get a decent burial.'

'An' get the fuckers what did it,' Wallace growled.

The sergeant, a heavy-set man with a red face, in BDs and a black beret, studied them with a worried look on his face.

'Sir, I've got to tell you, there's been a signal about your unit. Seems you haven't got authority to cross into the French Zone.'

Caine kept calm. 'That's not right, Sarn't,' he said. 'I've shown you our permission, and it's authentic. All we want to do is find our mates, identify them, and make sure they're buried properly, that's all.'

The sergeant hesitated. 'There's another thing, though, sir. That signal came from 216th Field Detachment, Royal Military Police, from SHAEF HQ in Paris. Seems they're coming up behind you.'

Caine noticed that the sergeant had deliberately avoided saying *coming after you*. He kept his face deadpan, didn't reveal any surprise. 'I think some wires got crossed, Sarn't. In any case, we can still go ahead and bury our lads, can't we? I mean, if the MPs arrive, they'll know where we are.'

The sergeant seemed to waver. Then he handed the papers back to Caine, winked at him.

'My brother was Airborne,' he said. 'Killed at Arnhem. We all lost mates and family in the war. If you find out who done it, give 'em one from me.'

'Will do, Sarn't.'

'Remember, though, sir. I ain't seen you and you ain't seen me. You crossed the river somewhere else, all right?'

'Right.'

They exchanged salutes. The sergeant ordered the barrier opened.

As the three vehicles trundled across the pontoons, Fred Wallace commented, 'Good to know there's some decent blokes left in the world, innit?'

CHAPTER TWELVE

Gaggenau, Baden-Wurttemberg, Germany. June 1945

Gaggenau was a leafy town of timbered houses with high-pitched roofs and modern flat-topped buildings of concrete and glass, standing on both sides of the Murg river. A thick forest lay on one side; on the other, a blunt, sheer-sided cliff rose out of the trees, like the fin of a giant fish. The place had been bombed in the war but not extensively. A few of the streets had been reduced to rubble. Backhouse knew that the main industry here was a Daimler-Benz factory – one of dozens the Benz corporation had set up to manufacture vehicles and machine-parts for Hitler. They'd even built one on French soil, across the Rhine, at Wallenbach, in Alsace. He wondered why the Allies hadn't pounded the Gaggenau plant to slivers.

The town was occupied by Free French troops. They were patrolling the streets in light tanks, jeeps and armoured cars, but no one stopped the SAS patrol or gave them any trouble. The military commandant, Major Gaston Marchand, a trim man in khaki service dress and a kepi, with a face of weathered sandstone and a waxed moustache, had taken up his post in an office at the town hall. He didn't seem surprised to see them. In fact, he seemed gratified. When Backhouse, Caine and Copeland marched into his office and saluted, he sat them down, offered them Gauloise cigarettes and coffee. 'I was in London with General de Gaulle,' he told them in passable English. 'I was treated well. I am glad to return the *hospitalite.*'

He gave their papers only a peremptory glance, then waved them away.

'You will need a base while you are here,' he told them. 'May I suggest the Dellinger villa? It is large. You will be comfortable there. And you will have Frau Dellinger and the two *Frauleins* Dellinger to do the cooking and housework for you.'

'Won't Herr Dellinger object?' Backhouse asked.

'Not really,' Marchand chuckled. 'Karl Dellinger is at present in the detention centre at Karlsruhe. He was a staunch Nazi, you see.'

There was silence for a moment. The three SAS officers drank coffee.

'Now,' Marchand said. 'You have come to identify the bodies of your compatriots, I think?'

Backhouse nodded. 'How were they discovered?'

'The day we occupied the town, I was approached by some locals who showed me to a place in the Erhlich forest.' He made a gesture towards the sprawl of woodland they'd seen driving into Gaggenau. 'They were some way inside, lying in craters made by Allied bombs. No doubt the bombs had been intended for the Daimler-Benz factory but had gone wide. The craters had been filled in with earth. In these holes, we discovered twenty-seven corpses. Twenty-six men and one woman.'

Caine sat up sharply at the word *woman.* Marchand noticed and stared at him.

'You know this woman?' he enquired.

'It's... possible.'

'That's one of the reasons we're here,' Backhouse cut in. 'We need to see the bodies, of course, to be sure, but we believe that some of them, at least, are comrades from our regiment. People we knew personally.'

Marchand looked startled. 'Ah, I see. So, for you, it is a personal issue, not like the Americans.'

'Americans?' Backhouse raised his eyebrows. 'What Americans?'

'You did not know? But of course, there is also an American war crimes investigation team here. We had to inform them because there were American prisoners of war also at Rotenfels – in addition to British and French ones.'

For the first time, Backhouse looked at sea. He stubbed his cigarette out in an ashtray on Marchand's desk.

'I'm sorry, Major,' he said. 'Could we go back a step? What is Rotenfels?'

Marchand puffed out his chest slightly, as if proud to have to explain. '*Rotenfels*,' he said, 'is – or *was* – a prison camp. One of those the Bosch pigs kept for special prisoners. Your parachute commandos, for instance. American pilots who had been shot down. Members of the Maquis – active Resistance-fighters, who operated from the forest. This is Germany, of course, but the SS brought the prisoners held at Rotenfels across the Rhine, in September 1944, when the Americans and Free French Army were closing in on them in France. The Boche referred to camps like this as *Nacht-und-Nebel* – Night and Fog – camps. This was meant to signify that anyone who was a prisoner there would vanish from the face of the earth.'

'You mean *death camps?*' Copeland swore.

'Precisely,' Marchand went on, smiling sadly. 'Charming people, the Nazis. *Vraiment charmants.*'

Caine could see that Backhouse was itching to return to business. 'So, of the twenty-seven bodies, how many were British?' he asked.

Marchand shook his head. 'I do not know. That is for you to decide.

Three of the bodies were those of French priests, I am sure of that. One of them was identified as that of a Monsignor Jean Bordes, whom we know belonged to the *Alliance Reseau*. That was one of the most active of the Resistance organizations. The other two priests were probably also members of the *Alliance*. There was the woman, as I have said. For the rest, we had to take the word of the German locals that some were French, some Americans, some British.'

'Who *were* these locals?' Copeland enquired suspiciously. 'Why were they so keen to inform you about the bodies?'

Marchand shrugged. 'It is an interesting question. I myself wondered at first why they – Germans – should come up voluntarily with this information.' He paused to take a puff from his Gauloise. 'On questioning, it turned out that they were the last of the... how do you say... *white-collar staff...* of the Daimler-Benz plant. They knew, I suppose, because that is where the prisoners worked, *vous voyez?*'

'*Worked?*' Caine gasped. 'You mean they were used as slave labour?'

'But of course,' Marchand shrugged again. 'That was the Nazi way, *non*? Yes, that is why the Boche brought them from France. They had been working at another Daimler-Benz factory, at Wallenbach, in Alsace, and must have had experience at their jobs. They were taken to the Gaggenau factory by lorry every day. To answer the second part of your question, I now think that these people were anxious to inform us because they felt guilty and did not wish to be blamed. *Apres tout*, the prisoners worked at the Daimler-Benz factory and therefore, as part of the management of that company, they were, in a sense, partly responsible for their deaths.'

Caine and Backhouse exchanged a glance. 'So, are these Daimler-Benz people going to be charged with war crimes?' Copeland demanded.

Marchand shook his head. 'I do not think so. They were employed by an engineering company. They had no control over who worked there or what happened to them. When I asked them how they knew about the bodies, they claimed they had only heard about the killings later.'

Caine clenched his fists. '*They knew,*' he growled.

'*Of course* they knew,' Marchand said. 'They were... what do you say... *accessories.* But it was wartime. If they had objected, they would have been interned as traitors – perhaps even shot also. If we are to prosecute all the accessories to Nazi war crimes – all those who turned their backs and pretended not to see – then half the people in Europe would be implicated.'

A smile of satisfaction spread over his face suddenly. 'They were not at all happy, though – those white-collar employees.'

'How come?' Caine asked.

'Because we made them dig out the bodies of the dead from the craters one by one and rebury them in the cemetery.' Marchand grinned. '*Mon dieu,* if the situation had not been tragic, it would have been *amusant.* You should have seen the looks on their faces.'

CHAPTER THIRTEEN

Marchand personally escorted them to the Villa Dellinger in his Peugeot staff car. It turned out to be a spacious mansion set in green, wooded grounds. An oldish woman with a marble face, grey hair tied back, met them at the door. Behind her were two pretty teenage girls with blonde hair and blue eyes, wearing headscarves and maids' aprons. All three of them looked scared stiff. The girls kept their eyes downcast, their hands clasped together in front of them, as if expecting punishment.

The old woman – Frau Dellinger – spoke to Marchand in a low voice.

Marchand shook his head. He knew little German. Backhouse spoke the language as well as he spoke French. It was he who translated.

'She's worried about the safety of her daughters,' he told the others. 'She's heard stories about how German women have been molested by the Allies.'

He was going to continue when Caine cut in. 'Tell her that no one here will touch her or her daughters.' He half-turned to the men behind him. 'I know I don't have to say this, but if anyone here so much as pinches the arse of one of these ladies, or says a word out of place, I'll roast 'em alive.'

'*Surprise*,' Fred Wallace muttered. Copeland grinned back at him.

Caine caught the look. 'It isn't funny, Harry,' he said. 'I've heard the stories. Thousands of German women have been raped and not just by the Ivans, either…'

'I'm not saying it's funny,' Cope said. 'Neither is Fred. It's just so Tom Caine, that's all.'

Backhouse spoke to the woman. 'I told her that she and her daughters are in no danger from anyone here, as long as there's no funny business,' he explained. 'No spying on what we do. No listening at keyholes. They'll do the cooking and cleaning, make the beds – all that stuff – but apart from that, they'll just keep themselves to themselves, and no one will interfere with them.'

Caine nodded. At a word from the mother, the two girls scurried away. She showed the men well-appointed bedrooms upstairs, bathrooms, toilets. There was a cosy parlour downstairs with a polished round table, a fireplace, comfortable armchairs. The mullioned windows overlooked a garden full of trees. The men leaned their personal weapons against the table. Most of them had M1 carbines as well as the Colt .45 automatic pistols in their belts, but Caine had the trusty Thompson he'd carried through almost every battle of the war. Copeland and Ronson both had .303 Lee-Enfield sniper rifles with telescopic sights. Big Wallace toted his Bren.

They lounged in the chairs, lit up cigarettes.

A few minutes later, the mother brought them tea in a giant steel kettle. The girls followed her in with eight mugs, sugar and milk, on a tray.

'This is the life, *innit*?' Wallace chuckled. 'I could get used to this.'

'Looks like a first-class billet,' Rhodes agreed.

'Aye,' Swan answered. 'These Nazi boys seem to have done all right for themselves.'

'Major Marchand told me this Dellinger owns a brewery,' Backhouse said. 'I imagine that's where the money came from. Don't get too comfortable, though. We're here to do a job, let's not forget that.'

When they'd finished their tea and cigarettes he drew them round the table. He spread a map.

'All right,' he said. 'This is what we know. A total of ninety-one members of 2nd SAS Regiment were dropped behind Nazi lines, on Op *Taunton*, starting in August last year. The op was terminated in October. They were to operate in the Vosges mountains in Alsace – about forty miles west of Strasbourg – to prepare the way for Patton's US Sixth Army, which was on the advance. What we didn't know was that a massive force of Jerries was also moving into the area to defend it against the Yanks…' At this point, Caine detected a tremor in Backhouse's voice. He evidently included himself in the *we*. He'd been IO of 2nd SAS, after all. It had been his job to know, although the failure of intelligence didn't lie squarely on his shoulders. What had happened to the vast network of spies and agents the British and Americans had in place – SIS, Int. Corps, RAF Intelligence, God knew who else; it was clear Backhouse felt some guilt over it, Caine thought. *That must be why he's here.*

The major took a long breath and went on. 'German forces included part of the 17th *Panzergruppe Grenadier Division* – a crack force – about five thousand strong. The SAS had only the support of the local Maquis. They did a damn good job of raiding the enemy, but they didn't stand much of a chance, especially when Patton got held up by logistic problems, and the Sixth Army didn't arrive on cue. About fourteen SAS men were reported killed in action, forty-six survived and got back home, but there are another thirty-one unaccounted for…'

'It don't add up,' Wallace declared indignantly. 'The Frogs only found twenty-seven bodies 'ere, and some of 'em was Frogs and Yanks…'

'And one was a woman,' Caine interrupted him.

He felt for the dead SAS lads, he felt for their families, but it was Blaney that obsessed him. He couldn't keep the feel of her body out of his mind. He couldn't forget the explosive way she'd kissed him when they'd met in his jail cell in Algeria. He couldn't forget the white curve of her neck, the pertness of those red curls, the way she'd insisted on wearing a man's BD, even during his court martial. He remembered the way the coarse uniform hugged her figure and how every man in court had stared at her. He thought about her softness, her care. He remembered how she'd sat by his bed for hours in Cairo when he was delirious. He thought of her brilliant mind, the toughness that lay under the soft mantle. He recalled the way she'd survived the near-fatal chest wound she'd taken from a deserter in Cairo, how she'd pulled through by pure willpower. He recalled how she'd stood, moodily tearful, outside the courtroom after she'd just got him off a charge of treason, thinking he was in love with another girl. He recalled how that mistake had been rectified once they'd both got back to London, and, without a single word, without any explanation, how they'd fallen into each other's arms.

'Yeah, one was a woman,' Wallace went on. 'So…'

'What about *her*?' Caine interrupted him again. 'What about Blaney? She wasn't on Op *Taunton*. So how does she fit into this?'

Backhouse stared at him with eyes that had gone eerily blank. 'All we know is that she was dropped blind in an area near the Vosges, in Alsace, France, in September last year,' he said, 'at the same time our chaps were operating in those hills. The operational zones were adjacent but not overlapping. We know her code name was *Empress Eugenie*. We don't know what her mission was, because SOE is being snotty about it. They won't tell us, but since SOE's a sabotage mob, we can safely assume it was to blow something up.' He paused and looked at Caine directly, speaking now in a softer voice. 'Her op was definitely in France, not in Germany. True, Marchand says the prisoners held at Rotenfels were brought here from France, but we can't be sure it's her buried in that cemetery, Tom. Don't raise your hopes.'

'*Hopes?*' Caine swore, his face suddenly wild. 'You think I *hope* it's her? I *hope* she's a million miles away, living the life of Reilly. I *hope* she abandoned her bloody kamikaze mission, did a bunk and left the bloody stupid war behind. That's what I *hope*. Knowing her, though. Knowing how faithful, and loyal, and determined, and committed she was, I know that *hope* is impossible. It's the last bloody thing in the world she would do.'

He turned away. For a moment everyone went silent. None of the men, not even his mates, had expected the outburst.

'I'm sorry you…' Backhouse began, but again, Wallace cut him short, ploughing on like a juggernaut.

'Yeah, one was a woman,' he repeated, as if Caine hadn't spoken. 'So, it don't matter 'ow thin yer slice it, if thirty-one of our lads is missin', they can't all be 'ere.'

'Must have been done in somewhere else,' Rhodes commented.

'Obviously,' Backhouse said. 'Before we start looking into that, though, let's find out who we've got.'

CHAPTER FOURTEEN

Over a breakfast of bacon, eggs, bread and coffee next morning, they heard the sound of engines gunning outside the house. Caine listened carefully, heard the crunch of tyres on the gravel as the vehicles came to a halt. He heard voices – men shouting to each other. They seemed to be speaking English.

'Five jeeps,' Wallace said. He raised a shaggy eyebrow at Caine. 'Not the bleedin' rozzers is it?'

Caine got up calmly, took his Thompson from where he'd leaned it against the table.

Backhouse stood, drew his .45. The others raised themselves, retrieved their weapons without a word. Backhouse nodded Caine forward. Caine gave a hand signal; the men followed him to the front door. He turned the knob and flung it open.

Not twenty yards away, five jeeps, almost identical to their own, were drawn up in perfect echelon, about five yards apart. Each jeep carried two or three men in khaki shirts, with cocked side caps. They had weapons pointing at Caine and Backhouse – mostly M1 carbines, Caine noticed. To his annoyance, he saw that some of the men were sitting in his own unit's jeeps; another was in the cab of their three-tonner. Two more had lifted Ronson's Matchless motorcycle down from the back of the lorry and were messing around with the gears.

Caine shifted attention back to the jeeps. He noticed that, on the bonnet of each, was painted a white star enclosed in a circle.

'*Yanks*,' he said under his breath.

Backhouse didn't seem flustered. 'Marchand told us they'd be here.'

On the bonnet of the centre jeep sat a corpulent man in a tin helmet. His face was broad, dark and humorous. He had high cheekbones and slightly slanted eyes. He wore a khaki dress shirt with a silver leaf on the shoulder straps. *Half-colonel,* Caine thought. The colonel was grinning at them, an unlit cigar stuck in his mouth.

He slid down from the bonnet and poised himself on legs like tree trunks, removed the cigar. 'Come out if you're comin' out, then,' he chuckled. 'Come on, Limeys, don't be shy.'

Backhouse holstered his automatic, stepped forward. He was wearing his Dennison smock and maroon beret. 'Tell your men to lower their weapons, please, *sir*,' he said. He nodded to the SAS jeeps and three-tonner. 'And would you mind not fiddling about with our property? We are supposed to be Allies, and it's really *not* polite.'

'*Rahlly not polite*,' the fat colonel chuckled.

He turned and ordered the men to put their guns away, told the boys in the SAS jeeps to leave them. He told the pair with the motorcycle to put it back where they found it.

He lurched up to Backhouse and held out a plump hand. 'Lootenant Colonel José Garcia, Commanding US No.2 War Crimes Investigation Team.'

Backhouse shook hands. 'Major Bill Backhouse,' he said. 'OC, 2nd Special Air Service Regiment War Crimes Investigation Team.'

The colonel raised an eyebrow. The name sounded Spanish, but he didn't look European, Caine thought. 'So, you boys are investigatin' only *one* unit?' he asked.

'We're investigating any war crime we come across,' Backhouse said. 'American, French or British. But some of the men murdered here were friends of ours.'

'Boy, you Brits sure take it personal, hey?'

For the first time, the colonel looked impressed. Then the smile faded.

'Thing is, I've heard bad reports about you guys.'

'Like what?' Caine enquired.

Colonel Garcia looked him up and down, noting the slim waist and the broad torso, the swimmer's shoulders, the polished stone-coloured eyes. He put out a boxing-glove hand.

'Captain Tom Caine,' Caine said, shaking. 'What reports have you heard?'

'That you caused some trouble at SHAEF. That the MPs are after you. That you're not wanted here in the French Zone.'

'Funny, the French haven't turned us out,' Backhouse commented.

'What do *you* think?' Caine asked.

Garcia paused for a minute. 'I think the red-tape bureaucrats can go take a runnin' jump,' he said. 'You're here to find your own boys, and that takes dedication. Besides, we can't do all the work ourselves.'

CHAPTER FIFTEEN

Garcia and his crew led the SAS team up the dusty white track to the *Waldfriedhof*, the cemetery where the bodies had been reburied. It was a crescent of rough green lawn, edged by trees, dotted with the tombstones of local families. Since hardly any of the corpses had been formally identified, their graves had been marked with wooden crosses, arranged in four rows.

The convoy pulled up in the gravel car park nearby. Caine saw that there were already some vehicles there – Marchand's Peugeot staff car, an armoured personnel carrier and a couple of three-tonners. All of them were marked with the double-barred cross of Lorraine, the emblem of Free French Forces. A host of men and women was already at work with picks and shovels, almost up to their thighs in the graves. Piles of fresh spoil lay along the pits, steadily increasing in size. The diggers were guarded by French soldiers in khaki tunics and kepis. Marchand stood with his hands on his hips, a Gaulois stuck in his mouth, glaring at the workers.

'Who are this lot?' Backhouse demanded, as the teams gathered round the French major.

Marchand removed the cigarette from his mouth. 'They are the Daimler-Benz white-collar staff. I told you about them, no? They were not *tres contents* about digging up the bodies and reburying them the first time. Now they have to go through it all again *ha! ha! ha!* They have been here since seven thirty. They are not – 'ow you say…'*appy bunnies.*'

Rhodes was keen to get a closer look. He slung his M1 carbine over his shoulder and strode over to the open graves. Caine followed him, his Thompson made safe, carried underarm. He noticed that some of the workers were wearing worn clothes. Others had on suits and ties, as if they'd been accosted on their way to the office. Many of them stopped work when they saw the SAS men approaching, muttering together, casting wide-eyed glances in their direction. They'd probably never seen maroon-red berets before, Caine thought. Maybe they associated the colour with blood. Maybe they imagined his unit was a British death squad, sent to kill them.

'Get on with your work,' Marchand bellowed. He stalked up behind Caine and Rhodes, with Backhouse and Garcia beside him. 'No one's going to shoot you. Even though that's what you deserve.'

'Excuse me, sir, but I do not think it is what we deserve,' someone said in heavily accented English. Caine saw that it was a youth who'd spoken. He was dressed in a dark suit, spattered with mud, frayed and torn in places. His tie was askew, and the collar of his once-white shirt was in tatters. The boy had close-cropped fair hair and glittering blue eyes. He was tall, crane-fly limbs, the frame of a skeleton. His face was sheet-white, his head lolled forward as if he couldn't keep it upright. He seemed to be having difficulty breathing.

Caine was certain he was sick – TB, maybe. Otherwise, the Nazis would have drafted him into the Hitler Youth or Home Guard or something, and he'd be either dead or a prisoner. On their last ops in Germany, Caine's squadron had come up against kids younger than him. They'd been among the hardest fighters.

Marchand opened his mouth to say something, but Backhouse beat him to it. 'Why exactly is that?' he asked, his voice soothing.

'Because we were not responsible for the deaths of these… these soldiers.' His breath came in wheezes. Caine suddenly felt sorry for him.

The boy stared into Backhouse's eyes. 'I am one of those who revealed to the French major where the bodies were,' he said, his voice almost a whisper. 'I showed him the places. Why would I do that if I am responsible?'

'No one said you're responsible,' Caine interjected. 'If we thought so, you'd already have been arrested. Yet you *knew* where the bodies were. How's that?'

The boy was about to reply, but at that moment there was a babble of voices and a surge of excitement. The diggers had reached the level at which the corpses had been buried. Caine and the others looked to see them lifting the first cadaver out, passing it from hand to hand. There were looks of disgust on their faces. The first corpse was followed by a second and a third, soon by others.

Garcia showed them where to lay the bodies out, in rows on the rough lawn. 'Handle 'em with care, now,' he told the Germans. 'These guys are our buddies.'

'*Doc Smithson*,' he yelled. 'Get over here. Have a look at these dead guys, will ya?'

A lean, serious-looking man with round spectacles separated himself from the crowd of American soldiers. He sidled over to Garcia, carrying a battered black case. He was older than the other GIs, Caine thought – wrinkled and balding with slender hands. He was wearing a chip-bag cap like the rest, but as he came closer, Caine saw that it bore the intertwined snakes and wings of the US Army Medical Corps. The man had silver lieutenant's bars on his shoulder straps.

'This is Charlie Smithson,' Garcia said. 'Fully qualified pathologist. He's a lootenant, but we call him Doc.'

They shook hands. Caine, Backhouse and Copeland followed Smithson, Garcia and Marchand over to examine the corpses. Backhouse called Rhodes. 'I knew some of the missing chaps,' he told Caine, 'but Dusty knew them all personally.'

As they reached the line, the Germans carried in another two cadavers. Caine counted fifteen altogether. 'These are all the bodies found in the first crater,' Marchand told them. 'We buried them in the first two rows. The other twelve were found in the second crater.'

Caine and Rhodes moved in for a closer look, gagging at the smell of putrefaction. At once, they were disappointed. The bodies were in a worse state of decomposition than they'd imagined. A couple had rags of clothing on them, but many were scarcely recognizable as human beings. Caine's gaze shifted down the line, seeking out the remains of the woman. She was the very last – the smallest and frailest of the corpses. From where Caine stood, she was little more than a skeleton.

He pointed to her. 'Can we start at that end, please Doc?' he asked Smithson. 'That's the only woman, and it's ladies first where I come from.'

Smithson glanced at the pips on Caine's shoulders. He nodded. 'Ok, sir,' he said. 'It makes sense.' He paused, examined Caine's face intently through thick lenses. Caine felt himself flush, realized he was afraid. Afraid it might be Celia Blaney lying there, a few yards away. Afraid it might not be.

Smithson's eyes were blue, slightly magnified by his lenses. There was sympathy in them.

'You knew this woman did you, sir? That's why you're here? To identify her?'

'That's one of the reasons,' Caine said. 'But until I've had a close look, I can't be certain.'

Smithson nodded. 'We'll start with the woman, Colonel,' he told Garcia.

'Go ahead.'

Caine and Smithson made their way along the avenue of corpses. No one followed. No one said anything. This particular cross was for Caine alone to bear.

CHAPTER SIXTEEN

Caine's first thought was that this couldn't be Blaney. This was the body of an old woman, a shrivelled up old hag with the rictus grin of a clown. Then he realized he was being stupid. Had he expected her to emerge from the earth looking exactly as she had when he'd last seen her a year ago, bursting with life? He forced back the images of Blaney that crowded into his head. Walking arm in arm with her down the Nile Corniche, kissing her in his cell in Algeria, remembering how they'd sat up the whole night, smoking Gold Flakes, while she'd patiently listened to his story. Blaney laughing, Blaney crying, Blaney's naked body spreadeagled on the counterpane of a London hotel, her red hair spilling across the snow-white pillow like fire. Caine deliberately blanked his mind. If this really was her, he would have the rest of his life to remember those images.

He'd been wrong about the skeleton, too; there was covering on the bone. The ribs showed from under skin as taut and thin as parchment, leg and arm bones were visible, wrapped in fragments of hide, like scorched brown paper. The hands and feet were nothing but bone joints and the remnants of sinew with shreds of tissue on them. The skull had skin on it too, but it was black and purple. The nose was missing, the eye sockets were empty. What was left of the lips was curled back in the chilling grin.

Caine shivered, gagged. He'd seen a lot of dead people. He'd seen so many men, women, and even children, die in front of his eyes – so many that death was almost familiar. This was different, somehow.

'You're not going to faint or throw up, are you?' Smithson enquired.

Caine pulled himself together. 'I don't think so,' he said.

He gritted his teeth. The corpse was laid on its back, vacant eye sockets staring at the sky. This woman seemed smaller than Blaney. True, she hadn't been unusually tall, but she'd had a full figure. This woman's pelvis and chest seemed too narrow to be hers. The pathologist was leaning over the body making little tut-tutting sounds.

'It's a pity they left them out so long,' he commented. 'The bodies must have decomposed more in those eight days in the sun than in the entire eight months they'd been buried.

For a moment, Caine was puzzled. 'What do you mean?' he asked.

'After the French found them and had 'em dug up, they left the corpses lying on the ground for eight days before they reburied them. Maybe they were trying to identify them, or maybe they just didn't know what to do. Anyway, if it wasn't for those eight days it would've been a lot easier for us.'

Caine cursed. 'So, there's no chance, then?'

Smithson adjusted his glasses. 'There's always a chance. Bodies exhumed after a much longer period than this have been identified. It just makes it harder, that's all.'

He leaned closer to the body, actually touched the skull. 'Cause of death not hard to determine,' he said. 'Gunshot wound to the head.'

He showed Caine a surprisingly large, odd-shaped hole in the white bone just above the right ear. He examined the opposite side of the skull. 'No exit wound,' he said. 'The bullet's still in there.' He pointed at the hole. 'See how it's almost cross-shaped, much bigger than you'd expect – and there's soot on the edge of the opening. That means she was shot at hard-contact range. To Caine's surprise, Smithson took a small tape measure from his bag and measured the length and breadth of the entry wound. He put the tape away, pencilled entries in a little notebook. 'The round was 9mm Parabellum,' he said. 'That's not an unusual calibre, but it *is* used in some handguns issued to the *Waffen-SS*.' He paused, leaned back. 'Someone put a 9mm pistol to her head and shot her. She'd have died instantly.'

Caine said nothing. 'What about the rest of the body?' he asked. 'Can you tell anything about that?'

The pathologist parted the corpse's thighs in a way that seemed almost obscene to Caine. He examined the pelvic bones. 'It's unlikely she ever had a baby,' he said. 'I can't be certain, but childbirth usually leaves some traces on the inner pelvis.'

'*Christ*,' Caine said. 'She'd never been married. She was only twenty-three…'

There was a wan smile on Smithson's face. 'You've already decided this is her, then? The woman you knew?'

For a second Caine was flustered. 'No,' he said. 'I just don't know.'

'She *was* probably in her twenties,' the pathologist went on, 'but that doesn't tell us much either. Did she have any distinguishing marks? Deformations? Had she suffered any trauma that might affect the bones?'

Caine thought for a moment. *Deformations? Blaney? She was beautiful, perfect.* Then he suddenly remembered that she'd been shot by deserters in Cairo. A bad wound, he remembered. Sucking pneumothorax. Would there be a trace of that?

Smithson looked doubtful when Caine explained it to him. 'Skin's too decomposed to make out scar tissue,' he said, 'and as she survived, the bullet probably didn't strike any vital organs or hit bone.'

As if on a sudden impulse, he made an incision on what was left of the skin of the chest, sheared it away. Inside the cavity, the organs were almost entirely gone. Caine blinked and turned away, straining to stop himself vomiting, clenching his fists tight to keep control. More images of Blaney flitted through his mind like spirits – her flaming hair, her soft voice, snatches of conversation. If she'd lived, they would probably have stayed together. She would have got old, yes – the glorious red hair might have faded to grey, but to him, she'd still have been beautiful. Not like this, he thought.

Once again, he forced the thoughts out of his mind, watched the pathologist. Smithson had cut through what remained inside the chest cavity, opened the ribcage wide and exposed a length of vertebrae. 'If she was shot in the lungs, the chances are that the bullet would have grazed her spine somewhere in this area,' he said. He peered at the bones a second time and shook his head. 'I see no sign of trauma. That's interesting, but it was always a long shot, if you'll pardon the expression. Since you say your friend survived the gunshot wound you told me about, it's almost certain the bullet passed right through her body, puncturing her lung, but otherwise not hitting anything vital.'

He sighed, sat back on his haunches. 'I'm sorry, Captain,' he said. 'I have to say the results of my autopsy are inconclusive. This might be your girl. On the other hand, the only evidence we have – slim as it is – suggests that it might not.'

CHAPTER SEVENTEEN

Wallenbach, Alsace, France. September 1944

For a second, no one spoke. It was bad luck that they'd run into the *Milice*, Blaney knew that. You could bamboozle Germans more easily than native French. If they arrested her and took her back to their base, the game might well be up. She didn't dare look at André, Rolande or Paul, but she wondered if they were considering violence. Even if they bumped the *Milice* off, they would be missed sooner or later. Others would come looking for them, find their bodies. They'd put two and two together. The operation would have to be cancelled. The bottom line was that none of the *Maquisards* was armed.

'*Mademoiselle?*' the older of the two repeated. 'Who are you, please?'

'My name is Giselle Tomalin,' she said, trying to keep her voice steady. 'I'm a travelling saleswoman from Paris. I sell cosmetics.'

The weasel-faced *Milice* made a clown's show of looking around him. 'Odd, *Mademoiselle*, I see no ladies here. You are in the habit of selling cosmetics to *men*, perhaps?'

Blaney forced herself to giggle. It sounded genuine she thought. She was about to add something when André cut in with a loud horse laugh. 'It's *Saturday*,' he chortled. 'My cousin can't be expected to work all the time. You know what Alsatian women are like – pestering her from dawn till midnight. Come on, Spreitzer, old man. Even you must get a day off.'

The *Milice* man started at the mention of his name. He looked more closely at André, and Blaney saw a smile crack his weasel face. '*Juran*,' he exclaimed. '*Maurice Juran*. By God, I haven't seen you since… Since…'

'Since we were *in there*?'

Spreitzer swallowed hard. 'Wasn't a lot of fun, was it?'

'Fun, it wasn't,' answered the man Blaney now knew was called Maurice. 'We did a good job, though. The Germans were pleased. You know, they told me that if it wasn't for me and you and a few others like us, they'd never have got it done on time.'

Spreitzer laughed. He moved forward to shake hands, kiss Maurice's cheek. 'Well, well, Maurice Juran,' he said. 'I remember that time you pulled me out from under a rockfall. God, you saved my life.'

'I don't know about that,' Maurice said modestly. 'You'd have done the same for me.'

'That doesn't change it,' Spreitzer said. 'How are you? How's your wife?'

'She passed away,' Maurice said glumly. 'Got caught in an Allied bombing raid.' He looked genuinely furious. 'Those bloody British and Americans. Tearing our country apart…'

Spreitzer seemed sympathetic. 'I'm sorry,' he said, then he glanced at Rolande. 'But this must be your son,' he said. 'I remember him. Henri. Little Henri.'

Rolande grinned and nodded like an imbecile. He didn't shake hands, though.

'Big Henri now,' Maurice said. 'He's a registered farm worker. The military wouldn't have him. He's got curvature of the spine.' He nodded at Paul. 'Simone is another cousin of ours. He's a farm labourer, too. Giselle here is a cousin on my wife's side. Thought she'd come down, see if she could flog a few lipsticks and powder puffs.'

Spreitzer turned his attention back to Blaney. 'So, you were brought up in Paris, *Mademoiselle*?' he asked. 'You don't speak Alsatian dialect?'

Blaney shook her head. 'I feel ashamed of myself. You know, they told me, when I was three years old, I used to chat away twenty to the dozen in dialect. My father was a welder, and we left for Paris when I was three. Only came back on rare visits. In Paris, the other kids used to make fun of me, and even my parents started speaking French, so I forgot it.'

The younger man said something to Spreitzer. He shook his head. Launched into a long tirade.

'Wants me to look at your papers,' he said.

'Oh, here,' Blaney said, picking up her bag and rummaging in it.

Spreitzer held his hand up. 'I told him. This is the cousin of a man who saved my life. I'm not going to insult him by asking for her papers.'

'Are you sure?' Blaney asked, her hand still in her bag. 'You're welcome. I wouldn't want you to get into trouble.'

Spreitzer shook his head, smiled grotesquely. He turned his gaze back to Maurice.

'So, they let you go with no problem?' he asked.

Maurice nodded. 'They were happy with my work,' he said, 'but it messed my lungs up, something terrible.'

'Yeah, you were always at the head of the line,' Spreitzer said. 'Always where the dust was thickest. Me, now, they asked me to join the *Milice*, so I said, why not? After all, Alsace is part of Germany now.'

Maurice nodded. 'Yes, we're all Germans now.'

Spreitzer studied them all again, taking in each face in turn, as if trying to work something out. For a moment Blaney wondered if the whole interaction had been a charade. Then he grinned once more. 'I know why you're here,' he said suddenly.

A cold tingle touched Blaney's spine.

'*Birdwatching*,' Spreitzer announced. 'See, I haven't forgotten. You used to love birdwatching in the forest, Maurice. You used to say it was the only way to get the dust out of your lungs. You took me along once or twice, do you remember? Still got that little telescope of yours?'

'Certainly have,' Maurice said, holding it up.

'Looks a bit worn,' Spreitzer said. 'Still, I remember it well. Woodpeckers, Alpine swifts, spotted crakes, nightjars... I still know them all.'

'That's it,' Maurice said. 'I thought my cousin might enjoy it as a break from selling cosmetics. That's why we all came up here on our bikes. You remember the day we saw a whole flock of cranes?'

Spreitzer nodded. '*Wonderful*,' he said.

'Yes,' Maurice muttered sadly. 'They don't come now. The war... you know.'

Spreitzer heaved a heavy sigh. 'I know. Still, best not to get too near the factory. They're a bit sensitive. I would steer clear of the place if I were you.'

Maurice agreed: the two of them shook hands. They said goodbyes.

In moments, they were shooting down the road on their bicycles, pedalling like bats out of hell.

CHAPTER EIGHTEEN

Gaggenau, Germany, June 1945

Caine walked back along the row of cadavers, leaving Smithson to examine the next in line. He glanced at the bodies as he passed. All of them, he noticed, had the same oversized entry wound on the right side of the skull. They'd been shot at hard-contact range, like the woman, but there was more. The wounds were so uniform, that they were almost a signature. He could have sworn that all twenty-seven people had been shot by the same man.

The bodies were all in the same state of advanced decomposition. Rhodes, Ronson and Swan, who'd known the lost SAS men, were studying each of them, trying desperately to find some semblance of their mates in what remained of the faces. Backhouse was moving steadily from corpse to corpse with Garcia and Marchand, so absorbed in searching for clues he seemed to have forgotten Caine. Copeland, Wallace and Trubman were hanging back, observing. The Daimler-Benz staff were working on the remaining two rows of graves, still watched by bored-looking French soldiers with cigarettes in their mouths.

Cope touched his arm. 'Find anything skipper?'

'Inconclusive,' Caine said. 'Body's too far gone in decomposition.'

It was the worst possible result, he thought. If there'd been a definite *yes* or *no*, it would have been better. The worst thing was not knowing.

Copeland thought it over for a minute. 'Autopsy's not the only way of identifying the corpses. There are people here who might have known her in life – that wheezy kid who talked back to Bill, for one. The prisoners worked at the Daimler-Benz factory. That kid was one of the people who showed Marchand where the craters were. He might be able to tell us something.'

Caine sighed. 'All right. His English seemed quite good. Can't hurt to have a word with him. Better ok it with Bill first, though.'

Backhouse and Garcia were kneeling next to the second corpse, watching the pathologist work, when Caine and Copeland approached them. Backhouse turned to look at Caine. 'Sorry, Tom,' he said. 'Smithson told me his autopsy on the woman drew a blank. I'm afraid we're going to have the same trouble with most of them. The colonel here…' he nodded at Garcia, '… reckons this might be a USAF pilot.'

'How can you be sure, sir?' Caine asked. Garcia had removed his helmet, laid it on the ground next to him, revealing steel-grey, crew-cut hair. He turned his bulging face to Caine. '*Sure*, I ain't,' he said. 'This guy had what's left of a pair of under-draws on him. US Air Force issue. That ain't proof, but it's better than diddly squat.'

Caine explained Copeland's idea to Backhouse. The major considered it for a moment, then looked at Garcia. 'Have you got any objection, Colonel?'

Garcia shook his head. 'Nope. Sounds like an angle. Make sure you quiz him about all the dead uns, though, not just the woman.'

'Roger, sir,' Caine said.

'And Tom,' Backhouse added, 'no rough stuff, eh? Let's leave that for the real villains.'

'Didn't even cross my mind,' Caine chuckled. 'In any case, that boy looks like a breeze might blow him down.'

The boy's name was Wolfgang Dellinger. 'Any relation to the Dellinger whose villa we're billeted in?' Caine asked him.

'Karl Dellinger's my uncle,' he answered.

They were sitting in the shade of a cedar tree, on upturned wooden crates. Wolfgang was trembling, but whether from fear or sickness, Caine wasn't sure. His face was deathly pale, and his blue eyes unnaturally bright. Every so often, he was wracked with fits of coughing.

Caine and Copeland moved back a little. TB was contagious – if that's what it was.

'I hear they sent him to a labour camp,' Cope said. 'What do you think of that?'

'My uncle was a member of the Nazi party,' the boy wheezed, 'but he wasn't a Nazi.'

'Easy to say now,' Caine commented. 'Now the war's over.'

The boy took several deep, hacking breaths before he answered. 'My uncle, he brewed beer only. Like every businessman in Germany, he had to join the party. If not, his brewery would have been taken away, given to someone else... someone who *sympathized*.'

Neither Caine nor Copeland said anything. Maybe what the boy claimed was true. Maybe the uncle had just been trying to stay on the right side of the Nazis, or maybe he'd been a committed Nazi from the start.

'How long have you been working at the Daimler-Benz factory?' Caine asked, changing the subject.

'Two years.'

'What's your position?'

'Management trainee.'

'Then surely you must have known these people.' He gestured to the rows of corpses and the figures swarming around them. 'You must have realized they were prisoners. You must have noticed that they were ill-treated and underfed. You were part of the management. The work they did for nothing made a profit for your company. Yet you never lifted a finger to help them.'

The boy croaked with what Caine thought must be ironic laughter. '*Help?*' he rattled. 'If I said anything – even one word, the SS would claim I was a traitor. Then it would be *me* in a labour camp.'

Caine took a long breath. This was getting them nowhere.

'So, in two years you never spoke to any of the prisoners?' Copeland asked.

The boy's glittering eyes fixed on him, puzzled. 'I said I worked for Daimler-Benz for two years,' he rasped. 'Not the prisoners. They came only a few months before the end. I heard they were brought from France. I think they worked at Wallenbach - another Daimler-Benz factory over there.'

Caine and Copeland sat up sharply. 'You're saying that these people – the twenty-seven who were shot – worked here for only a few months?' Caine stared at him in surprise. 'Why were they brought here?'

The boy shook his head. 'This I do not know. I know only that they were brought to work on a special project.'

'What special project?'

'It was a secret – an SS operation. I swear they never told us, not even the director. Maybe someone in head office knew, but nobody here. We received orders to let the SS use the underground hangars of the factory. They brought the machines... the equipment... from the Wallenbach factory in France, too. They installed it at night, when no one was there. The prisoners worked only on this project. I think they are… *were*… brought here because they already knew the work of the operation. They have… what you say… *experience*… no?'

He paused, out of breath, let his head droop between his knees, sucking in breath.

Caine and Copeland exchanged glances. It was starting to get interesting, Caine thought. He was desperate to ask about Blaney but restrained himself. He wasn't an expert on interrogation technique, but he judged it was better to take things one step at a time. That way they'd get not only the details but the bigger picture as well.'

'Where were the prisoners kept?' Copeland enquired.

The boy lifted his head. 'At Rotenfels – a prison camp near a village on the outskirts of Gaggenau. They were brought in every morning in SS lorries, taken back at night…' He paused. 'They worked hard, yes, but I do not think they were starving like you say. I think the work they did was important. The SS are not stupid. They did not bring special workers here to starve. What would be the good of that?'

Copeland nodded. 'Were there prisoners in Rotenfels before these workers came?'

'No. We hev no foreign workers at the factory before. I think Rotenfels was built only for these workers.'

Again, Copeland and Caine exchanged glances. '*Twenty-seven* people?' Caine exclaimed. 'Must have been a very special project.'

'Yeah. They didn't want anyone talking about it, either,' Copeland said. He glared at the boy. '*That's* why they shot them, isn't it? They didn't want anyone blabbing about the job? Isn't that right?'

The boy looked sick and miserable. He hung his head. 'I do not know. Perhaps. I know about the shootings only later. After the SS have gone.'

'Did you know the Allies were coming?'

'No, but we suspected it would happen, because the SS packed up and went.'

Caine realized he was getting angry. He took a breath, tried to consider it. Perhaps the boy was telling the truth, perhaps not. In a small place like this, word of the shootings would have got around. He was pretty sure that neither Wolfgang nor any of the other Daimler-Benz staff had been present at the murders because the last thing the SS would have wanted was civilian witnesses. The Daimler people might have known what was going to happen beforehand though – possibly even where. The jury was out on that one. He decided to leave it, shift to another tack.

'What were these foreign workers actually doing in the factory?' he asked. 'I mean, if you knew where the graves were, surely you must have wanted to see what they'd been working on? Can you show us the machinery?'

Wolfgang cackled. 'It is not there. You... no, I think it is the Americans... yes, the Americans. It vas last April, months after the SS had gone. They came in lorries, jeeps, motorcycles, with white stars in circles painted on them. They arrive only hours before the French take over. They are very eager. They demand to know where the SS project took place. They shout. They hit the director. They say they shoot him if we don't tell.'

'Did they ask about the dead prisoners?' Caine enquired.

The boy shook his head. 'No. Even though we tried to tell them, they were not interested in prisoners. They were not interested in going after the SS. Only the machines, nothing else. They knew they were here. They seem in a hurry. We show them the doors of the underground hangars – the SS welded them shut before they left. The Americans blew them open with explosive. They hev special suits with hoods and respirators. They took the equipment to pieces, carried it out, very carefully, like babies. They put the pieces in their lorries. They did not make any of us Germans help. They set more explosives inside the hangars – on timing mechanisms, I think. As soon as they were out of the factory, the hangars went *boom*. Then they jump into their vehicles. They drove off fast.'

He halted, out of breath. For a moment, Caine wondered if the boy could have concocted the story. It seemed fantastic. The Americans had arrived at the Daimler-Benz plant that April, only hours ahead of the French. They must have known exactly what they were looking for, as Wolfgang said. They must also have known the rate of the French advance. They had carefully calculated the time they needed to get in and out. They'd dismantled technology that was part of a secret SS project and destroyed the rest. Of course they'd been in a hurry. This area had been designated part of the French Zone months earlier. If the French had got there before them, they'd have been stuck. From what Caine had heard, the French had been quite prickly about the division of spoils, because they'd only been thrown the leftovers. If Yanks had been caught looting German machinery in the French Zone, it might have caused an international incident.

The boy laid his head between his legs. The last effort had been too much for him.

'Only two more questions, Wolfgang,' Caine said softly, using the boy's name for the first time. 'Then you can rest. First, there's the corpse of a woman among the dead prisoners. Just one woman. Did you ever see her when she was alive?'

The boy raised his lolling head with what seemed a last gargantuan effort. 'There was… a woman,' he whispered. 'Yes. I sometimes saw her when the prisoners were being brought from the lorries or taken back.'

'Can you tell us anything about her?'

'I never spoke to her because it is forbidden. She was young – maybe twenty-three or twenty-four. She speaks – *spoke* – both French and English, I think, because I see she talked to all the prisoners – French, British and American. I guess she was a *terr…* a member of the *Resistance,* but I do not know.

'What colour was her hair?'

'Light brown.'

'Curly or straight?'

'Straight.'

'What kind of figure did she have? Was she slim or…'

Wolfgang's eyes glittered at him curiously as if he would have liked to ask a question.

He didn't though.

'Slim. She wore glasses, but she was pretty, I think. Her name I do not know. I am sorry she is dead.'

Caine sat back. The youth's testimony was almost as inconclusive as the autopsy, he thought. Blaney was twenty-three and spoke fluent French as well as English. As a prisoner, she might have masqueraded as a Frenchwoman. She had a full figure but might have lost weight in prison. Men considered her pretty. Blaney never wore glasses, but SOE agents often disguised themselves so as not to get noticed. They might have given her false ones. Certainly, the first thing they would have done at SOE training school was get rid of those blazing red curls that made her stand out like a lighthouse beacon, but surely the dye or whatever they used would have grown out or washed out in a few weeks, revealing the original colour. Unless she'd been able to dye it again, of course, but that would surely have been impossible for a prisoner. He remembered, with a sudden pang, that her comrades in the Int. Corps used to call her *Red*.

He wanted to ask more questions, to push the boy, to wring the truth out of him. He knew deep down though, that it would get him nowhere. He had to accept that Wolfgang didn't have the information. Somebody must though. He'd been a POW himself and he knew by experience that the Jerries were meticulous about documentation. Someone at Rotenfels – the camp commandant, at least – must know who she was.

'Last one,' he said. 'Who was in charge of the camp at Rotenfels? I'll accept that you didn't know the prisoners' names, but you must have met, or at least seen correspondence with, the SS camp administration. Who was he and where is he now?'

The youth paused a little too long for Caine's liking.

'The war's over,' Caine said. 'The SS can't hurt you.'

Wolfgang closed his eyes, then opened them suddenly. 'The commandant? His name was Schuochwurte. *SS-Sturmbannführer* Werner Schuochwurte. His family was from Karlsruhe. I heard he works now on the black market. I can tell you no more.'

CHAPTER NINETEEN

Sitting round the table in the little parlour at the Villa Dellinger that evening, they ate chicken that resembled old rope, with roast potatoes. At least it was served on china plates. 'I think the old lady wrung the neck of her best cockerel, boys,' Taff Trubman chuckled, chewing on a chicken leg.

'Stop complainin' yer Welsh git,' Wallace growled. 'This 'ere's better than compo rations.'

'Yeah?' Dusty Rhodes grinned. 'Says who?'

'And it's *Sergeant* Git to you, boy,' Trubman chortled. 'I got promoted.'

'So what? I got offered me stripes more times than I've 'ad 'ot dinners.'

'The only stripes you've been offered are the ones on a convict's uniform,' Copeland tittered.

'Oh, '*is majesty* speaks,' Wallace countered. 'Made it to the dizzy 'eights of first looey, an' you'd think 'e'd won the bleedin' war on 'is own.'

Garcia rumbled with laughter. Backhouse had invited him to dinner at the villa to discuss the next step. The rest of the US team were encamped in their own tents on a green space in another part of town.

The colonel raised a glass. 'At least there's good French wine to wash it down with,' he declared. 'Here's to king whatever, and to the president of the dear old USA. Bottoms up.'

'And here's to the lads – and lady – who gave their lives for 'em,' Caine added, raising his glass. '*Fallen comrades.*'

The SAS team repeated the toasts, slurped wine. When they'd finished eating, Frau Dellinger and the two girls came to take the plates, silent as ghosts.

Afterwards, lounging in an armchair near the fireplace, Garcia lit a cigar. Copeland and Backhouse smoked the Players Navy Cut fags Caine gave them. The enlisted men sat round the table or on the opposite side of the room, smoking, cleaning weapons, discussing the identities of the cadavers they'd seen that day. 'One thing's for certain,' Rhodes said. 'Those corpses were stripped of clothing and their dog tags taken.'

'Yeah,' Wallace agreed. 'The Nazis didn't want nobody findin' out 'oo they was.'

'Must have been a rush job, though,' said Rhodes. ''Cause they missed a thing or two.' He held up a pair of dog tags on a slim chain and a watch he'd found attached to the skeletal wrist of one of the corpses.

'These discs belonged to Captain Crouch,' he said. 'Tell you the truth, I wunta known 'im. Name, rank, number, date of birth, blood group is all there though.' He handed them to Backhouse, who showed them to Caine and Copeland. 'That seems a pretty certain ID,' Cope said.

He handed the tags reverently back to the major.

Backhouse put them away, turned to Rhodes. 'Let's see that watch, Dusty.'

Rhodes handed it to him. Backhouse took it, laid it in the palm of his hand, turned it over. It was a G10, army-issue model – and it had a serial number.

'I'm tellin' you, it was Lieutenant Gill I took that off,' Rhodes said. 'I recognized 'is features. I'd have known 'im anywhere.'

'Och, you're gropin' in the dark, Dusty,' Swan said. 'Ye couldna' tell nothin' from what was left of that face.'

Rhodes glanced at Trubman. 'You send that signal off, Taff? The one with the serial number of the watch?'

'Certainly did, Sarn't Major. Sent it on a new frequency, to the War Crimes Team's own base, see.'

'You mean we got a *base* now?' Ronson asked.

The Welshman looked smug. 'Colonel Franks set up a WCIT signaller in a loft at Eaton Square, London, see. Comes directly under the MOD. OC is a Captain Yelchukov. Ex-SOE bloke – Russian, maybe.'

'Russian father, British mother,' Backhouse corrected him. 'Brought up in Blighty, English as cucumber sandwiches and high tea.'

'Franks reckons they're goin' to demob the whole SAS Regiment,' Rhodes said.

'Paddy Mayne ain't goin' to like it,' Wallace chuntered. 'Can't see that bruiser goin' back ter civvie street. Not with four DSOs to 'is name.'

'*DSO*s,' Trubman muttered. 'They gave Stirling one just for bein' in Auschwitz. Paddy should've had the VC.'

'Whaddya expect?' Wallace grunted. 'Stirlin's a nob *inni*? Paddy ain't. The war didn't change nothin'.'

'I 'eard you once knocked 'im down,' Ronson said. 'Paddy Mayne? 'Eavyweight boxin' champion. Ex-British Lions prop forward. An' you, Trooper Fred Wallace, knocked '*im* down?'

Wallace looked uneasy, lowered his eyes. Knocking down one of the war's most decorated heroes wasn't something he liked to boast about.

'It's true all right,' Copeland chuckled. 'Big Fred here knocked the colonel down. Ended up in clink for it, too.'

Wallace glared at him. 'That weren't Paddy's fault. It weren't 'im as called the Redcaps—'

'—Gettin' back to the subject,' Rhodes broke in. 'The QM branch is goin' to have a record of that watch – the serial number I mean – and they'll find out 'oo it was issued to. You know 'ow they are. Wouldn't give you a sack of dried lizard shit without signin' in triplicate.' He looked directly at Swan, his eyes twinkling. 'Betcha a *stein* o' best Jerry beer that watch is Lt Gill's, Jock.'

'You're on,' Swan said.

In a huddle by the fireplace, the officers were engrossed in their own conversation. Caine and Copeland had repeated what Wolfgang Dellinger had told them, leaving out the part about how the Americans had looted German industrial equipment in the designated French Zone. They'd decided to save that for Backhouse's ears only and let him decide whether not to pass it on.

'So, let's get this straight,' the big half-colonel was saying. He waved his fat cigar as if drawing a pattern in the air with smoke. 'You wanna go to Karlsruhe, in the *American* Zone, where my *own* office is based, snatch a Jerry, and bring him back into the *French* Zone?'

Backhouse looked relaxed in his shirt and short-sleeved pullover. He was hatless, his dark hair sleeked to one side. 'That's about the size of it, Colonel, yes. Unless you want to do it, of course.'

'Me?' Garcia rumbled. 'No way. I ain't gettin' mixed up with snatchin' no one, not even in the US Zone. Not without authorization. And that might take weeks.'

Backhouse's eyes had taken on the dreamy, far-off look Caine had become familiar with.

'Then *we'll* do it,' he said. 'We can't wait weeks for red tape – forms that might never come through. There are twenty-seven decomposing corpses out there. We need to find someone who knows who they are before it's too late. Don't forget, your fliers are among them. You're going to benefit, too.'

'I ain't forgotten,' Garcia smirked. 'I only said I ain't gettin' mixed up in it, that's all.'

'The ball's in your court, then,' Backhouse said.

Garcia heaved a great sigh. 'I like you guys,' he said. 'You ain't the usual nose-in-the-air, la-di-da Brits. Down-to-earth guys, like me. Grandma was Cherokee. You don't find too many US Army colonels with native blood. Not that I'm boastin', of course. You guys are vets, and you're dedicated to your buddies. My crew, they're good men, but they're just doin' a job. That's the difference, you see. All they're bothered about is findin' bodies. They ain't fussed about huntin' down war criminals.'

'So?' Backhouse asked.

'So, if you get caught, I don't know Jack about it. You were operatin' on your own, and you never told me nothin' – ok?'

CHAPTER TWENTY

Alsace, France. September 1944

Blaney sat huddled in the corner of the safe house, with her arms wrapped round herself. It was only September, but the nights could be chilly – it often snowed in October. She tried to stop herself thinking about Tom Caine, wondering if he might be back in London, searching for her. Maybe SOE wouldn't tell him she'd volunteered. She remembered how he'd told her of the days he'd spent scouring Cairo, hunting for any trace of Betty Nolan after their taxi crashed into the Nile and she'd disappeared. It seemed obvious to everyone else that she'd simply drowned, but Caine wouldn't accept it. In the end, they'd put him on the sick list as mentally unstable because he'd refused to believe she was dead. As it turned out though, he'd been right. Would he do the same for Blaney if he found her missing? She was certain he would. He'd accost every intelligence officer he could find, ransack every intelligence department fearlessly until they either clamped him behind bars or he found out the truth. Whatever the case, she wished he were here now, holding her.

Maurice and Rolande were sitting by the fire in their usual positions, smoking and talking in dialect. She guessed they were discussing the encounter with Spreitzer because his name kept cropping up. How trustworthy was he, she wondered? True, he had waived the chance of looking at her papers, and that made it unlikely that he'd report her presence at his base, but there was the other – the silent one. He hadn't seemed too satisfied with Spreitzer's conduct. Maybe he would rat on him, and the *Milice* would either inform the Gestapo or send out a search party. Still, it would be difficult, since André – Maurice that was – no longer lived where he had when Spreitzer had known him. Most people in Alsace considered themselves French, supported the Maquis and hated the Bosch. They would act blind, deaf and dumb, even if they knew something. To cap it all, there were dozens of safe houses, and they never spent more than one night in the same place.

She forced her thoughts away from Caine and Spreitzer, tried to focus on the problem. André's idea of penetrating the underground part of the Wallenbach factory through the ventilation shaft was a good one. If only the sentry and those damn floodlights hadn't stood in the way. She thought about air raids. Surely they'd have to switch them off if there were any reports of Allied bombers en route. All those lights blazing out of the night would be as good as yelling, *Here I am. Come and get me.*

'A diversion,' she said suddenly, in French. 'Some reason for them to switch the lights off, that's what we need.'

The men stopped talking and stared at her as if they'd forgotten she was there.

André – she still called him that to his face – considered it carefully.

'Not a bad idea,' he said at last. 'If we could get your RAF bombers to launch a feint, the Bosch would fall over themselves to get those lights off.'

Blaney was thinking about how Bomber Command detested SOE, though. She could imagine the face of their CO, Bomber Harris, if

SOE requested a dry run, with all the risks it entailed when the RAF could have hit the place themselves.

She shook her head. 'I don't think so. It was a bad idea.' She considered it again for a moment, and for no reason, the words *dummy war* came into her head. She remembered *Operation Bertram* in the Western Desert of Egypt. How 'A' Force – the Deception Service – had created an entire dummy army, tanks and all. They'd even *moved* Alexandria port into the desert, just by using patterns of lights.

'Not a *real* dummy bombing run,' she said suddenly. She realized the words were contradictory and chortled. 'A *dummy*-dummy bombing run.'

'This woman has gone mad,' André exclaimed.

She giggled again at their serious faces. 'The SIS have double agents,' she told them. 'They told us that in training. They've got W/T operators the Bosch think are working for them, sending false data all the time. Don't you see? We don't need an actual air raid. What we need is for the Bosch to *believe* an air raid is coming, on a certain date, at a certain time.'

She saw understanding creep into their eyes. 'You mean your base gets one of these… double agent wireless ops… to put it out that the factory at Wallenbach is going to be raided from the air on a specific date—?' Rolande said.

'— and *snap*,' André finished the sentence for him. 'Out go the lights.'

'It's got to be soon,' Blaney said. 'We've got to get a message to *Samson* today, so he can pass it straight to my HQ.'

Samson was the W/T Operator on *Circuit Boxer*. She'd never met him – they always communicated through a cut-out. All she knew was that he was an SOE man who'd been dropped in by parachute, like herself.

'Paul will take the message,' André said.

'Good. He's to tell them that the *ghost-raid* should be set for midnight, two days from now.'

André looked unconvinced. 'The fact that we do not want a *real* raid is going to take much explaining.'

'Tell him to request the raid as if it's the real thing and add the word *Pomegranate* as a postscript. They'll know what it means. In fact, there's no need to tell Paul anything apart from that message. The less people know, the better.'

'All right.'

'And by the way, André,' she laughed, 'I won't be doing in that sentry with any commando knife.'

'No? Who said?'

'I did. There was a Winchester rifle with a suppressor on it in the kit they dropped, remember? I'm a good shot. I'll take him down at a hundred metres in complete silence.'

André chortled. 'You may be a good shot, *Mademoiselle*, but you are not going to hit a sentry at a hundred metres with any kind of rifle on a pitch-dark night.'

Blaney laughed again. 'You're losing it, André. Two nights from now, there's a three-quarter moon. It's not going to *be* pitch dark.'

'It is if there's cloud-cover,' Andre smirked. 'I don't think you thought of that.'

CHAPTER TWENTY-ONE

Karlsruhe, Baden-Wurttemberg, Germany. June 1945

Werner Schuochwurte stood under the clock tower between platforms nine and ten of Durlach Railway station. He felt twitchy – the only trains that used the place now were run by the US military. In fact, the destination board fixed on the tower was in English and read *Karlsruhe Seventh Army*, a legend imposed over a list that might have come out of a storybook. *Strasbourg, Switzerland, Nancy, Dijon, Paris, Marseilles, United Kingdom* and *USA* – as if you could board a train here, and it would fly you, like a magic carpet, to any destination in the world. The platforms had once been roofed, but half the roof was missing – the section that had covered platform nine. He wondered why that half had gone and not the other. The clock itself had stopped at 9.35. Maybe that was the time of the air raid that had sliced half the roof off. Funny the Americans hadn't fixed it, though. Still, Karlsruhe had been hit badly by Allied bombing raids; it was half in ruins. They couldn't fix everything at once, he thought.

Civilians shuffled past in hats and long mackintoshes, but there wasn't much movement. The platform was wet – there'd been a light shower that afternoon. He was glad of it because it gave him an excuse to wear his own faded mackintosh – a deep pocket concealed the SS-issue Walther P38 he'd brought with him. Nine 9mm rounds in the clip and one up the spout. He'd been working on the black market ever since he'd been ordered to abandon Rotenfels concentration camp and burn his SS uniform. The trade could be rough. You didn't take chances – not on a dicey deal like this. That's why he'd brought along three helpers, Rudinger, Heidecker and Horch – all ex-SS men of one rank or another, all armed. He'd posted two of them behind the remains of shattered iron pillars, another in the shadow of a rusted luggage trolley. He hoped he wouldn't need them, but in this job, you never knew.

Bright moonlight fell through the missing half of the roof, glistened on the damp platform. Schuochwurte glanced at his watch. It was 8.46. The meeting was scheduled for 9 pm. Fourteen minutes to go. He shifted from foot to foot, his fingers curled around the handle of the automatic in his pocket. It was the same one he'd used to execute the Rotenfels prisoners. Perhaps he should have got rid of it – ballistics tests might one day prove that it had been used to kill them. They'd been well hidden though, and perhaps that day would never come. He stood up a little straighter; a tall, muscular man with sandy hair under the broad-brimmed hat. He was handsome – high forehead, straight nose, firm jaw, a determined expression in the blue eyes. No one could argue that he wasn't an *Aryan*, he thought. He'd fought with Heydrich's *Einsatzkommando* on the Russian Front. He was a Doctor of Law. He had no doubt about the superiority of the Germans, but even they couldn't do the impossible with the balance of power weighed so heavily against them: the British, the Americans, the Russians, the Canadians, the Australians, the Free French and all the rest. The money, he thought – the resources available to the enemy – it was all down to that. Why should he feel guilty about shooting a few prisoners? He'd been following orders from his superior. No blame could be attached to himself.

That morning, he'd received an unexpected phone call from a Frau Dellinger in Gaggenau. At first, he'd wondered how she'd got his number. Then he remembered. Karl Dellinger was the owner of a brewery – he lived in a villa in spacious grounds and had two pretty blonde daughters. He was a fervent Nazi – or so he'd claimed. Dellinger had entertained him for dinner on several occasions when he'd been commandant of Rotenfels and had sent him away laden with cigars, nylon stockings and cigarettes. On the phone this morning, Frau Dellinger told him a sob story about how her husband had been arrested by the French and put in a camp somewhere. That didn't surprise him. He was taken unawares though, when the woman had handed the telephone over to Hans Schumann – ex-*SS-Oberführer* Schumann – who'd been chief of the Gestapo in the region when Schuochwurte had been resident there. He remembered that the Dellingers had dropped Schumann's name into the conversation once or twice. Schuochwurte had never met him though. Schumann's voice sounded slightly hoarse and indistinct on the phone, but the meaning had been clear. The ex-Gestapo officer had heard that Schuochwurte was working on the black market. The Dellingers had hordes of stuff in their cellars, and Frau Dellinger wanted to get rid of it before the French winkled it out. If they could find someone to handle it, a small fortune was to be made. Should Schuochwurte feel that he was the man for the job, he must be at the clock tower at Durlach Station in Karlsruhe, that night at nine o'clock sharp. Then Schumann had hung up.

Schuochwurte had turned it over in his head. It seemed a bit rushed, and there'd been something slightly odd about Schumann's voice. But then there was the lure of the Dellingers' loot. *Someone to handle it.*

A small fortune to be made. That was what he needed right now. He'd checked: no military trains were due in that evening. He'd gathered his little gang together for security, and here he was.

At exactly nine o'clock, he saw a man walking slowly towards him from the station entrance – a man wearing a full-length mackintosh, like his, and black shoes. The man was hatless, he had dark hair slicked to one side. He was young and clean-shaven. His hands were dug deep into his coat pockets. As he came nearer, Schuochwurte saw something mournful in his eyes that reminded him of a bloodhound. The man was only two metres away when the ex-SS man realized this couldn't be Schumann. He was too young. Schuochwurte smelled a rat. '*Sie sind nicht Schumann,*' he said.

'*Nein,*' the man replied, '*aber ich bin der Mann, der mit Ihnen am Telefon heute Vormittag.*'

In a flash Schuochwurte saw the trap – the lure of the Dellingers loot, the slightly hoarse, slightly foreign quality he'd noticed in Schumann's voice on the phone. This man spoke fluent German, but he wasn't German at all.

He went for his weapon, screeched, '*Bleib Zuruck! Komm nicht die Nahe von mir!*'

The Walther cleared his pocket, but before he could even bring it to bear, a .303 round smashed through the very centre of his right palm, followed instantly by an ear-splitting *crrrrrraaackk*. He dropped the pistol. It fell on the wet platform with a clatter. Blood was already spurting from his hand when the pain hit him like a bludgeon. He screamed. In the same second, hands as big as dinner gongs seized both his arms, pinioned them behind him. He felt iron handcuffs click into place around his wrists. For a moment, the world swam out of focus. When it came back, the young man with the bloodhound face was holding a Colt .45 automatic to his temple. The soulful, sad-hound look had been replaced by one of venomous fury. '*SS-Sturmbannführer* Werner Schuochwurte,' he said. 'You are under arrest for war crimes committed while you were commandant of Rotenfels concentration camp.'

'Vat are you talkink about?' Schuochwurte demanded in English.

The man loosened his coat. Schuochwurte saw that he was wearing an English paratrooper's camouflage smock beneath it. 'I am talking about the cold-blooded murder of ten prisoners of war of the 2nd Special Air Service Regiment – *my* regiment,' the man answered. 'In direct contravention of The Hague Convention of 1907. I'm talking about the butchery of a total of twenty-six men and a woman, mostly civilians, by you, or troops under your command, you fucking Nazi pig.'

CHAPTER TWENTY-TWO

Schuochwurte's face was sickly pale. He tried to twist away. '*Sie! Sie Töten!*' he bawled. The arms that pinned him were like steel clamps, and the man they belonged to – who'd come up behind him in total silence – looked like an ogre from a Brothers Grimm fairy tale. His head was like a gnarled stump of wood, cut from an old tree, with a shock of gipsy-dark hair, a two-day growth of stubble and tiny black pig's eyes. This hulk of a man was also dressed in a British paratrooper's smock. He was wearing a big pistol in a webbing holster at his belt.

'If yer callin' for yer mates, forget it,' Wallace chortled at him. 'Fink we make an RV without doin' a recce? We ain't amatooers, mate. Those blokes ain't in any state to 'elp.'

They'd parked the jeeps in a bombed-out street near the station an hour earlier, leaving Taff Trubman to keep an eye on them and man the wireless. Swan, Rhodes and Ronson had fanned out into niches and corners around the station entrance, to watch out for Yank patrols. Backhouse had hugged the shadows, waiting for Schuochwurte, while Caine, Copeland and Wallace had cleared the platforms, boxing around the station buildings and crossing the rails from the opposite side. They had spotted the ex-commandant's three henchmen lurking in the darkness – men in presentable civvies with their hands in their coat pockets, two of them behind broken pillars and another crouching by an old luggage cart. The men's attention was focused on the station entrance and the clock tower. Caine's small team had come up behind them as quietly as ghosts and jumped them at precisely the same moment. The first the ex-SS men knew about it was when they felt Colt .45 muzzles pressed to their necks, and heard the words, 'Make any noise and you're dead,' growled in their ears. Just in case they didn't understand English, Caine and his men added the words, '*Mache Lärm und du bist tot.*' It was one of several phrases Backhouse had drummed into them on the drive from Gaggenau.

Caine and the others had searched and disarmed the men, gagged them with scarves and bound their hands. Then they'd waited by the prisoners until 8.40, when the tall man in the broad-brimmed hat and old mackintosh had appeared.

They watched the confrontation between Schuochwurte and Backhouse. Cope had the Nazi in his telescopic sights the whole time, his finger at first pressure on the trigger. The instant the Walther pistol cleared the Nazi's pocket, he put a round from his SMLE sniper's rifle smack through the fellow's palm. It hadn't been an easy shot, with only moonlight for illumination, and the SAS were never trained to shoot at limbs. It was short range for a Lee-Enfield, though, and not the hardest shot he'd ever taken, either. Almost before he'd squeezed the trigger, Wallace had been sprinting down the platform, moving with a speed and silence that Caine knew so well from the war years but which never ceased to amaze him in such a huge man. Wallace had had the handcuffs out of his pocket and on the chap's wrists before the Nazi even knew the giant was behind him.

Caine and Copeland left the trussed-up Jerries where they were and ran down the platform to support the others. Schuochwurte had screeched when the bullet hit him and jabbered once, but now Backhouse had his .45 automatic to the back of the chap's skull, and he wasn't jabbering anymore. They were almost at the station steps when Dusty Rhodes darted in, carrying his M1 carbine in both hands. 'Yank MPs,' he told Backhouse. 'Must've heard the shot. Comin' up the street, two hundred yards away and closin."

Backhouse told him to take Swan and Ronson, run ahead, get the jeeps started. They hustled Schuochwurte down the steps, almost carried him across the street to a broken pavement, conveniently screened by piles of rubble. The SS man began to struggle again. Wallace gripped his arm with a massive right hand, closed his left round Schuochwurte's mouth. Once behind the debris, they fell automatically into patrol formation, five yards apart, with Copeland on point and Caine at the rear. They heard Yank voices raised and the patter of boots coming in their direction. They rounded the corner into the side street to find the jeeps already manned, motors gunning. They shoved Schuochwurte into the passenger seat of the first vehicle and leapt in where they could. At almost the same moment a dozen men in BD, with white helmets and blancoed gaiters reeled around the corner. A whistle blew. '*Military Police,*' a voice yelled. '*Halt!*'

'Fat chance o' that, *Buddy,*' Wallace belched.

The jeeps were already lurching off, zigzagging down the street, with Swan and Rhodes at the wheels. Rifles *whomffed* and cracked. Rounds whizzed off the shattered masonry. Caine knew the MPs were deliberately shooting wide.

The jeeps spun round a corner, out of rifle shot. Clinging onto the roll bars in the back with Wallace, Caine felt a surge of elation. 'Just like old times, eh Fred?'

'No it ain't, Skipper,' Wallace grunted sourly. 'In the old days, I'd 'ave bin be'ind a pair o' Vickers Ks in the back 'ere and blasted the bleedin' lot of 'em.'

CHAPTER TWENTY-THREE

They cleared the city limits without being stopped, halted in a field outside long enough for Backhouse to dress Schuochwurte's wound. When he complained about the pain, Backhouse gave him a syrette of morphia. After that, the ex-SS man lolled in the passenger seat and fell asleep.

They sped on south, weaving around checkpoints as they had on their way across France, leaving the US Zone behind them. They pulled into Gaggenau just before first light and drove straight up to the cemetery. Trubman had maintained radio silence throughout the operation – Backhouse didn't want to get Garcia involved. When they halted in the gravel park, Schuochwurte was snoring loudly.

Wallace shook him roughly awake, dragged him out of the jeep. When the Nazi was on his feet, the giant unlocked the handcuffs. Schuochwurte massaged his bandaged hand with a sigh. They had a quick brew – tea with cold tinned bacon and hard tack biscuits. By the time they'd finished, dawn light was hanging on the foliage of the forest trees. There was an eerie rustling in the branches as they escorted the ex-commandant along the rows of cadavers. It was like some macabre inspection parade, Caine thought.

They halted him by the final corpse – the obscenely grinning remains of the girl who might or might not be Celia Blaney.

Schuochwurte had scarcely glanced at the bodies. He kept his head high. His features showed not the faintest sign of remorse.

Backhouse faced him. 'Do you deny having murdered these people?' he demanded.

'*Yes*,' the ex-SS man replied. 'I did not murder them. I *executed* them, according to instructions given to me by my superior. These instructions were directly in keeping with the *Kommandobehfel* – the commando order – issued by the Führer, Adolf Hitler, in person. I have committed no crime.'

Backhouse said nothing. Apart from Rhodes, who spoke some German, and Copeland, who'd learned a little, he was the only one who'd understood. He turned to the others. 'I'm taking him to the craters where the bodies were found,' he said. 'Captain Caine, you and Lieutenant Copeland will come with me. You too, Sarn't Major Rhodes.' He paused. Caine wondered why he was being so formal. It sounded almost as if he were going to hold a full-blown trial in the forest.

'Sarn't Swan.'

'*Sah?*'

'You'll take charge of the covering party. Conceal yourselves, stay awake. There might be repercussions from last night.'

'And if there's any bother, *sah?*'

'Fire a red flare and run for it with the jeeps. I don't want fighting and I don't want anyone arrested. We've got work to do and it's far from over. If you have to bug out, meet us on the main road to Strasbourg on the other side of the forest – the way we came in.'

'Very good, sah.'

They marched Schuochwurte into the forest. It was a good half hour before they reached the two craters where the bodies had been found. They were still open, with the damp spoil piled next to them. The holes were six feet deep, both muddy in the bottom from a recent shower.

Backhouse halted the ex-SS man on the rim of the left-hand crater. The one, he'd been told, where the bodies of the ten SAS men and four American pilots had been found.

'This is where you killed them?' Backhouse demanded. 'You shot them here?'

If he'd been expecting any change in Schuochwurte's demeanour, he was disappointed. The man looked as haughty and self-righteous as ever.

'This is where I *executed* them,' he said. 'According to my orders.'

'You killed them all yourself?'

'The others were too… squeamish,' he sneered. 'They were afraid of the *Americans*, they said. So, yes, I shot them all myself.'

'With this?' Backhouse displayed the P38 Walther he'd picked up from the platform in Karlsruhe. The grip still held a trace of blood.

'Yes, with that. As tests will no doubt confirm.'

'How many men did you have with you?'

'A full company – almost the entire guard staff of Rotenfels. There were some Russian prisoners. We brought them to fill in the holes.'

'What happened to the Russians?'

'I don't know. If you're thinking I shot them, you're wrong. They were moved somewhere when we evacuated Rotenfels.'

'How did you kill the prisoners?'

'They were made to take off their clothes. I called for them to be brought forward in threes. I made them kneel at the edge of the crater, shot each in turn at the base of the skull and pushed the bodies into the hole.'

Caine felt frustrated that he couldn't understand what was being said.

MICHAEL ASHER

Schuochwurte's apparent composure infuriated him. It was as if the ex-SS man was proud of what he'd done, and what was more, expected to get away with it. Caine clamped his knuckles. He saw the dark looks on the faces of Copeland and Rhodes. He knew they felt it, too.

'*Speak English*,' he told the prisoner. 'You're an educated man. You know English, don't you?'

The ex-SS man sent him a disdainful glance. 'I am a Doctor of Law, not an ignorant soldier. Of course I speak it.'

'You didn't recognize any of the bodies we showed you?' Backhouse asked in English.

Schuochwurte shook his head. 'They were too far gone in decomposition. And, of course, as I mentioned, we removed their uniforms and any personal items before they were shot, to prevent identification.'

He's so bloody smug, Caine thought. *He doesn't even realize he's dropped himself in it.*

'Seems like you missed a few things,' Rhodes growled. 'Lieutenant Gill's watch, for one. Captain Crouch still had his identity discs on. Some of them were wearing bits of military-issue clothing. Did you know that?'

'As I have said, my men were rather… unenthusiastic. They seemed to believe the Americans would be here at any moment. So, yes, perhaps they were a little sloppy.'

He paused, nodded at the crater. 'Your British *parachute commandos*, captured in the Vosges mountains, in France, were in here. With them were the four American pilots, also captured in France.' He stopped again, nodded towards the second crater. 'That hole was for the French. Seventeen terrorists active in the Resistance – the *Alliance Reseau* – including three Catholic priests… and, oh yes… also the woman.'

Caine opened his mouth to speak, but Backhouse made a sharp sign at him. Caine swallowed his words.

130

'Yet you cannot recall the names of any of the people you... *killed*,' Backhouse demanded disdainfully. 'An educated man like you?'

For the first time, Schuochwurte looked irritated. 'Of course, I knew some of them,' he snapped. 'There was a list of names, but I was instructed to destroy it, again to prevent identification. They were only at Rotenfels for two months before I received orders to execute them, after all.'

'I see,' Backhouse said, nodding, 'and where did they come from?'

'From Natzweiler-Struthof, a large concentration camp in Alsace. Natzweiler was the only special camp on French soil – tens of thousands were held there at one time or another. Rotenfels, though in Germany, was a sub-camp of Natzweiler. It was a small camp, built especially for these prisoners. Originally, they were working at the Daimler-Benz factory at Wallenbach, about sixteen kilometres from Natzweiler – I think it was the only Benz plant in France. When the American Sixth Army got too close, though, equipment from the Wallenbach plant was moved across the Rhine into Germany. It was installed in the Daimler-Benz works here at Gaggenau. These prisoners had acquired certain skills at Wallenbach – I assume they had learned how to operate the machinery. When it was moved, they were moved with it.'

'*Certain skills*,' Backhouse repeated, as if mulling over the words. 'So, the work here must have been important. What was it?'

Schuochwurte shook his head. 'This I do not know. It was work for the Reich, that's all I was told.'

Backhouse wasn't sure whether he was lying. He didn't think so, though. The man had been frank about everything else, including the fact that he had personally murdered twenty-seven people. What admission could surpass that?

Backhouse looked at Caine. He knew Tom was bursting to ask about the female prisoner. He nodded at him.

Caine took a breath to stop himself from launching into it too quickly. He didn't want to betray his personal interest, as he suspected he had with Wolfgang Dellinger. 'It seems odd there was only one woman amongst your prisoners,' he said. 'Surely you must at least know something about *her*.'

Schuochwurte took a breath. 'As it happens, I do. Her name was Jeane-Louise Luscher. She was French – one of the leaders of the *Alliance Reseau*. She had been giving us a headache for years with her terrorist activities – since 1940 or '41. The Gestapo got her in '42, but she escaped by squeezing through the bars of her cell window – imagine that. She was flexible as a gymnast. She returned to Alsace in 1944, to help the American Sixth Army. That is when we got her for the second time. She did not escape again.'

'What was she like?'

'Brunette. Glasses. Luscher is a common name in Alsace. She spoke French, English and Alsatian dialect – a debased form of German. That, I think, was her mother tongue.'

Caine felt relief welling up inside him like a slow-burning fuse. He tried not to show it. Names, of course, could be invented, but if the Nazis had known of this woman for four years and if she'd really been captured in '42, then she couldn't be Celia Blaney. Caine knew Blaney had been brought up in France, but in Paris, not Alsace. He was certain she didn't know Alsatian, which, as the SS man had just stated, was a dialect of German, not French. Even if she'd learned a bit of it at SOE training school, she could never have passed as a native speaker. Then there was the slimness, the flexibility. Blaney had been fit but no sort of gymnast – she'd had a full figure. Even if she'd lost weight as a prisoner, he knew for a fact that in 1942 she'd been with Field Security in Egypt. Now he was certain. The skeleton found in the crater wasn't hers. The explosion of relief he felt ballooning inside him never came though. At that moment, he realized he was no better off than he'd been before. He knew that the woman this man had killed wasn't Blaney, but he was still no nearer to finding out what had really happened to her.

'These ten parachute commandos, as you call them,' he said on impulse. 'They weren't the only ones captured in Alsace, were they? We know some were killed in action, but thirty-one men were captured. Where are the rest of the prisoners? What about the special agents sent to work with the Resistance – some of them were women. Some are missing.'

Schuochwurte shrugged, unconcerned. 'The bodies you have seen are the only personnel sent to Rotenfels,' he said. 'The ones I was responsible for. I heard there were others at Natzweiler. I assume they weren't needed here. There were also spies there – British spies dropped by parachute, and yes, at least one of them was a woman. Natzweiler was not only for ordinary cases. It was also a *Nacht und Nebel* camp.'

'What happened to the woman?' Caine demanded, before he could stop himself.

He knew he'd put a foot wrong. Schuochwurte was watching him curiously, a half-smile on his lips. 'You are interested in this woman, eh, Captain? She was your *liebchen*, no? You thought the woman found here was her. Now you know she is not…'

'Answer the question,' Caine snapped.

The SS man shrugged again, as if it were a matter of no importance. 'How should I know? I expect she was executed, as were all the other special prisoners.'

'Did you ever see her? What was she like?'

Again, that infuriating smile. 'I saw her once… from a distance. She was… I remember she had red hair. It had been hidden under some sort of brown dye, but that soon grew out …'

Caine opened his mouth to ask another question, but Backhouse evidently felt he'd had his innings.

'What about the other SAS men?' he cut in.

Schuochwurte sighed. 'On 22 November 1944, I received a message that the American Sixth Army was closing in on the Wallenbach-Natzweiler area in strength. Two days later, on 25 November, I received a further message instructing me to liquidate all prisoners at Rotenfels. I was an SS officer, part of a chain of command, acting under direct orders. If you want to find out what happened to those personnel not moved to Rotenfels, may I suggest you make enquiries at Natzweiler, in France. I would not have expectations, though.'

He stared from Caine to Backhouse triumphantly. 'That is all I can tell you. I am sure you will bring a case against me, but as I have said, I am a Doctor of Law, not a peasant. The fact that you kidnapped me from the American Zone will perhaps render null and void any case. Even if it does not, since I was simply following orders in executing these prisoners, I have, as I keep saying, committed no cri—'

He was cut off by a blood-curdling bellow. Caine jumped, realizing it had come from Rhodes. His normally placid face was contorted with rage – hatred so intense it had made him a demon. He hit the SS man only once, but with a punch like a wrecking ball. Caine couldn't believe it had been generated by that slim figure. Schuochwurte reeled, stumbled, fell back headlong into the crater, hit the bottom with a thud and a splash. They looked down to see him spluttering, wallowing in the ooze like a hog, blood pouring from his nose and lips, spitting out, dirt, fragments of teeth, muddy water.

'That's where you belong, you fucking piece of shit.' Rhodes spat at him. '*Committed no crime*? You murdered my mates, my friends – soldiers captured in uniform. You murdered prisoners of war, entitled to dignity and protection. *No crime* my dick. You're guilty as shit and you're going to swing for it.'

He picked up a clod of earth and was going to hurl it hard at the floundering man when Backhouse stopped him. 'Ok, Dusty,' he said. 'It's not going to make our case any better.'

They watched, expressionless. Schuochwurte attempted to scramble up the walls of the crater, hampered by his bandaged hand. Each time, he slithered back, splashed and gouged in the filthy water.

'You think you are better than me?' he gasped at last. 'You attacked a helpless prisoner.'

'Yeah, only there's a difference,' Rhodes snarled at him. 'You've got a chance of gettin' out of that pit. Our mates didn't. Now just imagine what it'd be like if we decided to fill the hole in and leave you down there. That's what you deserve, you Nazi arsehole.'

When they finally pulled him out, he stood amongst them, shivering. His face was covered in blood, snot and mud. His civilian clothes were soaked and spattered with dirt.

Backhouse had taken out the ex-SS officer's P38 and was toying with it, flipping it from hand to hand, weighing it playfully.

Schuochwurte watched the action. He tried to assume his previous poise of dignity, but he was breathing hard. When he spoke this time, his voice sounded hollow. '*I... hev... done... nothing... wrong. I... vas...just... following... orders.*'

'You can tell the judge that,' Backhouse said, examining the Walther pistol abstractedly, 'but personally I doubt if you'll get away with it. After all, you're a *Doctor of Law*, and you know all about these things, don't you?' He stared straight at the ex-SS man with eyes like drill bits.

'Tell me, *Herr Doktor*, if you believed these executions to be legal, why were they done in secret? It took us almost half an hour to reach this spot. It's deep in the forest. You chose a place where there would be no witnesses, where your crimes would be hidden. Legal executions are not carried out in secret. If you really believed in the legitimacy of Hitler's commando order, these so-called executions would have been carried out, at the very least in front of official observers. You said that all items of uniform, or anything that might allow the prisoners to be identified, were removed. You said that you destroyed the list of names, for the same reason. Again, if you really believed you were committing no crime, why would you be afraid they would be identified? You, *Herr Doktor*, knew full well that Hitler's so-called commando order was a worthless piece of crap, illegal under The Hague Convention of 1907, and the Geneva Convention of 1938. You knew that using prisoners of war as slave labour is not only similarly illegal, it is also *against* the so-called commando order, which specifies that enemy saboteurs must be killed within *eight days* of capture. I know. I've read it. It seems to me that you used that piece of verbal diarrhoea very selectively, so I wouldn't bank on making a defence of it.'

He smiled truculently. 'And in case you're interested, I too was a lawyer – actually a barrister – in civilian life. I studied at the University of Cambridge.'

Schuochwurte gritted his bloody teeth, the whites of his eyes bulging at Backhouse. He said nothing.

'The strangest thing of all,' Backhouse continued, fingering the Walther again, examining the stock with interest, 'is how a *highly gifted* person like yourself failed to realize that when the Allies invaded Germany - as they were bound to do - and your crimes were discovered – as they were bound to be – you'd be branded a war criminal and hunted down.'

136

Once again, he glared at Schuochwurte. His voice remained even, his eyes blazed. 'You are perfectly aware, I think, that the murder of these twenty-seven prisoners had nothing to do with any commando-order nonsense – that was just an excuse. It was connected with the work those prisoners were doing in the Daimler-Benz factory at Gaggenau and the need to keep it secret. Now, you may or may not have been told what they were doing. Whatever the case, I am sure you're aware who does know. I'm guessing that it would be the same person who gave you the order to kill the prisoners. Since you obviously *do* know who that was, I'd like you to tell me.'

Schuochwurte was casting about desperately, his eyes popping from their sockets as if he was seeking a way of escape. Suddenly, with astonishing speed, he snatched the Walther pistol from Backhouse with his left hand and leapt away. He backed towards the trees. Before he'd taken two paces, Caine, Copeland and Rhodes had their weapons trained on him. Backhouse didn't move. He stood there, smiling.

'This time I won't be aiming for your hand,' Copeland grunted.

Schuochwurte shot him a withering glance. He raised the Walther slowly. Cope took the first pressure, knowing the man – a right-hander – would be shooting left-handed and that he could blast the Jerry's head off before he even got the barrel steady. Then Schuochwurte turned the barrel against his own face, lodged it under his chin and pulled iron. There was a flat *ppooomphhh* – Caine found himself wondering if the prisoners this man had murdered had heard the same sound, realized it was impossible. The ex-SS man had used his non-shooting hand, though, and it had been shaking. It was a bad shot. The 9mm round had passed through his jaw and emerged from his right eye socket, bursting the eyeball, knocking it out. Schuochwurte collapsed on the wet earth, dribbling blood, gagging. What was left of the collapsed eyeball dangled obscenely from the optic nerve.

Backhouse and Caine were the first to reach him. By then it was too late. The bullet had severed his jugular artery and blood was pumping from it in long, dark spritzes. Backhouse pulled a field dressing from his smock, tore it open, lodged the pad against the wound. The German was already lying in a pool of thick gore. Backhouse knew he'd lost too much blood already. He leaned over the man. The single eye blinked at him. '*Swine*,' he whispered. '*British pigs.*'

'Pigs, maybe,' Backhouse said, 'but no one here has ever shot a prisoner of war in cold blood. Not yet anyway.'

'I hev told you,' he slurred. 'I was given an… *order.*'

'You didn't say who gave it to you,' Backhouse said.

The Nazi's eye went out of focus. '*Boelcke*,' he rasped. There was a vacant smile on his face. 'But… Boelcke… is too clever for you. You will *never* get him… *never.*'

Caine saw the fury come back into Backhouse's eyes. At the same moment, Schuochwurte's body convulsed as the last gush of purple blood spurted from the neck wound. His remaining eye misted over and went rigid.

CHAPTER TWENTY-FOUR

'Where the 'ecks the bleedin' Jerry?' Wallace demanded. He was in the driving seat of the leading jeep, steering with one massive hand while the other yanked on the throttle. The two vehicles sped down the white road to Gaggenau in wafts of dust.

'Don't ask,' Backhouse yelled over the engine noise, gripping the forward roll bar to stay in his seat. 'Just drive like hell.'

He craned his neck to look back at Copeland, who was clinging on like a limpet in the back, his head lodged between Backhouse and Wallace.

'You did that on purpose, Bill,' Cope bawled.

'*What?*'

'Showed him the pistol. Gave him a chance to grab it.'

'Why the hell would I do that? Blighter might have shot me.'

'Oh yeah? You knew very well I could have dropped him before he even got the barrel up.'

'He killed himself, Harry. We didn't kill him.'

'No, we didn't, but we've still got a dead German lying in the forest, with a nine-millimetre gunshot wound in the neck. He's also got a hole in the right hand made by a round from an SMLE sniper rifle that they could quite easily trace back to me. He's got broken teeth, a bruised face, and a body covered in blood and shit.'

Backhouse seemed unconcerned. 'That man had it coming,' he said. 'Judging by the way it ended, I think he knew that.'

They passed through the open gates of the Villa Dellinger, along the drive towards the house.

Their three-tonner was still parked outside. Next to it was an American jeep.

The two SAS vehicles pulled up behind them. For a minute, no one moved. Then Backhouse stepped down. 'Stay where you are, Fred,' he said quietly to Wallace. 'Keep the motor running.' He nodded at the Jeep, glanced at Caine. 'Looks like we've got company.'

Caine slipped out of his seat. He slung his Thompson, pulled out his .45 Colt in a smooth cross-body draw. He crouched down and examined the gravel to see if he could spot any tracks – the first reaction of a desert veteran. The area was so churned up with the coming and going of vehicles, though, that he learned nothing.

He moved up beside Backhouse. The major had his own pistol out. 'Cover me a minute, will you, Tom?' Backhouse said. 'I need to have a word with Taff.'

Caine nodded, crouched on one knee, his eyes fixed on the front door. Backhouse moved round to the tailboard of Caine's jeep. Trubman was perched by the wireless set. It was switched on, but he hadn't been transmitting during the snatch operation. He'd been listening in on various frequencies, hadn't touched the key.

'I want you to get comms with Eaton Square ASAP,' Backhouse told the signaller. 'Tell Captain Yelchukov to contact CROWCASS in Paris…'

'CROWCASS, sir?'

'It's a registry of wanted Nazis SHAEF have set up. I want Yelkuchov to find out if they have any record of a chap called Boelcke – that's B–O–E–L–C–K–E…'

Trubman scribbled down the name on a signals pad with a stub of pencil.

'First name unknown, but the fellow must have been a high-ranking SS officer if he gave Schuochwurte the order to kill our men. I want to know anything Yelchukov can find out about him. Most important – where he is now.'

'Got it, sir. Anything else? Only you know it takes a long time to get comms, see, especially when you're on the move. The bumpin' of the vehicle plays havoc with the antenna and you have to get it—'

'—That's your business, Sergeant,' Backhouse cut him off. 'Yes, there is something else. I need that intelligence by tomorrow if not sooner. I also need Yelchukov to get hold of the dental records of all the men missing on Op *Taunton* and bring them to France in person. Tell him to get on a plane to Strasbourg. I expect him to RV on the French side of the Rastatt Bridge on the Rhine by sunset the day after tomorrow…'

Trubman scribbled furiously. 'Isn't that a bit of a tall order, Major? I mean…'

'Yes, it's a tall order. So what? I don't care if he has to jump in by parachute. I want him there. I want that information. I want those records.'

Trubman's cheeks developed pink spots. Rhodes had told him that Backhouse could be the most awkward critter on earth when he wanted. This was the first real sign he'd seen of it.

'Very good, sir,' he said.

He turned away, started resetting the antenna, recalibrating the set.

While the rest of the crew covered them from the vehicles, Caine and Backhouse took turns to move, crossing the distance between the gravel drive and the house door with deft precision. They stood outside.

Backhouse was about to knock when it opened. Both he and Caine brought their weapons to bear, double-handed, arms extended, SAS style.

Frau Dellinger stood there, face ashen, eyes wide with terror. She'd been reluctant to play a part in Backhouse's deception on the telephone the previous morning when he'd masqueraded as Schumann. She had clearly expected repercussions. Backhouse had explained over and over that the SS were finished. They couldn't harm her. It was only afterwards that he'd wondered if it was the return of her husband she feared.

They lowered their pistols, stood up. The trembling lady stood aside. They moved through the hall into the little parlour they'd been assigned. Ensconced comfortably in an armchair by the fireplace was the hefty figure of Lt Colonel José Garcia. He was wearing his tin helmet tilted back, with the chinstraps unbuckled and hanging down. He had the stub of an unlit cigar in his teeth and a huge Colt revolver, in his plump hands, pointed straight at them. His slightly slanted eyes were narrowed. He did not look a happy man.

When he saw them, he let the pistol drop, took the cigar out of his mouth, heaved himself up. 'You guys sure stirred up a hornets' nest,' he drawled. 'The CIC's been here. Lucky they came to me first. Told 'em I had no idea where you'd gone. They'll be back though. The three-ton truck outside was a dead giveaway.'

'*CIC?*' Caine repeated. 'What's that?'

'Counter-Intelligence Corps. Outfit in charge of all post-war operations, including war crimes. They say armed men kidnapped a German civilian from Darlach railway station in Karlsruhe last night. One shot fired. Ran off when MPs arrived. Found three more civilians trussed like chickens, gagged with British tank corps scarves, hands tied with parachute cord. He peered at Backhouse. 'You wouldn't know anythin' about that now, wouldya?'

'Nope,' Backhouse said. 'Why would we?'

'Turns out these guys were wearin' camouflage smocks, like the Brit Airborne.'

'That rules us out then,' Caine smirked. 'We're SAS, not Airborne.'

'Anyone can put on a camouflage smock,' Backhouse said. 'Do they have proof?'

'I guess not,' Garcia growled, 'but if I was you, I'd beat it right now. Those boys don't give up easy, and they'll be back.'

'At least it's not our own lot,' Caine commented.

'Oh yeah, that's another thing,' said Garcia. 'Those guys from SHAEF I told you about? Your Brit MPs? CIC had another message from 'em. They're on your trail but didn't have the right paperwork to cross the Rhine. They're holdin' fire, waitin' for it. I reckon it was them that put the CIC onto you.'

Backhouse was casting around the room, looking for anything they might have left behind.

Seeing nothing, he stuck out his hand. 'It's been a pleasure, Colonel. You're an officer and a gentleman.'

Garcia shook with his fat mitt, grinning. 'Likewise, Major.'

They saluted.

'By the way,' Backhouse added, as if it were an afterthought. 'You'll find a dead Nazi war criminal in the forest, near the craters where they dug up the bodies...'

'*Aw, shit.*' The grin faded from Garcia's lips.

'We didn't kill him,' Backhouse said. 'Chap shot himself with his own weapon. Ballistics tests will prove that. They'll also show that the same weapon was used to kill all twenty-seven of the prisoners, including your four USAF pilots. The man admitted it openly, not under duress. If it comes to it, there are four witnesses to that. Name of Werner

143

Schuochwurte – ex-SS officer, ex-commandant of Rotenfels concentration camp…'

'*Great*,' Garcia growled. 'Just dandy. How'm I gonna explain to the CIC how he got there?'

'Don't know anything about it?' Caine suggested.

'Last point,' said Backhouse. 'You remember what I told you about the prisoners being moved here to continue the work they were doing at the Daimler-Benz factory at Wallenbach?'

'Yeah. You find out what the work was?'

'No, but I do know this. The day before the French moved in, an unidentified American unit pitched up here in a hurry. They dismantled the equipment and took it away. Apparently wore special protective clothing. They obviously knew exactly what they were looking for and where to find it *and* calculated on getting here before the French.'

The colonel looked baffled. Caine and Backhouse were already on their way out.

'See you on the other side, Colonel,' Caine said.

'*Nossir*,' Garcia chortled. He stuck the cigar stump in his mouth, shook his broad head. 'Not if I see you first.'

CHAPTER TWENTY-FIVE

Wallenbach, Alsace, France. September 1944

'*Eight, seven, six,*' Blaney counted off the seconds silently. She was lying next to André, Rolande and Paul in the grove of Aleppo pines, almost directly opposite the sentry post. To her delight, the night had turned out to be perfect for the op, with a brilliant three-quarter moon, basking smugly in a cloudless sky. Blaney had been tempted to tease André about it, but had contented herself with an inward smile.

The Winchester sniper rifle was nestled in the pit of her right shoulder; she had already zeroed in on the German guard with her telescopic sights. The suppressor on the barrel made the weapon feel slightly out of balance, but for now, she'd rested the muzzle in a tuft of sword grass. She hoped desperately that she could make the shot. If she failed, either the sentry would realize he'd been shot at, or else he wouldn't notice anything at all. In the first case, he'd sound the alarm. In the second, she might have to take him out with a commando knife. *What am I talking about? I can always make a second shot.*

It was two days since Paul had passed the *Pomegranate* signal to *Samson.* It had been acknowledged, but that was all. The fate of the raid now depended, not on the Brylcreem Boys, but on the Secret

Intelligence Service, MI6, who was known to despise SOE even more than Bomber Command did. The hands on her elegant little watch were approaching midnight. It had taken them three hours to crawl, through the moonlight and the floodlight beams, the several hundred yards to the ravine from the edge of the wood. Since all of them had been carrying weapons and haversacks containing explosives, detonators and other sabotage equipment, not to mention water, ropes and tackle to help them with the climb, they had been obliged to progress at the rate of slugs.

They had reached the grove over an hour earlier, lain there unmoving in the shadows ever since. *Now comes the moment of truth*, Blaney thought. She didn't know what the procedure would be at the Benz plant in the event of an air raid alert. Would they black out in advance or wait till the last moment before switching off the lights? Would they take the rumour seriously or wait till they heard the rumble of aero engines? Would they delay it till someone eyeballed enemy bombers or shuftied them on a radar screen? She'd given orders that the ghost raid should be set for midnight, so she already knew the answer to the first question. It was only seconds to 0000 hours, and they hadn't been switched off yet. Blaney wondered if the *Pomegranate* message had got through to the right channels. If it had, had it been acted on? If it had been acted on, had it been detected by the enemy? There were so many variables in this battle of phantoms, that nothing could be sure.

She focused on her watch. '*Five, four, three,*' she counted off. The lights were still on. The sentry still at his post. Occasionally he shifted, paced a few yards to the left, a few to the right, but he never ventured far from his spot in front of the ventilation shaft. Blaney could sense the tension in the three men lying beside her – charges waiting to go off. '*Three-two-one. Zero.*'

Nothing happened. The glare of the floodlights remained.

'*Merde*,' André whispered.

'*We'd better…*' Blaney never discovered what Rolande had been about to say. At that moment the floodlights snapped off in unison, leaving the ravine in the dimmer light of the moon. An air raid siren began to wail from somewhere far off. Blaney felt an irrepressible pulse of gratitude to Lurgan and even to the SIS. Some double agent had risked their life for this.

Paul had already started to move to the edge of the ravine, pacing rapidly in the moonlight. His job was to scale the cliff on the other side and make a hole in the barbed-wire fence with wire cutters. He would sever the electric cable connecting the floodlights, make sure they didn't come on again. He would then move right and make another hole, fifty metres further down the line, as an emergency escape route. He would attach a rope there, shimmy down again, fix up quick-ascent ropes on the other side. Meanwhile, André, Rolande and Blaney would cross the ravine carrying the demo kit.

Blaney had to wait thirty seconds till her eyes adjusted from the intensity of the floodlights to the softer light of the moon. She counted off the time impatiently, then fitted the stock of the rifle firmly into her shoulder. She peered through the sights. The guard was a dark stickman in the moonlight. He hadn't shifted from his place, but he had raised his rifle in both hands and was gazing up at the stars. Blaney aimed at his midriff, then brought up the muzzle a fraction, centred on his chest. She took the first pressure. Squeezed iron. *Sorry, Fritz*, she thought.

The rifle kicked, made a faint hiss. By the time she heard the sound, though, the bullet had already ruptured the Jerry's heart. She saw him fall, saw André and Rolande moving towards the ravine, carrying heavy knapsacks and 9mm Sten sub-machine guns. She laid the Winchester down, picked up her own Sten, slung it over a shoulder, ran after them.

The descent wasn't as difficult as she'd first anticipated. They'd practised it several times in a gorge of similar height. If anyone discovered them training, they could always fall back on what they'd come to call the *ornithologist alibi*. André had calculated that it would take six minutes to get down. In fact, they were squatting by the river in only five. The water was a dark gush, flecked with white foam, but as André had told them, not as bad as it looked. Their main concern was keeping the sabotage kit dry, especially the time pencils. Items small enough had been inserted in rubber condoms. Larger components had been carefully wrapped in canvas. Paul had evidently crossed with no problem – he had disappeared into the shadows on the opposite side.

Rolande was the first to step into the current. Blaney almost chuckled when she saw it was only up to his thighs. Of course, he was much taller than she was. When she stepped into the water, it was surprisingly cold and almost up to her waist. Rolande put out his hand to steady her. It was soft – too soft for a farm labourer – which was why, she'd understood later, he hadn't shaken hands with Spreitzer that day. She caught the glint of his smile in the moonlight and felt encouraged by it. Over the past few weeks, they'd become close. She knew he wanted to become her lover, but he'd never been pushy about it. He was good-looking, clever and gentle. She liked him, but he wasn't Tom Caine. She appreciated his support now though. The bed of the stream was uneven and slippery, and there was constant pressure from the fast-flowing current. The real risk was that one of them might miss their footing, slip over, get washed downstream. If that happened, some of the demo kit would almost certainly be ruined. Canvas wasn't very reliable when it came to total immersion. The Nobel's 808 plastic explosive they carried would be all right, but the detonators and time pencils might not.

They made their way across the stream slowly, feeling for every step. It was slow going, but the stream wasn't wide, and within minutes, Rolande was pulling her out on the opposite bank. They waited for André to clamber out, made way for him so that he could lead them up the narrow chimney that he'd spotted while working on the ventilation shaft. He'd never climbed it before, but it proved to be fairly easy, with convenient handholds and footholds. Going was ponderous in the semi-darkness though. When they reached the top, they found that the rock shelf was narrow. They moved along it in file, Stens at the ready, André leading, till they found the body of the guard. André and Blaney squatted down to examine him. He was lying on his back, eyes wide open, staring at the sky – a youth of no more than eighteen, weak chin, pointed nose. The expression frozen on his face was one of mild surprise. '*Hitler Youth*,' André whispered. 'I told you the guards here were not of the best.'

Blaney staved off a feeling of remorse by remembering what he'd said about the tens of thousands of slave labourers from Natzweiler who'd been starved, worked to death, beaten, tortured and hanged at this factory. *Still, it wasn't his fault. He was only a kid.* There was hardly any blood apart from a trickle from the youth's left nostril. The shot had passed through the breast pocket of his field-grey uniform, straight through the heart.

André made the sign of the horns at Blaney with the index and little fingers cocked. It could mean a lot of different things, but Blaney knew this time it meant *damn good shooting* and felt embarrassed. She'd just killed a young lad, and for the first time, André was giving her praise.

Rolande was already crouching by the iron grill. As they moved up to him, he put his Sten down, slipped off his haversack and unbuckled it. André inspected the lock on the grill. It was a large, heavy brass padlock, but nothing that a small charge of Nobel's 808 wouldn't take care of. The grille consisted of iron bars as thick as a man's forearm, with two-inch spaces in between them. It was a door that swung outwards, with hinges on the inside. The door was attached to a strong iron frame, embedded in the solid rock. André put his ear to one of the gaps in the bars. The hum of the turbines was clearly audible. He got a whiff of scorched metal like a burned-out clutch plate. The smell gave him unpleasant memories. He shivered.

Rolande took out a piece of 808 he'd already cut and moulded roughly into shape, held it out in two hands to André as if it were a sacred offering. André took it, pressed it against the lock. He accepted the detonator and attached it with extreme care. Blaney watched their movements with admiration. She wondered how many times they'd practised this, to get it so perfect. Last of all, Rolande needed to give André the time pencil. They were SOE issue, colour coded according to the time delay required. '*One minute?*' Rolande suggested.

André shook his head. '*Thirty seconds,*' he mumbled, with a hard glance that seemed to add, *we haven't got all night.*

This time, it was Rolande who performed. He squeezed the ridge on the timer until the copper casing bent inwards, set it in place and picked up his haversack. '*Come on,*' he said.

They retreated about thirty yards along the edge of the ravine, lay flat, waited. They seemed to lie there for so long that Blaney started to think the time pencil must be a dud. Then there was a low *barooooomfff* from the direction of the grille. Blaney felt hot air warp. Just as they got up, Paul approached them silently from behind. 'All set up for a quick getaway,' he muttered. 'If anything happens to me, you'll find the opening fifty paces down and a rope secured. There are four ropes on the other side.'

André nodded. They approached the grille, Stens ready. The lock had been completely blown off.

André opened the grille door; it creaked. Evidently, no one had used it in a while, the hinges hadn't been oiled. When it lay open they hesitated at the entrance, staring up the dark tunnel to where it curved round into an eerie luminescence of orange light. The hum of the turbines sounded louder now, but Blaney still found it hard to believe that no one had heard the explosion. It was Sunday, half past midnight though, and there would only be a skeleton guard on the place. Hopefully, with the air raid warning, any sentries in the cross-tunnels would have gone topside to help with the AA defence. Of course, you never knew. As André had commented wryly, the opposite might happen: the anti-aircraft gunners might scarper down into the tunnels to escape the bombs. Knowing the Germans though, this seemed doubtful. Jerry soldiers were generally well-disciplined and steady, even the Home Guard and the Hitler Youth.

André nodded again to Paul. He would remain at the entrance to cover their withdrawal once they'd set the charges. He took up a position in the shadows. The other three paced quietly along the tunnel in Indian file, with André in the lead. They were wearing their overalls and black stocking caps, with rubber-soled boots, their faces blackened with burnt cork. All of them were carrying No 36 grenades and smoke canisters to cover their retreat if they got bumped. André – five yards ahead of Blaney – peered into the darkness, his Sten firmly at the shoulder, trying to block out horrific images from the time he'd worked here. He knew he had to stay focused and present, like a fox in the forest, poised to run or fight.

It was no more than a hundred metres to the place where the tunnel curved round, almost at right angles – the place from where the strange orange luminescence glowed. He remembered the bend but beyond that, didn't know what to expect. The last time he'd seen the cross-tunnel the machinery hadn't yet been installed. Even Giselle hadn't been told exactly what the machinery looked like. There were no photos or sketches of it. She'd told him only that they were likely to find a number of units – no more than six. On each of them, a separate charge had to be laid. André paced slowly, the rumble of the turbines and the nauseating scorched-metal smell increased in intensity with every step.

When he came to the bend, André crouched down and let Blaney pass into lead position. Not knowing what or who she might find, she edged round the bend into that oddly luminous orange light.

CHAPTER TWENTY-SIX

Nothing in Blaney's briefing had prepared her for what she saw. She'd been expecting units of conventional machinery – of a sophisticated kind, perhaps, but ordinary all the same. What she saw was something different. There were no separate units but a continuous wall of white metal, divided into cells, each tall enough for a man to stand up in. Every cell had an oblong window of what looked like bulletproof glass. She didn't know if submarines had portholes, but if they did, this is how they might look, she thought. Except that, from each window there came that orange glow – it was the only light in the room. The walls were festooned with light bulbs and connecting cables, but the lights were switched off. The turbine hum was as loud as André had predicted, but the turbines themselves weren't visible. Instead, there were sectioned pipes a foot in diameter – bloated steel caterpillars leading down from the roof to each cell. Blaney thought the pipes must be connected to the turbines and, judging by the heat around the units, must be blowing cool air.

The floor around the cells was covered in studded metal sheeting, to prevent slipping, she supposed. She moved towards the nearest unit, her boots clicking slightly on the metal. She beckoned André and Rolande after her and saw their faces drop as they took in the scene. André's eyes bulged. For an instant she thought he was going to say something. She drew a straight finger across her mouth.

Closer to the glow it was as if a fire was burning on the other side of the window. The glow was almost fire-coloured but there was no flicker, so it had to be some kind of internal light. The cell was hung with wires leading to a control console, on which there were what looked like pressure gauges, switches, red and green panel lights. The oddest thing, though, was the fact that there were holes either side of the windows, just large enough, just wide enough apart, and at the right height, for a person to insert both arms. Beyond the window she could see what looked like protective sleeves – frames of metal rings covered in fabric, like the arms of a deep-sea diver's suit. But instead of gloves, the arms terminated in three-pronged steel pincers. Blaney put her left hand tentatively into the adjacent hole and waggled it. The arm beyond the window moved. She withdrew her hand quickly. Obviously the protective arm covers were there to allow an operator to lift, move or manipulate whatever was inside the cell without touching it. Whether they were intended to protect the operator against heat, cold, or something else, she didn't know. *What the heck is inside the cell, anyway?* She pressed her nose against the glass. All she could make out were some smooth, flat ovals of a dark substance in the tangerine-coloured light. Nothing special at all. The whole set-up gave her the shivers.

André and Rolande were crouching on the steel plates, already removing the demo gear from their haversacks. Blaney went down on one knee by the first cell, slipped off the straps of her own pack and laid it on end. Suddenly she froze. She grasped the Sten in her right hand with the hollow butt lodged against her stomach. Her left hand grasped for the smoke canister clipped to her belt. As André had told them, the constant drone of the turbines cut out ambient noise. Blaney wasn't aware she'd heard anything; she had a *feeling* someone was there. André and Rolande noticed her movement, stopped what they were doing.

They had only just grabbed their Stens when a dozen figures hustled round the opposite bend. Blaney had been thinking about diving gear – it was as if her imagination had come to life. The figures were dressed from head to foot in one-piece suits of some shiny material. They wore rubber boots, like Wellingtons but closer fitting, and their heads were entirely covered in what looked like something between a respirator and a diver's mask. They were all carrying Walther pistols in rubber-gloved hands. If they had opened fire at that moment, Blaney thought later, she and her two comrades would have been dead as rats. Strangely, though, the men didn't fire. It occurred to Blaney that there was something in this room they didn't want to hit. The smoke grenade was already in her hand. She had teased the pin out, almost without noticing. She tossed it. Voices croaked behind the masks, too indistinct for her to make out. The smoke canister hit the steel. A dense white curd of phosphorous smog steamed out. Within a second, visibility in the tunnel was down to zero. Blaney could hear the suited figures blundering into each other, cursing. They never fired a shot, though. *They're not going to fire.* The smoke wafted back on the three of them. Blaney coughed, pinched her nose with the thumb and forefinger of one hand, squeezed iron with the other and let go a burst from her Sten.. She deliberately fired high – she could no longer see André and Rolande in the swirling fog of smoke. She didn't want to hit them by accident. '*Allons! Allons!*' she yelled. '*Laissez-nous sortir!*'

André and Rolande backed into her, almost sent her flying. Their Stens were cocked but neither opened fire. Blaney glimpsed a gnarled hand raised in the smoke and realized there was a No. 36 grenade in it.

She screamed, '*Nooooo!*' Too late. The grenade had already gone. She grabbed André by the back of his collar, tried to drag him round the bend in the tunnel. Instead, he fell flat on his face. She and Rolande did the same. Blaney just had time to see the weird diver figures floundering out of the smoke when the grenade exploded with a deafening blat. Fire blazed, black claws snatched at the whorls of white, shrapnel shards spat, glass fragments whizzed over their heads. She glimpsed frog-suited men bowled over like skittles. Before she could stop him, André was up, running to the window of the nearest cell – the one his grenade had just shattered. He thrust his bare hand through the broken glass. This time it was Rolande who grabbed him. '*Leave it alone,*' he roared. '*For God's sake leave it alone.*'

'*Come on,*' Blaney bawled.

She was already backing round the bend, out of the smoke. A moment later, Rolande followed, pulling André with him. To Blaney's relief, his hands held nothing but his Sten.

They turned and ran down the air shaft, pursued by slivers of smoke. Then pistol shots were whanging around them, shearing off the stone floor, wheezing off the walls. Paul was still crouching in the shadows where they'd left him. '*Covering fire,*' Blaney squealed as they belted past. She heard the steady throb of rounds as Paul fired at the advancing men, heard the pause as he chucked a grenade, heard a last burst of fire as he emptied his magazine, heard the booming crump as the grenade exploded in the tunnel. Then Paul was behind them, all running for their lives along the rock shelf, past the hole in the barbed wire, to the second hole he had made further on. They slid down the rope, one after the other, splashed across the river, dimly aware of gunshots buzzing like hornets from above them. They shimmied, with wet hands and feet, up the escape ropes Paul had secured on the other side. When

Blaney neared the top of the ravine, Rolande stretched out a big hand and hoisted her up. Then they ran like gazelles towards the wood from which they'd reccied the target – it seemed like days ago. Shots still rang out behind them, but it was clear the Krauts were shooting blind.

CHAPTER TWENTY-SEVEN

'What the hell *was* that?' Rolande demanded. They were sitting on stools around the hearth in a safe house, drinking coffee laced with rum. The house was part of a farm tucked snugly into the forest, half derelict, cobwebbed, smelling of ratpiss. It was almost sixteen kilometres away from the Daimler-Benz factory at Wallenbach. They'd covered most of the distance by bicycle, hidden the bikes, done the last two kilometres on foot. Outside the tiny window, fool's dawn was a crimson line hanging above the jagged domes of the trees.

'They never told me,' Blaney said. There was a bitterness to her tone that made Rolande look up.

'It didn't matter though, did it?' she went on. She glared at André, fought back words of reproach. She met Rolande's eye – a silent message passed between them. Rolande stared at André, who was examining his coffee cup; his eyes far away.

'Why did you do it?' Rolande asked him softly.

'Do what?' André spoke without looking at him.

'You know what. Why did you throw that grenade? In that confined space it could have killed us all. Then, instead of pulling out, you went and put your hand through the broken window... into that... whatever it was. *Why?*'

André still wasn't looking at him. 'I worked there,' he said. 'I saw thousands die to build those cross-tunnels. I wanted to know what the Bosch were making there... what was so important they thought it worth all those lives.'

'You must have realized it was dangerous,' Blaney said, unable to rid her voice of its critical tone. 'Those protective arms with pincers. The thick glass windows. Those Jerries. The fact that they never opened fire until they got round the bend. Did you think they were wearing frog suits for fun?'

'I don't know what I thought,' André growled. 'Maybe that we'd failed to carry out the mission. Maybe I couldn't leave without something to show.' He paused. When he glanced at them, Blaney saw his eyes were bloodshot.

'They were tipped off, you know.'

'How can you be sure?'

'They were ready for us. With those suits on. They knew the air raid was a bluff. They were there less than a minute after we arrived. They didn't know which way we'd come because we never told anyone. They knew the date, time and target, though.' His eyes bored into Blaney.

She stared back. 'Are you suggesting...?'

'No,' he shook his head wearily. 'You didn't come here to commit suicide. *Samson* knew though. SOE base knew.'

'Are you saying *Samson's* messages were intercepted?'

'I don't think so. They would have got him before now.'

'Then you're saying there's a mole in SOE?'

André considered it. 'Perhaps,' he said. Blaney noticed his speech was slightly slurred. 'Not necessarily, though. The ghost raid – your SIS people knew too, no?'

Blaney bit her tongue. 'The SIS double-cross us? Why would they do that?'

'How do I know? Maybe they do not want that place destroyed. Maybe this is why RAF bombers were not tasked to raid the place.' He smiled faintly. 'Oh yes, I have heard about a new incendiary bomb they have that spurts liquid fire. A bomb that can clear out underground tunnels. Word gets around, even in the Maquis. I did not mention it, but I knew.'

His eyes went out of focus. Suddenly he turned away, vomited on the floor. He took a gasp of air, threw up again, retching, coughing, spitting saliva. When he looked up, Blaney saw his face was ghostly. He laid a shaky right hand on his temple. 'I have a headache. I don't feel well.'

Blaney saw fear in Rolande's eyes. 'Did you touch that... that... stuff... inside the cell?'

He nodded guiltily. 'It did not feel hot. Just like... metal.'

Blaney felt the pulse at his wrist. It was racing. 'You'd better lie down.'

In the next room, they found a rickety bed with motheaten sheets, stained blankets, a mattress gnawed by mice. 'Just lie down for a minute,' Rolande said. 'Let it pass.' Blaney poured water from a pitcher into a chipped mug, forced André to drink. The first mouthful made him retch again. The liquid trickled out of his nostrils. He managed to swallow a few more gulps and keep them down.

They returned to the tiny parlour. The sun was up, exploding deep-fire brilliance over the trees, shafts of light piercing the foliage like golden spears. Rolande was about to say something to her when there were shouts from the direction of the dirt track leading to the farm. Rolande snatched his Sten and peeped over the window sill. The glass was dirty but clear enough to see figures in *Wehrmacht* field-grey and coal-scuttle helmets advancing up the drive. To him, they looked like the same Home Guard veterans and Hitler Youth who'd been left to guard the Daimler-Benz factory. The soldier at point was an old man with a grizzled face. NCO insignia. He was evidently not well trained because he was coming right up the middle of the track. Although the soldiers behind him were spaced out at intervals, they were making no attempt to use cover.

A double tap. Paul, firing from the outhouse, where he'd been posted sentry. The oldish Jerry did an elegant pirouette, collapsed in a heap in front of his men. He made no sound, there wasn't even a trace of blood. The rest of the Jerries started running around like disturbed ants, yelling, firing Schmeisser sub-machine guns and rifles in every direction.. It was such a confused reaction that Rolande laughed. His chuckle was cut short when a brace of Schmeisser rounds shattered the window into shards. He and Blaney ducked.

Blaney popped up, fired a burst from her Sten into the melee. Jerry men and boys fell; some screamed. She couldn't tell whether they'd been hit or were just having hysterics. *They're amateurs. Most've never been shot at before.*

As she ducked down behind the sill, Rolande took her place, lodged the barrel of his Sten on the opposite corner of the window. He fired four rounds – the sub-machine gun jammed.

'*Shit.* What do they make these things out of?'

'Exactly what you said,' Blaney grinned. 'Oh, and baked-bean cans. It's a well-known fact.'

'You'd be better off eating the beans and farting at the Bosch.'

They broke into snorts of laughter. It was brought to a sudden halt once again when more Jerry rounds pinged off the wall near the window, grazed air with a bluebottle buzz.

Blaney swung the muzzle of her Sten over the window rim, firing blind. 'Those boys are green as grass. Doesn't make any difference if you aim or not.'

Rolande kicked his useless Sten across the room. It hit the wall, firing a sudden burst at the ceiling.

'*Ah*,' he chortled. '*Now* it shoots.'

They both hiccupped with laughter again.

Rolande drew a 9mm automatic pistol from his pocket. He pumped a few half-hearted rounds through the window, peered after them. Kraut shots were still hitting the wall and the window frame. Chunks of stone whizzed, chips of wood snickered.

'They're closing in,' he said. 'They may be green, but there's at least a platoon of them. We can't kill them all.'

Blaney was listening. Over the shooting, she could hear a voice swearing and cursing in dialect. '*Paul*,' she said. 'They've got Paul.'

She looked at Rolande. 'There must be a mole in *Circuit Boxer*,' she said. 'How did they know we were here?'

Rolande opened his mouth to speak. A stray rifle bullet struck him in the neck, passed through his windpipe, emerged the other side and zipped off the wall. Rolande dropped his pistol, fell on top of it, clutched at his neck, gasped for air. Blaney popped up at the window again, was about to loose half a magazine at the bawling Jerries, when she saw that they'd got hold of Paul. The slim youth was thrashing and screaming obscenities, trying to twist out of their grip. There were too many of them. '*Comrades!*' he bawled in French. '*Shoot! Shoot the Bosch bastards! Don't worry about me.*'

Blaney checked herself. Unless she took aimed, single shots, she'd be almost certain to hit Paul. Whatever bravado he came out with, she wasn't going to do that. She knelt down near Rolande. Blood was spurting from both sides of his neck, his head was already lying in an expanding wine-coloured lake, thick as treacle. His eyes were open but dim. He was struggling to speak.

'*Oh Jesus,*' Blaney said. She laid down her Sten, fumbled for a field dressing, knowing that it was too little, too late. She opened the double-sided pad and held it tight against his neck with both hands. There came a pounding at the farmhouse door. The Krauts were hammering at it with big stones. Despite everything, Blaney had to grin to herself. The door wasn't even locked.

But when she kissed Rolande, there were tears in her eyes. 'I'm sorry,' she whispered in his ear. 'So sorry, my dear friend.'

'*Get out of here,*' he croaked.

The Bosch were still shouting, still banging frantically on the door. All they had to do was lift the latch.

'Can't leave André,' she said.

'Ah yes. Tell my father... say... he was a miserable pig... but I sort of... *liked*... him *tu sais?*'

He tried desperately to focus on her. The Jerries had finally fathomed that the door was unlocked. It creaked open. Blaney saw a twitchy youth of about sixteen with a mouse-like face, pointing a rifle at her.

She glanced down at Rolande for the last time, heard him whisper something.

It sounded like *Liberte.*

CHAPTER TWENTY-EIGHT

Baden-Wurttemberg, Germany. July 1945

They'd put twenty kilometres between themselves and Gaggenau when Backhouse called a halt in a copse, deep enough to conceal the two jeeps and the three-tonner from the main road. He sauntered round to the back of Caine's jeep, where Taff Trubman was working on the wireless, headphones squinted across his mole head. 'Any word from Yelkuchov?' he asked.

The signaller blinked at him through thick lenses. 'You know, these sets are very sensitive, sir. I mean, it's hard to pick up sigs when you're on the move, see. Especially with a driver like Wallace, goin' like the clappers. I told, him, I said, *slow down, you great lummox, I can't get a clear signal*, but would he listen? Still, it's not so bad as in the desert, when—

'—Yes, I understand all that, but did you *get* a message from Yelchukov?'

'Well, as a matter of fact, I did and—'

'—About Boelcke?'

Trubman poked his glasses closer to his nose. 'Captain Yelchukov has been onto CROWCASS in Paris. A chap called Franz Joseph Boelcke was arrested by the Counter-Intelligence Detachment of the American Third Army Group in December 1944…'

'That's got to be our man. Did Yelchukov find out where he is?'

Trubman nodded. 'At the French detention centre, Strasbourg.'

Backhouse looked delighted. 'All right, did he confirm he can get the dental records from Wivenhoe and make the RV?'

'He said he'll do his best, sir.'

'That's good enough for me. Roger him and send my personal thanks.'

'Right you are, sir.'

Copeland was standing by the driver's seat of his jeep, smoking a cigarette, looking nervous.

'Hadn't we better get a move on, Bill?' he said. 'Those CIC blokes might come after us.'

'Hold your horses, Harry. We need to talk.'

He held up his closed fist for an 'O' group. The men sat down on their backsides in the grass, lit pipes and fags, smoked. Backhouse blew out a jet of smoke, studied Copeland, shifted his bloodhound gaze to Caine.

'We've got to go back,' he said.

'*What?* The CIC boys will eat us alive.'

Backhouse shook his head. 'First of all, the job we came for isn't finished, and we can't dump it on Garcia. We're fairly sure we've identified the dead woman. Ditto the US pilots, but we still haven't identified most of the SAS.'

'How *could* we identify them?' Copeland asked.

'Apart from odds and ends like Gill's watch, Crouch's ID tags, bits of clothing, the only sure way is dental records. Yelchukov is bringing them out.'

'What are you going to do when the CIC want to know why there's a dead Jerry lying in the Erhlich woods?' Cope demanded.

Backhouse watched him, unblinking. 'What proof do they have it

165

was us? The MPs in Karlsruhe saw a couple of jeeps without numbers or markings. They saw men in Airborne smocks without headgear or insignia. They found three thugs tied up with para cord and gagged with Tank Corps scarves...'

'Those geezers could identify us,' Wallace boomed, 'an' what about the 'ole in that SS bloke's 'and what 'Arry put there? They could prove what weapon fired that.'

Backhouse smiled a Cheshire cat smile. 'Maybe, but that weapon won't be around anymore...'

'I'm not parting with my SMLE,' Copeland butted in.

'There's more than one SMLE in this outfit,' Backhouse countered, 'and more than one sniper. Ronson here had nothing to do with shooting that man... and as for the trussed-up thugs, only you 1st Regiment boys were directly involved. We – I mean the 2nd. Reg lads – only covered you...'

For a second, Caine sensed treachery. 'Now wait a minute...' he began.

Backhouse held up a hand. 'If you think I'd sell you out to the Yanks, Tom, you're a bad judge of character. All I mean is that you and your 1st Regiment crew, the only ones who could be positively identified, should make yourselves scarce.'

'What about you?'

'We'll go back to the Villa Dellinger. After all, we were officially assigned it by the French. We'll stay and face the music. If the Yanks come looking for trouble, they'll find it. I doubt they'll be able to pin anything on us, as long as Garcia doesn't snitch, and I don't reckon he will. We'll keep on till we've ID'd all the men, then we'll RV with you in France.'

Caine considered it, glanced at Copeland. 'Sounds like a plan.'

Cope nodded. 'This business is starting to look like it's more to do with Nazi secrets than dead POWs.' he said. 'Why did SHAEF try to stop us investigating war crimes when the Americans were already doing it? What work was so important to the Nazis it had to be moved across the Rhine from Alsace when the Allies got too close…?'

'And why did these *workers* have to be moved?' Backhouse went on. 'What did they know that meant they had to be killed before the Allies arrived?'

'Maybe you're readin' too much into it,' Rhodes interjected. 'Maybe they just did it out of sour grapes. You know, like sendin' them doodle-bugs to bomb London, even though they musta known they'd already lost the war.'

'Yes, but then why were the Americans so interested in what they were doing?' Backhouse demanded. 'Interested enough to break protocol and loot a factory in the designated French Zone – an operation finely calculated to get there only hours ahead of their Allies.'

The major steepled his fingers. He looked like a vicar in church, Caine thought. He actually closed his eyes as if meditating. He opened them again.

'You're right, Harry,' he said. 'There's more than Hitler's commando order going on here. Something the Americans know about – *some* Americans, probably the big cheeses, and SHAEF too – but we don't…'

'An' they don't *want* us to know, neither,' big Wallace croaked. 'They don't give a monkey's about war crimes… about the Nazi bastards 'oo murdered our mates. Them CIC wallahs is scared Schock… whatever 'is name were… might of told us sommat they din't wan' us to 'ear.'

'Yeah, if they're so damn concerned, why didn't they pick up Schuochwurte before?' Rhodes demanded. 'All senior ex-SS officers are on the Allied arrest list – especially ex-POW camp bosses. The SS has been declared a criminal organization. SHAEF set up that new registry in Paris – CROW… something.'

'CROWCASS,' Backhouse corrected him.

'Yeah, exactly. Schuochwurte must 'ave bin on that register. He was there under the Yanks' noses, and they never laid a finger on the bugger.'

'Garcia hinted at it himself, didn't he?' Caine said suddenly. '*We're just doing a job… All they want us to do is find bodies… They ain't fussed about huntin' down war criminals.*'

'That's right,' Backhouse said. 'I wish I knew what the hell is going on.'

'*Power,*' Copeland said. 'The Americans want something they think the Nazis have. Something that will increase their power. They don't want the other Allies to have it. Maybe they'll share it with us Brits, or maybe they'll just give us a few crumbs off the table in return for our cooperation. The Frogs aren't in the game. The Ivans – forget it. They're the new enemy.'

Caine's mind was already elsewhere. He'd always known the war was corrupt. Not that he'd wanted to see Jerries running around in England – *or* Ivans for that matter. That was as far as it went, though. He didn't give a damn for the balance of power. He was recalling what Schuochwurte had said about the female spy he'd glimpsed at KL-Natzweiler. *I remember she had red hair. It had been hidden under some sort of dye, and her features had been remodelled with wax, but, of course, they soon discovered that.* Blaney – it had to be. Schuochwurte had said she'd almost certainly been killed. He felt a new heaviness in his chest. Had he really expected anything different? It was the uncertainty of it that was getting to him. This was Betty Nolan in a coma all over again. He couldn't feel free, couldn't mourn Blaney – not till he was sure. He felt a sudden surge of fury. Why the hell had she done it? Why had she been stupid enough to volunteer for something so dangerous, when the war was almost over? She'd been in Field Security, copped a gunshot wound. She'd already done her bit.

He heaved a long sigh. 'Ok, Bill,' he said. 'You go back, finish the job. I reckon you can handle whatever the Yanks throw at you.'

'Right,' Backhouse said. 'You cross the Rhine by the bridge at Rastatt. It's been rebuilt and it's guarded by the French First Army. You shouldn't have any trouble with them. Yelchukov's flying out from London to Strasbourg with the dental records of all the missing SAS men from Op *Taunton*. He'll pick up a vehicle and a driver there. You'll RV with him on the French side of the bridge after first light, day after tomorrow.'

Caine felt surprised but didn't show it.

'Yelchukov found out that Boelcke is on the CROWCASS register. Franz Joseph Boelcke. Suspected ex-SS officer. Nothing else known.'

'So Schuochwurte was telling the truth...'

'Looks like it. Boelcke was arrested by our friends, the CIC. According to the records, he's now residing at the French Detention Centre in Strasbourg. I want you to go and get him.'

'You mean me and Yelchukov?'

'No, I need Yelchukov here with the dental records and personnel files. You'll have to do it yourself, Tom.'

'I don't speak Frog.'

'Someone there is bound to speak English. I want you to get Boelcke out...'

'Wait a sec, Bill. We don't have authorization for that.'

Backhouse chuckled. 'You didn't wait for authorization when you killed those three Brandenburgers with a rusty knife. *Who Dares Wins*, remember? Get him out, take him back to Natzweiler, find out what happened to Blaney and the rest of our boys. For Christ sake, don't kill him, don't use undue force, don't give him a chance to top himself...'

'Not like you did with Schuochwurte, you mean?'

Backhouse studied Caine with his sad-hound eyes. 'It was an accident. I don't want any accidents with Boelcke – at least not before I get there.'

Caine suddenly recalled what Schuochwurte had said about Boelcke just before he died.

He's too clever. You'll never get him. Never.

'Why did Schuochwurte say we'd never get him? He must have known the chap had been arrested?'

'Yes, I thought about that, too. Maybe he meant that we'd never get anything out of him, or maybe he just wasn't aware. Anyway, I've got a hunch that if anyone can tell us what the Nazis were *really* doing at Wallenbach and Gaggenau, Boelcke'll be the one.'

'I don't give a toss what was going on,' Caine said. 'All I care about is what happened to the rest of the SAS men captured on *Taunton* and to Celia Blaney.'

CHAPTER TWENTY-NINE

Gestapo Headquarters, Strasbourg, France. September 1944

It was an ordinary-sized bathroom, with a bath of chipped and stained porcelain and light coming in through a barred, opaque window. Four men were crowded in there with her – two of them Gestapo, one French *Milice*, the fourth, a senior SS officer. The SS officer was the one they deferred to – a tallish man, fit-looking, forty-odd, dark hair with a widow's peak, carefully shaven jowls, eyes like diamonds. His gaze was keen – he seemed to study Blaney, to examine her, to dissect her. He looked more like a science professor than an SS man, she thought, but his rank insignia showed that he was an *SS-Standartenführer* – a full colonel. At his collar he wore the ribbon of the Knight's Cross – the highest award for service to the Reich. *...well in with Hitler,* she remembered André saying *...wears the Knight's Cross on his jacket. An SS concentration camp commandant who's also an engineer or scientist... Boelcke, I think it was. That's it...* SS-Standartenführer *Franz Boelcke.*

Knight's Crosses weren't ten a penny. This chap was the right rank, and he looked just what André had said he was – a self-opinionated and arrogant intellectual rather than a soldier. If he *was* Boelcke – and she was almost sure of it – he was not only the commandant of KL-Natzweiler, the only Nazi death camp in France, he was also in charge of whatever strange alchemy was going on at Wallenbach – a process that had led to the starvation, death by overwork, beating, hanging, torture and murder of tens of thousands of slave workers. *Wears an SS uniform, acts like a civilian… used to see him sometimes… it was him who ordered the starvation and the killings… didn't do it with his own hands… the bastard enjoyed it… used to watch.*

Blaney shivered.

'Take your clothes off,' a Gestapo man said.

She hesitated, her dove-grey eyes downcast. The men were leering at her. One of them was thin and sallow-faced, the other squat and overweight. The Frenchman, a swarthy, red-faced, middle-aged fellow with glittering eyes, licked dry lips. Blaney forced her mind away from them, away from her body. In interrogation resistance training, she'd been taught to – *disassociate* – that was the word. Why should she feel humiliated standing here naked? *After all, they're not even real men.* She removed her overalls with dignity, then her underwear, let them fall to the floor at her feet. The men stared at her breasts, the V of red pubic hair at her crotch. The *Milice* collaborator wet his lips again, visibly aroused. Boelcke's eyes moved from the wedge of pubic hair to the scar tissue on the milk-white skin of her chest. 'A gunshot wound,' he said in French. His voice was deep but cultivated. 'You have been shot, I think?'

Blaney stared back at him, said nothing.

Boelcke smiled sadly. 'We know you were one of the group who tried to sabotage Wallenbach,' he said. 'What was the purpose of this attack? Who are you working with? Two *Maquisards* died in the firefight when you were captured. Who organized it? Where did the sabotage equipment come from?'

Blaney stayed silent, sieved inferences from Boelcke's words. Two

Maquisards had died in the firefight. *Rolande and Paul.* No mention of André. That might mean he'd escaped. *Who are you working with?* Boelcke wanted to know whether she was SOE or Resistance, whether the op had been planned in London or Alsace. *What was its purpose?* If orders had come from London, how much did the British know about his Wallenbach operation? If he needed to know how much they knew, it must be of some importance.

Blaney said nothing. Taking a deep breath, she unbuckled her elegant Swiss watch with fingers that were only slightly shaky, slid it carefully on the shelf over the bath. She knew what was coming: the water treatment, the *bagnoire*. She'd been warned about it. It wasn't going to be pleasant. As the three men dragged her to the end of the bathtub, though, she felt no fear or horror. She was curious to find out how well she would stand up.

The men gripped her bare legs. They tipped her face forward into the bathtub, feet protruding. Someone lashed a thick rubber belt around her ankles. The plug was already in. Another man turned on the tap. Cold water splashed over her. The level rose quickly until it covered her nose and mouth. She forced herself not to shudder. But by the time the water level had reached her ears she couldn't stop herself. She tried to raise her head: all three men were holding her down. The water covered her completely now. She was suffocating, drowning, groping for air. There was water in her nostrils, in her mouth. She began to fight, but the men held her arms and upper body in an iron grip. Her feet were too tightly bound to kick. She was totally immersed, battling for her life. Her struggles became frantic, heaving, drawing on strength she didn't know she had. She saw why they needed three men to hold down a single girl. She was breathing in water. It was in her lungs. She shook her head violently. That was enough. She couldn't take any more. As they yanked her head out, she reminded herself of her instructions. *Don't speak too quickly. Never offer more than they ask. Every answer you give must be a lie or distortion. If they know too much, don't say anything.*

Boelcke was leaning over the side of the bath towards her. She could see in his face closer up that, for him, this was more than duty. He was excited. He was getting off on seeing a naked girl tortured... *didn't do it with his own hands... the bastard enjoyed it... used to watch.*

He cocked an eyebrow.

'*It was...*' she coughed, let water and spit dribble from the side of her mouth. 'It was... a Maquis job.' She spluttered, spat, coughed again.

'Who was the leader?'

'One of those your men killed at the farmhouse.'

'How convenient. So, he can't tell us anything. What was his name?'

'I don't know. He never told me.'

Boelcke scowled. His eyes narrowed.

'What was the purpose of the attack? Why did you choose that particular cross-tunnel?'

'I don't know,' Blaney said. Tears were ribbing down her cheeks, mingling with the bathwater. They were real. Suddenly she noticed that Boelcke was staring at her nose. For almost the first time, she remembered the wax modelling SOE had done on her features – to make her less conspicuous. The mould was coming loose. She could feel it.

Boelcke lifted his hand – a small, delicate hand – and pulled the remains of the wax off her face. She gasped as the adhesive ripped savagely at her skin.

He examined it for a moment, held it up, boomed with laughter. '*A false nose,*' he declared in German. 'We have here a clown, gentlemen. A clown with a false nose. Those clowns thought they could get away with foisting a clown on *us*.' The other men roared. Boelcke threw the wax on the floor, scrutinized Blaney with new eyes. He touched the scar on her chest with a fingertip. His touch was light but probing, like a doctor's. Finally, he grabbed her mousy hair, forced her head down, examined her hair roots.

'*Red*,' he announced triumphantly. 'Like her pubes. They dyed the hair on her head but forgot the tuft between her legs. I told you they were clowns.' He brayed with laughter again. 'She was wearing spectacles when she was arrested. Where are they?'

One of the Gestapo men handed over her glasses. Boelcke held them up to the light, gazed through one of the lenses.

'Plain glass,' he chuckled.

He took a step backwards, as if staring at a new person. There was more than interest in the gaze – there was lust. With the false nose gone, it was as if he was noticing her body for the first time. Blaney looked down, her skin was turning to goosebumps. She started to shiver.

'I don't think you are Maquis at all,' Boelcke said. 'Only the British sabotage organization would go to so much trouble to make you look insignificant…'

He lowered his face till it was only inches from hers. 'You are a British saboteur – at least, you are working for the British. This is not the first time you have been in action. You were wounded in the chest once. A big calibre round, like a .45. Not a civilian weapon. You are an experienced agent. I don't know if you are French or English, and I don't care. Your attack on Wallenbach was planned by British Intelligence…'

He stopped himself abruptly. *Realized he's giving too much away,* Blaney thought. *To others present, not just me. Only a handful of people know what's really going on at Wallenbach. The Nazis are keeping it under their hats. That proves it's important – perhaps very important.* She pictured the strangely-lit cells, remembered the creepy feeling they'd given her, remembered that weird stuff inside. André had touched it: it had made him sick. *A weapon. Some kind of advanced weapon the Bosch think might win the war, even now.*

Boelcke had stepped back. 'Let's start again,' he said. 'Who are you? Who sent you to attack the plant at Wallenbach? What were your orders?'

Blaney clamped her lips, stared at the floor. This time Boelcke looked annoyed.

'Let's see how you like another dose,' he said.

The three men plunged her head under the water. She tried to resist, but each of them was heavier than her, and they were all exerting their full weight and strength. It went on longer this time. It seemed to go on and on. Blaney started to think that Boelcke meant to kill her, he didn't care what she knew. Her heartbeat throbbed in her ears, built up to a screeching climax. She felt her head would crack, pop like a balloon, felt she would go insane. Then suddenly her mind went numb. Her body went limp. There was water in her mouth, water in her nose, water in her lungs. She was drifting away, floating down a long, dark tunnel.

At that moment the men dragged her head up. She took in a gulp of air so deep she thought it would never end. She coughed, hacked, sputtered, spat water, let liquid trickle from her nostrils.

Boelcke was grinning. 'A close one,' he said. 'Now, who are you working with? *Talk.*'

'*All… right.*' Blaney took in ragged breaths, retched, stared at Boelcke with bulging eyes. As they had instructed her, if captured and tortured, not to try and hold out forever. The Nazis had taken her fighting, they'd discovered that her appearance had deliberately been altered. They knew she was a foreign agent all right. The point was to tell them nothing else. '*All… right…* the scheme was planned by… British Intelligence. They briefed me, dropped me in by parachute.'

For the first time, Boelcke seemed slightly perturbed. 'What was the purpose of the raid? Why sabotage the plant from the ground when they could have bombed it?'

Blaney felt tears coursing down her cheeks again. 'I don't know,' she stammered. 'They didn't tell me. They only told me what I had to do...'

'*Liar*,' Boelcke bawled. He turned to the waiting men. 'Bring the bottle,' he ordered.

One of the Gestapo men came up with what looked like a green wine bottle with a screw cap. He filled it from the bath tap.

'*Hold her*,' Boelcke snapped. Blaney was still sitting in the cold bath-water. She felt rough hands grab her arms, pin them back. '*Handcuff her*,' Boelcke went on.

Blaney felt iron manacles fixed round her wrists, felt her head jerked back. Boelcke took the bottle. She guessed what was coming, tried to keep her mouth closed, but the men wrenched it open with their fingers. Boelcke stuck the neck of the bottle into her mouth, poured water down her throat, kept on pouring until she couldn't breathe. She felt water spill down through her windpipe into her lungs. She tried to cough but couldn't, strained against the cuffs, couldn't move her arms. She tried shaking her head from side to side, found the men were holding it like a vice. Boelcke drew the neck of the bottle from her mouth, ordered the men to pull her head back until it was almost parallel with the bath, then poured water carefully into each nostril. Once again, Blaney tried to squirm but couldn't move. Boelcke poured water down each nostril, then pinched them together. While the men stretched open her mouth again, he poured more water down her throat.

Blaney's head was spinning. She was upright, yet she couldn't breathe. The world was ratcheting in and out, sighing and pumping like a pair of bellows. Once again, her heartbeat was a shrieking siren in her ears.

Her vision dimmed. Boelcke's face went out of focus. Before she went into the dark, she must have convulsed violently, because when she opened her eyes the men were feeling gingerly in the bathwater for pieces of the bottle she must have knocked out of Boelcke's hands. It had evidently smashed on the bottom of the bath.

Boelcke was watching her with a half-grin on his smug face. 'All right,' he said. 'Perhaps you don't know what it was you were sent to do. You are an enemy agent, however. I am sending you to Natzweiler. That is a *Nacht-und-Nebel* camp. No one will hear of you there. No one will come looking for you. No one will know where you have gone.'

Blaney clamped her lips, shivered. The men hauled her out of the bath.

Boelcke had the men drape her, still handcuffed, over the edge of the bath. He told them to remove the rubber belt strapping her ankles together, spread her legs from behind, and leave.

The three men went out, smirking at each other, shut the door behind them.

When they had gone, Boelcke dropped his uniform trousers and pants and grasped a stiff erection in his palm. He squatted over her, forced it between her legs from behind, rammed it up inside her. He raped her brutally for half an hour. Blaney clenched her teeth. Not a moan nor a whimper escaped her.

CHAPTER THIRTY

French detention centre , Strasbourg. July 1945

'*Boelcke*,' the sergeant repeated. A spindly youth with thick glasses, bumfluff moustache and a pale, dark haired, high-domed forehead, he examined lists of handwritten names in a neatly kept ledger. He wore French uniform, but from the way he spoke English, Caine guessed he must have been brought up in the USA or at least spent some time there.

Caine and Copeland stood in front of the desk, observing the sergeant's long finger with its broken nail, descending the list.

The detention centre in Strasbourg was a rambling camp built to house Nazis and French quislings arrested after the war. Neither Caine nor Cope knew anything about Boelcke, except that he was suspected ex-SS and, according to Schuochwurte, was the one who'd given the order to kill the prisoners held at Rotenfels. That must mean he was a high-ranking officer.

They had removed their Dennison smocks. They wore clean battledress with shirts and ties, maroon-red berets, badges of rank, SAS insignia. They were back on the wrong side of the Rhine though – in France - and neither had forgotten that the Redcaps were still after them. There were American forces about, too. They had no particular desire to run into the Counter-Intelligence Corps, or to be asked awkward questions about a dead ex-SS man in the Erlich forest at Gaggenau.

They'd crossed the river at Rastatt that morning, a little further upstream from the pontoon bridge they'd used going the opposite way. It had only been a few days, but it seemed forever. Rastatt bridge – an age-old crossing point on the Rhine – had been repaired after hits from Allied artillery and bombers. As their jeep rumbled across, the SAS men saw water traffic: boats and commercial barges laden with coal, ore and wooden poles, plying in both directions. The French infantry unit guarding the bridge let them through with hardly a word.

Just past the checkpoint on the western bank, a lone figure stood on the edge of an open field. He waved them down. The man was bare-headed and wore an army trench coat, buttoned up to the throat. '*Yelchukov*,' he announced, extending a hand as Caine hopped out of the jeep. 'Captain. Yuri.'

Caine shook his hand. The man wasn't tall but looked muscular. He had the warm, sympathetic features of a chap whom nothing could ruffle, who found the world faintly amusing. Dark hair, a hint of foreignness in the slant of his eyes, but when he spoke, it was one hundred per cent, cut-glass English. Over his shoulder, Caine saw a jeep parked in the field, a uniformed driver at the wheel.

'*Caine*,' Caine said, imitating his manner. 'Captain. Tom. You're our man at Eaton Square?'

'Holding the fort,' Yelchukov chuckled. He winked. 'Actually, the fort is only me and a wireless op. I don't think the War Office even knows we're there.'

'How do you get funding?' Caine enquired.

'If I told you that I'd have to kill you.'

Over cigarettes and mugs of tea, brewed by the driver, Caine gave him a briefing on the Karlsruhe snatch, Schuochwurte, the CIC, Garcia. In return, Yelchukov showed him the briefcase full of personnel files he'd brought, including dental records. He plucked out a buff-coloured folder and handed it to Caine. 'Honorary Lieutenant Celia M. Blaney,' he said reverently. 'First Aid Nursing Yeomanry, No. 2 Field Security Section, Intelligence Corps.' He looked away, slightly embarrassed. 'Thought you might need it.'

Caine took the file. 'Thanks,' he said.

'For a moment, Yelchukov eyed him thoughtfully. Then he said, 'I don't know if this means much, but I had a quick dekko at the files of the lost SAS men. The only two you positively identified at Gaggenau were Lieutenant Dill and Captain Crouch, am I right?'

'Yep, and then only because the Bosch had done a sloppy job. They'd forgotten to remove Crouch's dog tags and Dill's watch...'

'I know. It was me who traced the serial number of the watch issued to Dill. Thing is, I was wondering why these particular SAS men were singled out as workers. Maybe it was just random, but I tried to find out if there was any connection between Dill and Crouch in the files – anything they might have in common.'

'And was there?'

'Interestingly, there was. Both of them had been specialists in explosive projectiles – rockets, I mean – before joining the SAS. Both were originally commissioned in the Royal Army Ordnance Corps. Maybe it was another long shot, but bearing that in mind, I went through the files again to see if any of the lost SAS men had similar backgrounds. It was quite surprising. There were infantry, cavalry, gunners – what you'd expect – but quite a few came from support units – especially Ordnance and Engineers. It might be a coincidence, of course, but guess how many of them came from those arms?'

'Just tell me,' Caine sighed.

'Ten,' Yelchukov said. 'Exactly the number of SAS men found at Gaggenau.'

Caine pondered it. It was a thought. If Yelchukov's idea was right, then perhaps these particular SAS men had been singled out because they had some expertise in ordnance work. Whatever the case, it didn't seem to matter much. They were still dead.

They shook hands and the two jeeps sped off in opposite directions, Yelchukov across the Rhine towards Germany and Gaggenau, Caine west to Strasbourg and the French detention centre there.

The administration office was in good order. There were real filing cabinets and neatly stacked volumes on steel shelves. A portly man in a loose-fitting French uniform was writing at a desk behind the sergeant – an old half-colonel with overlong grey hair and a bushy moustache stained yellow with nicotine. He was studying a file, writing intently, as if he didn't even realize they were there. Caine had the feeling that he was listening carefully though.

'Here we are,' the sergeant said suddenly. 'There *is* a prisoner on the list called Boelcke. Franz Joseph – suspected SS officer.'

'Good. We'd like to talk to him,' Caine said.

The sergeant flushed. Small red patches appeared on his hollow cheeks. 'I'm afraid that won't be possible, sir.'

Caine turned stone-polished eyes on him. 'Why not?'

'Boelcke is no longer with us.' The sergeant's look was apologetic.

'What?' Copeland burst in. 'You mean you let him go?'

'No, I mean he escaped.'

'*Escaped?*' Caine repeated. 'From a place like this?'

'We do have a number of escapees…'

'Nazi war criminals?' Copeland cut in. 'How could you let that happen?'

'This is a holding centre, sir. We keep suspects here till there's enough evidence to compile a case against them. If there's no evidence, we let them go. If they try to escape… well, we aren't Nazis. We don't shoot them in the back.'

His expression was suddenly so challenging that Caine didn't know whether to laugh or slap him on the shoulder. After all the Hun had done to France, they didn't shoot escaping Nazis in the back. It said a lot for their sense of justice, but it was practical too. What they needed from this Boelcke was information: dead men told no tales.

'How come he got away?' Copeland demanded.

'No prison is completely watertight. The Bosch reckoned Colditz Castle was escape-proof and—'

'—Thirty or forty blokes got out, I heard,' Caine cut him off again. 'How did Boelcke do it?'

'I don't know, sir – not exactly.'

'You never tried to recapture him?'

'He hadn't been convicted of war crimes.' The sergeant was looking straight at Caine now. The dark eyes behind the thick lenses were harder. 'Most ex-SS men have a blood group tattooed on their arm. Boelcke didn't have one. It's not even certain that he *was* SS…'

Caine raised his eyebrows. 'You seem very clued-up about him all of a sudden, for a man who didn't seem to recognize the name when I asked.'

The red spots on the NCO's cheeks deepened. 'It's coming back to me now.'

'Really?' Caine could hear the sarcasm in his own voice.

'So how *did* he escape?' Copeland demanded again.

'If I recall rightly, he was with a working party – we have prisoners out repairing roads and things. He disappeared. Wasn't at the roll call at the end of the shift.'

Caine nodded. 'So why no pursuit?'

'We don't have the manpower. With respect, sir, this isn't wartime. There aren't any friendly forces they can run to. Escapees usually turn up sooner or later.'

The sergeant closed the ledger, laid his white hands upon it. 'That's really all I can tell you. Sorry for your wasted journey.'

There was something the man wasn't saying, Caine knew it. The way he'd let out the information in penny packets. The red flush. Caine felt like throttling him but restrained himself.

'What about his file?' he snapped.

'What?' The sergeant looked as though Caine had slapped his face.

'You must keep files on the detainees, surely?'

The sergeant seemed about to deny it, when Caine nodded at the filing cabinets behind him. 'Should be under 'B', shouldn't it?' he said.

The sergeant stood up with obvious reluctance, shuffled over to the cabinets, opened one of them and flipped through the folders inside.

Caine was fully expecting him to say that there was no file, but instead, the sergeant drew out a slim manila dossier, slammed the drawer of the cabinet, slouched back to the table. He slapped the file down in front of Caine, opened the cover, riffled through the very few pages. He stopped at the last page. There was a photograph of a man with dark hair, slightly balding with a widow's peak and fine features. He wore civilian clothes and was lounging at a table in what looked like a street cafe. He wasn't smiling; there was a distinct look of haughtiness on his face. Caine and Copeland focused intently on the photo, memorizing the expression, the features, the build. The sergeant pointed to a stamp beneath the portrait, a rectangular frame enclosing the word *Escaped* in large letters. Then he shut the file with an audible snap, whisked it out of their sight.

'Thank you,' Caine said. He nodded at Cope.

They had almost reached the office door when someone said, 'Wait a minute.'

Both of them turned. It was the old half-colonel who'd been sitting behind the sergeant. He was shambling towards them. The sergeant had gone. A door to what must have been another office was standing open.

The colonel's eyes were blue and wary. He pulled on his nicotine-stained moustache as he spoke. Again, his accent was American. Caine began to wonder if this really was a French place at all, or whether it was run by Yanks in French uniforms.

'Franz Joseph Boelcke held the rank of *SS-Standartenführer*,' the colonel said. His voice was whispery, probably from too much smoking, Caine thought. 'He was high on the CROWCASS wanted list because he was commandant of the Natzweiler camp in the Vosges, near Schirmeck – the only Nazi concentration camp in France. A lot of the prisoners there were French Resistance, but they had people from all over Europe – Russians, Norwegians, Polish, German Jews. There were some Allied POWs there too. Commandos, pilots, saboteurs – that kind of thing.'

Caine and Copeland surveyed him. The colonel's face was a grid of wrinkles – inscrutable, almost oriental, Caine thought.

'He escaped before he could be tried, but there's evidence he was responsible for the death by starvation of thousands of slave workers. They were hired out to the Daimler-Benz engineering plant at Wallenbach. A few were moved across the Rhine to Gaggenau, in Germany, when the Allies came too close for comfort. Some say he ordered beatings of captured troops and civilians. There was also torture and public hangings of prisoners who refused to work. If convicted, Boelcke would have got the death penalty. He knew it… probably why he did a bunk.'

Caine and Copeland watched the ancient-looking officer with interest. The question that wouldn't go away was why, if Boelcke was a major war criminal, there'd been no hot pursuit after his escape.

The colonel seemed to have anticipated this. 'Boelcke's dead,' he said. 'Made his way back to Schirmeck – the town nearest to Natzweiler camp – and put a bullet through his own head. Probably just couldn't live with the horror of what he'd done.'

Caine and Copeland considered this new revelation.

'Where'd he get the suicide weapon—?' Copeland began.

'—How can you be sure it was him?' Caine interrupted him.

The colonel didn't look flustered. 'The weapon – stole it? Got it from one of his former cronies? Who knows? There are plenty of Nazis and Nazi collaborators still running round out there in the Vosges. His body was identified by locals who'd survived the camp. There were a few.'

'And Boelcke's body?'

'Buried at Schirmeck.'

The colonel studied their faces. 'May I ask why you're so keen to find him?'

Caine paused. Their reception here hadn't been entirely straight, but he saw no real reason to hold back. Whatever Kemp had said at SHAEF, their mission was official.

'We had a tip-off that he might have been responsible for the murder of men from our regiment, at least one female special operations agent and others.'

The colonel nodded slowly. 'Quite possible,' he said. 'Pity you'll never know. You've been led on a wild goose chase, gentlemen. Boelcke is no longer with us. May I suggest you give it up as a bad job, go back to where you came from?'

Caine thanked him, saluted. He and Copeland marched out.

The others were waiting for them at the jeep – Trubman tinkering with the wireless in the back, Wallace lolling against the bonnet, smoking a cigarette, cradling the Bren in the crook of one cylinder-sized arm.

The giant threw away the cigarette butt and stood up when he saw them coming.

'You didn't get 'im, skipper?'

'Boelcke's dead,' Caine said. 'Escaped and topped himself – according to our informant, that is.'

'Why would 'e do that?'

'Why not?' Copeland said. 'Hitler did.'

'Guilt,' Caine said. 'He was the ex-commandant of Natzweiler, responsible for the deaths of thousands of slave workers. Our lads too, probably.'

'*Guilt?*' Wallace snorted. 'If those buggers felt any guilt, they wouldn't of donc it in the first place. An' all right, a bloke in clink might top 'isself... but you said this geezer got away. It don't make sense.'

'None of it makes sense, Fred. We get two different stories from a sergeant and a half-colonel, both in the same room. One says it's not even certain Boelcke was SS, the other that he was an *SS-Standartenführer* commandant of a Nazi death camp. We get contradictions, information in snatches, sugar lumps fed to gee-gees.'

'Yeah, I mean, why didn't that sergeant just say he was dead from the start?' Cope agreed. 'Why go through that *let me see, oh yes, we have him on the list, but I'm sorry it won't be possible to talk to him* shit?'

'And the escape,' Caine added. 'The details were a bit bloody light, weren't they? *Never turned up to roll call.* Boelcke was commandant of the only Nazi concentration camp in France, an *SS-Standartenführer* – a full colonel. Why didn't they look for him?'

Cope nodded. 'The old bloke knew we didn't believe the sergeant.

Rather than let us go away suspicious, he filled us in. Only he didn't fill us *right* in.'

'He wanted to get rid of us.'

'I had that feeling, too.'

'Ever since we set foot in SHAEF, they've been trying to stop us.'

'Who?' Wallace boomed.

'I dunno,' Caine said, 'but it stinks, the whole kit-and-caboodle. *Give it up as a bad job*, the colonel says. *Go back to where you came from*. Well, I'm not going back where I came from. I'm going to Schirmeck. If Boelcke is dead, I want to see his grave for myself.'

CHAPTER THIRTY-ONE

Strasbourg–Schirmeck road, Alsace, France. July 1945

Five minutes after Caine's jeep left the detention centre, Sears-Beach's wireless operator handed him a message.

From: Act/OC 211st Field Detachment RMP, SHAEF, Paris.

To: OC 211st Field Detachment RMP.

SAS WCIT group reported leaving FDC 1112 hrs. Turned south-west on Schirmeck road. 4 SAS pers. One jeep. No mounted weapons. Stop.

Sears-Beach hadn't felt this excited since they'd pulled him out of mothballs as understrapper of a penal camp in the back end of nowhere. From a major in the Military Police, with the post of Deputy Provost Marshal, he'd been reduced to a subaltern in the Provost Corps – the army's turnkeys: a dump unit for misfits and dead-ends. He'd squandered the best years of the war sweltering in a hole in the desert, not much better than a prisoner himself.

Caine was to blame. Wheedling himself in with nobs like Stirling, Mayne – even Monty. It was Caine's fault that he'd ended up in that pig-shit corner of hell.

It was the image of Stirling that stopped the pinwheel of anticipation in his gut, though.

Guilt.

He tried to ignore it. Couldn't. *Wasn't my fault. Wasn't my fault they sold him to the Hun. I planted a few bad eggs on Caine's mission in Tunisia in '43, maybe. That was strategy – a double–bind op from the Int. boys. Not me. Sometimes men have to be sacrificed. That's war. How was I to know that two of those turds would fight to the death for Caine? Even that traitor Quinnell. He'd been a bloody IRA terrorist, for Christ's sake. Until the chips are down you never know which way a man will jump.*

He still hated Caine. The man was an arrogant, ignorant peasant who'd found an opportunity in wartime to wallow in violence. Not only against the enemy, either. He'd once been court-martialled for threatening to kill a superior officer. Not to mention assaulting *him* – Sears-Beach – just because he'd called that Nolan bint a *tart*. It was the truth, anyway. *Honorary Captain Elizabeth Nolan, GM and bar.* My arse. *Some nightclub slut G(R) picked up in Cairo and made use of. Dead now. Good riddance.* And Caine was a bloody nutter. Aged sixteen, he attacked his stepfather so viciously he had to join the army to escape borstal. If it wasn't for that, and the war, he'd still be behind bars in Blighty now. Well, the war was over. Caine was about to get what he deserved.

The major shifted his feet, slung his Sten over his shoulder, lit a cigarette. He smoked it pensively, his eyes never leaving the road. He'd positioned his four-jeep MP detachment exactly at the point where flat farmland gave way to thick forest, about twenty klicks south of Strasbourg. The road behind him wound up through the woods into rolling, round-topped hills that ran on in serried ridges, dotted with hamlets and farms. Some were bald, grey crags with sheer-sided faces. Most were covered in forest, like dense green fur. At that moment the jeeps were hidden under the trees to his rear. They were manned by eight Military Police NCOs, all heavily armed and ready for action. He'd chosen the men personally and taken care to include Sargeant-Major Brunton, the bullish WO2 Caine's man had knocked down.

Sears-Beach regretted that it hadn't been Caine himself who'd attacked Brunton, or kicked the other MP, Lance-Jack Scarbett in the testicles. Then he'd have had a clear-cut case. Brunton's description told him it must have been that Wallace baboon – the *Gunner*, they called him. He was another dangerous lunatic who ought to have been strapped in a padded cell years ago. The major wasn't even sure he could pin unit responsibility on Caine. To his fury, there'd been a superior officer present – a Major Backhouse, formerly a barrister-at-law, ex-Int. Officer, 2nd SAS. No fool by the sound of it and no peasant either. It was he, not Caine, who officially commanded the SAS War Crimes Investigation Team.

That muddied the waters a bit, maybe, but Backhouse was still in Germany. Caine could be held responsible till further notice. Sears-Beach bristled again with anticipated satisfaction. This time Caine wouldn't escape. This time he'd got him. If he cut up rusty, like he was apt to do, so much the better. Men could be badly wounded – even killed – resisting arrest.

He glanced at his watch then back at the road. It was in a bad state. He reckoned it took a jeep about an hour to get here from Strasbourg. The message had come through at twelve minutes past eleven. Provided there weren't any delays, Caine and his men should be here by noon.

Sears-Beach congratulated himself on his foresight, his careful planning. *Whatever they told Caine at Strasbourg, I knew he would head straight for Schirmeck.*

It was the nearest town to the disused Natzweiler concentration camp. If Caine was investigating war crimes, it would be an obvious place to start. The major guffawed suddenly. *Caine investigating war crimes? Should start by investigating himself.*

He hadn't seen the man since '42, but he knew him well. *All big time and braggadocio.* There was no way a man like Caine was going to slink off back home when there was another chance of playing the hero.

'*Sir.*' He was roused from his thoughts by the barrel-chested Sgt. Major Brunton – the MP Wallace had knocked down. For a week, the WO2 had been sporting a livid black circle around his right eye: it had faded now. Brunton had expostulated at great length about what he was going to do to that *bloody gorilla* once he got hold of him. The fact that Wallace was a head taller and built like a bulldozer didn't bother him, he said. Sears-Beach had made sure the MP crew would outnumber the SAS men three to one.

'OP south reports vehicles approaching,' Brunton said. 'Two jeeps, four three-tonners. Yank Army transport column.'

Sears-Beach had posted a brace of two-man observation teams with orders to conceal themselves to the north and south, about two klicks from his position. The teams consisted of a Bren-gunner and a spotter, with binos and a short-range voice radio.

'Let them pass,' the major said. 'Tell the men to keep their heads down.'

Brunton saluted, stomped off. A moment later, Sears-Beach heard the drum of engines, took in a whiff of diesel fumes, heard the rumble of tyres on the hard dirt road. He squished his cigarette butt with a boot, squatted in the bush, watched the convoy trawl past – jeeps in the lead, lorries following. GIs with half-shaven faces rode in the vehicles, looking well fed and cheerful, in olive drab fatigues and pudding-bowl helmets. They were travelling fast, hauling a shroud of dust.

Sears-Beach popped his head out of cover and watched the convoy until it disappeared around a bend. He stood up, angled a shufti at his watch. Twenty-five minutes since Caine's crew had turned onto the Schirmeck road. The SAS jeep should be here soon.

Five kilometres to the north, Caine was watching the forest-line approach. It was a barrier of oak and beech, maple and spruce – an undulating sea of foliage, a million shades of green, exploding with the imperial bloom of summer. The trees climbed the hillsides, pines grew ramrod straight from ridges and interlocking valleys, bare stone crags emerged out of the forest. Caine judged the highest peaks at five or six thousand feet. It was warm. The washed-out blue of the sky was visible only in patches through giant rolls of cotton-wool cloud, ragged at the rims.

He was sitting in the passenger seat, Copeland driving. Trubman and Wallace were in the rear. Cope was doing his best to keep up speed, but the dirt road was rough, full of potholes and corrugations that made the vehicle judder. For the first twenty kilometres out of Strasbourg, the way had taken them across flat, cultivated land – penny-packet fields divided by hedgerows and copses, grapevines trooping the colour, staked out in parade lines between villages of red-roofed, half-timbered houses and square-towered churches of white stucco. There were few people about. The area had seemed half deserted.

As they approached the treeline, Wallace tapped Cope on the shoulder twice. Caine glanced at the big Gunner, saw his eyes focused on a bend in the road ahead. Copeland didn't take his gaze off the track, just geared down, braked, pulled over. They'd worked together too long for Caine or Cope to question Wallace's senses. He had the keenest eyesight of anyone they'd ever met. His hearing was as highly tuned as an echo sounder, his sense of smell so acute he could identify the brand of cigarette someone was smoking at two hundred yards. Wallace had sensed something; that was good enough.

The jeep came to a halt and the giant stood up in the back.

'*Diesel*,' he grunted. He turned his left ear towards the bend, opened his mouth, showed an array of broken teeth. '*Motors*. Cantchou 'ear 'em?'

Caine strained but heard, saw nothing.

'Small convoy,' Wallace added. 'Couple of jeeps; three – no mebbe four – three-tonners… unladen.'

'*Yeah?*' Copeland mouthed, 'and what did the drivers have for dinner last Sunday?'

A moment later, both Caine and Copeland heard the purr of engines, smelled motor fuel. A moment after that, the small American convoy swept round the bend – two unarmed jeeps leading, four lorries in the rear.

'Not bad, mate,' Cope grinned at Wallace. 'Couldn't you have given us a bit more detail, though?'

In the old days, they'd have been cammed up, with their twin Vickers cocked well before the convoy came into sight. *In the old days*. Wallace often called them the *good old days*. There were no more Kraut or Itie convoys to be banjoed. *More's the pity*, he thought.

Caine expected the Yank vehicles to pass without even acknowledging them. Instead, one of the jeeps pulled across the road towards the SAS jeep – a pork-faced sergeant at the wheel, a dark-complexioned lieutenant next to him. The rest of the vehicles slowed to a halt. Men in drab fatigues and pot-shaped helmets jumped down, pissed, drank water, lit up cigarettes.

The lieutenant had a lean face, keen brown eyes, a day's stubble. He slipped out of the passenger seat, came over, saluted Caine with the palm down gesture that – in British forces, anyway – was only used by the Royal Navy. The Yank eyed the maroon-red berets and the SAS insignia. He wore a pistol in a leather holster on his belt.

'Draper,' he said. 'Lootenant, US Logistics Corps. You boys Brit Airborne?'

'Special Air Service,' Caine told him. 'Same difference, more or less. I'm Caine. We're a war crimes investigation team. On our way to Schirmeck to investigate the murder of our mates by the Nazis.' He paused. 'Road all clear?'

Draper scratched his chin. 'As a bell, Captain. You'll get through. Climb's quite steep from the treeline, but you should be there in half an hour.'

'What are you, Lieutenant?' Caine enquired. It was nosy, but after all, he'd told Draper *their* business.

'Supply convoy. Just delivered a stack o' stores to the CIC base in Schirmeck. I guess you'll wanna parley with 'em. Doing the same kind of job as you.'

Caine nodded, stored this data away for further consideration. *A CIC post in Schirmeck. No one told us. A big one, too, if it needed four three-tonners to carry its supplies.*

The subaltern was about to head back to his jeep. Before getting in, he stopped, turned about.

'Almost forgot why I came over,' he chuckled. 'Just where the road hits the forest, there's some guys hidin' in the trees…'

'*Hiding?*'

'Yeah. I guess they wanted to stay outta sight. Thought we never saw 'em. Only got a quick flash, but there's four jeeps, eight, ten men. Not our boys. Not French. Yours, I'd say. Not cammed up, just lurkin'. Battledress, peaked caps, red covers…'

'*Redcaps,*' Wallace groused. 'Military Police.'

The lieutenant narrowed his eyes. 'You wouldn't know anythin' about that would ya?'

195

'Nothing at all,' Caine answered. 'Sounds like they're preparing a roadblock though.'

'For you?'

Caine shrugged. 'We're on authorized business.'

The lieutenant nodded. 'There's funny stuff goin' on at Schirmeck,' he said.

'What kind of funny stuff?'

'Ain't gotta clue. Too much said already... oh, and by the way, there's another thing. They've put out an observation post on the right side of the road by a clump of bushes, about a mile and a half from here. Same lot I'd guess. Two-man team with an LMG and a radio. They got another OP about the same distance on the other side.'

'Thanks,' Caine said.

The American nodded. 'Ok, war's over. Still gotta watch it though. I've heard stories of armed bands hidin' out on the Spanish border – ex-SS guys refusin' to surrender. Might be bullshit, but you never know.'

CHAPTER THIRTY-TWO

Caine sat still for a moment, hooded his eyes, let a flood of thoughts wash through him. '*Sears-Beach*,' he said suddenly. 'Got to be.'

Copeland and the others stared at him.

'Tracked us from SHAEF to the Rhine, couldn't cross into Germany,' Caine went on. 'Decided to wait for us in France. Knew we'd head for Schirmeck.'

'Must have a stoolie in Strasbourg,' said Cope. 'Probably that old poser of a half-colonel who told us to go home.'

Caine nodded. 'All right. Harry, you and Fred debus here and take that OP out. I don't want Sears-Beach – if that's who it is – knowing we're on the way.'

'Right you are, skipper.' Copeland drew his SMLE sniper weapon from the seat brace and swung out of the driving seat. Wallace jumped down from the back, his Bren already in his pancake-sized hands. 'No shooting,' Caine told them. He squinted at Wallace. 'Remember, Fred. Minimum force.'

The gunner gave him an indignant look. 'Whaddya mean? That Redcap was goin' to welt 'Arry with a pick 'elve.'

Caine grinned. 'Minimum force,' he repeated. 'Just make sure they don't let the buggers know we're on the way.' He twisted round to face Trubman, still squatting by the wireless. 'We're going straight down the road to the forest line,' he said. 'It'll be a roadblock, like that Yank officer said, not an ambush. You're driving, Taff.'

'How you going to get past four jeeps?' Cope demanded.

'Persuasion.'

'With Sears-Beach? The bloody traitor who tried to sabotage our Tunisia mission? Have you forgotten that?'

Caine shook his head. 'Nope,' he said.

He watched Copeland and Wallace head off cross-country through fields of grapevines and sunflowers. Trubman climbed into the driver's seat, gunned the engine.

Sears-Beach heard the motor from a kilometre away, couldn't understand why there'd been no word from the OP. He'd already ordered his men to move their vehicles out of the trees, had them drawn up in a wedge, completely blocking the road. He positioned himself in the middle, stood rigid and watched the SAS jeep as it spun round the bend. The first surprise was that it carried only two men – driver and passenger. The signal from Strasbourg via SHAEF had specified four. Both men were clad in Dennison smocks and maroon-red berets. The driver wore glasses. Sears-Beach recognized the mole-headed signaller, Trubman. The officer in the passenger seat bore the unmistakable swimmer's shoulders and blunt, freckled face of Tom Caine. *Where are the others*, the major wondered. *That bumbling ape Wallace. Mister clever-dick Copeland. No alert from the OP – two men missing from the SAS crew?* Sears-Beach smelt a rat.

It was too late to do anything. His eight men were spaced out in and around the vehicles. They were armed with batons, pistols, Sten sub-machine guns.

The SAS jeep ground to a halt about twenty yards away. Sears-Beach watched Caine get out and stand up straight. He was carrying a holstered pistol. He said something to Trubman. The driver nodded, kept the motor idling.

Caine squared his shoulders at Sears-Beach, began to stride directly towards him. The major watched him. With every step, memories flooded back. It was this man, not the Jerries, who'd ruined the war for him. He recalled the carnage at Bir Hakeim in '42, when both he and Caine had been serving in 51st Middle East Commando. He'd ordered Caine to abandon some wounded men on a ridge. Caine had argued that they'd been promised they wouldn't be left behind. Sears-Beach had insisted. Caine had ignored him, got big Wallace and know-it-all Copeland on his side, brought most of the wounded back alive. He'd endangered the whole commando, disobeyed a direct order. Worst of all, he'd ended up getting lionized for it. They'd even chosen him – a *sergeant* for God's sake – to lead the top-secret *Runefish* op, to bring back that G(R) tart Nolan. No one had expected him to get out of that one – especially with a battalion of Brandenburger special-duties troops on his tail – but he had. They'd given him the DCM. He'd even got his commission back.

Sears-Beach had personally repaid him, though, the time he'd marched Caine into a police cell in Cairo and had him beaten to a pulp by some of his MPs. *They said he was fast. Not fast enough to get out of that one.* The pleasure faded when he recalled how Caine's SAS boss, David Stirling, had threatened him. *Him*, Major Sears-Beach – the then Deputy Provost Marshal of Cairo. *You lay so much as a finger on one of my boys again, I'll send Paddy Mayne to cut off your prick and ram it so far down your gullet, you'll choke to death.*

Mayne. Another nutcase Sears-Beach would have had locked up for life. If Caine was a thug in uniform, Mayne was a professional delinquent who thought he could do just as he liked because he used to play rugby for Britain. Mayne had once knocked Sears-Beach down the steps of Shepheard's Hotel, Cairo, in full view of the GOC Eighth Army, Bernard Montgomery. To his indignation, the GOC had actually taken the bruiser's side. Sears-Beach had ended up in the Provost Corps.

The boomerang had come round for Stirling though. *Hubris*. He'd accompanied an SAS patrol into Tunisia – as if a sabotage patrol needed a half-colonel in command. Out for glory. Got more than he bargained for. Stirling was the darling of Cairo's Silver Circle Club, matey with the PM's son, Randolph Churchill, had a direct line to Winnie himself. No idea how many enemies that had made him. Word had got around that all special operations units in the Middle East were to be disbanded, reformed into an SAS unit, with Stirling as top dog. Stirling – a twenty-six-year-old who'd been classed as an incorrigible Guards subaltern a year earlier, a gambler and a boozer who'd spent so much time off nursing a hangover, he'd been on the carpet for malingering. Stirling had gone to Tunisia for vainglory, had fallen into a trap set for him by Sears-Beach and others. Things hadn't come off entirely as planned. Two men had got away. They'd been picked up later by Caine and co. Stirling had been bagged, though. All his friends in high places couldn't get him out of Colditz. He'd rotted there for most of the war.

Caine came closer. His boots crunched on the gravel. Sears-Beach could see the familiar eyes like water-buffed, grey pebbles. There was that look of rigid, unstoppable purpose in them. The major shifted slightly, remembered again how he'd insinuated three convicts into Caine's Tunisian op. The ex-cons were supposed to bring back a Jerry black box containing some radar gear that would win the war. They'd leave Caine and his boys to face the music. To his fury, Caine and his pet Copeland had got out of it almost unscathed, though only by dumping their mates, Wallace and Trubman. Those two had been captured – both badly wounded – and ended up as POWs in Italy. They'd got out, though – obviously. That was Trubman, sitting as large as life at the wheel of the jeep, not twenty yards away.

Sears-Beach didn't know why he himself had been restored to grace and returned to his rightful unit, the RMP, to the rank of major. The order had come through Military Intelligence, though they must have known about the black box incident. Sears-Beach had always wondered how he, and the others involved, had got away with it. Like the Stirling affair, he guessed there were wheels within wheels. He'd been judged capable of keeping his trap shut when things weren't quite kosher. He had no idea why SHAEF didn't want Caine and this Backhouse chap poking their noses into war crimes, but evidently they didn't, and his grudge against Caine was useful to them. It wasn't his to reason why.

Caine halted in front of him. Their eyes locked. Caine's face was as desert-honed and unreadable as Sears-Beach recalled. He looked older than when the major had last seen him; there were lines round his eyes – a certain hollowness that hadn't been there before. To his surprise, Caine stamped to attention and gave him a sharp salute.

Sears-Beach took a step back. He fumbled a return salute, a clumsy flick of the fingers.

'Major Sears-Beach,' Caine began. 'It's been a long time.'

The voice, like the face, was expressionless. So neutral, in fact, that after all the bad blood between them, the hairs on the back of Sears-Beach's neck prickled.

'Spare me the auld lang syne, Caine.' He grimaced, showed the slab-like front teeth Caine remembered. He marvelled that someone hadn't knocked them out by now.

'I'd prefer *Captain* Caine if you don't mind, sir,' Caine said.

'Really? Well, I *do* mind. You are under arrest for allowing a man under your command to assault a warrant officer of the Royal Military Police. You made no attempt to stop or apprehend him, as was your duty. In fact, you were complicit in his escape. You were also an accessory in the misappropriation of vehicles ordered impounded by SHAEF. Remove your weapon at once and hand it over.'

Caine didn't budge. His face stayed blank as stone.

'The order to impound our vehicles was illegal,' he said. 'We were, and are, acting under instructions from a superior officer at UK Base. I have the authorization with me. I can show you.'

'As far as I'm concerned, Caine, you can wipe your arse with it. You and your fat friend over there are under arrest. Give me your pistol and tell that Welsh sheep-shagger to switch off the engine and surrender his weapons.'

'That *sheep-shagger* was awarded the Military Medal for bravery – twice.'

Sears-Beach looked unmoved.

'Tell me, Major,' Caine said, keeping his voice steady. 'Do you see the man who allegedly assaulted the warrant officer here?'

Sears-Beach stuck out his chin. 'That doesn't mean anything. You allowed him to get away with it. You're a commissioned officer. You're responsible for ignoring the offence and for leaving SHAEF in impounded vehicles.'

'I've told you – that order was illegal. As for being responsible, that would only be true if I had been OC of the unit, which I wasn't.'

Sears-Beach didn't look flustered. He'd been expecting this.

'You may not have been OC, but under military law, you were instrumental in a breach of military discipline. Now hand over your weapon. You're for the glasshouse, where you've always belonged. I hope they throw away the bloody key.'

Caine blinked hardglass eyes. 'I'm afraid I can't do that, Major. I've got a mission to carry out. I might need my weapon.'

A half-grin played around the corners of Sears-Beach's mouth. He'd been hoping for this. 'Then we'll have to do it the hard way.'

He went for his pistol. For anyone who knew Caine well, it was a very unwise move. The last British officer who'd tried to pull a pistol on him had ended up in a wheelchair. Caine regretted it, had no wish to repeat it. He didn't draw his weapon. He took a step forward, fists a whiplash blur. Before Sears-Beach's .45 Colt was even in his hand, Caine's bunched right knuckles caught him under the chin – a blow so hard that if Caine hadn't pulled it, might have broken his neck. Sears-Beach's head snapped back just as Caine slugged him hard with his left. The major's eyes dimmed. He staggered. Caine hit him a third time – a straight-arm crumpler direct to the chin. It sent him sprawling against the bonnet of the nearest MP jeep.

Caine spun round, ready for the rest of the crew. All eight of them had drawn their batons. They hurled themselves at him from both sides. Caine took in the bullish WO, Brunton, saw his stick raised, saw the gritted teeth. Caine caught the broad man's wrist with a grip as tight as a monkey wrench, twisted it with a jerk that made the MP screech, made him let go of the baton. More MPs were on him, yanking back his arms. He tried to throw them off but there were too many. His legs were swept from under him, his head thumped against the bonnet of a second jeep.

'Turn him over,' he heard Sears-Beach croak.

Six MPs were holding him – the other two were standing back, observing, Stens cradled in both hands. Caine resisted, grabbed at one of the Redcap's batons. The MP gave him a crack across the shoulder: it hurt. The Redcaps turned him on his back across the jeep's bonnet. He saw Sears-Beach standing over him, his immaculate BDs dishevelled. Blood dripped from the major's nose and lips, his chin red and swollen where Caine had punched him. He spat out saliva, and – to Caine's satisfaction – fragments of teeth. His eyes looked dim.

'All right,' the major said. 'You want it the *really* hard way.' He leaned over Caine's face, let blood drip onto his smock. 'Someone up there doesn't like you and your friends nosing about occupied Europe,' he said. 'If you were to… *disappear*… I don't think you'd be missed.'

He was breathing hard. Caine didn't know if it was excitement, pain, or the fear of doing something so obviously illegal. He noticed that the major had put away his pistol and was playing with his old toy – a silver-knobbed swagger stick. Caine had memories of that stick – or at least one like it. He remembered the time – two or three years ago – when Sears-Beach had poked him with it. Caine had snatched it off him, snapped it in half like a twig, thrown it away. There wasn't much chance of doing that this time, though. Not with half a dozen MPs on him. Sears-Beach was holding the stick by the narrow end, knob extended. Caine eyed it warily. The knob seemed lightweight enough, but it could kill. The look of sheer loathing in the major's eyes told him that it was on the cards. Out of the corner of his eye, he shuftied his jeep, Trubman still at the wheel. Good. He'd told the signaller not to budge, whatever happened, whatever he saw. Not unless he was personally threatened. The Welshman had followed his orders to a tee.

'Very inconsiderate of you, Major,' Caine grunted. 'If you kill me, you'll be involving your men here. They'll be accessories to the murder of an officer.'

'I think they can live with that.' Sears-Beach managed a bloody grin. 'I've told them all about you.'

'And have you told them about yourself? Have you told them how you deliberately sold Lieutenant Colonel David Stirling to the enemy? Sold out the best special service officer we ever had for a black box that turned out to contain a germ-warfare agent? One that might have wiped out the whole of GHQ? Your OC is not only a traitor, boys, he's also a bloody stupid one. He was so keen to get rid of someone he didn't like, he never stopped to consider why the Hun might be offering something for nothing...'

Sears-Beach took a step closer. His eyes smouldered, his breath came in rattles. 'That's a damn lie, Caine. If I was involved in anything like that, why didn't they court-martial me, eh? There *was* no black box, that's why. It was a figment of your imagination. Did you know, men, that Mr Caine here got a dose of some Nazi nerve agent when he was up the Blue? Pronounced off his rocker by the Cairo MO?'

None of the MPs answered. 'Well now, Caine, nutcase or not, you're going to pay the price for resisting arrest.'

He swung the stick, raised it for a crushing blow. Caine saw the major's knuckles whiten, saw his teeth gritted as he prepared to bring it down. At that moment a gunshot thumped out from the trees on the right side of the road, sliced the stick neatly in half. The weighted end dropped off, hit one of the MPs on the head. His *oww* was drowned by a second bullet – one that knocked Sears-Beach's field cap clean off, sent him ducking, clutching at his skull. Not a mark on his head, Caine noticed. He marvelled at the precision of that shot. Hitting the stick alone was no mean shooting, but only a real sniper could have shot off a man's cap without even grazing the wearer's head.

Copeland, he thought.

CHAPTER THIRTY-THREE

Cope was enjoying himself. He'd never learned trick shooting – it was a new challenge, like the round he'd put through Schuochwurte's hand at Karlsruhe. SAS snipers were trained to kill, not to perform circus stunts. If they'd been Jerries, he wouldn't have risked it, but in these circumstances, precision marksmanship was fun. Copeland was crouching next to big Wallace in the trees. They'd crawled and monkey-walked to within a hundred metres of the roadblock. You couldn't bring off shots like that from much further away.

The OP had been easy meat for desert vets like Cope and Wallace. There hadn't been a lot of cover – only the occasional clump of thorny bushes – but they knew how to make use of what there was. The two MPs on stag had sited themselves in a shallow cleft, all their attention on the road. *Rule number one: always cover your arse*. Both lay prone – one with a Bren on a bipod, the other manning a compact voice-wireless. Cope and Wallace had crawled the last fifty feet, jumped them before they even knew what was happening. When the Bren gunner had tried to turn his weapon on them, Wallace had stopped him in his tracks with a giant bunch of fives, knocked him off his feet. Copeland had cracked the W/T operator across the side of the head with the stock of his SMLE, just hard enough to stun him for a moment. By the time the two MPs came round, they'd been disarmed and gagged, their hands tied behind their backs with parachute cord. The SAS men had smashed the wireless for good measure, dismantled their weapons, thrown the parts away. Then they'd vanished – into thin air. A minute later a jeep swept past their position, with two occupants who didn't spare a glance at them. The MPs' eyes bulged – there was no way of warning their OC.

Now, from the bushes, Cope watched Sears-Beach grope for a hole in his head, feel for blood that wasn't there. Copeland could read his face like a book: a fraction of an inch lower, the shot would have blown his brains out. The major's features wavered between relief that he hadn't been hit and fury that whoever was shooting was playing games with him.

Copeland and Wallace watched MPs dive for cover, watched Caine roll off the bonnet of the jeep where he'd been pinned. Cope dropped a few rounds over the heads of the Redcaps, put a couple through jeep windscreens. Unlike the screens on SAS wagons, they weren't bullet-proof. The crackle and slew of glass shards were enough to keep the rozzers' heads down. Then Cope started on the front tyres – Sears-Beach had obligingly lined up his jeeps with regimental precision. Copeland sighted up on the first, squeezed metal, felt gas blow, felt the stock jug his shoulder, worked the cocking handle, shifted the muzzle, fired again. Four shots in four seconds punctured the nearside front tyres of all four jeeps. He heard the long *sisssssss* of escaping air, saw vehicles list. Then he worked the muzzle back, put rounds through the offside tyres. This was more difficult as they were harder to see. Again, he didn't miss a trick. The jeeps sank, bonnet forward, as if they were kneeling to some invisible master. Wallace crouched on massive haunches, fired his Bren from the shoulder. The only other chap Copeland had ever seen manage that was Paddy Mayne. Wallace fired fast squibs, double taps, bursts of three, at the jeeps' bonnets: Tracer rounds seared air, .303 bullets drilled through metal, small volcanoes of black smoke erupted, the bonnet of the last jeep was wrenched back in a rip of blinding flame.

MPs were shooting but shooting blind. *Greenhorns*, Wallace thought. No combat experience. Despite the tracer, they hadn't located the shooters' position. They didn't have the killing instinct, either. They were scared to hit anyone in case it turned out to be *blue on blue*. They'd set their SMGs on single shot. Any idiot knew the Sten was only effective on automatic.

Wallace whipped a smoke grenade off his belt, bowled it overarm with the force of a wicket-crusher. It hit one of the ruptured bonnets, sheared off in a comet's tail of billowing white phosphorous. The MPs coughed, spluttered, lumped into each other, staggered, popped off rounds skywards.

Just before the smoke enveloped him, Copeland saw Caine on his feet, saw him make a *close on me* sign to Trubman. The jeep engine grumbled, the vehicle belted straight towards Caine. As it vanished into the pall, Wallace got an impression of Trubman, hatless, dust goggles clamped over his eyes, mole-shaped head thrust forward, bent over the steering wheel, clutching it tight. He heard the ringing *clunk* of steel on steel as the winch apparatus on the front bumper barged MP vehicles out of the way like dodgem cars. There were yells and curses, more blind cracks and thumps. Trubman let the motor idle – Copeland guessed Caine was vaulting aboard. He heard the jeep lunge forward, grate and screech in first gear.

'Come on, mate,' he told Wallace. 'Time to move.'

Wallace pitched a last double tap, lumbered after the heron-legged Cope, through the undergrowth, heading for the road.

They emerged from the trees just as the jeep nosed out of the smoke.

Trubman was gripping the wheel as if he thought it might get away from him, his eyes under the goggles almost maniacally ferocious. The jeep raked to a halt next to them. 'What you waitin' for, then?' he squeaked. 'Bloody *Christmas*, is it?'

Cope climbed into the back. Wallace leaned over Trubman, clamped his Bren into the dashboard brace. Two figures appeared abruptly from the shadows of the trees. They wore BDs and red-topped MP caps. One was carrying a Sten SMG, the other a Bren.

Caine remembered the second OP – the one Sears-Beach had posted to the south. He'd forgotten about it in the rush. The spotters must have heard the row and come to investigate. He'd made a mistake, but by leaving their post they'd made a worse one. Both Redcaps were tall and clean-shaven – the man with the Sten was all balls and beef, with a neck that bulged over his shirt collar; his oppo was lean and athletic. The lean Bren gunner kept his weapon at waist height. Wallace turned his grizzly-bear mass towards them. He was armed only with his holstered .45 pistol: it was too late to snatch his Bren back. The Redcap with the Sten raised his weapon slightly: Wallace didn't shift. *Let the buggers come.* From what he'd seen so far, they didn't have the guts to shoot him down. Then he recognized the Sten gunman, the same lance-jack whose nuts he'd kicked hard back at SHAEF. He could tell the MP hadn't forgotten him, either. It took a lot to forget Wallace – or a kick like that. He'd have bet the poor sod's knackers still looked like boiled beetroot. There were shouts from Sears-Beach's crew behind, ghost movements in the smoke. Wallace didn't move. He let the beefy lance-jack step towards him, saw that the man had dropped the muzzle of his weapon. It was pointing at Wallace's groin. The MP was two yards away. 'Old Testament got it right,' he growled. 'Eye for an eye. Ball for a…'

Wallace kicked him in the kneecap. This time, he wasn't holding back.

The arsehole was going to shoot *me*. The MP's knee joint caved in with a sickening snap of bone. The man screamed, staggered, fell squirming into the dust. Wallace kicked the Sten away with a size-thirteen boot, turned to face the MP holding the Bren. In that second, the chap cocked the working parts and took one step closer. Wallace wrenched the machine gun out of his hands, rammed the stock into the man's guts hard. The Redcap let out an *oooooofffff*, collapsed, gasped for breath. Wallace unclipped the curved magazine hurled it into the trees, ejected the round in the breech, removed the barrel, lobbed it in one direction, threw the body of the gun in another.

The jeep was already moving. Copeland hauled the big man into the back as Trubman worked the accelerator. The vehicle shot forward in a spume of dust. There were shouts and a few desultory shots from the smoke pall behind them.

CHAPTER THIRTY-FOUR

Schirmeck, Vosges Mountains, Alsace, France. July 1945

If not for the war, Schirmeck might have been a fairy-tale town. Set in a natural cradle between the Bruche river and interlocking wedges of pine-covered hills, it was a medieval warren of ornate wood-timbered houses with pitched roofs and dormer windows. There were older buildings of solid pink granite, sprawling around a central boulevard – the *Grand Rue*. Most of the shops that had once flourished along the main street were boarded up. There were two churches of the same rose-coloured stone, with spires and stained-glass windows, and a railway station built to look like a castle, with a grand clock tower over the entrance. Along the station road – the *Rue de la Gare* – stood five-storey stone buildings with arches and low stairways leading up to great doors. Among them was the *Hotel des Postes*, a major attraction in pre-war days when weekenders from Strasbourg had flocked to the Vosges to enjoy the ski slopes and the mountain air. Allied bombing hadn't touched the town, but an air of neglect hung over it. Holes in the red-tiled roofs, rubble in the street, ornamental trees like dried-out skeletons. Under some of them were parked American light tanks.

Boelcke hurried across to the *Hotel des Postes*, keeping his eyes downcast, scarcely looking left or right. There were few pedestrians and almost no traffic, except the occasional Allied military vehicle. What scared him most was being spotted. He had grown a beard and wore ragged peasant clothes, but officially he was an escapee from the detention centre in Strasbourg, and he had no wish to go back there. They had enough on him for a statutory death sentence. CIC chief Captain Jack Skinner had told him there were at least eighteen surviving witnesses with evidence against him, and not all of them were ex-inmates of KL-Natzweiler. One was the man who'd supervised work in the granite quarries for the masonry contractor he'd employed. Another was the ex-foreman of the prisoners who'd built the cross-tunnels at the Daimler-Benz plant – a chap called Maurice Juran. The rest had been slave labour at the Junkers aero-engine factory near Struthof. They'd been overlooked when the camp had been evacuated – they were still living there when the French and Amis had taken over in November '44.

Boelcke knew he should have made sure they were all dead before the CIC had arrested him – the contractors, too. Luckily, he'd had something of outstanding value to trade – his knowledge of the *Uranprojekt*. CIC interrogators had soon realized that he was much more than a former SS camp commandant. A brilliant mathematician and physicist, an outstanding engineer, he'd been trained at the Universities of Gottingen and Munich, had a doctor's degree in physics, had been a member of the *Uranverein* – the Uranium Club – since nuclear fission had been achieved in 1939. Heisenberg, Bohr, Pauli, Schumann, Gerlach, Hahn – he'd rubbed shoulders with all the big names in the nuclear research business at one time or another. In the end though, it was him, Franz Boelcke, who'd developed the only functioning hot cell. He'd been a member of the Nazi Party since the twenties and was an honorary member of the SS, but only because he'd wanted to stay in with whoever controlled the budget. Now it was the Americans, and he was ready to suck up to them if it meant continuing with the *Projekt*. He gave no more of a damn for Hitler and the Third Reich than for the tens of thousands of slave labourers who'd died at KL-Natzweiler. What had they been but brainless sheep, compared with those like himself, a man helping to create the most devastating weapon in history? *Of course* the Amis wanted it. *Of course* they didn't want their Allies to have it – especially the Russians. That's why they'd gone to so much trouble to get him here, why they were ready to overlook the suffering he'd caused, the tens of thousands of deaths he was responsible for.

The iron grilles that covered the double doors of the hotel were open. There was no guard, only two MPs in uniform at twin reception desks in the lobby. Boelcke told them he had an appointment with Captain Skinner and was shown to his office.

Originally it had been the hotel manager's office, but when the SS had taken over, it had become the headquarters of local Gestapo chief Rauss. He'd been carted off to Strasbourg detention centre when the Free French and the American Sixth Army had arrived. Skinner's 430th Detachment of the Counter-Intelligence Corps had commandeered the hotel as their office, though they slept in a villa on the outskirts of town.

The room hadn't changed much, Boelcke thought. Same glass-panelled partition, green drapes, worn Persian carpet, polished table, standard lamp, telephone, upholstered chairs, side table, typewriter. The portrait of Hitler had gone, so had the Swastika hangings. They'd been replaced by the American stars and stripes and the French tricoleur. The captain sitting at the table opposite him, Skinner, was a man with a square face, a wave of blonde hair, blue eyes and a gravelly voice. He wore creased olive drab fatigues and his style was easy-going. Boelcke had been expecting someone not much different from his Gestapo predecessor. Quickly, though, he'd begun to discover that the American was much more than a policeman in uniform. He was educated. He hardly even thought of himself as a soldier. His father was the director of a railway company, with thirteen acres on Long Island. He'd never wanted for much in his life. He'd attended an exclusive boarding school in Massachusetts, had studied physics at Harvard – up to doctoral level. That was what they had in common. Skinner hadn't fought in the war. He was here for *Uranprojekt* – he was as fascinated by the vast potential of nuclear fission as Boelcke was. They got on well, discussed relativity theory and quantum mechanics, even Heisenberg's uncertainty principle.

Skinner gave him a Lucky Strike cigarette took one himself. He lit them both, considered what to tell the German. He decided to plunge right in.

'Something awkward has come up, Franz,' he said. 'A British war crimes investigation team got hold of your name. They're investigating the disappearance of some of their men – parachutists captured in uniform last September. Oh, and a girl – a British agent – dropped in at about the same time.'

Boelcke tried to look indignant. He studied his cigarette, shook his head. 'I know nothing about it.'

He thought of the men – British parachute commandos – who'd worked on his *Projekt* at the Daimler-Benz plant. Bright men, *intelligent* men, all with technical experience. They'd been highly useful to him. He'd had them transferred to Gaggenau when the enemy had got too close, and then, when everything looked lost, he'd ordered them shot.

He'd done the same thing with the commandos left at Natzweiler. A woman? Several female agents had ended up in the camp. They had been executed by lethal injection. Their bodies had been burned in the crematorium. There had been another woman, though – the one with the flaming red hair…

'I didn't think so,' Skinner said, cutting off his thoughts.

Boelcke had long ago discovered that Skinner wasn't much interested in the human side of the *Projekt*. Organizing those men and women – getting labour out of them on minimum rations, keeping the process going – had been a work of art in itself.

'In any case, they found out you escaped from Strasbourg detention centre,' Skinner continued. 'They're on their way here.'

Boelcke blew smoke, shrugged. 'Franz Boelcke is dead,' he said. 'The man sitting opposite you is Hermann Schmidt, a poor ex-*Wehrmacht* soldier who was himself a prisoner at KL-Natzweiler, awaiting a death sentence for insubordination.'

Skinner shifted uneasily. 'I've told you, there are witnesses. Survivors of the camp, contractors you employed. They could identify you. These Brits are special service troops, decorated war vets. They know their business. They're from the same regiment as the men who… *disappeared*. It's a personal thing. They're not gonna give up till they've found out what happened to their buddies.'

Boelcke shrugged. 'The *Projekt* is more important than a few parachutists.'

'Maybe it is. But executing troops captured in uniform while they were POWs is a big no-no under Hague Rules.'

Boelcke's face was impassive. He reminded himself once again that he'd made a mistake. He should have done the lot of them – everyone who'd ever been a prisoner in KL-Natzweiler. He should have blown up or set fire to the camp, erased every scrap of evidence. Then he remembered why he hadn't. He'd hidden his papers and records there – years of work, years of calculations. He'd sealed them in an oil drum, hidden it in a cesspool. If it weren't for those papers he wouldn't be here. Of course, Skinner had the documents now – that had been the price of his escape from the detention centre. The CIC was examining them. They were in German though, partly in code, and the mathematics was advanced. They'd never understand them without him.

'Why put you in SS uniform?' was one of the first questions Skinner had asked him. 'You're a scientist. Why give you all that extra stress when you had such important work to do?'

'The KL-Natzweiler project was conceived as an industrial process,' Boelcke had explained. 'Himmler wanted concentration camps built where there were quarries. The prisoners could be used as slave labour, for money. Natzweiler was sited next to a granite quarry, where the first prisoners worked. Later, when the camp population got bigger, they farmed them out to industry – the Junkers aero-engine factory, for instance, and the Daimler-Benz plant.'

'Must have been very economical,' Skinner said dryly.

Boelcke appeared not to have picked up the sarcasm. 'It was ideal,' he said. 'You see, prisoners were sent to Natzweiler from all over France, Holland, Poland, Russia, Scandinavia – everywhere. They were undesirables, Resistance, homosexuals, perverts, Maquis, spies, saboteurs – even German traitors. Some of them were classed as *Nacht und Nebel* – usually Maquisards, parachute commandos, special operations people – they were supposed to disappear.'

'Whose brilliant idea was that?'

Once again, Boelcke didn't seem to have picked up the irony in his interrogator's voice.

'Hitler's. It *was* brilliant, too, because if you execute types like that openly, it turns them into martyrs and heroes. If they vanish without trace, interest in them soon dies.'

'Clever,' Skinner said.

He'd quizzed Boelcke extensively about his background, knew he'd been brought up in Baden-Baden, knew about the ultra-strict Catholic schoolmaster father, who'd beaten and humiliated him in front of his younger sisters. He knew how he'd turned away from religion, gravitated to the Nazis in his teens. How he'd been an outstanding student of maths and physics, won every prize. He knew about the work he'd done on the *hydrodynamics of turbulent flows* for his doctoral thesis. He knew about his membership of the Uranium Club.

He also knew that Boelcke was almost totally self-absorbed, a perfectionist. He had no friends. He was a loner, obsessed with the problems of atomic physics. Personally, Skinner wouldn't have had qualms about standing the guy against a wall and riddling him with lead. But this was for the greater good, he told himself. If the Ivans got hold of the *Uranprojekt*, it might end in a war even more terrible than the one that had just ended. They reckoned sixty million people had died. With the kind of weapons they were developing now, the next one – if it happened – could be a hundred times worse.

'It wasn't just the *Nacht und Nebel* prisoners, though, was it?' Skinner had commented. 'I mean, you worked the ordinary prisoners to death, hardly fed them. When they were too weak to do any more, you let them die of exhaustion or typhus or whatever, and drafted a new lot in.'

Boelcke nodded. 'It *was* very economical,' he said. 'Of course, we needed some skilled workers for the manufacturing process – both at Junkers and Daimler-Benz. They had to be hand-picked. Every stage of the process had to be carefully overseen so that wires didn't get crossed. They decided to appoint one man in overall charge – me.'

Since the first days of his debrief, Skinner hadn't quizzed Boelcke any more about KLNatzweiler – the starvation, the torture, the beatings, the hangings – nor the fact that he'd been responsible for it all. The fact that he'd not only thought it necessary but had secretly enjoyed it – enjoyed holding the power of life and death, enjoyed the feeling that he was playing a major part in creating a new weapon. Boelcke didn't believe that Skinner really cared about dead prisoners. What he cared about was the *Projekt* – how far the Germans had got with it. While he kept them guessing, he'd be worth his weight in gold.

'Can't something be done about these British war crimes people?' Boelcke asked. 'Don't you have the authority to stop them?'

Skinner said nothing. Only that morning, part of the British SAS War Crimes Team had broken through a roadblock set up by their own Royal Military Police. Just four men, but they'd caused havoc, opened fire, put all the MP vehicles out of action. He could throw the book at them, of course: there'd already been a similar incident at SHAEF in Paris when they'd been ordered to stop their operation. On the other hand, the CIC had to tread carefully. These SAS guys were damn good. Nothing seemed to bother them. They were war heroes. They were searching for their own comrades, who'd been murdered by Nazis like Boelcke – a crime punishable by death. It would be easy enough to arrest the Brits, silence them maybe, but a lot of questions would be asked. The CIC was already sailing close to the wind, helping known Nazi war criminals escape from custody, giving them false identities, smuggling them out of the country. He frowned. Arresting the Brits might be on the cards if all else failed, but whichever way you looked at it, it would still open a can of worms. The CIC's main object was to keep *Operation Big* under wraps.

Skinner stubbed out his cigarette in a crystal ashtray. He shook his head. 'We'll have to get you out,' he said. 'It's the only way. If we cause too much of a kerfuffle with these SAS guys – make it too obvious we're trying to stop them – it might draw attention to the *Projekt*. We don't want that.'

Boelcke considered it. He'd returned to Schirmeck on Skinner's orders, to retrieve his records from the Natzweiler camp. He had no special wish to be here.

'How will you get me out?'

'The Spanish ratline,' Skinner said. 'We've already sent some of your guys that way.' He paused. 'It was the Resistance and the Brits who created it originally, to get escaped POWs and pilots out of the country. Then it was taken over by your lot – with a little help from the Vatican. Across the Pyrenees, into Spain, then Portugal, by ship to Argentina.'

'How does it work?'

'You go by lorry, car, maybe bicycle, till you get to Perpignan. There's a villa there – the *Villa Stauffer*. It's used as a base for the ratline. From there you climb the Pyrenees, cross the Spanish border. You use safe houses on the way to Perpignan. You'll have a guide to lead you through the mountains, of course. Everything will be taken care of.'

'What if someone comes after me?'

'Like you said, you're already dead.'

'Yes, but if these Britishers are as dedicated as you say, they might not accept that.'

Skinner paused. 'It's possible,' he said. 'But there's insurance. A group of ex-*Waffen-SS* are holding out in the forests among the foothills of the Pyrenees. They use the *Villa Stauffer* as an occasional meeting place. We could have bombed 'em out of existence months ago, but they protect the ratline, and that's useful when we want to get guys like you out of the country. They have no idea we're involved, of course. I'd keep quiet about that if I were you. Anyway, if these Brits *do* come lookin', they'll almost certainly run into the SS renegades.' He winked at Boelcke. 'We'll still smell like roses,' he said.

CHAPTER THIRTY-FIVE

They camped in the forest that night, well away from the road. The more Caine thought about it, the less keen he was on reporting to the CIC in Schirmeck. Copeland and Wallace had made sure that Sears-Beach couldn't follow them – at least for the time being – but the MPs would have been in wireless contact with Schirmeck by now. The Logistics Corps officer had said there were *funny things going on*. Caine didn't know what that meant, but he wasn't going to walk into any more set-ups. He had a list of court-martial offences as long as his arm to answer for when they got back to SHAEF. If it wasn't for Blaney, he might have called it off. Schuochwurte had talked about a red-haired woman, though – a British agent – at Natzweiler. It was a slim chance, but Caine wasn't going back without finding out what had happened to her – or the twenty-one SAS men still unaccounted for.

He had scoured the map and found a track that they took from the main Strasbourg road at the village of Russ, bypassing Schirmeck and re-joining the road again at Rothau. They saw a neat railway station of pink granite there. 'That's where they brought the prisoners,' Wallace boomed. 'I'd bet money on it.'

Caine squinted at the map. 'Yep. According to this, Natzweiler is about six klicks from here – uphill all the way. The Krauts must have made 'em walk that last stretch.'

The road led through pine forest, hemmed in by stony banks. It twisted and turned up a hill named *Mont Louise* according to the map. There were a few timber-framed stucco cottages on the way, half derelict, all deserted. 'Nazis probably cleared everyone out to make a safe zone,' Copeland commented. 'Wouldn't have wanted locals eyeballing them.'

The camp had been built on a bald table, tilting down at a twenty-degree angle towards a broad swath of pine forest. It was encircled by woodland, but there wasn't a single tree in the compound itself. It was a four or five-hectare oblong, with a double barbed-wire fence. Watchtowers stood at intervals along the perimeter – *towers* was a bit grand for what they were, Caine thought. They were wooden structures like top-heavy cabins, sagging over the fence, on the point of collapse.

The wire-and-timber gate stood open. It was guarded by another teetering tower of wooden slats. A narrow strip bearing the words *Konsentrationzlager Natzweiler-Struthof* was fixed on the frame above the open gates. Inside, there was what looked like a guard hut. Beyond it, Caine counted fifteen wooden blocks, eight on one side, seven on another, each pair slightly below the previous one, built on stepped terraces. At the bottom of the slope stood another cluster of buildings – offices, kitchen, hospital wing, prison block, Caine supposed. Beyond that, at the very bottom of the slope, was a dense wood.

Copeland halted the jeep. They jumped down, stared about. There was no sound but the wind moaning across the exposed plateau, like far off, tortured voices. A door creaked somewhere, a shutter rattled. Caine tried to imagine what the place must have been like when it had been crawling with thousands of starved, sick, vermin-infested prisoners. For so many, this was the last place they ever saw. He reminded himself that those *people* had probably included SAS men. Celia Blaney, perhaps. A cold finger touched his spine. He tried to blot out the thought but couldn't. Was this where Blaney had ended her life – abused, tortured, reduced to the state of an animal? He couldn't bear to think about it. Neither could he stop.

'Must be bloody freezing in winter,' Copeland commented. 'Wind must cut through the place like a scythe.'

'No picnic in summer, either,' said Trubman. 'Not an inch of shade, see. Nazis must have built it here on purpose. Prob'ly hoped the prisoners would flake out just from the overcrowding.'

Copeland shuddered. 'Disease, too. Must have gone down like flies.'

They climbed back in the jeep, motored down to the buildings at bottom of the slope. This section was divided from the rest of the space by another barbed-wire fence. Again, the gate was open and they drove in. Caine, who had been a POW in Italy, like both Trubman and Wallace, had no difficulty in identifying the hospital wing – an L-shaped hut, the colour of lead – or the prison block, the kitchen, the camp office. At a lower level, down two flights of stone steps, lay another wooden hut that hadn't been visible from above. This one, Caine noticed, was distinguished by a black iron chimney stack, as tall as a ship's funnel.

'What the heck is it?' he asked.

'Bloody obvious,' Wallace said. 'That's where they burnt the bodies. Bleedin' crematory, innit.'

The four of them descended the steps, carrying their weapons and approached the door. Caine found it unlocked. Inside, there was an almost sickeningly sweet smell of smoke. At first Caine took the giant contraption inside the hut to be a boiler. It looked like a giant deep-sea diver's helmet stuck on top of a great iron cupboard. Then he realized there were two doors of six-inch steel, standing open, revealing a space lined with oven bricks. It hadn't been designed for burning fuel. The furnace itself lay underneath the oven space, and separate from it, an aperture, outlined with soot-black traces of fire. It was a crematorium, as Wallace had guessed, large enough to cram in three bodies at a time. Rusting bars extended from inside. At first Caine thought they were exhaust pipes. Then he realized, with horror, that they formed part of a movable metal frame. It must have been used to slide corpses into the oven.

'You were right, Fred,' he said. 'This is where they burned the dead prisoners.'

'Thousands,' Cope muttered. 'Tens of thousands, maybe. Reduced to ashes, just like that.'

Caine wasn't squeamish. All four of them were decorated soldiers and they'd seen more than their share of carnage. But somehow this was different. It was the premeditation. The lists. The numbers. So efficient. So organized. So perfectly calculated to make sure no one survived. The starkness of it. Gathering thousands of people and systematically murdering them in cold blood. To kill in the passion of war was one thing. This bureaucratized mass murder was much worse. The simplest of peoples killed other men at times. Only civilized men could reduce murder to an industrial process. He was about to turn away when he sensed a movement behind the oven. He raised the muzzle of his Tommy gun, cocked it, drove the working parts forward with a *clack*.

'Who's that? Come out. I know you're there.'

He glanced at the others. Each of them had brought his weapon up before Caine had even finished his sentence. There were metallic snaps as Wallace and Copeland levered rounds into chambers.

'*Come out*,' Caine repeated, 'or we'll come in and get you.'

'*I em not armed*,' a young man's voice answered. '*I kom out. Do not shoot.*'

Caine frowned. The accent sounded German – but then the people of Alsace spoke a kind of German, didn't they? He wasn't sure.

'All right,' Caine said. 'Show yourself.'

A head poked out from behind the oven – a spring-loaded jack-in-the-box of a head. It was a youth, ashen-faced, bulge-eyed, with a sparse beard and a tuft of dirty blonde hair. The figure emerged with his hands up – he was no more than eighteen or nineteen, lean to the point of emaciation. He wore wooden flip-flops and a ragged French uniform two sizes too big. Caine noticed that the boy had rolled up his sleeves and trouser legs.

The youth's lips were cracked, his teeth yellow. He was shaking like a leaf.

'Don't shoot,' he hissed.

'Who *are* you?' Caine demanded, letting the muzzle of his Thompson drop. 'What the hell are you doing here?'

'My name is Hartmann – Hans Hartmann. I em… vell… sort of… caretaker… here.'

'Hartmann sounds like a German name,' Copeland said. He, too, had let his weapon drop, but he was eyeing the boy warily.

'*Ich bin Deutsch*,' Hartmann said. 'I em from Baden-Baden. I vas *Jugend* – Hitler Youth.'

Caine's fingertips fidgeted around his trigger guard. Some of the hardest fighting the SAS had experienced in Germany in the final weeks of the war was from the Hitler Youth.

'So you were one of the guards here?' he enquired.

The youth's laugh was a fractured cackle. '*Never*,' he coughed. 'I vas prisoner. I vas sentence to death.'

CHAPTER THIRTY-SIX

Hartmann led them over to the kitchen block. He'd set up a little den for himself there, with a bunk and some tins of US rations. Caine's eyes probed automatically for weapons – didn't see any. The boy lit a Primus stove, put on a sooty kettle for tea. 'Sit down,' he said.

There was a broken table in the room with some unsteady-looking chairs.

Caine and Copeland eyed each other.

'I'd better keep watch on the wireless,' Trubman said.

'Yeah,' Wallace nodded. 'An' I'm goin' to stand stag. Don't want no one creepin' up behind us, do we?'

'Like who?' Caine said.

'These days,' Hartmann cut in suddenly, 'you ken never tell.'

They stared at him. *Here we are talking to a Kraut*, Caine thought. *And he's warning us to be on our guard.*

Trubman and Wallace left. Caine and Copeland sat down at the rickety table. Over cracked mugs of bitter tea, without milk, Hartmann explained that he'd still been living at the camp when the French and Americans had moved in the previous November. 'They didn't know vot to do vith me,' he explained. He flipped his tuft of long hair to one side with slender fingers. 'I vas not the only German prisoner here at Natzveiler, but the rest vas dead or had been taken bek to Germany. I asked the French to let me stay. I vill look after the place, I said, in return for food.'

'But why not go back to Germany?' Caine asked.

'I do not *vant* to go back…'

'Why?'

'It vas the Germans, my own people, who sent me here.'

'What for?'

'I vas *kaporal* in charge of a patrol of *Hitler Jugend*,' he said. 'I knew the enemy – I mean the Americans and French – vere near. I vas ready to fight. Then the SS took from us our rifles – *Gewehr* rifles. They give us instead cut-off shotguns. I tell the boys, these veapons are… *verboten*… how you say?'

'*Illegal*,' Caine answered. He thought guiltily of Fred Wallace's sawn-off Purdey – the one he'd carried right through the desert campaign. How he, Caine, had once used it to save his own and Copeland's lives. 'Sawn-offs, we call them. They're forbidden under Hague Rules.'

'*Ja*, off course, I know this. I am not a *dumbkopf*. I tell my boys – we vill throw these veapons in the river. If the Americans catch us with them, they vill kill us. The boys agree. So ve throw them in the river. Ven SS come bek, they ask vere is the guns? *Ve threw them in the river,* I say, *because they vas illegal.* Then the SS arrest me. They say I destroy official property. The truth is that they vas scared of the same thing themselves – that the Americans find illegal veapons and kill them. They vas more afraid than us. They sentence me to death and send me here to KL-Natzweiler.'

He hesitated, slurped tea.

'Is ven I get here, I see vot they do. I see… *terrible* things… *terrible*. I vould not believe if another told me, but I see myself.'

'What kind of things?' Copeland enquired. A faint note of suspicion remained in his voice.

'I know ven I arrive this place is bad, very bad,' Hartmann said. He gulped down more tea. 'I do not understand *how* bad, till von day I vas vorking in stone quarry. Is von kilometre from kemp. Pink granite. They say they need it for Nazi buildings at Nuremberg.' He coughed suddenly. Tea dripped from his nose and the side of his mouth. He wiped it away with a shaky hand.

'At first ve vork in the quarry. Every day we get up before sunrise. Is cold, very cold. They give us only a mug of hot vater – vith just taste of coffee – ven ve get up. Mid-morning, they give us two thin slices of bread, with maybe a piece of sausage thick as a fingernail... Many die of hunger, but SS do not care. They say there is too many people to feed anyway...'

'*Bastards*,' Caine breathed. He couldn't believe it. The British might be bad, but they wouldn't have treated people so inhumanely. Or would they? Maybe it was because they had never been in the same position. It was the Jerries who'd occupied Europe. It was Hitler who'd started the war.

'Von day, a big block of granite drop on the foot of a prisoner,' Hartmann said. 'A Russian prisoner. His foot vas crushed. He vas very brave. They bring German doctor – Streiber. They call him doctor, but I think he is butcher... horse doctor, maybe. He cut the Russian's foot off vith a saw. There is no... vot you say...?'

'Anaesthetic?'

'Yes. But still, the Russian is brave. Streiber and the guards, they laugh when they see the foot come off. They throw it round like a football. Is a big joke. Ha! Ha! Then, Streiber gets a bottle of iodine. He pours iodine on the vound. *All* the bottle. The Russian screamed... *loud*.

Streiber laughed till the Russian passed out. The guards laughed. They bring him to infirmary. Ven he vake up, he start screaming again. The guards make fun of him. I vas cleaner in the infirmary that night. I see them. They poke the Russian in his... vound... vith sticks. They tell him *shut up* and they laugh. They poke him more. He scream more. They laugh more. Then he pass out. Next morning, he vas dead.'

'*Jesus wept*,' Cope said.

The boy wiped tears from his eyes, slugged tea. 'This is only *von* thing I see,' he said, 'but is then I know there is no humanity here. I see many horrible things here – *horrible*. Even if prisoners was too veak to valk to quarry, they make others carry them on their backs. Ven they get there, they cannot vork, of course, so the guards make them lie on the ground vithout shirt. They put one sharp stone under their back, another on their stomach. Then they pour cold vater over them and laugh. That is nothing to vat they do at hospital, though. Sometimes if prisoners vas too sick to vork, they send them to hospital, but not for cure. No. They do things to them. Doctors like Streiber. *Doctors*. One woman, they remove a nerve of her leg to see vot vill happen. Of course, vot happen is that she cannot valk. Others they infect with typhus to see how long it vill take them to die... all day there is beating, vipping, torture, vomen taken for rape by SS men at Struthof Inn. If people get sick, they burn them in the oven, sometimes ven they vas still alive...'

He swallowed hard. 'I understand it all. SS bring us here to die. This is not prison. This is kemp of *death*.'

The boy stopped talking. He set his mug down on the table. His hand shook. His eyes were wide, anaemic blue.

'I need to ask you something,' Caine said. 'Were there any British parachutists here? You mentioned women. Was there a British woman – a special operations agent – a girl with red hair?'

'*Giselle*,' Hartmann almost cut him off. 'There *vas* a red-haired voman, yes. They keep her in punishment cell. She vas French not British. They say she vas saboteur. Giselle Tomalin vas her name.'

'Could have been Celia's cover,' Copeland muttered.

Caine's heart was racing. Cope was right, of course. All SOE agents had cover names as well as their official code names. Blaney had been *Empress Eugenie* on the broadcast network, but he had no idea what name she'd actually used on the ground. Blaney would never have admitted she was British – not when she'd been brought up in France, anyway. He felt sure now. Blaney had been in this camp. This was the closest he'd come to her. He didn't know if he wanted to hear more.

Copeland took advantage of Caine's pause. 'What about the parachutists?' he said.

'*Ja* there vas British parachutists here,' Hartmann said. 'They call them *kommandos*. SS vas mad because they make much trouble. Some – maybe ten or so – vork at Daimler-Benz at Vallenbach. Is not far. The rest they keep in cells.'

'What happened to them?' Caine asked. He leaned forward. 'Them and this *Giselle*? Where did they go?'

Hartmann shook his head. 'They vas taken away,' he said. 'Ven the SS hear that American and French armies vas near, they get scared. Then they hear Strasbourg vas taken by Allies. The *kommandos* that vork at Benz vent first. Von day, they vas gone. Later, Giselle vas gone, also. Then SS hear that Strasbourg vas capture, and the rest of the kommandos vas taken avay, too.'

The boy stared at Caine's knuckles. Caine dropped his gaze, realized he was squeezing the mug so hard that his fists had turned white.

'When *was* this?' Copeland asked. 'I mean, when did the last of the commandos… disappear?'

'It vas... I think... November... last year. Ven ze Allies vas vey close.'

'And you have no idea where they were taken?'

Hartmann shook his head. 'Sometimes there vas rumours ven people vas disappear. This time, nothing.'

'Who knows then?' Caine demanded. He didn't blame the boy, but for God's sake, *someone* must know.

'There vas von person who know,' Hartmann said. 'The *Kommandant*.'

'And who was that?' Cope asked.

Hartmann's eyes seemed to drift out of focus. 'His name is Boelcke. *SS-Standartenführer* Franz Joseph Boelcke. He is the von that know.'

Caine banged the table so hard that the youth jumped.

'That's no good to us,' he grunted. 'Boelcke is dead.'

'*Dead*?' Hartmann repeated. 'Boelcke *ist nicht todt*.'

'They told us,' Caine insisted. 'Put a bullet through his own skull. He's buried here.'

Hartmann scoffed. 'Boelcke is not buried here. He came here von day, *ja*. I vas scared to see him. I vonder *vy* he vas not dead. I hide. I vatch. He vas with Americans. American soldiers. They... they search the cesspool by the infirmary. They fish out an oil drum.'

'An *oil drum*?'

'*Ja*. Boelcke show them vere, I think. They load the oil drum on lorry and off they go. He vas not shot himself. He is happy. The Americans is very happy too.'

For a moment, Caine couldn't believe it. Then he recalled the strange behaviour of the French military at Strasbourg detention centre. The contradictions. The roadblock put in place by Sears-Beach. It was starting to add up.

'How do you know he didn't kill himself later?' Copeland enquired.

The boy gave a hollow chuckle. 'I go to Schirmeck to get food,' he said. 'I hev a bicycle. Last time I go – only two days ago – I *saw* Boelcke in the street. He did not see me. I votch him enter *Hotel des Postes*. That is base of American intelligence in Schirmeck.'

'Are you sure it was him?' Cope asked.

Hartmann suddenly spat on the floor. His eyes blazed. 'You think I forget that man? After vot I see here? Never. It was Boelcke. *SS-Standartenführer* Boelcke. He is not dead. That pig is vorking for Americans now.'

CHAPTER THIRTY-SEVEN

They slept in a field that night and next morning drove to Schirmeck. There was a checkpoint at the entrance to the town, manned by MPs in white helmets. Copeland pulled the jeep off the road, some distance away, cut the motor. He stared at Caine. 'You sure we're doing the right thing, skipper?'

'I've thought about it,' Caine said. 'Boelcke's the only one who knows what happened to Blaney… and to the rest of the 2nd Regiment lads. If he's here, we've got to find him, make him talk. I don't reckon we've got any other choice.'

Copeland nodded, swallowed hard. 'You can bet SHAEF will have put the Yanks on the alert, after we shot up the roadblock…'

Caine took a breath. 'Maybe I should go in alone, Harry.'

'Get lost, skipper,' Wallace's bearish voice growled behind them. 'Don't even say it.'

'We're in it together, boys,' Trubman piped up. 'We've been through more than this. What about that bloody bridge, eh? Held back a *Totenkopf* battalion, didn't we? These Yanks haven't even been in combat.'

'Yeah,' Wallace chuckled. 'We're SAS ain't we?'

'All right,' Caine nodded, 'but I reckon we should put on our crap-hat berets. Draw less attention.'

The sergeant at the barrier seemed friendly, but Caine didn't like the way he examined the dented front bumper – the winch gear, damaged when Trubman had rammed through the roadblock. *He knows*, Caine told himself.

When he explained their business, the MP told him that they should report to 430th CIC headquarters at the *Hotel des Postes* on the Station Road, ask for a Captain Skinner. He gave them directions. Caine nodded, returned the NCO's salute. The man lifted the barrier. They drove into half-deserted streets.

The place seemed quiet enough. Caine liked the way the view was dominated by green hills in all directions, the houses, some half timbered, others solid pink granite. There were a few civilians, the occasional Yank jeep, but no one took any notice of them. They cruised up the road as far as the station itself, surveyed its clock tower, with the slate roof like an exotic hat. They turned and drove back towards the *Hotel des Postes*, which they'd passed on the way. Across the road, the Bruche river was lined with trees, untended, grown wild. Caine told Copeland to drive slowly along the avenue until he found what he was looking for – a niche among the trees where the jeep could be concealed.

Caine jumped down, nodded at Copeland to follow. 'You man the wheel, Taff,' he told Trubman. 'Fred, you keep lookout. What time is it?'

'Ten thirty-five, skipper.'

Caine glanced at his watch. 'Ok, if we're not back by eleven thirty, beat it.'

Wallace grinned, showing broken teeth. 'Yeah, right-o skipper,' he said.

Caine didn't answer. He knew there was no more chance of his mates dumping them there than of Hitler being resurrected.

He and Cope marched across to the hotel.

*

'Boelcke?' Skinner said. He was staring across the table at Caine, who was sitting in the same chair the man he was looking for had vacated only the previous morning. 'Franz Boelcke is dead. It's true he escaped from the detention centre in Strasbourg and returned here—'

'—Why would he?' Copeland butted in. As there wasn't another chair, he was standing at Caine's shoulder. He felt better that way. Jack Skinner spoke American with a clipped accent. He seemed cultivated, exuded smarminess. Cope didn't trust him an inch. 'He's not *from* here, is he?'

'No, he was German, but—'

'—Why come back here? A place he might be recognized? Why not leg it back to *Deutschland*?'

Skinner scratched his head beneath overlong blonde hair. His instinct about these boys had been right. They were keen as Tabasco sauce.

'I guess he left something here,' he said. 'Something he figured he might use as a bargaining chip.'

'What?' Caine asked.

'All I know is that I'm called to the old Natzweiler camp one morning. I find a dead fellow there. Guy's dressed as a peasant. One shot – in the head – looks like he topped himself. Walther pistol, 6mm, SS issue. Maybe he'd hidden it there earlier...'

'Came back here to do himself in?' Caine said. There was a touch of sarcasm in his voice.

'Maybe he didn't find what he was looking for,' Skinner answered. 'The bargaining chip or whatever it was. Realized he had no chance. There was enough evidence to get him strung up. We'd have found him sooner or later.' He paused. 'He's buried in the camp cemetery, alongside a lot of folks he put there, one way or another.'

Skinner stared at Caine. 'Why're you interested in Boelcke, anyway?'

Caine pulled on his chin. 'Ninety-one of our men – SAS Regiment – were dropped in these mountains in August last year. Op *Taunton*, it was called. Their objective was to carry out acts of sabotage with the Maquis, behind enemy lines, to prepare the way for General Patton's advance with the Sixth Army. Only forty-six of them made it back. Fourteen were killed in action. That's fair enough. But thirty-one were unaccounted for. Almost certainly murdered by the Hun. Soldiers captured in uniform. That's a war crime. We found ten at Gaggenau in Germany – or I should say the French found them, and we went in to identify them…'

'…and to find out who's responsible,' Cope added.

'Gaggenau,' Skinner repeated. 'We have a war crimes team there, too.'

Neither Caine nor Copeland commented.

'And you think Boelcke was responsible for… executing them?'

Caine hesitated, wondered how much Skinner knew. *Does he know about Schuochwurte? I'd bet money he does.*

'No idea,' Caine lied, 'but I reckon he knew where the bodies of the rest of our men are – the ones that weren't at Gaggenau, I mean. And there was a girl…'

'A *girl?*'

'A woman. A British special operations agent dropped here last year. She also disappeared. I wanted to know if Boelcke could tell us what happened to her.'

Skinner sighed. 'I'm sorry,' he said. 'I admire your dedication, but what you were told in Strasbourg was true. Boelcke's no longer with us. I'm sorry it's been a waste of time.'

Knowing he'd been dismissed, Caine rose. The CIC officer rose too. He was wearing the usual US olive drab battledress, with a .45 pistol on his belt. He and Caine shook hands. 'Just one thing, Captain Skinner,' Caine said. 'How did you know the dead man was Boelcke?'

Skinner looked taken off guard. 'There were locals… survivors of the camp… they knew him.'

Caine nodded. 'And those people were still living there, were they… at the camp?'

'What do you mean?'

Caine's stone-ground eyes bored into the CIC officer's face. 'I mean how was the body discovered? You said you were called there. Who called you? I wondered if survivors are still living there?'

Skinner's eyes dropped for a moment. Then he raised them again. 'A farm worker, or someone at Struthof nearby, heard the gunshot, went to investigate, found the body.'

'Did this chap know who the dead man was?'

'No. The farm at Struthof was evacuated during the war. We called some camp survivors. There are several around. They identified him.'

Caine smiled. 'I see. Thanks, Captain,' he said.

Skinner smiled back. The smile was as hollow as Caine's, and faded almost immediately. At that instant, something in Skinner's eyes came down like a shutter. Caine saw at once that Skinner knew they'd seen through his charade.

The CIC officer took a step back, went for his pistol. '*Boys!*' he yelled.

The door flew open: two MPs stood there. They carried M1 carbines, levelled at Caine and Copeland. Their faces were set hard. The order hadn't come as a surprise, Caine thought.

Skinner pointed his pistol at Caine. 'You're both under arrest,' he said. 'If you resist, I'll shoot you.'

Caine and Copeland exchanged glances. They might just have fought their way out, but it would mean killing or wounding Allied soldiers. Caine raised his hands. Cope lifted his palms half-heartedly, a bored expression on his face.

238

'I had hoped it wouldn't come to this,' Skinner said. 'If you had any sense, you'd just have accepted what I told you and backed off quietly. I know about everything you've done – even shooting up an MP squad on the way here. Put all their vehicles out of action. I was prepared to let it go—'

'—Rather than draw attention to the fact that you're protecting Nazi war criminals,' Caine cut him off. 'We know you're lying, Skinner. Boelcke's not buried at Natzweiler. He didn't do himself in. He's alive and kicking. You sprung him from Strasbourg detention centre, probably with inside help. Boelcke has something you want – something valuable.'

Skinner remained po-faced. 'Drop your gun belts,' he said. 'Do it slowly, and no one gets hurt.'

Caine unclipped his web belt, let it fall to the floor. He heard the thud as Copeland did the same.

Skinner nodded to the MPs. One moved forward and collected the belts: Skinner and the other covered him.

'You're way out of your depth,' Skinner said. 'You have no idea what's going on here or how big it is.'

Caine stared back at him, unblinking. 'I don't give a damn,' he said. 'Boelcke deliberately worked thousands of people to death. You're quite aware of that. He tortured them. He had them hanged when they refused to work. He had men and women brutally beaten. He murdered our comrades. Is there anything bigger than that?'

Skinner's face remained expressionless. 'I'm going to hold you in detention till I can hand you over to SHAEF,' he said. 'Then you'll face a court martial.' He paused. 'Where are the rest of your men?'

Now it was Caine's turn to look nonchalant. 'Couldn't tell you,' he said.

CHAPTER THIRTY-EIGHT

A jeep with US markings was parked outside the door of the hotel when Caine and Copeland were marched out with their hands on their heads. There was a driver – a flabby-faced private wearing a side cap, who turned to watch the solemn procession moving towards him from the doors of the hotel. Caine glanced hastily towards the place in the trees where they had concealed their vehicle. He detected no movement. He guessed Wallace's eyes would be riveted on them, hoped the big man wouldn't do anything rash. He didn't want to give the Yanks a reason to start shooting.

The street was almost deserted. No other American military in sight. Caine noticed an old woman leaning against the wall of the hotel, about twenty yards away. She was wearing an ankle-length coat of threadbare black. A faded scarf half covered a face that was a mass of blotches and wrinkles. She looked as though she was ill, had stopped to catch her breath. She had one gnarled hand braced against the wall for support, the other was buried under her coat, as if she was trying to ease a stomach pain. Caine noticed that the old lady's visible hand was unusually large and hairy. Skinner's attention was still focused on his two prisoners. The MPs flanked them, carbines at the ready.

They were only a few paces from the vehicle when the driver stiffened. Caine caught a movement out of the corner of his eye, turned his head to see the old woman standing up straight. She had withdrawn her hand from inside her coat. She was holding up what looked like a grenade in one fist, a pin in the other. Her scarf had fallen away from her blotchy, ravaged face. She was smiling.

'*Down!*' Caine bawled. He and Copeland pitched and rolled in the street, just as the old woman sent the grenade skittering along the road like a bowling ball. Skinner pulled steel, fired a quick double tap. The woman dropped, hit concrete, lay still – a pile of old rags. The two MPs went into a crouch, weapons trained on the woman's body. The driver flipped out of the driving seat, screeched '*Grenade!*' Skinner hurled himself down just as the bomb thumped with an ear-punching boom. For an instant, Caine's senses went out of focus, as if he'd just been hit on the head. He felt the ground tremor, heard a kettle-drum bang in his ears. The windscreen of the MP jeep shattered. Bits of glass spattered around them.

Caine's consciousness returned with a blinding headache, eyes streaming, ears bumping like bongos. His limbs felt numb, and for a moment he thought he was paralysed. He couldn't understand what had happened. The grenade had fallen only yards away, yet he hadn't been hit. He'd blacked out for a second when it crumped, but in that instant he'd seen no smoke or fireball. He wondered if the blast had been too near. Perhaps the old lady had placed it with expert precision, aware that the explosion would luft upwards in a V-shape vortex. That would have done hardly any damage to the group – a deliberate distraction, rather than a deadly attack. You would need to have an expert's eye for that though, and he still recalled no flame, no wave of shrapnel. He didn't see any blood, either. There were no dead, nobody seemed to have been wounded. Caine couldn't work out what had really happened, but he didn't care. He snatched the carbine from the nearest MP, jumped up, took a step over to Skinner, still lying on his face. He knelt, laid the muzzle of the carbine against the captain's forehead. Skinner tried to raise his pistol. Caine stamped on his fingers hard, but not hard enough to break them. '*Aaaaagh, Christ!*' Skinner screamed. Caine stuck the muzzle of the carbine into the cleft under his left ear. 'Order your boys to ditch their weapons.'

'Goddamit, you're up shit creek!' Skinner croaked.

Caine prodded harder.

Out of the corner of his eye, he saw that the order was unnecessary. Copeland had the other MP's carbine in his hands and was relieving the driver of his pistol. He'd also retrieved their own gun belts – the ones Skinner's men had confiscated. The air smelt of burnt-out electrical circuits, rather than cordite. There was no smoke in the air.

A motor gunned. Caine cast a glance, expecting enemy action, but instead saw their own jeep emerge from the trees on the other side of the road. Trubman was at the wheel. Wallace was in the passenger seat, his Bren locked on the pintle mount. The jeep scudded right at them, and suddenly Wallace opened fire. Caine ducked instinctively. *What the hell is he doing?* he thought. *He could kill us all.* He could see squirts of orange fire pulse from the muzzle of the machine gun but felt no whizz or twang of rounds. *Blanks*, he almost chuckled to himself.

'Lie flat,' Caine shouted at the Americans. 'Don't move a muscle.'

He knelt down, grabbed Skinner by the collar of his battledress, hauled him up.

A second later, Trubman brought the jeep to a halt beside them. Caine dragged Skinner over to it. Copeland covered the three prone bodies.

Caine saw Wallace's uneven teeth bared in a tigerish grin.

'Meet Captain Jack Skinner, Fred,' he said. '430th Detatchment, Counter-Intelligence Corps.'

''E don't look so intelligent to me,' Wallace chortled. He leapt out of the seat, hefting a hank of parachute cord. It was as if he'd been expecting this. 'Nice to meet you, sir,' he said, pinning Skinner's arms behind his back. The fingers of the captain's right hand were swollen where Caine had stepped on them. He winced as Wallace tied his wrists.

'You're kidnapping an officer of the United States Army,' he protested. 'You're…'

'Come on for Chrissake,' Copeland yelled from behind them. 'We haven't got all day.'

'Not leaving without Maurice,' Wallace said. He saw the puzzled look on Caine's face and nodded at the pile of rags lying on the concrete – the old lady who'd tossed the grenade.

Blood was pooling around her, she was still moving.

'*Maurice?*'

'Our French mate, Maurice Juran. Where'd you think he got that grenade?'

Wallace tied Skinner's hands to the passenger seat. Caine sprinted over to the old woman – the *man* – Wallace had called *Maurice*. How did Wallace know his name? Caine put that question aside for another time. There were shouts, the patter of boots, khaki-clad figures in pudding-bowl helmets moving up the street. They weren't shooting yet. Caine guessed that they didn't know who they should be shooting *at*.

'Come on, skipper,' Cope bawled again, 'we'll soon have the whole garrison on us.'

Caine knelt in spreading blood, pulled off the scarf, saw a man's unshaven face, ravaged by sores and scabs, blotches of red and purple. Skinner's bullets had hit the bloke in the neck and chest. The man's lips moved. 'No touch,' he whispered in broken English. 'No come near. I am dead. I touch *stuff* that… Boelcke… make… at Wallenbach. I believe they execute him. Then I see him. *Here*. With Americans. *Laughing*. He have beard. He have peasant clothes. But was that snake. Was *him*.'

His eyelids fluttered. The sound of boots and voices was growing nearer. 'Take her or leave her!' Copeland shouted. 'We've got to go.'

Maurice opened his eyes. '*Go*,' he murmured. 'Leave me. I was dead already. Find your comrades. Find Giselle. Follow the ratline.'

Caine's eyes opened wide. He was about to ask something when a gunshot cracked over his head. He ducked.

Maurice closed his eyes, took a raucous breath. After what he'd said, Caine didn't dare get near enough to make sure he was dead.

Trubman was revving the jeep engine, ramping her into gear. Copeland had jumped into the back. When Caine vaulted in beside him, the tyres were already screaming.

CHAPTER THIRTY-NINE

They got out of Schirmeck on a dirt track Trubman found, by what Caine put down to either luck or intuition. It wasn't guarded by the Yanks. It took them back to the Strasbourg road, a leafy tunnel winding through deep forest. As soon as they found a convenient side road, Caine told Trubman to follow it. They bumped across ruts and potholes for about five miles before they found a derelict peasant cottage.

Copeland and Wallace cleared the house thoroughly. It looked as though it hadn't been used for years. There were gaps in the roof, doors hung off their hinges. There was no furniture inside, but sticks of broken chairs and rubbish were strewn across the floor. Birds had nested in the fireplace and the house smelt of ratpiss. They avoided the place: it was too obvious for good cover. They concealed the jeep in a mossy clearing under the trees nearby. By now, the news that Skinner had been snatched would have got around: there might even be spotter planes out.

Caine jerked the captain out of the passenger seat, sat him down on the moss-covered ground.

'Untie my hands,' the CIC man snapped. 'Let me go. You can't even imagine what shit you got yourselves in.'

'*Shit?*' Wallace snorted. '*You* can't even imagine what shit we *bin* in. You're a hundred per cent proof rear echelon office wallah, if ever I see one. Ok, you just shot an unarmed civvie. Feeling tough are yer?'

'That woman… guy… whatever… chucked a grenade at us, in case you didn't notice.'

'An' in case *you* didn't notice, not one of us even 'as a scratch. Why d'yer reckon that is? You ever bin in a real battle, Captain? Ever seen yer mates with their guts 'angin out like spaghetti? Ever 'ad to put a round through a dyin' chum's 'ead? Ever seen yer muckers blown to slivers, bombed by yer own *side*? There ain't a single man 'ere who ain't bin decorated at least twice for bravery. There ain't one who ain't bin wounded. Three of us 'as bin POWs and escaped. It's a miracle any of us …'

'…That's enough, Fred,' Caine cut in. 'The captain isn't interested in the story of our lives. Untie his hands. He's not going anywhere. Not just yet.'

Reluctantly, the big man untied the para cord. Skinner let out a sigh of relief, massaged his swollen fingers.

'Sorry about that,' Caine said, 'but you *were* going to shoot me.'

Skinner looked angry, choked something back.

Trubman had already lit a Primus stove and was getting a brew on. Copeland stood guard, scanning the skies through the foliage, his sniper rifle in his hands.

Wallace made a move to join Trubman. Caine stopped him. 'Sit down,' he said. 'I want to know about that chap – *Maurice*. Who was he? Where did he come from?'

There was a touch of guilt on the big gunner's face. He sat down cross-legged opposite Caine and Skinner. He placed his Bren across his tree-trunk legs. Caine took out his cigarette case, gave them each a smoke, lit theirs, lit his own.

Skinner smoked begrudgingly. 'I was wonderin' about that myself,' he said. 'At first, I thought it was an attack by subversives. There're still people in Alsace who collaborated with the Nazis, even fought for the *Wehrmacht*. People who don't like the presence of Allied troops. We get incidents from time to time.' He glanced at Wallace. 'Ok, you say none of us was even scratched. What type of grenade was that? Never seen anything like it.'

Caine examined Wallace's Neanderthal face curiously.

'Stun grenade,' Wallace said with a cat-got-the-cream look. 'Causes concussion. For a sec, you can't see nothin'. Yer ears is ringin'. Feel anythin' like that?'

'Seemed like I blacked out for a second,' Caine said. 'I didn't see any flash or smoke, but the ground seemed to move.'

Skinner nodded. 'Same for me. There was no shrapnel. No fragmentation.'

'That's the beauty of stunners,' Wallace said. 'They don't do no real 'arm. Remember Crumper? 'E made 'em as a try-out, but they was never official issue. I snagged a few off Ordnance for D-Day ops last year. Never used 'em. Thought they might come in 'andy on this stunt.'

Caine blew smoke and thought of Crumper, the brilliant SAS artificer who'd invented an infra-red night sight and other gadgets way ahead of their time – the man they'd left in the desert, who'd died covering their withdrawal.

'So how did this… *Maurice*… come to get his hands on it?'

Wallace heaved a long sigh, looked Caine in the eye. 'I gave it to 'im, o' course. Maurice was ex-Resistance. Chief of a circuit called *Boxer*. 'E spots us driving round the town, don't 'e? Clicks we're British. Even knew we was SAS. Comes up to us when we was 'idin in the trees. Wouldn't get nearer'n five yards, though. You see 'is face? Like a pound of raw liver? Reckoned 'e'd picked up some lurgi that was killin' 'im. Didn't want us to get it.'

Caine paused in the act of taking a drag on his cigarette. 'He mentioned Wallenbach. Said Boelcke was making something at the Daimler-Benz plant there. Some *stuff.* He touched it.'

Skinner looked interested all of a sudden. He held his fag between two fingers, unsmoked.

'Yeah, 'e reckoned 'e'd bin sick ever since,' Wallace went on. 'Guess what else? Maurice touched that stuff, whatever it was, on a sabotage op ordered by SOE. The mission was led by a woman, name of Giselle. She reckoned to be French, but she parachuted in from Blighty in an 'Alifax.'

Caine looked stunned. '*Giselle Tomalin.* The girl Hartmann talked about!'

'Yeah, the red'ead…'

'*Blaney.*'

'Bingo.'

Caine stubbed out his cigarette absent-mindedly, lost in a momentary reverie. He looked around, noticed that both Copeland and Trubman were listening intently. Now he knew what Blaney's mission had been. He also knew that a redhead named Giselle Tomalin had been a prisoner at KL-Natzweiler. All of them, even Skinner, watched him in silence, anticipating his next question.

'*She was captured,*' Wallace said, a step ahead of him. 'Reckon we knew that already.'

Caine said nothing, waited for the big man to continue.

'Not on the Wallenbach stunt though. Maurice told us they was bumped and scarpered. There was four, includin' the girl, and they all got out. The Krauts tracked 'em down to a safe 'ouse. She was taken prisoner after a ding-dong. Two Maquis blokes with 'er copped it – one of 'em was Maurice's son. Maurice was already sick, hidden in a back room, 'e said. They never found 'im.'

'How did he get away with it?'

Wallace ground out his cigarette stub. 'Lucky, I s'pose. The Yanks and Frogs was already gettin' nearby then. Mebbe the Gestapo didn't 'ave time to waste lookin' for saboteurs, an'—'

'—What happened to her?' Caine butted in. His eyes glittered. He couldn't hold the question back any longer.

Wallace paused, looked down, then straight at Caine's face. 'Maurice didn't know,' he said, ''an I believed 'im. Like I said, 'e were sick from whatever it was 'e touched at Wallenbach. All 'e 'eard was that some of our lads – SAS lads – was bein' used as workers at the Daimler-Benz plant, and they wasn't buildin' no motor cars. They was workin' on whatever it was that Boelcke was makin' there…'

'The ones who were moved to Gaggenau,' Cope muttered from a few yards away. 'The ones Schuochwurte murdered.'

'Yelchukov told me that ten of the 2nd SAS prisoners came from support arms, mostly Ordnance and Engineers,' Caine said. 'Nothing surprising there, but they all had experience with technical stuff. That's exactly the number we found at Gaggenau. Might be a coincidence, might not.'

'I reckon not,' Wallace nodded his shaggy head. 'Rest of 'em was done in 'ere – at Natzweiler or somewhere else in the Vosges. Maybe this… Giselle, too. Sorry, Tom. Maurice was ninety-nine per cent sure they was murdered, but 'e 'ad no idea where, or where they was buried. Said the only one 'oo knew was Boelcke.'

Another momentary silence. Caine let out a long sigh. 'So we're back where we started. Unless we find Boelcke.' He stared at Skinner, his eyes hard as rock salt. 'Captain Skinner, maybe you'd like to help us out?'

CHAPTER FORTY

Skinner stared back. He looked indignant rather than afraid. Caine knew he was confident the SAS weren't going to torture him, and he was right. Caine was ready to fight his way out of stickies with minimum violence, but there was no way he was going to torture an Allied soldier. He'd already stepped on Skinner's hand. He felt bad enough about that. Caine opened his mouth to say something. Wallace ramped in again.

'Maurice told me that Boelcke enjoyed seein' people bein' 'anged and tortured,' he said. His voice was grave. He was looking directly at Skinner. 'Said he used to torture and rape women personally. Got a kick out of it, you might say. The prisoners at Natzweiler came from all over Europe. Some of 'em wasn't *supposed* to get out alive. Boelcke made sure almost none of 'em did. Used thousands to build underground tunnels at the Daimler-Benz plant at Wallenbach. 'E deliberately starved 'em, so as they couldn't work for more than a week or two. Then they dropped dead. Anyone 'oo complained they wasn't up to it was lashed an' beaten. If they refused to work, they was 'anged in public. Boelcke 'imself was always there to see it, big grin on 'is face, Maurice said. When one lot flaked out, 'e burned the bodies in the crematorium an' just drafted the next lot in, worked 'em to death and on and on. Treated 'em like

animals – *worse* than animals.' He paused. 'I done my share o' killin',
Captain. I seen some sickenin' things in the war. But that… that's the
most disgustin' thing I ever 'eard of.'

His eyes seemed to smoulder. Skinner tried to drag his gaze away;
failed. 'Mass murder, Captain. Not shootin' the enemy in combat. A
bloke's got some honour when 'e dies fightin'. These folks was redooced
to slaves. Boelcke organized the slow torture and murder of thousands.'

Skinner seemed to find his tongue. 'Boelcke was carrying out orders,'
he said. 'Isn't that what *you* do? Isn't that what all soldiers do?'

'Maybe,' Wallace said. 'Thing is, 'e enjoyed it.'

Skinner scratched his nose. 'How could you possibly know that?'

'Maurice said Boelcke wasn't a pukka SS man. Not even a soldier.
He were a boffin – a scientist, engineer – maybe both. Designed the
whole place at Wallenbach, the whole process 'isself. See, Maurice were
drafted in as a miner to 'elp supervise buildin' the tunnels, and 'e knew.'

'So he was a Nazi collaborator,' Skinner said acidly. 'Why trust what
he said?'

'I reckon that's obvious,' Caine butted in. 'Maurice gave his life to
rescue us. You shot him.'

'You know why 'e 'elped us?' Wallace went on. ''Cos he hated you
Yanks for collaboratin' with a fuckin' pig like Boelcke. For lettin' 'im
off the 'ook. See, 'e saw all this close up when 'e was workin' on the
tunnels there. 'E was lucky enough to get away with it, 'cos 'e weren't
a prisoner at Natzweiler, and they needed 'is expertise. 'E weren't no
collaborator, though. 'Ated Boelcke.'

He paused. 'When the skipper and 'Arry 'ere didn't come out on time,
we knew sommat weren't right. I thought up the grenade job. Maurice
volunteered – *insisted*. Said 'ed always thought you Americans stood for
justice, equality and democracy – all that crap. Thought you was the

good blokes. 'E couldn't believe it when 'e saw you was all matey with a war criminal like Boelcke. 'E watched your office, 'e said. Saw Boelcke go in an out day after day – smug look on 'is face. He nearly 'ad a go at the bugger isself a few times, 'e said, but 'e was too sick. Then, when 'e saw us Brits in town, 'e thought we might 'elp.'

Wallace took in a deep breath. Caine saw tears in his eyes. If it was an act, it was a damn good one, he thought.

'Now,' Wallace continued, leaning his massive torso forward. 'Ask yerself. Do you *really* want to go on protectin' a geezer 'oo's condemned thousands of men and women to a slow, agonizin' death, and *enjoyed* doin' it? You've already shot dead an 'ero of the French Resistance, a man 'oo believed in your country – a man 'oo thought you was liberators. I don't know why you're pally with Boelcke, an' I don't care. Maurice said there was others – wanted Nazis - always in and out of yer office. To them people in Schirmeck, you ain't lookin' much different to the Gestapo right now. Search yer conscience, mate. You know where 'e is, don't yer? Do the right thing.' He sat back on his great haunches. Wiped his eyes with a boxing-glove hand.

Skinner looked down, shifted uncomfortably. For a moment, Caine thought he wasn't going to speak.

'Boelcke's a brilliant man,' he said suddenly, his voice low. 'A physicist. He's been working on atomic fission since before the war. I don't suppose any of you know what that is, do you?'

'It means breaking atoms,' Copeland spoke from behind. 'Everything's made up of atoms. Bloke called Rutherford proved you could smash them, and it would release an incredible surge of power.'

'That's right,' Skinner said, nodding. 'When you do that, though – smash atoms, I mean – that surge of power makes things... *radioactive*. It's like getting burned, or maybe you could say like an infection. It spreads. It can contaminate others. That's what Maurice had – *radioactive poisoning*. The mission he took part in was an attempt by your SOE to sabotage the process Boelcke was working on – it was called a *hot cell*. No point going into detail, but the end result would have been a bomb – an *atomic* bomb. It's impossible to describe how devastating that would be – the most powerful weapon ever known.'

'And whichever country had it would be the most powerful *country* ever known,' Copeland said dryly. 'It would control the world wouldn't it?'

Skinner flushed. 'The Russians are already working on atomic fission,' he said. 'Imagine if *they* got the process before us. Imagine they got hold of men like Boelcke, used their know-how. You want to see Stalin control the world? You think Hitler was bad? He wasn't a patch on how Stalin would be if he got his hands on an atom bomb. Maybe you're right about Boelcke, but it was a choice of two evils. Surely you can see that?'

Caine weighed it up. He remembered the young man in Gaggenau who had told him about how the Americans had nipped into the town ahead of the French, looted the works, carried out equipment. He thought of how obstacles had been put in their way ever since they'd arrived at SHAEF in Paris. The MP roadblock they'd barged through. The Command – even British Command – must have known that their search would eventually lead them to this… *hot cell*… operation. To Boelcke. He felt a pulse of pure rage at the establishment. He thought of the SAS soldiers, of Blaney, used and squandered, discarded for something considered more important.

You're way out of your depth. You have no idea what's going on here, or how big it is.

'*Why?*' he demanded.

Skinner gave him a curious glance. 'I've told you …'

'...*Why* did they send a lone girl... a woman agent, I mean... to sabotage the Wallenbach plant? Why not use a bomber squadron? Blow the place to pieces?'

'Good point, Tom,' Wallace agreed. 'I forgot sommat. Maurice said the girl – Giselle – asked Blighty for a ghost raid, like a hoax raid... put out over the air, to fool the enemy into thinkin' a real bombin' raid was on the way. The idea was that they'd switch the arc lights off. He reckons the Krauts knew they was comin'. There was a tip-off, 'e said.'

'The buggers knew what Boelcke was doing,' Caine snarled. 'Not just the Americans, the British, too. That's why they never ordered a bombing raid in the first place. Either SOE were acting on their own, or the High Command let Blaney go in as a sort of decoy, to convince others it was a legitimate target. What they really wanted to do was to preserve it until they – or the Americans – could loot it. Blaney would have requested the ghost air-raid by wireless. What if there was a mole in the SOE signals network, passing messages to the Secret Intelligence Service – MI6? Maybe it was *them* who leaked it to the Nazis: maybe they didn't *want* the Wallenbach plant blown up. When the Yanks got too near, the Jerries moved this... *hot cell*... across the Rhine to Gaggenau. They moved the men who'd worked on it – *our* men, all with technical expertise – with it. They knew too much. When it looked like it was all over – last November, the Nazis finally abandoned the Natzweiler camp. Boelcke sent orders to Schuochwurte to kill the prisoners moved to Germany. He murdered our chaps here for good measure. They must have done Blaney in for the same reason. She'd seen this... *hot cell*. She had to go.'

There was silence for a moment. They eyed each other. Trubman poured tea into enamel mugs, added Carnation milk and sugar, handed them round.

Caine sipped his tea. It was gratifyingly hot. He watched Skinner sip for a few moments, then said, 'what's a ratline, Captain?'

'What?' Skinner looked startled. 'Isn't it something they use on ships?'

'I think we've got past the bullshit stage,' Caine said. This time there was the merest hint of threat in his voice. 'The last thing Maurice said to me was, *Find your comrades. Find Giselle. Follow the ratline.*'

The question hung in the air. Skinner looked at them, looked away. He seemed to come to a decision. He cleared his voice.

'All right, I'll tell you. Ratlines are escape routes, originally run by the Resistance and Brit intelligence department MI9, for extracting downed aircrew, escaped POWs – those kind of guys. After the war, ratlines were taken over by the Nazis, to exfiltrate personnel on CROWCASS – the wanted list – ex-SS men, Gestapo -'

'You mean war criminals?' Caine cut in. 'Men like Boelcke?'

Skinner flushed again. 'All right, yeah. Men like Boelcke.'

Caine gasped. 'And you CIC people *knew* about it?' Are you telling me that you're actually *helping* Nazi war criminals escape?'

Skinner sat up straight, glared at Caine, irritated now. 'Listen, Caine. First of all, I'm *telling* you, aren't I? I don't have to do that. Second, yes – your British Secret Intelligence Service, MI6, are in it up to the hilt. Sure, they leaked the intel on the SOE sabotage raid to the Jerries. We're Allies, *remember*? I told you we can't afford to let men with specialist knowledge like Boelcke fall into the hands of the Soviets. Too much is at stake. This way, if there's any trouble… well, we can get them out.'

Caine made a concerted effort to control his fury. He could see it all now. When the CIC had got wind that the SAS War Crimes Team was looking for Boelcke, they'd spirited him away down one of these ratlines. It must have been recently, because according to Wallace, Maurice had seen Boelcke in Schirmeck, at most, a couple of days back. Hartmann, too.

'So *why* are you telling us?' Caine demanded.

Skinner scratched his head. 'I don't know. Conscience maybe. Everything you say about Boelcke is true, I know that. Every time I had to deal with him it made my skin crawl. He's a mass murderer, a sadist, like you say. Showed no remorse at all. Tunnel vision – the *Project*, the *Project* and the *Project*. That was all that mattered. Didn't give a shit about the Nazis, Hitler, the SS – only about who was sponsoring the *Project*. He's responsible for the horrific deaths of thousands – maybe tens of thousands. You think I *approve* of that? I was following orders. Yes, I helped him escape from the detention centre. Yes, I put on a friendly act with him, yes, I put him on a ratline. I did it for my country,– and our Allies – not because I liked it.'

'So why the sudden change of heart?' Copeland enquired from behind them. 'Not long back you were swearing he'd shot himself.'

Skinner glanced at him, then back at Caine. 'Let's say we got what we needed.'

Caine shook his head. 'Oh yes, that sealed oil drum hidden in a cesspool at Natzweiler. What was in it? All his secrets, I'd guess.'

Skinner's eyes went wide with surprise. 'How did you—?'

'—A little bird,' Wallace growled. 'You 'ad a witness, did you know that?'

Skinner shook his head.

'So you can afford to write him off?' Caine said.

'It's not like that—'

'—Who cares,' Caine cut in. 'Just tell us the route of this… *ratline*… and we'll leave you in peace.'

'Perpignan,' Skinner said. 'Then across the Pyrenees into Spain – Madrid or Barcelona, usually. Spain was neutral during the war, but not *that* neutral. A lot of Allied escapees got interned as illegal immigrants. One route goes through Switzerland and out via Lyon. There's a string of safe houses on the way. I can't tell you exactly where they all are, but the most important one is a villa outside Perpignan – the *Villa Stauffer*, named after the charming lady who founded it – Spanish citizen, German born. It's no longer inhabited – at least not by the family – but it's the base for the Pyrenees crossing. The escapees get fixed up with *passeurs* – guides – there.'

'When did he leave?'

Skinner gave him an embarrassed glance. 'Yesterday morning.'

'*What?*' Caine was staggered. 'You sent him off when you heard we were coming, didn't you?'

Skinner looked down.

'We could still catch 'im, skipper,' Wallace boomed.

'No,' Skinner said. 'He went off in a car. He'll be well on his way to Perpignan by now.'

Caine got up. 'Thank you, Captain,' he said sourly. 'Pack up, lads. We've got a long way to go.'

Trubman had already slid the map out of its pouch. He and Copeland had unfolded it on the bonnet of the jeep. They were peering at it. 'I reckon it's getting on for six hundred miles to Perpignan,' Trubman declared. 'We're going to need more petrol, see.'

'We better get moving then,' Caine said. 'Maybe we'll find some on the way.'

They packed up in minutes, drove off, left Skinner sitting under the tree with water, rations and cigarettes. It wouldn't take him long to walk to the main road. His people would find him sooner or later, Caine thought. Would he be quick to let on what he'd revealed? He didn't know, but they'd have to make allowance for a pursuit.

257

The CIC officer watched them go, with a sullen expression, until the jeep careened out of sight around a bend. Then his face broke into a grin. '*Perpignan, here we come,*' he chuckled, mimicking Caine's British accent. 'And you'll never guess what's waiting for you there.'

CHAPTER FORTY-ONE

KL-Natzweiler-Struthof, Alsace, France. September 1944

A gang of men in ragged uniforms like pyjamas was digging an entrenchment along the road. Two SS guards marched Blaney towards the camp gates. They'd just climbed the steep, winding track from Rothau, about six kilometres below, and they were breathing hard. They seemed out of condition, she thought.

The prisoners were using picks, shovels and wheelbarrows, but they moved like automatons. Closer up, she saw that most of them were so emaciated that their cheekbones were sharp ridges in their faces and their eyes bulged like marbles from their skulls. SS guards in field-grey uniforms yammered at them ceaselessly. Two of the SS men held huge black Alsatians on leashes. The dogs snapped, growled, barked at any prisoner who attracted the attention of the guards.

Blaney was wearing a tweed coat and skirt, wooden-soled shoes. She carried her suitcase in one hand and had a black coat draped over her arm. Prisoners gaped at her as she passed. She saw a few mouths fall open in small 'o's of surprise as if the men had never seen a woman before. But mostly their features were incurious, the eyes blank and fish-like. The lack of feeling in them made Blaney shiver. It was as if they were already dead. Then, only for a moment, before the guards roared at them to get on with their work, Blaney realized with a shock that she knew one of the faces. She'd been trained in memorizing features and she was sure of it. The man was Brian Appleyard, a chap who'd been in her group at Beaulieu. He'd been brought up partly in France, like she had, and as a fluent French-speaker he'd also been earmarked for F Section of SOE. Appleyard, she remembered, was a gifted artist. Their eyes met for a fraction of a second, but there was an instant spark of mutual recognition. Appleyard's face was as wasted as those of the other men, but there was something about his eyes that suggested he hadn't given up.

Just before they escorted her through the gates, one of the SS guards – a squat man with trousers an inch too long and a face like a cabbage – pointed to what looked like a farmhouse, lying about two kilometres down the hillside. It was a square, dirty-white building with a pitched roof of grey tiles, standing by the side of a road. On the other side of the road lay a much bigger structure – three stories, a broad façade, with many windows and a rear wing that extended far back to the edge of a pine forest. '*Struthof*,' the wrinkled SS man commented in French. 'The big building is the *Struthof Inn*. People used to stay there for skiing and hiking before the war. Now it's an SS barracks. The smaller building across from it used to be a ballroom. Now it's the gas chamber. You're *Nacht und Nebel*, aren't you? That's where you'll end up.'

He chuckled. Blaney wondered why he'd said it. She knew that she'd been sent here to die one way or another. At Beaulieu, they'd made no bones about her fate if she was captured. The SS guard must have said it out of pure sadism. It always amazed her to find people so capable of pointless cruelty. This man must have been an ordinary man before the war – butcher, baker, candlestick maker? Perhaps he had a wife and children. Did war turn people into inhuman monsters? Most prison guards, she knew, belonged to *SS-Totenkopf,* or *Death's Head* battalions, like the one Tom Caine and his handful of men had held off from that bridge in Tunisia. Maybe they were specially chosen for their truculence. The thought had led her back to Tom Caine. Sooner or later, everything seemed to come back to him.

The gates were wooden, flimsy-looking, with the words *Konzentrationzlager Natzweiler-Struthof* blocked in above them. The camp itself consisted of rows of huts, built on a steep incline, falling away to what looked like administration buildings, some out of sight at the bottom of the slope. Beyond that there was a forest. From inside the gate there was a view over the interlocking ridges of hills, some wooded, others bare, purple stone. As the guards escorted her down the slope, she saw squads of prisoners being marched to and fro, stumbling along with the same spiritless movement as those she'd seen working on the entrenchment. On one side there was a wooden gibbet, built on a platform with four or five steps. A hanging rope, with a noose on the end. It swung slightly in the breeze. Hangings at Natzweiler were public affairs, then. There was no comfort here, she thought. This was the end.

They took her through, into a second compound at the bottom of the slope and into what she assumed was the jail block, where prisoners were kept in solitary confinement. Another guard thrust a striped prison dress at her and took away her things. Since she'd been captured, she'd been interrogated, beaten and tortured nine times. She'd never said a word about *Circuit Boxer,* never mentioned André-Maurice, never said more than she had done at the *bagnoire* when Boelcke had raped her repeatedly.

She hadn't seen Boelcke since that time. One thing she was sure of – he'd enjoyed it. She knew he was the *Kommandant* at Natzweiler and wondered if their paths would cross again.

The room was small. There was a thin mattress with a filthy blanket, a slop bucket in one corner. Light probed in a single beam through a tiny barred window with no glass. She thought of the cell in Algeria where, the previous year, she'd talked all night to Tom Caine before his court martial. Back to Caine again. That place had seemed dismal, but it had been luxury compared with this.

She held up the prison dress, saw that the letters NN were stencilled in big, spidery red letters on the back. NN – *Nacht und Nebel* – Night and Fog. It was a quote from Goethe, she knew, her death sentence. She put the dress on and huddled in the corner of her cell. She'd told herself that she wouldn't cry, but she felt tears trickling down her cheeks. It wasn't for her, she thought. She'd known what to expect the moment she'd been captured. She could have swallowed her L-ration – her cyanide pill – but she hadn't thought of it at the time. Maybe she just hadn't had the guts. Agents did sometimes escape, didn't they? Maybe she'd felt, somehow, that there might be a chance of seeing Tom Caine again. These tears were for him.

Someone tapped on the outside wall. She stopped crying, listened.

'This is *Rex*,' a man's voice said. '*Rex Quondam.*'

She almost laughed. '*Rex Quondam. Once King.* Why did SOE always favour pompous royal or imperial titles for their operational code names? *Rex Quondam* was a famous Latin quote found on the tomb of a man who was supposed to be King Arthur. It was the operational code name of Brian Appleyard.

'Who are you?' the voice came again, urgently. 'I can't stay long. To get here, I had to sneak from block to block. Who *are* you?'

Blaney was on her guard. She'd been warned about Nazi stool pigeons. She remembered what André-Maurice had told her about two Jerries who'd tried to penetrate another circuit by posing as downed American aircrew. All that had given them away was that one of them had mispronounced *New Jersey*. That was enough. They'd both ended up with holes in their heads, floating in the river. Maurice had said that afterwards, the circuit chief had never been quite sure if they actually *had* been Americans. It was a tough business. You couldn't afford to take the chance.

'Who *are* you?' the voice came even more urgently. 'Listen, I need to know who you are.'

It was Appleyard's voice, she was certain of that, but why was he asking who she was? Then she realized he was asking for her cover name. He couldn't call her Celia Blaney, of course.

She stood up and positioned herself close to the wall. 'I'm Giselle Tomalin,' she said. 'I was captured in a fight with the Jerries. What about you? Aren't you a *pianist?*'

'Lasted all of three months. Got triangulated.'

Blaney hesitated. 'And you're still here?'

Appleyard's voice was equally hesitant. 'The SS officers like my portraits. I never thought being an artist would save my life...' He broke off. 'Look, there's no logic to it. They can hold you for months for no good reason or bump you off the same day.'

'Is there any chance of escape?'

'There's always a chance. There *have* been escapes. They try to hush it up, but word gets round. Some escapees are recaptured. Others aren't.'

'So how do they do it – bump you off, I mean?'

When Appleyard didn't answer, she added, 'Come on, I want to know.'

'All right. I'll tell you the truth. With women... it's usually quick and quiet. They want to keep it under their hats. Thing is, they know the Allies are getting closer, and they're desperate. There are some British parachutists here – dropped in to stir up trouble in the Vosges, with the local *Maquisards*. Did a good job, but about thirty were captured. Ten of them worked at the Daimler-Benz plant at Wallenbach. A few days ago, they disappeared.'

Blaney bit her lip. She didn't need to ask what *disappeared* meant. The *Kommando Order* – to execute soldiers captured in uniform was illegal under The Hague Convention. Obviously, they'd done away with them in secret. They didn't want any witnesses. The Hague Rules didn't apply to her or Brian, though. They were saboteurs and spies.

'You said there were about thirty. What happened to the rest?'

'Kept in solitary, somewhere in the camp. No-one ever sees them.'

Blaney gulped. *No, Caine couldn't be one of them*. That was impossible, she thought.

'There are rumours that the local Resistance – the *Alliance Reseau* – is planning a general uprising,' Appleyard went on. 'That they're going to attack the camp. The Nazis have had us digging entrenchments round the place – you saw us working on one today. Not to defend them against attack, though. The machine gun emplacements are all facing *inwards*. They must be terrified of what the prisoners here would do to them if… Anyway, if you're lucky… if *we're* lucky…'

'And if not?' She was proud that there was no tremor in her voice.

'The gas chamber,' he replied. 'That's where it usually is… for… for those they want to… keep quiet about. It's outside the compound, you see.'

Somewhere a dog barked.

'*Christ*,' Appleyard growled. 'Those bloody dogs. Good luck. Better go.'

Appleyard didn't return. For the next few days, Blaney stayed in her cell, using the slop bucket. Occasionally, a timid-looking young German – just a boy – brought her tin jugs of thin soup. He said his name was

Hartmann. To Blaney's surprise, he was a prisoner here, too. Since he was Jerry, though, he was considered a *trustee*. She was perfectly aware that he might be a stool pigeon – she was careful never to talk about herself. But he spoke English well, and he was someone she could listen to.

He'd been a member of the Hitler Youth, he told her. They'd sentenced him to death for destroying Nazi property – some half-useless and illegal weapons, which he and his patrol had thrown into the river. It wasn't really the act of throwing away weapons the SS resented, he thought, it was the tacit admission that Germany had lost the war. They were so terrified, they refused even to think about it. Hitler had been wrong. The Thousand Year Reich had been the delusion of a sick mind. A few weeks back someone had tried to blow the Führer up. Blaney thought of the entrenchments Appleyard had worked on – the machine gun emplacements facing into the camp. She remembered what André-Maurice had told her about the thousands – tens of thousands – of slave workers from Natzweiler who'd died building those tunnels at Wallenbach. The six-year Nazi occupation of France had generated a tidal wave of hatred. The Allies were close. The Nazis must know that soon the dam would break, and the wave would sweep them away. They must be petrified.

Blaney couldn't help being curious about the British parachutists Appleyard had mentioned – the ones kept in solitary confinement somewhere in the camp. She wondered if Hartmann knew anything about them. She resolved to ask him next time they met.

In the morning the camp bell rang three times. It was the curfew bell Hartmann had warned her about. The prisoners had to stay inside their blocks. All day there was noise and commotion. She heard lorry engines grinding, men shouting wildly in Alsatian dialect, women shrieking, dogs barking, guards cursing in German. Then there was the shooting, the ruckle of sub-machine guns, the *pop* of small-calibre pistols – single shots, like the slam of a door. Shrieks of terror, bellows of rage, voices pleading. Blaney bit her knuckles. Once she saw Boelcke himself, hurrying past the punishment-wing in his black SS uniform and cap, followed by two other officers. As she peered out at him, he turned his head towards her. Blaney ducked quickly out of sight but knew it was too late. He'd recognized her.

The hubbub continued for hours. The next time she dared to peer out of the window she saw two women in peasant dress – not prison garb – being dragged past by three or four SS men. The women were young, wiry-looking, struggling against their captors defiantly, jabbering in dialect. Two German Shepherd dogs snapped savagely at their heels. She lost sight of them after a moment, but Hartmann had told her that beyond her field of vision lay steps that led down to the crematorium. A moment later Blaney heard the flat percussion of pistol shots. The screaming stopped. Not long afterwards, she glimpsed a gush of red flame. She knew it came from the crematorium. She'd seen that gush many times over the past few days.

When Blaney awoke the following morning, there was silence. The curfew bell didn't ring at nine. Hartmann slipped into her cell with soup. 'The *Alliance Reseau*,' he whispered. He glanced around furtively.

'*What*?'

'The French Resistance. The SS found out they vas planning to attack the camp – that is vy the entrenchments vas dug. They vas gathering in Schirmeck forest. The SS surround them, capture them. There vas about two hundred – men and vomen. They bring them here and they kill them all. Some vas shot. Some vas hang. Some vas gas at Struthof. All the bodies vas burn in the crematorium.'

Blaney knew it wasn't the right moment to ask him about the parachutists: she decided to wait until next time.

She never saw Hartmann again.

In the afternoon, not long before sunset, two SS guards arrived and ordered her out of the cell. One of them was the same cabbage-faced man who'd escorted her from the station at Rothau – the one who'd made the remark about the gas chamber. Blaney didn't ask where she was being taken.

They marched her uphill between the blocks. The gibbet still stood where it had on the day she'd arrived. The noose still swung ominously at the end of the rope. There wasn't a sign of blood, no hint that anything out of the ordinary had happened here, she thought. There were no prisoners around. She wondered if they had been ordered into their huts again, so as not to witness her final march. She glimpsed faces behind windows, though. Just for a moment, she thought she glimpsed Appleyard's features. *There's always a chance,* he'd said. *People have escaped.* Blaney guessed that this would be her first and last chance. A breath of wind blew her hair against her cheeks. She ran a hand across them – they felt hollow and bony where she'd lost weight. The sun was a gold pool, lying between skeins of ruffled cloud. There was a tincture of pink over the outlines of the hills. The hillsides were burnished copper and deep green.

Just inside the camp gate a vehicle was waiting – a jeep-like thing Blaney knew was called a *Kubelwagen*. The driver started the motor, the guards made her huddle in the back. The driver put the vehicle into gear, taxied up to the camp gate. Men in grey uniforms opened it, nodded grimly at the guards. For an instant, Blaney experienced a surge of hope – perhaps they were taking her down to Rothau to be transferred to another camp. Then the *Kubelwagen* turned off down a side road. She guessed where it led. The sun dipped beneath the rims of hills. Blaney tried to conjure up a clear, untarnished image of Tom Caine in her mind: the broad shoulders, the polished stone-grey eyes, the blunt nose, the freckled skin that would never take a tan.

Suddenly, there were lights ahead. The vehicle pulled up between two buildings. Only the one on her left was brightly lit. It was the Struthof Inn – the place she'd glimpsed on her first day in the camp, standing directly opposite the gas chamber. The hotel was an impressive L-shaped building with four great arch-shaped windows on the ground floor and smaller ones on the second. Dormer windows emerged from its steeply pitched roof. The hotel was built on a stone platform, with steps leading up to a wood-framed door. An old birch tree stood outside and Blaney saw there were rustic tables and iron chairs scattered around it. Light spilt in bright streams from the windows. Blaney heard the sound of men's voices, rough shouts, drunken cackles, the clink of glasses, an accordion playing a romantic melody – men were droning along with it, out of tune. She tried to imagine what it must have been like here in winter, before the war – bright snow, dark pines, excited young skiers from Strasbourg, children throwing snowballs, building snowmen, laughing, sliding, skating, playing on toboggans. *Before the war.* Many of those people would be dead now – perhaps some had been prisoners at Natzweiler. Others might have become *Milice* or fought for the Bosch.

The guards hustled her out of the vehicle, left her standing on the right side of the road, opposite the hotel, facing the gas chamber. She was wearing only her prison dress, and it was chilly. She wrapped her arms round her shoulders. The place was a crude oblong, grey in the half-darkness, silent and brooding. Most of its windows were boarded up, except for a small one beside the door. An unnatural wan blue light showed through it. Although there were two chimneys on its tiled roof, Blaney noticed a steel flue pipe that had been fitted under its eaves. The place was so quiet, it seemed disused. Blaney suddenly remembered what Hartmann had said that morning. *Some vas shot. Some vas hang. Some vas gas at Struthof.* She shuddered. The place had been working all the previous day: hundreds of people had been gassed to death while German guards drank and made merry at the inn across the road. It seemed as if they were still celebrating.

Blaney bowed her head. She'd volunteered for SOE. She could have waited for Tom Caine to come home. It suddenly hit her, for almost the first time, that she had no idea if he was dead or alive. If he was dead, maybe they would be together on the Other Side. If there was one.

Suddenly the wrinkle-faced guard grabbed her by the arm, wheeled her round. Instead of marching her towards the gas chamber, he hustled her towards the hotel, through the patches of light, up the steps, through the massive door. There was an atrium with deer heads and paintings: faded winter landscapes. The man let her go, urged her forward with a terse nod of the head, towards the room where the chatter and the music were coming from. Suddenly she was there, among a horde of men in SS uniform. They had taken off their caps, their field-grey tunics unbuttoned. They were drinking and smoking. Some were slopping beer from enormous steins. Many were red-faced, others staggering, trolling out the words of the tune one of them was playing on the accordion. As she entered, men ogled her, cheered, wolf-whistled, made what she assumed were obscene remarks in German. Blaney wondered if this was what she'd been brought here for, after all. To be handed around and pawed by these men – perhaps gang-raped before she died.

To their apparent disappointment, though, the guard nudged her towards a staircase that opened out of the room, up broad steps covered by a carpet that had, in places, worn through. They emerged onto a wide landing from which the doors of the hotel rooms opened.

For the first time Blaney felt the urge to ask what was happening. She opened her mouth; the guard glowered at her. He caught hold of her arm again and ushered her to one of the doors. It was number twenty-one, Blaney noticed. The door had oblong wooden panels, the paint peeling. Like the stair carpet, it had seen better days.

The guard knocked, called out in German. There was an answer from inside. The guard opened the door, pushed Blaney in.

The room was large, with a four-poster bed, a Persian carpet and plush velvet hangings. A low fire was crackling in the fireplace. Sitting in front of it, on a brocaded chair, with a glass of cognac in his hand, sat *SS-Standartenführer*, Franz Boelcke. She remembered the receding hair, the widow's peak, the clean-shaven face, the penetrating eyes, the arrogant smile, the look of easy superiority. The guard saluted. Boelcke ignored him. He eyed Blaney up and down.

'So… *Mademoiselle* Tomalin, I think,' he said in French. 'I so much enjoyed meeting you in Strasbourg that time. Of course, I'm a busy man, and it quite slipped my mind that you were due to be sent to Natzweiler until I spotted you there the other day. You are a *Nacht und Nebel* prisoner, of course, there is no getting away from that. In the meantime, though, I thought we might become… *reacquainted.*'

CHAPTER FORTY-TWO

Alsace, France, June 1945

They headed south out of the Vosges, avoiding main roads where they could. The weather had turned colder, the sky glowering, with cloud like matted fleece. Boelcke had fewer than two days start on them, but they had no way of knowing which route he had taken or where he might stop. Assuming Skinner had been right, the only place they could be sure of catching him was the Villa Stauffer at Perpignan.

In a village near Besancon they ran into an American supply unit – jeeps and six-ton trucks. The Yanks seemed to be bartering with the locals, exchanging cigarettes and petrol for milk, fresh meat, sausage, cheese. The men were dressed in olive drab fatigues. They didn't turn a hair when Caine's jeep drew up. After a five-minute discussion with a nonchalant master sergeant, Caine bought not only two hundred gallons of petrol in German-style jerrycans, but also a jeep trailer to carry them in. 'What you guys doin' here, anyways?' the sergeant asked them.

'Chasing Nazi war criminals,' Caine told him.

The sergeant guffawed. 'The war's over. Time to make a dollar,' he said.

Once they were deep into the cultivated land of Haute-Laon they halted in a wood. Wallace erected the canvas cover over the jeep. The

271

new trailer came in useful – there was room in it for other equipment besides the petrol: the jeep had been cluttered. Caine told Trubman to write and transmit a message to Backhouse in Gaggenau. He told the major the whole story – how they'd been given the runaround at Strasbourg, how they'd gone to Schirmeck anyway, broken through the MP roadblock, what they'd learned from Hartmann, how Skinner had tried to arrest them, how they had turned the tables on him, thanks to a *subversive incident*. Finally, he explained how Skinner had admitted that Boelcke was alive and currently on a ratline organized by the CIC, across the Pyrenees to Spain, how they hoped to catch up with him at the *Villa Stauffer* at Perpignan in two or three days' time. He had Trubman encipher the message, send it by Morse code, labelled *Secret*. He wanted a record of what had happened, but it had to stay in safe hands for now.

Afterwards he and Cope lit cigarettes while Wallace finished off hooking up the eyelets on the cover.

'Sounds bad, doesn't it?' Caine said. 'I mean, when you put it all together like that. Then add on what happened at SHAEF, the Schuochwurte incident, and we're in for the high jump.'

'I'm not so sure, Tom,' Cope said. 'Boelcke's a war criminal. If he stood trial, he'd be sentenced to death. What Skinner did – organizing his escape, not only from a detention centre but also from the country – was illegal. Skinner said the CIC had done the same for others. They wouldn't want that broadcast publicly. Think of the outcry.'

'Yeah,' Wallace commented. ''Specially the Ivans.'

Caine lit a cigarette, considered it. 'Why the hell did Skinner admit it, then?' he said, almost to himself. 'It wasn't fear. It was obvious we weren't going to lay a finger on him. Why not keep his mouth shut?'

'At that point, he just wanted to get rid of us,' Copeland suggested. He knew almost before it was out that it didn't really make sense.

'It were me, weren't it,' Wallace crooned from the other side of the jeep. 'Tugged at 'is 'eartstrings didn' I?'

Caine puffed smoke. 'Yeah,' he said. 'Must have been that, Fred.'

He didn't sound convinced, Copeland thought.

CHAPTER FORTY-THREE

Franz Boelcke cycled the last few kilometres to the *Villa Stauffer* from the safe house in Perpignan, where he'd spent the night. He was still bearded, dressed in his peasant attire and wooden clogs. He carried nothing but a small haversack and documents issued by the International Committee of the Red Cross. They identified him as Carlos Dalba, a Spanish citizen living in France, who had been interned by the Nazis during the war. The villa was surrounded by spurs covered in swathes of forest. It was a solid-looking lump of a house, built of grey stone slabs, with wood-framed windows and a vast oak door that opened onto low steps. A gable extended on the left side, with shuttered upper and lower windows. The walls were covered with strands of brown and faded ivy. Dormer windows sprouted from the roof.

The villa stood at the very edge of the Pyrenees. The mountains soared above it, their lower slopes a continuous deep-pile green carpet, penetrated in places by granite outcrops like hooks and claws. Higher up, beyond the treeline, the forest gave way to cliffs of ribbed and fluted rock, glittering like polished steel. Higher still, wild peaks reared, standing at thousands of metres, jagged ridges laced with snow, knotted and knapped into sparkling facets, like rows of giant stone-age tools.

Boelcke could not tear his gaze away. The mountains were mysterious, dark, haunting, he thought – he'd been told that he would have to cross deep, snow-ridden passes, ford icy rivers, scale sheer-sided ravines. There were bears and wolves up there, they said.

Boelcke left his bicycle under a lone pine tree, half a kilometre from the villa as he'd been instructed, and continued on foot. Before he had even reached the great oak door it swung open. A giant of a man peered out. 'Ah, the ratline,' he growled in German. 'Deserting the sinking ship, eh? Come in. Come in. We like your type here.'

Later, sitting in an uncomfortable, straight-backed antique chair by a moribund fire, in a vast but sparsely furnished room inside, Boelcke handed over his ICRC documents. He felt as if he were being court-martialled. The giant, who introduced himself as *Herr Strauber*, sat facing him, surrounded by a semi-circle of Germans in clothes that were a mixture of civilian and military. Strauber called them his *escort*. They were armed with Schmeisser sub-machine guns and Gewehr rifles, British .303s and Stens, M1 Carbines from the USA. The men were part of his band of *Werwulf*, Strauber said. They didn't live in the villa: that was maintained by a skeleton staff. They were nomads – almost all of them ex-*Waffen-SS*. They wandered the foothills of the Pyrenees, using the villa only as a rendezvous point. These days, Strauber confided, it was too dangerous to stay in one place.

Strauber's manner fluctuated between aloof and hearty. He cracked jokes that weren't funny and stared around to see who laughed. His eyes remained cold. He was a huge man, with a broad, scarred face and crew-cut hair of coppery blonde stubble. His features were carved stonework, his eyes ice-water blue. He looked exactly what he was, Boelcke thought – an ex-*Waffen-SS* officer – except that instead of an SS uniform, he wore a mottled hunting jacket, torn twill trousers and brown boots, caked with mud. In place of a Schmeisser he carried a Mannlicher hunting rifle. He clasped it over his knees with one vast, gnarled hand.

Boelcke's impression was that Strauber was trying to convince himself and his men that the war wasn't over, that this was only a temporary setback for the Third Reich. The fact that he used the word *Werwulf* to describe his followers was pure bravado. There *had* been talk in the SS of forming stay-behind parties called *Werwulf,* intended to make guerrilla sorties against the Allies if they occupied Germany. Little had come of it though. From the very start, the SS had been conditioned to believe that no Allied invasion of the Fatherland could ever succeed. It was hard for them to change those feelings now. *Werwulf* had got little further than talk.

Strauber hinted that by using the ratline, Boelcke was *deserting* to the enemy – an act of betrayal. Boelcke thought it ironic that the man's existence depended partly on money he was paid for facilitating the escape of people like himself, mostly high-ranking ex-SS officers, wanted by the Allies. He evidently didn't know that many of these escapes were organized by American Intelligence. Strauber's services in protecting and maintaining the ratline was paid for by the enemy.

Still, Boelcke couldn't help feeling that he was on trial. These renegades might be men in denial, but they looked tough and determined. They weren't bandits. Despite appearances, they maintained military order. There were no wild beards, no unkempt hair. Boelcke could see that they still considered themselves *Waffen-SS*.

He had brought cash, but he needed more than their assistance in crossing the mountains. A coded message, from Skinner he guessed, had been waiting for him at the Perpignan safe house: the British war crimes team that had followed him to Schirmeck had discovered that he hadn't shot himself at Natzweiler. They were tracking him. They knew about the *Villa Stauffer*, and they would probably be there by next morning. Although Skinner hadn't said so, it was clear that he was expecting Boelcke to arrange a surprise for them.

Boelcke surveyed the faces – the faces of fanatics, men who believed what they'd been told about the superiority of the German race. He wondered how best to bend them to his purpose. He suddenly decided to tell them who he really was.

'Of course, the name on my ID papers is assumed,' he said. 'I am *SS-Standartenführer* Franz Boelcke, ex-*Kommandant* of KL Natzweiler-Struthof.'

If he'd been expecting the men to click heels and give him the Nazi salute, he was disappointed. Strauber immediately rolled up his sleeve and showed him the blood group tattooed on his bulging bicep. '*O negative*,' he announced. 'Not many of those around.' Then he turned the almost colourless eyes on Boelcke. 'Where's yours?'

'I never had one,' Boelcke admitted. 'I was appointed, but never inaugurated officially.'

After that it got worse. Strauber asked him questions about SS training. Boelcke couldn't answer them.

'You don't sound like any SS man I've ever met,' the giant concluded.

The men murmured angrily. Boelcke wondered if he'd made a mistake.

'It's true I didn't do SS training,' he said. 'That is because I am a scientist. I was working on a special project for the Führer. The SS is a brotherhood – I swore an oath of personal allegiance to Herr Hitler, just as you did. I was given SS rank for a *Projekt*, which I ran at Wallenbach, with prisoners from Natzweiler concentration camp. An SS officer is not made by a blood group tattoo.'

Strauber glowered. For a moment, Boelcke thought the giant might hit him.

'If you are masquerading as a member of our sacred brotherhood…' he gasped, 'I will…'

'No, it's true,' a voice piped up suddenly. Boelcke looked to see a young, slim man –probably a Hitler *Jugend* – with slightly whimsical features, staring at him. 'I was a guard at Natzweiler, just for a few months, but I recognize him,' the boy said. 'This is *Standartenführer* Boelcke. And it's right what he says about Wallenbach. We used to escort workers to the Daimler-Benz plant there every day. I think he's a scientist or engineer or whatever, because he used to supervise the work himself.'

'*Thank you*,' Boelcke said. He dared not add, '*I remember you*,' in case this might be a trick. The truth was that he couldn't remember having ever seen the youth before in his life.

Strauber handed the ICRC papers back to Boelcke. 'We don't use rank titles here,' he said. 'So I'm going to call you *Herr Dalba*.' He paused. 'All right, I'm ready to accept that you might be one of us, but then how did you get these papers? Only the Allies can get documents like that. You are passing secrets to them, perhaps? Secrets about this special project you were working on at Wallenbach? Selling secrets to the enemy is treason.'

Strauber was again staring at him icily. The men had gone silent. Boelcke shrugged. 'They put me in the detention centre at Strasbourg, interrogated me several times, but I refused to talk. I escaped from a work party. Before that, though, I did learn something of importance to you.'

'What?' Strauber demanded.

'That they have decided to end your little spree of freedom here. Your *Werwulf* are the only SS troops who have yet to surrender, and they feel you are an embarrassment. They are sending a force here to demand you give yourselves up. The advance guard will arrive tomorrow.'

The men growled and swore. Strauber held up his massive hand for silence.

'How do you know this?' he demanded.

'I received a message from a contact working for the American Counter-Intelligence Corps in Schirmeck,' he said. 'The man is one of us. He tells me that the advance guard belongs to the elite parachute *kommando* group that caused so much trouble in the Vosges last year. They will ask for your surrender. If you refuse, the rest of the force will close in on you and wipe you out.'

Strauber's eyes narrowed. 'You say these *kommandos* will be here tomorrow?' he demanded.

'Yes.'

'There will be no surrender. They will see how *Werwulf* can fight.'

CHAPTER FORTY-FOUR

Through his binos, Caine watched the boy collect the bicycle where it had been left, leaning against a lone tree, on the track about half a klick from the villa. He was lying on a bed of needles in the dawn shadow of massed Aleppo pines. Although he was near enough to see the road and the bicycle, perhaps a hundred yards further on, the place still commanded a good view of the house.

A sea wind had blown up in the night, the ground was humid. They'd driven straight up the road from Perpignan, making use of the roar of the wind in the trees to disguise the sound of their motor. They'd got as close to the villa as possible before turning off into the forest. While Wallace and Trubman had stayed with the vehicle, Caine and Copeland had sidled through the trees for a closer shufti at the target. The wind had passed now. A sun like a runny egg yolk was spreading through layers of cloud towards the sea.

The boy looked young – maybe sixteen – but he was tall. He had a lean, ferret-like face and spidery limbs. He wore wooden clogs, a cloth cap and an old jacket buttoned up against the early-morning cold. They had watched him saunter up the track from the direction of Perpignan and head straight for the bicycle. Either he'd left it there himself, Caine thought, or he'd been sent to collect it. He knew exactly where it would be.

'You reckon Boelcke might have left that bike to be picked up later?' Copeland asked. He was scanning the youth with his telescopic sight.

Caine lowered his binos. 'There isn't much going on at the villa – no movement, no smoke. Maybe we should have a word with that kid.'

They moved quietly to the edge of the forest, only a yard or two from the track. The youth looked comical as he rode towards them. The bicycle seat was far too low for him, which meant that his knobbly knees stuck up, giving him the appearance of a mechanical grasshopper. Caine had to suppress a chortle. He stepped out into the road, jabbed the muzzle of his .45 Colt pistol at the lad.

The boy was so astonished that he lost control of the handlebars. The bike wobbled and crashed heavily on its side. The youth squawked, scrambled from under the frame, picked up his cap, cursed in French. Before he was on his feet, Caine was standing over him, the Colt in his hand. 'I don't speak French,' he said. 'You speak English?'

The youth rose slowly, eyeing the weapon. He replaced his cap, glared at Caine. 'A *leetle*,' he said. 'Why you do that, *Monsieur*? I sink ze war is finish now?'

'Not for everyone,' Caine said. He raised the Colt. 'I don't want to hurt you, but I need to talk. If you're going to get… *funny*… I might have to…'

The boy cocked his head to one side, looked puzzled. 'What do you mean, *funny*?' he asked.

Caine had him pull the bike off the road and hide it among the trees. Then he moved him on to where Copeland was waiting in a sheltered dell. Cope had a grim look on his face. When Caine ushered the youth up, he slid out his bayonet. 'Sit down,' Copeland told him. 'You look sensible…' He glanced at the bayonet. He always kept it polished and razor-sharp. '…But I'm sure you'd like to go home with your balls intact.'

The youth sat on the floor of pine needles. Caine squatted in front of him, Cope stood close behind with his SMLE slung over one shoulder, the bayonet in his hand.

'What's your name?' Caine demanded.

'Pierre,' the youth answered sullenly.

'All right, Pierre. I want to know who that bicycle belongs to and what it was doing there.'

The boy examined him with wide eyes. 'Is just a bicycle. Is my bicycle, of course, who else?'

Caine guffawed. 'No one who'd seen you riding that thing would believe it's yours. It's about ten sizes too small. Now come on. Who owns it and how did it get there?'

The youth sighed. 'My uncle Renard, he leave it there yesterday. He tell me to get it today.'

'Who is your uncle Renard?' Caine enquired. 'What does he do and where does he live? Why would he leave it there for you to bring back?'

The look of indignant innocence in the boy's eyes faded. 'You are not police,' he said. 'You are American, maybe British soldiers. War is over. This is France.' He made a move to get up. Copeland grabbed his arm, twisted it behind his back, placed the sharp edge of the bayonet against his throat.

'You're right,' he snarled. 'We are British soldiers. Commando soldiers. We killed a lot of people in the war. For us, the war is not over. We don't care who we kill.'

'*Bien, bien,*' the youth said. Cope shoved him down hard.

'Start talking,' Caine said.

The boy sighed again. 'A man borrow the bicycle yesterday to go from Perpignan to *Villa Stauffer*. I tell him to leave it by that tree, and I will collect.'

'Who was that man?'

The boy's eyes were cold: he was concealing something.

Copeland touched the skin on the youth's neck with the very tip of the bayonet. The boy jumped.

'All right,' he hissed. 'He is on ratline. He go Spain across mountains. Is arrange he sleep last night in *Villa Stauffer*. *Passeur* – guide – will meet him today. I know nothing of how is organize. My job only to collect bicycle.'

'But you knew when the guide would meet him,' Caine commented. 'Did you see this man?'

'Of course I see him when he take bicycle. I tell him to leave it by last lone pine on road before villa.'

'What did he look like?'

Pierre thought for a moment. 'Is older than you, but not *very* old. Dark hair, a little bald, not too much. He have a beard and dress like farmer but is not farmer. His hands is soft, not farmer hands. Also he have a look…' The youth's voice faded.

'Yes?'

'He have… I mean, the way he speak. Like he is… *big boss*. Like all others is dirt. Like only *he* is important.'

Caine nodded. 'You didn't like him much?'

'Is not my job to like. Only give bicycle.'

'What was his nationality, this man?'

'He say is Spanish, but he don't speak French like Spanish people. I think he is German. Most men on line is German. He stay one night at safe house in Perpignan, then come to villa yesterday. Guide arrive today. They start before sunset.'

'Who is the guide?' Caine asked. 'Local man?'

'His name is Rene. He is not from Perpignan – come from village near here. He know the mountains better than anyone. They always use Rene.'

'So Rene and this man – they've already met?' Copeland asked. 'They've discussed terms – I mean money?'

The boy shook his head. 'Of course not. They will meet today.'

'Who else is in the villa?' Caine demanded.

'Old couple who look after it. Caretakers. Till owners come back.' He gazed at Caine curiously. 'Why you want to know about this man?'

'He murdered our friends. In the war.'

The boy shrugged. 'Many soldiers killed in war. Is not murder.'

'He killed them after they'd been captured.' Caine said. 'That's murder.'

The boy looked deflated as if he had been tricked. Any vestige of resistance had faded from his eyes. 'I didn't know,' he said. 'I didn't know that.'

'All right,' Caine said. '*Merci*, Pierre. You've been very helpful, but I'm afraid we can't let you go.'

The boy's eyes dilated with sudden terror. '*What*? *You…*' He launched into a torrent of French that even Caine knew was obscene. He lifted his hand. 'We're not going to hurt you. We just want to make sure you don't tell anyone. We'll release you in a few hours, I promise you that.'

They had just finished tying him to a tree with parachute cord when an idea occurred to Copeland. 'Hey Tom,' he said. 'You remember how you got into that villa in Italy, the one that was guarded by a company of Krauts?'

'The *Villa Montefalcone*,' Caine said. He thought of the vast, ancient edifice in the foothills of the Apennines, riddled with passages and secret tunnels. 'What about it?'

Copeland hauled him out of the youth's earshot.

'You got in disguised as a peasant woman, didn't you?'

Caine pulled on his chin. 'Not exactly, Harry. I got near enough, but only because the guards were asleep. They woke up quick enough. I had to fight.'

He'd rescued the Countess Emilia, though, he told himself. *Emilia Falcone.* He hadn't thought of her in a while. In Italy, it had seemed that something might happen between them. But ever since Betty Nolan had died it had been Blaney, Blaney and Blaney. He glanced wistfully towards the villa. He had to know what had happened to her. The answer lay behind those walls.

'Why not try the same stunt here?' Cope said. 'Put on Pierre's clothes, make out you're the guide? Boelcke has never met him, and there's only him and a couple of caretakers. It's not like you've got to get past a bunch of Krauts.'

Caine thought about it, shook his head. 'First, I don't speak the lingo,' he said. 'Second, what if Pierre's not telling the truth, or doesn't know the full picture. Third…'

'*Third?*'

'Pierre's about six foot two. I'm five-nine. I'm going to look like a bloody scarecrow in his clothes.'

Cope thought it over. 'You don't have to do a lot of talking. Just say, *Bonjour, je suis Rene, le passeur.* Don't go in. Ask for Boelcke to come to the door.'

Caine shook his head. 'No way, Harry. How am I going to say all that in Frog, and *sound* like a Frog? It's going to look fishy if I don't go in, too.'

'Just cautious, maybe. We'll get the jeep as near as possible. Fred and Taff will be with you like greased lightning.'

'What are *you* going to be doing?'

'I thought I'd work round to the rear, cover the back door. Just in case Boelcke tries to do a bunk that way.'

Caine stared at him. 'Why would he?'

'If Pierre doesn't know the full picture,' Cope chuckled, 'or if he's not telling the truth.'

CHAPTER FORTY-FIVE

Caine strode up the gravel drive towards the villa, looking more confident than he felt. In the end they'd togged him out in Pierre's jacket and cloth cap, over his own battledress trousers and boots. Plenty of folk wore mixed military and civilian clothes these days. A guide would have had some sort of kit, they'd thought, so he was carrying the most battered rucksack they could find. In his pocket he carried one of Crumper's flashbang grenades, snagged from Wallace. Under his jacket he wore his holstered .45.

As the sun rose the mountains changed hue from soot to ash-coloured to metallic blue. Jewels glittered in tiaras and necklaces of snow on the peaks. Caine could have watched the landscape all day, but he kept focused on the house. This wasn't war, but things could still go pear-shaped. Boelcke might be armed and ready to shoot, for instance. If Caine slotted him before he got the chance to talk, they would never find out what had happened to Blaney, or to the rest of the SAS.

It was comforting to know that Fred and Taff weren't much more than a couple of hundred yards behind him. The jeep was cammed up, out of sight in the nearest wedge of trees. They'd stripped off the cover and the four of them had pushed it into place. Luckily there had been a slight downhill gradient and it hadn't been that hard. Copeland had taken his SMLE and a haversack, worked through the woods to the rear of the house. He had a Very pistol with him in case he needed to signal to the others. He also had a couple of Wallace's flashbangs. He'd been impressed with the effects of the stun grenade back in Schirmeck. Not much good for real fighting, perhaps, but for this kind of stunt, ideal.

By the time Caine was halfway down the drive, Copeland had already found a covering position fifty-odd yards from the back door. It was smaller than the main door, but there were as many windows here as on the other side, all of them shuttered. He laid the muzzle of his SMLE on a mossy mound, covered himself in his poncho, scattered leaves and pine needles on it, settled down to wait.

Caine was within twenty paces from the main door now. He scanned the windows on the ground floor. He counted five – all of them had the shutters closed. He looked at the next tier of windows – only three, again shuttered. There were two shuttered windows on the projecting gable, and two dormers nested in the slope of the roof. Caine noticed that one of them was slightly open. For a split second he thought he spotted movement there – so quick that he might have imagined it. He was sure he hadn't though. Boelcke might be on the lookout, but from the top storey? It didn't feel right. Caine experienced a feeling he hadn't had in a long time – a sense he often got before the shooting started. It was as if time had slowed to a stop and the world had gone quiet. He saw with perfect clarity the muzzle of a rifle appear at the open window, knew it was aimed at him, dropped the rucksack by its quick-release catch. He broke into a plunging run, straight towards the door of the villa. It was only after he'd made five paces that he heard the crack of the rifle and dimly registered the whine of the ricochet from the gravel behind him. His left hand was already on the stun grenade, working the pin with his thumb. His right hand was on the stock of his pistol. Two more shots. Caine swerved and zigzagged. He was five paces from the main door when it began to open. Caine saw it happen in slow motion, saw Kraut faces revealed as it swung outwards, saw weapons raised. Before the door was fully open he'd hit the dirt, rolled, heaved the grenade right inside. The grenade kettle-drummed. The ground shuddered. The door quivered on its hinges, blew forward, hung lopsided. He saw Kraut eyes go dim, saw men clutch at their ears, saw men tumble. His Colt was magically in his right hand. He picked targets, pulled iron, fired with both eyes open. He saw a Jerry stagger back, saw the pink rosebud blossom above the bridge of his nose, saw gore gush, saw eyes burn out, saw another, a blonde young man, drop his Schmeisser, clutch at a crimson groove in his neck, saw blood, like dark glue, ooze through scrabbling fingers. Caine heard men bellow, saw them stagger, couldn't take in details. He'd fired six rounds, knew each one had found a mark. A hundred-pound weight lumped his left shoulder, his head looped. A scythe of acid creased his upper arm. A Jerry youth with a smooth red face was moving in on him with a grin on his lips, pointing a Gewehr rifle. Caine made to swing his pistol, then realized it was no longer in his hand. He blinked, waited for the next shot. He had walked straight into the trap Skinner had laid for him, even though, deep down, he'd known something was wrong from the start. He was alone in a nest of enemies when he'd thought the war was over. This time there was no way out. He should have known he'd never get away with it. The boomerang always came back.

The Kraut's finger squeezed the trigger. At the same moment, his head volcanoed sideways in a cone-shaped trail of brain and mush that slavered against the house wall, trickled down in runnels. His shot shaved past Caine's ear, flipped off the wall with a shriek.

Caine found his pistol, swung round in agonizing pain, saw big Wallace in the jeep, five yards away, caveman face twisted, gipsy hair flying, shuddering off tracer non-stop from the Bren on the pintle-mount. Trubman was at the wheel next to him, wearing a paratrooper's helmet, digging into a haversack, pinning and lobbing smoke canisters, rolling No. 38 Mills grenades. He hadn't even heard the jeep approach.

'*Get in for Christ's sake!*' Wallace hollered. Caine wobbled to his feet, lumbered towards the vehicle. Smoke bombs hissed, grenades exploded, swells of gold and black molasses furled. Rounds pittered against the walls. More windows opened. Jerries with all kinds of weapons crossfired bursts and single shots in a latticework of tracer. A round singed a cheek of Caine's backside as Trubman yanked him in. The signaller hit the throttle hard in reverse – the tyres kicked up avalanches of small stones.

The whole house-front was hidden by smoke. Krauts were shooting through it. Trubman twisted the steering wheel, turned on a sixpence, thrust into first, shot off towards the Perpignan road. He eased into second, accelerated. Caine lolled and bounced in the back, grovelling in his own blood. A burst clattered against the side of the jeep. A round twanged off Trubman's helmet, another cleaved two inches of meat off his tricep. He howled. Blood slicked the steering wheel. He clung onto it, ash-faced, hard as death. Wallace pulled the Bren from the front mount with biscuit-tin sized hands and tried to clip it onto the rear pintle. The air around them was ripped open like wrapping paper. A rocket sheered past, hit dirt in front of them, heaved up in a pulse of oil and fire. Shrapnel twanged Trubman's helmet, peppered Wallace's giant arm, drenched his smock in gore. '*Bloody hell*,' the big man croaked. 'A *Panzerfaust*.' He was still fighting to fix the Bren into its clip, ignoring the blood welling from his arm. His great hands were slippery with it, he rubbed it into his face and hair. The Bren clicked home. Wallace, half-turning in his seat, saw two vehicles bouncing out of the smokescreen behind them. '*Kubelwagens*,' he gasped. '*They're chasin' us.*'

CHAPTER FORTY-SIX

The wound in Caine's buttock stung, but it was only a graze. The one in his shoulder hurt like hell – it was more serious, and it was still bleeding. He was struggling desperately to slap a field dressing on it and stay in the jolting vehicle.

'*We dumped Harry,*' Trubman moaned. He looked as if he was going to faint. If that happened they'd be dog meat, Caine thought.

'Harry'll be all right if he keeps his head down,' he said. 'We're not leaving him.'

He realized they were approaching the place where they'd unhitched the trailer. When they'd first stopped there, they'd woven a path through the trees, halted in a small clearing. He decided to make for there. They needed that fuel, anyway.

'Turn off here, Taff,' he said. 'We're not going any further in this state.'

'What about them Jerries?' Wallace demanded.

'We've still got a chance. Maybe they won't find our tracks.'

The trailer was still there, where they'd left it, covered in a tarpaulin. Trubman stopped the jeep, almost fell out of the driving seat. Caine climbed down heavily, groaning. He drew his Thompson from the forward brace, then groped for the medical bag in the back. He took a long swig of water from his canteen, pulled down his BD trousers, patched up the wound in his backside. He strapped a field dressing on Wallace's arm. The big man did the same for Trubman. 'It's only a—'

'—scratch, I've heard it,' Trubman chuntered. 'Next it'll be *it ain't nowt like we took at that bridge in Tunisia.*'

They both roared with laughter. They looked so bizarre, cackling in mirth, only the whites of their eyes showing through a crust of congealed blood an inch thick, that Caine burst out laughing too. He must look the same, he thought. He gave them both morphia shots and had Wallace give him one. He glanced at his watch. The patching up had taken about seven minutes. Those wagons hadn't been far behind. He listened for the sound of motors. 'You hear anything, Fred?' he asked.

Wallace listened. 'There's *Kubelwagen* motors to the south,' he growled. 'They're goin' slow. They know we've given 'em the slip an' they're lookin' for us.'

'Who *are* those buggers?' Trubman piped up. 'They weren't wearin' uniforms or insignia…'

'This ain't the time for an inquisition,' Wallace grumped. 'We got about ten minutes before they find our tracks, I reckon. They might miss 'em, but I wouldn't bank on it.'

There was a rise on one side of the clearing. It might be defensible, Caine thought. He pointed to it, winced as pain shot through his shoulder. 'Can you set up the Bren there? Fred? Taff, how many No. 38s have we got? If we could string a daisy chain…'

'Forget it, Tom,' Wallace said. 'I'm down to two mags of .303…'

'There's no grenades left,' Trubman nodded. 'I used them all at the villa.'

Caine removed the fifty-round magazine from his Thompson. In wartime, he'd mostly carried the hundred-round mag, but he'd never expected to run into opposition like this on a war crimes investigation. The mag was full – he hadn't fired the weapon since they'd arrived in France.

He clipped the mag back on its lug. 'Well, I'm not just going to wait for those—'

'—*Quiet*,' Wallace was holding up a blood-caked hand, straining his ears. 'I can hear sommat else.'

'*What*? Not more of the…'

'A motorcycle,' he said. 'Probably a Matchless… you hear? Sounds like a bleedin' sewing machine.'

Caine thought of the Matchless Flint Ronson used for scouting ahead of the column – the one Backhouse carried in the three-tonner. Ronson was at Gaggenau, though – and that was in Germany, six hundred miles away. It was a vain hope – the morphia playing tricks on him, he thought.

'There's more,' Wallace said. His voice was excited now. 'There's a column followin' it. Six jeeps an' a three-tonner, I reckon. Comin' from the north. They're gonna run straight into those *Kubelwagens*.'

Caine and Trubman listened, holding their breath. Almost at once, Caine picked up the bluebottle buzz of the motorbike and then, a moment later, the distant sound of massed engines. The motorcycle slowed, stopped. There was silence for a few moments. Then the engine sparked to life, dopplered off fast in the opposite direction. A second later, Caine heard the motors of the *Kubelwagens* coming nearer from the south.

'The bloke on the motorbike spotted 'em,' Wallace said. 'He's gone back to report.'

For a split second no one spoke. The engine drone grew louder.

'It can't be,' whispered Trubman.

'It bloody well is,' Wallace said.

CHAPTER FORTY-SEVEN

Backhouse was in the leading jeep. Yelchukov was driving. Dusty Rhodes was manning a Browning .50 machine gun, mounted on the back. The major clocked Ronson leaning the Matchless into the bend towards them, knobbly tyres churning dust, saw the angle of the rider's posture, eyes narrowed behind the goggles, knew he'd clocked something important. Backhouse stood up, waved the convoy to a halt. Ronson braked next to him so abruptly that the bike almost tipped over. He lifted his goggles, spat dust. 'Two *Kubelwagens*,' he said. 'Comin' towards us from the direction of the villa. Goin' slow. Lookin' for somethin'.'

Backhouse cocked his head to one side. 'I take it they're hostiles,' he said.

'Can't rightly say, sir,' Ronson grinned, 'but they've got Spandaus mounted, and they're both flying SS banners.'

That was good enough for Backhouse. He made the sign for *action stations*, heard the sharp ratchet of iron on iron as the men cocked .50 Brownings, twin Vickers Ks, Thompsons and M1 carbines. Backhouse sat down, glanced at Yelchukov, still placid-faced, still hatless, still wearing his WW1-style trench coat. '*Once more into the breach*,' Yelchukov beamed.

'Or *breeches*,' Backhouse chuckled. 'Here we go.'

*

They'd been on the road almost non-stop since the day after receiving Caine's coded message sent from near Besancon. They'd maintained radio silence though. Backhouse already knew a few things Caine didn't, such as the presence of a renegade force of ex-*Waffen-SS* men, holding out in the forests at the foot of the Pyrenees. The int had come indirectly, through Garcia, from the CIC. They didn't know Backhouse knew, and he wanted to keep it that way. There was a reason the Yanks hadn't rounded up those Nazis, and Backhouse had a good idea what it was. When Caine reported that Boelcke was on a ratline, passing through the region, authorized by the CIC in Schirmeck, Backhouse had smelt a very big rat. Caine had known all about Boelcke's involvement in the CIC's atomic salvage programme but hadn't mentioned SS men running free in the area around the *Villa Stauffer*, where the ratline was based. Backhouse had put the pieces of the jigsaw together, and the picture hadn't looked pretty. In any case, they were here to find dead SAS men, and that meant getting hold of Boelcke – alive. Yelchukov had used his Whitehall influence well – it had taken only a day to get extra jeeps, men and weapons flown in from Wivenhoe. Garcia had declined to accompany them, but he'd lent them a couple of jeeps, extra fuel, three Browning .50s, four bazookas and a crate of grenades. This was on the understanding that they came back with information on any US personnel who'd been held at KL-Natzweiler. Garcia had advised him strongly to keep the whole thing off the air. 'Don't underestimate the CIC,' he told him. 'They're good at eavesdroppin', and they're dab hands at decipherin' codes.'

*

Caine and his three-man crew checked their weapons, climbed painfully back into the jeep. With the wound in his shoulder, Caine couldn't drive. He delegated the task to big Wallace, who maintained he was just about up to it. Whatever happened, they weren't going to miss out on this. They were only halfway to the road, when they heard the *chunka-chunka-chunka-chunk* of heavy machine guns, heard ricochets whine, heard rounds go *plip* against tree trunks, whiffed cordite drifting through the trees. 'Oh Christ, we're missin' it, boys,' Trubman groaned.

There was a nostalgic smile on Wallace's face. '*Those geezers've got Vickers Ks*,' he said.

*

Strauber was manning the Spandau on the back of the leading *Kubelwagen* when they heard the motorcycle. They waited for it to come into sight, but it never came. Instead, a minute later, they heard it humming off the opposite way. Strauber's driver pulled up suddenly.

'There's a convoy coming towards us,' he told Strauber. 'Can't you hear? Maybe the main force.'

'*Main force?*' the big German repeated. Then he remembered. Boelcke had said that the advance party would be followed by a larger one. He hadn't said it would be there on the same day though. Strauber was wondering how many other things Boelcke hadn't told them. He was still wondering how he'd got hold of those Red Cross documents.

The second *Kubelwagen* pulled up beside them. The senior rank was a tall, hollow-cheeked man with thin lips and an arched nose. He held a Schmeisser sub-machine gun across his knees. There was a *Panzerfaust* rocket launcher in the forward bracket. Like Strauber, he'd ordered the black SS banner broken out. It flapped idly from the back of the vehicle.

'Maybe we should retreat?' he said.

The word *retreat* set Strauber off like match paper. '*Retreat?*' he yelled. 'There will be no retreat, no surrender. The war is not over.'

'Maybe not, but if this force is in strength, it would be best to scatter into the forest…'

'The time for scattering is finished. This is time to fight…'

They were still bickering when Backhouse's column swept around the bend in the road three hundred yards away – six jeeps armed to the teeth, riding two abreast. Strauber levelled the Spandau; the gunner in the second jeep did the same. Backhouse's machine guns were already stuttering, blazing trails of ball and tracer straight at the Jerry vehicles. The racket was thunderous, the wall of fire irresistible. The gunner in the second wagon was hit six times before he could get a burst off. His broad chest popped like an airbag, ripped apart in writhing maggots of cloth-wrapped burning flesh. He slumped across the Spandau, his finger pulling steel convulsively. The weapon jiggered five rounds, went high. Two black holes appeared in his temple: the back of his skull dissolved into beetroot-coloured slush.

Strauber gritted his teeth, pulled iron, released a pulse of crimson tracer a split second before .50 rounds from the Browning, manned by Dusty Rhodes, crushed his shoulder bone and ripped off most of the third finger on his left hand. Strauber's driver was already reversing. The SS man in the passenger seat leaned forward with his Schmeisser going *rat-tat-tat-tat* when a .303 round burst his left eyeball and whizzed out of his ear in a spiral of bone and blood. The man's other eye blanked and he toppled sideways out of the vehicle. The driver of the second *Kubelwagen* reversed past Strauber's. At the same time, the tall, arch-nosed soldier in the passenger seat stood up. He had the *Panzerfaust* on his shoulder and a grim expression on his face. Whoffs of earth and smoke from grenades that had fallen short spigotted up from the road: the ground juddered. There was a *whoosh* from one of Backhouse's rear jeeps – a red rip that seemed to tear the air open, so slowly Backhouse could see the big bazooka rocket spinning on its trajectory. It hit the bonnet of the *Kubelwagen* a fraction of a second before the Jerry fired the *Panzerfaust*. The vehicle seemed to leap vertically off the ground. Then a gaping mouth opened in a terrifying grin that cracked the machine into groping tentacles of shrapnel, flesh and fire.

Strauber's driver was hit in the bicep. A bullet had drifted past the engine block and blown off part of his knee. He was screaming in agony as he went into a swerving turn. Strauber fought desperately to hang on in the back, cursing the driver as a coward, retching, gasping for breath, floundering in his own blood. Rhodes could have finished Strauber and the driver at that moment. Instead, he sprayed a long burst through the black SS flag, ripped it to shreds, left only the last vestige of a singed black rag on a pole. The *Kubelwagen* skidded off towards the villa. An instant later it was out of sight.

Backhouse let it go. He called a halt in front of the burning wreck, jumped out of his jeep and almost retched at the stink of scorched oil, red hot metal, burned meat. At that moment, Caine's jeep burst out of the forest purlieus with the giant gunner at the wheel. Dusty Rhodes swivelled the .50 Browning, took in Wallace's blood-smeared, matted hair, the faces of Caine and Trubman, pale ghost features under packs of caked gore. Rhodes pointed and hooted with laughter. Wallace pulled up beside Backhouse. 'What the 'eck kept yer?' he said.

CHAPTER FORTY-EIGHT

Copeland had lain there for over an hour. He wondered what was happening. Something had gone wrong, that was clear. Caine was supposed to walk up to the house, snatch Boelcke, load him into the jeep, drive off. Simple. It hadn't gone like that, though. There'd been a sudden whip-crack of fire, rounds spattering everywhere, grenades crumping, smoke wafting, men howling in German, thumps, thuds, the *piuuuewwey* of ricochets. He'd heard the jeep roar up the drive, heard the *tack-tack-tack* of Wallace's Bren. *It was a real firefight.* From nowhere, he'd heard two other vehicles starting up. Then the *whompppp* and *whooooshsh* of what had to be a *Panzerfaust.*

There'd been more than just Boelcke and a couple of caretakers in the house. Caine had run into a whole enemy unit – at least a platoon. If they were the Bosch – and who else could they be – what were they doing, armed and free, in France, six months after Germany had surrendered? A renegade band? The CIC man, Skinner, had talked about almost everything. Funny he'd never mentioned that.

Copeland heard vehicles rumble off at speed. The shooting had petered out. No more than half an hour later, though, there'd been a short, savage engagement not far to the north. A little while afterwards, a vehicle had limped down the drive to the villa – a Kraut *Kubelwagen*, not a jeep, he thought. It sounded as though it had been damaged.

He wondered if he should move. His limbs were cramped and numb. He'd missed out on the action. For all he knew, Caine and the others might be in trouble – wounded, dead, captured. He stopped himself. Patience was a sniper's quality. Sooner or later, someone was going to walk out of that back door.

*

They spread out in open formation opposite the villa, halted just out of effective range of Schmeisser fire. Caine sat in the passenger seat of the jeep next to Backhouse's. The morphia had made him light-headed, but at least the pain was gone. He had the forward Browning trained on the middle window in the façade, where he'd spotted what he thought was a light Spandau. Behind him, the phlegmatic Sergeant Swan manned the twin Vickers Ks. Caine scanned the windows – many of those that had been shuttered, when he'd made that perilous walk down the drive, were now open. The muzzles of weapons poked through. Occasionally he spotted eyes, the outline of heads popping up for a shufti. His assessment was that the villa was defended by more than twenty men – roughly platoon strength – but they weren't heavily armed. Some of the Germans had rifles with a greater range than an SMG. Caine was surprised there were no potshots. The Jerries were waiting for an order, he thought – or maybe they were just wary. They could obviously see that the jeeps were armed with twin Vickers or .50 Browning heavy machine guns; some carried both. They could see that the men in the jeeps wore the smocks and maroon-red berets of British Airborne commandos. Many of the Brits had Bren-guns, and one man in most of the vehicles had a bazooka. The ex-SS men had seen the way the advance guard had fought. Three men and one vehicle had caused dozens of casualties, and against all odds, they'd survived. What had gone on when the two parties had met in the woods, on the Perpignan road, probably wasn't clear. Maybe it had been an ambush. What they *did* know was that only one of the *Kubelwagens* had come back, riddled with bullet holes and reeking black smoke. The gunner and the driver were alive, both wounded. The Spandau machine gun mounted on the back of the wagon was out of action. The *Kubelwagen* now stood, abandoned, outside the main door of the villa, like a giant insect with a crushed and broken back.

In the main hall, a medical orderly was strapping up the stump of Strauber's finger. 'At least it's not your shooting hand,' he commented nervously. He had already dressed Strauber's shoulder wound. It was bad, but the finger was giving the big SS man more trouble. As soon as he'd stopped the bleeding, the orderly administered a stiff morphia shot. Across the hall, Boelcke observed the process impassively. Next to him stood a short, wiry-bodied man, with a black beard, a pointed nose, foxy eyes. He was dressed in a hooded, windproof smock, wore a woollen cap comforter and carried no weapon other than a knobbly stick. His rucksack – a home-made job of multiple pockets, pouches and leather-reinforced straps – stood squarely on the stone floor next to him. He was the guide Rene Laforte – the man Caine had attempted to impersonate. He had arrived in the interval after the battle and had been astounded by the carnage, the dead and wounded ex-SS men, blood still dripping down the outer walls, places where chunks of stone had been blasted out. Rene, a French mountaineer from a nearby village, had guided scores of men – and some women – across the Pyrenees on what was referred to as the *Lasca* ratline. The odyssey usually began from the *Villa Stauffer*. He had never seen anything like this.

Rene watched Strauber anxiously. 'I think we should get moving,' he told him. 'Before anything else happens.'

The big man made an attempt to grin, held up his good hand. '*Listen*,' he hissed. From somewhere outside, a man was talking German through a bullhorn. 'I think it's too late,' he said.

*

'I'm speaking for the Supreme Headquarters Allied Expeditionary Forces, Europe,' Backhouse announced through the bullhorn, 'now occupying Germany.' Though Caine didn't understand any more German than he did French, Backhouse's fluency always amazed him. 'The war is over. Hitler is dead. He shot himself in Berlin last April. His successor, Admiral Donitz, President of the German Republic, ordered all Axis units to surrender months ago. Millions of your comrades have done so and are being treated well. By refusing to surrender, you are not only violating the orders of your leader, but you are at risk of squandering your own lives for nothing…'

He paused.

'We have overwhelming firepower. We are the spearhead of a much larger force, supported by aircraft and tanks. They will wipe you out…'

In the hall, Strauber sprang to his feet, shoved the orderly out of the way. With his damaged hand, he knew he could no longer hold his Mannlicher. Instead, he drew a Walther pistol, flexed it in his right. '*Don't listen to the lies!*' he bawled at his men. 'The war is *not* over. No state of peace has been declared. Our wireless reports say that thousands of German troops who surrendered are being deliberately starved to death, not only by Russians but by Americans and British too. We are *Werwulf*. No surrender.'

Men cursed. Nobody fired. Gasping for breath, keeping low, he ran to the window where the only light Spandau the band still had was set up.

'…but whatever you have been told,' Backhouse's metallic voice droned, 'we are not here to ask for your surrender. That is not our concern. We are here only to arrest Franz Joseph Boelcke. We know he is in there with you. Boelcke is a war criminal, responsible, among other atrocities, for the murder of British prisoners of war, captured in uniform. We do not hold you in any way responsible for these acts. Turn Boelcke over to us, and you are free to go.'

Again, Strauber heard grumbling. 'There is no *Werwulf*,' someone said. No one suggested handing Boelcke over to the enemy, though.

'*We* are *Werwulf!*' Strauber roared.

He pointed his Walther at Backhouse. Even though he knew the jeep was beyond the range of the weapon, he squeezed steel. The pistol blammed. The 6mm round kicked up a spurt of dust and gravel, yards short of the vehicle.

'*Open fire!*' Strauber yelled, gazing around desperately. He locked eyes with the Spandau gunner, a pale man with watery blue eyes. The gunner looked away. No one opened fire.

Backhouse put down the bullhorn, gave the signal to advance. The jeeps began moving slowly towards the villa, opening into wider formation. They moved slowly, menacingly, tyres crunching on gravel. The SAS men, bent over their weapons, were completely focused. To the watchers in the house, they looked blissfully unafraid.

Suddenly there came a burst of Schmeisser fire from one of the upper windows. The rounds hit the windshield of the last jeep to Caine's right, fizzed across the armoured glass, wheezed off in a scatter pattern. The SAS man in the passenger seat yelped and clutched his arm: bright blood blistered. The reaction was instantaneous. All three pairs of Vickers Ks in the three right-hand jeeps opened up at the same time. The air was a cyclone of fire. The guns shimmied, *rat-tatted* lines of tracer and incendiary that wove a web of filigree around each other, red and green, splashed like a tidal wave against the frame of the window, carved it to shreds, snaked in through the opening, clove the SMG shooter into packets of bloody flesh. The German was already dead when he hit the wall. Incendiary rounds bounced off the ceiling beams inside, gashed the rafters in spirals of fire. A moment later, grenades in the dead shooter's belt went up, sent a javelin of flame through the aperture: spaggots of steel chunked off masonry, left the window a grinning demon mouth full of orange light.

Instead of galvanizing the defence, it was a signal to abandon the house. The room hit by the incendiaries was a blazing mass of flame and smoke. The fire was spreading. The Vickers fell silent, the jeeps ground on ominously towards the villa. Ghost heads faded from windows, weapon muzzles withdrew. The gunner opposite Strauber shook his head, pulled his weapon back, slung it from his shoulder, turned made for the back door. Strauber held up his pistol, framed the retreating man's back in his sights. Then he lowered the weapon. Men were converging on the hall from all directions, running in from passages and staircases. Strauber caught a glimpse of Boelcke heading in the same direction with the guide, Rene, not far behind. Both were carrying rucksacks. *Boelcke*. A taut nerve broke, twanged in his mind.

CHAPTER FORTY-NINE

Harry Copeland saw the door open at last. Rag-arsed Jerries, in mixed civvies and uniform, pelted through, some in small groups, some alone. He'd heard the shooting a moment earlier; three pairs of Vickers Ks fired from jeeps, he reckoned. *Where the hell had* they *come from?* The Krauts weren't in a blind panic. They weren't elbowing each other out of the way. They just wanted to get out of there fast.

Cope ignored them. He eased the butt of his SMLE into his shoulder, scanned the door with his telescopic sights. He smelled fire, saw smoke drift across the roof: the villa was burning.

He counted fifteen, seventeen, eighteen men, armed with various weapons – Jerry, Yank, Brit. Cope's limbs were aching, and he longed to move. *Not yet. Not till Boelcke appears.* A gangly, pale-faced man with a Spandau slung from the shoulder emerged. Copeland let him go.

Next out of the door was a man with a greying beard and farmer's clothes. He was wearing a woollen hat and hiking boots, hefting a rucksack, with a pistol in his hand. After him, came a trim-looking little bloke in climbing gear, with a neat black beard. He was also carrying a rucksack but had no weapon other than an alpenstock.

The first man was Boelcke. There was the beard, and the peasant clothes, but Cope was sure of it. He had studied Boelcke's features in the photo at the Strasbourg detention centre carefully, and his memory for detail was excellent. He guessed that the other man was the guide. Instead of following the retreating Krauts, the pair made straight for Cope's position in the trees. They weren't running, but they were moving fast. Copeland was about to shout out to Boelcke to stop when someone did it for him. A man as huge as Fred Wallace burst through the door about twenty paces behind them, roaring, '*Halt, or I'll kill you!*' in German. He was holding a Walther automatic, pointed straight at Boelcke. His face was a mask of fury.

Boelcke stopped. The guide froze, backed away from him. The giant approached with an ungainly stride. Cope saw that his left hand was bandaged, and that the left side of his hunting jacket was soaked in blood. The giant's face was round and clean-shaven, his hair a stubble. He was tall and looked immensely strong. He was within ten yards of Boelcke when the ex-*kommandant* raised his pistol. The big man was quicker. He fired a double tap at chest height. Boelcke was knocked off his feet by the blast.

It was all Copeland could do to control himself. *Shit. Shit. Shit.* He had almost *seen* the shots strike Boelcke's chest. *Vital organs.* If Boelcke was dead, they would never find out what had happened to the other SAS men, to Celia Blaney. The giant closed on the bleeding body, his pistol still trained. To Cope's relief, Boelcke squirmed, tried to get up. Blood soaked the front of his jacket, though it didn't look as if a main organ had been hit.

The guide watched as if hypnotized. The big man ignored him.

'*Gut, ich bin froh, dass du nicht tot bist,*' he growled. Copeland had learned enough German before the D-Day ops to understand him. 'I wanted to tell you to your face that you are a stinking traitor, Boelcke.

You lied. You said those British commandos were coming for us. They were coming for *you*. You led them here, hoping we would deal with them, so you could escape. You used us, Boelcke. You aren't one of us. You never could be. Even when they demanded we hand you over to them, not one man agreed. Not one. *Du bist ein dreckiges Verräterschwein.* A man like you could never understand…'

Boelcke coughed phlegm tinged with blood. He tried to speak but the big man cut him off. 'I wondered where you got those Red Cross documents. I knew only the Allies could have provided them. You sold out, Boelcke. Not to the British – to the Americans. The British wanted you for what you did to their comrades in the war, so the Americans organized your escape. The British were still on your trail though. You brought them to us, hoping we would kill them.' He laughed bitterly. 'It didn't work out that way.' He paused, wiped slaver off his mouth with his wounded hand.

It was a remarkable piece of deduction, Copeland thought. Almost perfect. Except for the fact that it was the CIC who'd arranged the whole thing – that was clear. Skinner had sent the SAS team after Boelcke – even told them where they could find him – confident that this band of renegade Nazis would stop them. At that moment, he could not decide which of the two – Skinner or Boelcke – he despised more.

The big man was pointing his Walther at Boelcke again. '*Jetzt bist du dran zu sterben.*'

Copeland already had the big man in his cross hairs. He felt sorry for him – he would rather have had Boelcke in his sights. He watched as the muscles tightened in the man's face. He shot him once, through the head.

Cope threw the poncho aside, scrambled to his feet. Pins and needles pulsed through his legs. He fumbled in his haversack, drew out the Very pistol. There was a cartridge in the breech. He held it at a high angle, groped the trigger. He heard the *whoosh*, didn't wait to see the purple octopus explode in the sky. He moved towards the little group covering the guide – the only one left standing. The man had dropped his stick. His posture was still frozen, his face waxen with shock. Copeland didn't think he had much to fear from him, but you could never tell.

He checked that the giant was dead. The .303 bullet had entered the side of his head just above the ear. There was a large, clean exit wound on the opposite side. Copeland was pleased with the shot: no suffering – instant death. He gave the guide an intimidating stare. 'Sit down,' he ordered. 'Stay there.'

Boelcke was bleeding from the chest, gagging for air. His eyes were glassy. Cope wondered if he was still compos mentis. 'What's your name?' he asked in English.

Boelcke had to think for a moment. 'My name is… Franz Joseph Boelcke. I held the rank of… *SS-Standartenführer*. I vas *Kommandant* of… KL-Natzweiler-Struthof…' He tried to laugh, coughed blood. '*What… nonsense…*' he gasped. 'I am physicist… I vas von of first… to develop hot cell.'

At that moment a jeep screamed round the side of the villa, headed straight for Copeland's position. There were two men in it: Tom Caine in the passenger seat, Bill Backhouse at the wheel.

CHAPTER FIFTY

Caine's smock was greasy with blood, his face drawn. He'd evidently been wounded in a firefight, but Copeland didn't ask for details: Boelcke was dying, there wasn't time for that. It was Backhouse who slit open Boelcke's shirt with a clasp knife, examined his chest. Though the bullets had missed the heart, he was losing blood fast. The wounds looked bad – he was covered in gore. Caine brought the medical pack from the jeep: Backhouse applied field dressings. He shook his head. Without immediate surgery, it would only be a matter of time.

'You are going to die,' Backhouse told Boelcke. 'A surgeon with a fully equipped field hospital might save you, but oddly, I don't see one here. Even if there were one, I wouldn't let them... *you... you.*' His voice broke. Caine could see the fury blazing in his eyes, the rage – usually well-concealed – that he'd glimpsed in that room at the *Victory Club* the first time they'd ever met. Caine saw that Backhouse's right hand was clenched tightly around the butt of his holstered pistol. He touched the major's arm. Backhouse turned his head. For a split second, Caine glimpsed the stranger lurking in his eyes. '*Bill,*' he said gently. '*Bill.*'

Backhouse started, blinked. The hand on the pistol butt loosened. The burning rage died. 'It's all right, Tom,' he said. 'I'm all right.'

Both of them squatted down by Boelcke.

'Just answer this,' Caine said. 'Last year, you had thirty-one British parachute commandos in the Natzweiler camp. You sent ten of them across the Rhine to Rotenfels, near Gaggenau, in Germany. In November, when it was certain that the Americans would liberate Natzweiler, you phoned Schuochwurte and told him to kill all the prisoners held at Rotenfels. The remaining twenty-nine parachutists disappeared from Natzweiler at the same time. We want to know what happened to them.'

It seemed that Boelcke was trying to laugh: instead, he spluttered blood. 'I had… them… executed,' he croaked. 'I was acting on the orders of the Führer… the *Kommandobehfel…*'

'We don't care about that,' Backhouse snapped. 'Where are the bodies?'

Boelcke made a gurgling sound. He blinked. Caine and Backhouse exchanged a glance. After all they'd been through, all the trouble they'd got themselves into, surely Boelcke wasn't going to die on them now?

'Where did you have them killed?' Backhouse asked again.

'At Moussey… in the Vosges. You vill find… their bodies there.'

He retched, coughed blood.

Backhouse leaned back on his haunches. 'Moussey,' he sighed.

'There was a girl,' Caine said, leaning forward, trying to keep his voice steady. 'A pretty, red-haired girl. Her name was Giselle Tomalin – a special operations agent. Where is her body?'

Boelcke managed to chuckle, blood ran out of his nostrils. '*Giselle* yes… yes *Giselle*… she was… a pity.'

'Where *is* she?' Caine almost shouted.

'I cannot… help you.'

It was Caine's turn to clench his fists. He was tempted to hit the man. 'What do you mean?'

Boelcke coughed again. His eyes were out of focus, veined in red. *Come on, for Chrissake,* Caine thought.

Boelcke took a rattling breath as if making a last tremendous effort. 'Many people died at… Natzweiler,' he gasped. 'It vas for the *Projekt* you see. You must understand… the *Projekt*… vas important.'

Caine made an epic attempt to keep his voice calm. 'Yes, I understand,' he said, 'but I must know what happened to… Giselle.'

'I do not know… vere she ist now.'

Caine was about to cut in again when Backhouse shook his head sharply. Then Caine understood. Boelcke had used the word *now.*

'Giselle… *escaped,*' Boelcke grunted. 'She got *avay.*'

Caine stared at Backhouse. *Got away.* His head swam. He felt faint with shock.

'From… the… Struthof… Inn. A guard… came in. She snatch… his veapon. She vas… quick. She… jump out… of vindow. She steal car… We never… find… her…'

Boelcke's eyes dimmed, the pupils were pinpoints. 'It… vas… for… the *Projekt*… you see… you understand… the *Projekt*… vas… all… that… mattered…'

His body jerked. There was a sound in his throat like the scrape of metal. Blood trickled from the side of his mouth. His eyes were open, focused on the sky.

Caine grabbed his arm, shook it. '*Where did she go?*' he yelled. '*Where is she?*'

Backhouse's hand closed around his wrist. '*Tom,*' he said softly. 'Tom. He's dead.'

Caine let go of Boelcke's arm, ranged Backhouse with wild eyes. 'I'll never find her,' he said, almost sobbing. 'After all this. I'll never find her now.'

'I think I can help you,' a voice said. Caine, Backhouse and Copeland all looked up. It was the guide who had spoken. In reasonably good English, too. They had forgotten he was even there.

'My name is Rene Laforte,' the man said. 'I am a *passeur* – a professional mountain guide. I have taken many people across the Pyrenees, during and after the war. They pay me. I do not care what nationality or who they are.'

'So you're a mercenary,' Caine said. 'How does that help us?'

The man tugged on his trim black beard. 'In October 1944 – last year – I was working for the Maquis. The *Alliance Reseau* started the ratlines across the mountains, long before the Nazis used them – and the Americans, of course…

All three SAS officers were staring at him now.

'It was not long before the Allies liberated Alsace,' he said. 'The Maquis arranged for me to guide a woman across the mountains. She was a pretty girl, perhaps twenty-three or twenty-four. Very tough. She spoke French like a Frenchwoman, but I had the feeling she was not French. I took her through the passes, across the border, into Spain. When we parted, she told me that she would make for Barcelona rather than Madrid. She thought the weather would be nicer there.'

'What was the name of this girl?' Caine whispered.

'Her name was Giselle Tomalin. The thing I remember most about her was her hair. It was beautiful – the colour of fire.'

CHAPTER FIFTY-ONE

Catalonian Coast, south of Barcelona, Spain, August 1945

She sat on the beach, watched the sea. Rodriguez let her go there in the afternoons when she finished at the café – as long as it wasn't too far, he said. He wasn't being possessive, she knew that. It was just that she forgot things. She couldn't remember how long she'd been working there. There was a lot she couldn't remember. Some bad things had happened, but they were shadow-images from long ago and far away. Another person's story, another person's life. Sometimes the sea was as still as a blue table. If the sun was out it was a weave of colours. When she paddled in the shallows it was like walking through a rainbow. She collected sea shells. Sometimes she brought a net and caught little fish.

On other days, there was a high wind from the east that tussled her ponytail of flame-red hair. Then the sea went wild, surging in, wave after wave, booming and sighing, white spray exploding over rocks. She watched seagulls caught in the air currents, flapping their wings madly just to stay where they were.

She liked the wild sea, but she liked it better when it was gentle. She liked the lap of low rollers, little white fingers tickling the beach, the soothing scourge of surf. Sometimes, in the roiling whirl of waters, she

315

glimpsed images: a woman floating out of the sky on a dandelion seed, men in frog suits, a dark cavern with a row of orange cats' eyes. She saw a man with a weathered face and rough hands in a peasant's cloth cap. She thought his name was André – or was it Maurice? Another man, tall and handsome, called Rolande. She saw men with trolls' faces trying to drown a woman in a bathtub – pouring water down her throat. She was sitting in a prison cell. There were screaming voices all around her, gunshots cracked like fireworks, a gush of crimson flame from a building she couldn't see, a sickening stench of scorched flesh. There was a room full of drunken soldiers, an accordion playing the funeral march, men singing a dirge, lurching, staggering, leering at her, a soldier sitting in a big room by a fire, drinking brandy: an arrogant-looking man with a widow's peak and balding hair. There was a younger soldier carrying a tray of something, a pistol hanging from his belt, a holster he'd forgotten to close.

She was holding the weapon in her hand, pointing it at the soldiers, they were staring at her, wide-eyed, surprised, *scared*.

She jumped from a first-storey window. She tried to roll, but she hurt her head. Nothing seemed quite real after that. She was driving a vehicle, swerving madly down a steep road. She left it somewhere. She ran into the woods. There were friendly peasant faces, a cosy farmhouse, hot soup by a warm fire. There were other houses, huts, cottages in the forest. There were other faces, other voices. Places faded from her mind: people flitted around her like phantoms. She rode a bicycle. She walked. She was quiet. When people talked to her, she shook her head. There were forests, mountains – beautiful, majestic, gleaming peaks. A man called Rene, with a trim black beard and a knobbly walking stick: wading through rivers, trudging through snow, shivering under a blanket, a wolf howling somewhere, a bear shambling away.

Then the café. A fat man called Rodriguez, his plump wife, Maria, their children, Mariana, and José. They gave her a tiny room. She worked for only her keep. She looked after the children, did the housework, did the washing, swept the floor, waited at tables in the café. It was mostly locals. Families came at weekends, on a bus from a nearby town. She was quiet. She didn't need to say much. At first, men bothered her – tried to touch her. Once she scratched a man's face. No one troubled her after that. Rodriguez looked after her, warned them off.

The police came to question her – the *Guardia Civile* – men on horses with funny hats. They looked at her papers. One of them spoke French. He asked questions she couldn't answer. Finally, he tapped the tip of his forefinger against the side of his head.

They rode off on their horses. They never came back.

It was getting chilly on the beach. The sun was drifting through layers of cloud that reminded her of soft wing-feathers. The tide was creeping higher. The cry of a seagull woke her from her daydream. She got up, brushed sand off her dress. She put on her wooden-soled shoes and climbed up the shingle towards the path.

There was a man standing there, watching her. She had the intuition that he'd been watching her for some time. At first he was in shadow, but as she came closer, she saw that he was wearing a faded mountaineer's smock, tweed trousers, thick socks tucked into hiking boots. He had unusually broad shoulders, a slim waist. He held strong-looking hands loose at his sides. His face was blunt and freckled, his eyes like polished grey stones. There was no cruelty in them, though.

She didn't feel afraid. She knew she'd seen him before.

In another person's story, another person's life.

*

Caine had been watching Blaney for half an hour – something had stopped him from approaching her. He told himself that he just wanted to be sure it really *was* her, but he'd known it from the first second. After so long, thinking about her, longing for her, craving her touch, despairing for her, believing her dead. Now he'd found her, she seemed unreal – fragile. He felt that if he touched her, she might fall to pieces.

It had taken him a month in all to track her down to this small village on the Catalonian coast. Backhouse had tried to stop him, of course. A British officer entering Spain illegally? It would cause an international incident. They'd lock him up, throw away the key. It was Copeland who'd come up with the idea of using Boelcke's bogus Red Cross papers. Caine was younger, but the documents were mostly handwritten, and a little doctoring did the trick. Backhouse relented, gave him cash, took Copeland, Wallace and Trubman off with his own crew to search for SAS bodies at Moussey. Nothing more had been heard of *Werwulf.* They would die in the forest, give themselves up, blend in with the locals, get hitched with French girls, perhaps get arrested one at a time.

For a week he'd trekked through the mountains with Rene. There hadn't been any trouble: Rene knew how to dodge the border police. When they'd parted, the guide had given him the same contact address in Barcelona he'd given Blaney nine months earlier. It had taken a train ride and some enquiries to discover that Giselle Tomalin had decided to wander south, down the coast of Catalonia, looking for a place by the sea, where perhaps she might find work. The contact in Barcelona told Caine that when he'd suggested she report to the British Embassy in Madrid, she'd stared at him blankly. '*Moi, je suis Francaise,*' she'd said. She was *odd*, he added. Sometimes she forgot things.

Before leaving, Caine had managed to put a phone call through to a number in Strasbourg Backhouse had given him. It was Yelchukov who answered. Backhouse and the team had uncovered the bodies of twenty of the twenty-one SAS men – and some French Resistance and USAF pilots, too – at the village of Moussey in the Vosges.

That was all Caine needed to know.

Now Blaney was here, standing in front of him, her hair as flaming red as ever, tied up in a ponytail with a scarf. She wore a simple, floral dress. She looked a little more careworn, a little older, her rose-ivory cheeks were flushed. Her dove-coloured eyes hadn't lost their softness though.

They stared at each other. Then Blaney burst into tears, threw her arms around him. He held her tight, a precious being, a being he would never let go of again. Her lips were on his neck, he could feel the warm flow of her tears.

'I can't *remember*,' she sobbed. 'I hit my head when I jumped out of that window. I know I know you, but I can't *remember*.'

Caine nuzzled her. 'It's ok,' he said. 'It's all right.'

He pulled her arms away gently, took her by the hand, led her away from the beach.

'Where are we going?' she asked.

'Home,' he said. 'Where else?'

Perhaps she didn't know him. Perhaps she never would. Perhaps they'd have to start again. Or perhaps her memory would return, all at once, or little by little. He didn't care about that now. She was alive, she was Blaney, and he loved her. The war was over. For the answer to any other question, there was eternity to find out.

www.ingramcontent.com/pod-product-compliance
Lightning Source LLC
Chambersburg PA
CBHW052016240626
47153CB00006B/1834